O.L.D.

A GOOD WAY TO DIE

Thanks for reading.
Now let's save the world!

7-22-20

O.L.D.

A GOOD WAY TO DIE

Christopher Kügler

KLOCKWORK PUBLISHING
BELLEFONTE, PENNSYLVANIA

Klockwork Publishing
www.klockworkpublishing.com

Book Layout © 2017 BookDesignTemplates.com

ISBN: 978-1-7349869-0-7
Ebook ISBN: 978-1-7349869-1-4

To my beloved Xenia: thanks for believing in me.

"Imagine a room awash in gasoline. And there are two implacable enemies in that room. One of them has 9,000 matches. The other has 7,000 matches. Each of them is concerned about who's ahead, who's stronger. Well, that's the kind of situation we are actually in. The amount of weapons that are available to the United States and the Soviet Union are so bloated, so grossly in excess of what's needed to dissuade the other that if it weren't so tragic, it would be laughable."

—Carl Sagan, ABC News Viewpoint, November 20, 1983

PROLOGUE

It was the air fresheners — at least that's what he'll tell himself later. It was the air fresheners that first clued him in that something wasn't right...

•••

November 1983

Ronald Wilson Reagan — the fortieth President of the United States — stares out the window of Marine One. Watching the treetops below, a blur in the fading light, his mind swims about in one alarming truth: he has absolutely no idea where he is.

Or where he is going.

Or what he is doing.

He *should* know, of course, being the Leader of the Free World and all. But, looking back inside the cabin, his eyes darting up and down the empty rows of ugly plaid seats in front of him, he doesn't have a clue. And — even more perplexing for the Commander in Chief — there isn't even anybody to ask... *not even his beloved Nancy.*

Dagnabbit, he thinks, convinced this was all explained to him in detail this morning, in his daily briefing.

If only I was paying attention.

Now all the president can do is sit back and watch the air fresheners dangle on the seatbacks in front of him. Those air fresheners, they're a ten-cent solution to a million-dollar dilemma. One hangs from the back of each and every seat, pine tree-shaped and strongly scented.

You've seen them, you've smelt them, and Marine One — the president's dedicated transport — reeks of them.

The helicopter itself is a beast: a Sikorsky SH-3 Sea King, the same make and model that pulled the Apollo astronauts out of the Pacific. This particular ride is as iconic as the presidential seal that emblazons its sides. Just close your eyes and picture Richard Nixon waving his peace-signs before turning and flying off into his soon-to-be-pardoned sunset.

Sandwiched between the fuselage and the massive, sixty-foot long rotor blades are the helicopter's twin turboshaft engines. And despite the staggering amount of money the United States Marine Corps has spent over the years trying to stop the jet fumes from drifting down into the cabin, drift they do.

And when it comes to the first lady, Mrs. Nancy Davis Reagan, the former Hollywood starlet turned White House decorator, these fumes — and their habit of lingering on one's chic, custom-made clothing — is downright unacceptable.

These air fresheners are the Marine Corps' desperate attempt to mask said fumes. But they're not just any scent. No no. Just as the first lady is picky in regards to the dining china presented to foreign dignitaries, she too is picky in regards to air fresheners. And, for those whose whole existence in the federal government is to appease the first lady, her air freshener of choice is the refined scent of jasmine.

PROLOGUE

It was the air fresheners — at least that's what he'll tell himself later. It was the air fresheners that first clued him in that something wasn't right...

• • •

November 1983

Ronald Wilson Reagan — the fortieth President of the United States — stares out the window of Marine One. Watching the treetops below, a blur in the fading light, his mind swims about in one alarming truth: he has absolutely no idea where he is.

Or where he is going.

Or what he is doing.

He *should* know, of course, being the Leader of the Free World and all. But, looking back inside the cabin, his eyes darting up and down the empty rows of ugly plaid seats in front of him, he doesn't have a clue. And — even more perplexing for the Commander in Chief — there isn't even anybody to ask... *not even his beloved Nancy.*

Dagnabbit, he thinks, convinced this was all explained to him in detail this morning, in his daily briefing.

If only I was paying attention.

Now all the president can do is sit back and watch the air fresheners dangle on the seatbacks in front of him. Those air fresheners, they're a ten-cent solution to a million-dollar dilemma. One hangs from the back of each and every seat, pine tree-shaped and strongly scented.

You've seen them, you've smelt them, and Marine One — the president's dedicated transport — reeks of them.

The helicopter itself is a beast: a Sikorsky SH-3 Sea King, the same make and model that pulled the Apollo astronauts out of the Pacific. This particular ride is as iconic as the presidential seal that emblazons its sides. Just close your eyes and picture Richard Nixon waving his peace-signs before turning and flying off into his soon-to-be-pardoned sunset.

Sandwiched between the fuselage and the massive, sixty-foot long rotor blades are the helicopter's twin turboshaft engines. And despite the staggering amount of money the United States Marine Corps has spent over the years trying to stop the jet fumes from drifting down into the cabin, drift they do.

And when it comes to the first lady, Mrs. Nancy Davis Reagan, the former Hollywood starlet turned White House decorator, these fumes — and their habit of lingering on one's chic, custom-made clothing — is downright unacceptable.

These air fresheners are the Marine Corps' desperate attempt to mask said fumes. But they're not just any scent. No no. Just as the first lady is picky in regards to the dining china presented to foreign dignitaries, she too is picky in regards to air fresheners. And, for those whose whole existence in the federal government is to appease the first lady, her air freshener of choice is the refined scent of jasmine.

Frustrated, he turns to the nearest man.

"Son," he says. "You mind telling me what's going on here?"

The man stares at him, nervous. The others shift uncomfortably. "Mister President," the man says, trailing off. "Umm..."

"Yes?" Reagan asks, impatient.

The man swallows. "Sir," he says, his voice cracking.

Reagan studies him. Noting the man's struggle for words and sweat beading on his forehead, the president assumes the worst.

"This is it, isn't it?" Reagan asks.

"This is what?" the man asks, confused.

"War," the president says, drawn out. "We are at war."

Taken aback, the man glances at the others. One of the men shrugs back at him. Reagan, not waiting for any sort of confirmation, dramatically staggers back, grabbing the handrail for support...

We. Are. At. War.

Since his inauguration over two years ago, these are the four words the president has feared most. The Cold War, a perilous extension of World War Two that has pitted the U.S.A. and U.S.S.R. in a dangerous standoff, armed with thousands of nuclear weapons locked and loaded in a deadly game of chicken, has left the world on the brink of total annihilation.

We are at war, Reagan tells himself again.

Those commie bastards.

The president abruptly steps away from the helicopter, startling the armed men. He looks up at the night sky, watching the stars twinkle above him, peaceful and serene. A shooting-star streaks across his view.

An incoming warhead? the president wonders, then nods.

"This is it, huh?" Reagan asks, turning back to the men. "Well," he says, straightening up. "Be sure to hit 'em with everything we got, boys." Feeling the need to lighten the mood — comedy was always his forte — the president continues: "Give me liberty... or give me *Mutually Assured Destruction.*"

Reagan chuckles to himself. But he realizes the men are staring at him, stone-faced.

"That's a joke," Reagan adds.

But the men say nothing.

Reagan frowns. *Something isn't right*, he thinks.

Taking a moment, the president recalls the events of his day, thinking of everything that had led to him being here and now. There was breakfast with Nancy, a crunchy bowl of Raisin Bran cereal. There was — yet another — drawn-out meeting on the economy. Vice President Bush blabbing on about last night's episode of *Dallas*. And then...

The unexpected arrival of Marine One.

There was confusion in the West Wing, his staff flustered and panicked, culminating in them rushing him out the door. The president dozed off not long after takeoff. He woke up clueless and confused.

The air fresheners... The missile facility... The armed men... The war...

Something isn't right.

"Move it, old man," a voice barks, shoving the president from behind. "This way," the man orders, pushing Reagan toward the access building. The armed men that greeted the president follow behind, their boots crunching on the gravel.

"Inside," the voice says, forcing the president into the security center. Fluorescent lights flicker over a bank of CRT monitors, each one displaying another closed-circuit security camera from somewhere within the complex.

Reagan — always the narcissist — catches a glimpse of himself in one of the monitors. He pauses to admire his image in profile before noticing the man pushing him around, standing behind him. And the president's jaw drops.

Towering over him is Nash, a steroid-raging brute of a man. Reagan turns, looking up into the man's eyes. But with unbridled hatred, Nash stares down at the president.

"Get in the fucking elevator," Nash says.

The elevator shaft descends ninety feet to the hardened, underground bunker below. Built of concrete and steel, missile bases like this were made to withstand indirect nuclear blasts.

The president reminds himself of this as they ride the elevator down — but a nuclear attack seems to be the least of his worries, not with the way he's being treated and roughhoused. The hoist cable moans as the car stops at the bottom of the shaft. The door opens. And Reagan peers out.

"Move," Nash orders, pushing him off the elevator.

The president stumbles out and finds himself in the facility's main corridor: a ten-foot diameter tunnel, every inch of which is the same lime-green. Every twenty feet, concrete bulkheads reinforce against the earth above them. The tunnel leads a hundred feet or so to the first of three visible access points, each separated by massive hydraulic blast doors.

Nash shoves Reagan along the walkway and a handful of guards follow close behind. Stepping through the various sections of the facility, they approach an intersection of two corridors.

Curious, Reagan glances to his left, spotting the facility's power generator and air filtration system — nothing alarming down that way. But to his right, the president spots the signage for the silo itself...

The missile, he thinks, uneasily.

"Keep moving," Nash says, pushing the president through the third access point.

Reagan finds himself in another, albeit smaller tunnel. At the end of the corridor awaits a room labeled *Launch Control Center*.

The president hesitates as they approach the blast door. He looks inside and finds the room devoid of any launch equipment. There's no guidance computer or communication station or anything. Instead, an old worn-out couch — lumpy and stained — sits front and center. In front of that is an old black and white television.

Reagan's eyes light up as he recognizes what's on screen: *Bedtime for Bonzo*, a 1951 feature starring Reagan himself.

"Get your ass in there," Nash barks, pushing the president inside. He forces a jar of jellybeans into Reagan's hands and shoves him down onto the couch.

The president, enamored by his own visage on screen, hardly notices the abuse and instinctively grabs a handful of jellybeans — his absolute favorite — throwing them into his mouth.

Nash backs out of the room. But as he steps one foot out the door, Reagan snaps from his trance...

Something isn't right.

Thoughts of Nancy flicker in the president's mind. As much as Reagan would love sitting around watching television all day — especially television with his own face plastered on screen — the first lady would not approve.

Nancy, he thinks. *My beloved Nancy...*

"Now hold it right there, son," Reagan says, pausing Nash. "What about Nancy?"

Nash looks the president over, sitting there like a fool, his hand deep in the jar of jellybeans. A cruel sneer creeps onto his face.

"Oh. Don't worry, sir. She'll be dead soon enough!"

And with that, Nash bursts into laughter.

Reagan stares at him, stunned.

"What does that mean?" the president asks, meekly.

Nash cackles his way out of the room, slamming the blast door shut behind him. The mechanical locks clunk into place, leaving the president alone and imprisoned.

It's now that Reagan realizes, with absolute certainty, that something is wrong...

Something is very, very wrong.

Ronald Wilson Reagan — the fortieth president of the United States, the Commander in Chief, the Leader of the Free World — has just been kidnapped.

PART ONE

The dream is always the same.

Steven Leonard, thirty years old, sits at a banquet table at a fancy reception. His tuxedo, his hair, they're perfect. Sitting across from him are his loving parents — they're always in the dream. Next to Steven is his date — she tends to change. Today, she's blonde. Sometimes she's brunette. Blue eyes, brown eyes, whatever. The details don't particularly matter, she swoons over Steven all the same.

A hush falls upon the room as a distinguished-looking individual steps up to a lectern. "And the winner of the 1984 Pulitzer Prize goes to," the man says, the audience holding its collective breath. "Steven Leonard."

There is uproarious applause as Steven, squinting in the spotlight, takes the stage.

"Thank you. Thank you all," Steven says into the microphone, his parents beaming with pride, his date hopelessly in love...

• • •

Steven Leonard opens his eyes, smiling. Whether it's night or day, that dream keeps him going, keeps him moving. And now, sitting behind the wheel of his hand-me-down Chevy Vega, Steven is closer to making that dream come true than he ever could have imagined.

Before him, at the end of a winding mountain road, awaits a beautiful cabin home, rustic and grand.

I found it, Steven thinks. *I actually found it.*

Though this cabin marks the end of an hours-long drive from Ithaca, New York, it signals the beginning of a far greater journey — one that Steven hopes will culminate in his very own Pulitzer, the highest honor to be bestowed upon the country's finest journalists and, in Steven's case, would-be journalists.

Past recipients of the prize include such powerhouse investigative reporters as Bob Woodward and Carl Bernstein, the two who broke the Watergate scandal, and Seymour Hersh — Steven's personal favorite. Hersh broke the story of Project Azorian, a top-secret C.I.A. mission that attempted to raise a sunken Soviet missile submarine sixteen-thousand feet beneath the ocean's surface, an engineering feat on par with landing a man on the moon.

Today, however, Steven hopes to top them all.

Today, if all goes well, Steven Leonard will reveal to the world the existence of Hunter Gunne, secret agent extraordinaire. A man single-handedly responsible for saving the world a startling number of times...

That is, of course, if Steven can convince this secret agent that not only does his story need to be told, but Steven is the man to tell it.

Unlike Woodward and Bernstein, who worked for *The Washington Post*, and Hersh, who worked for *The New York Times* — both pillars of investigative journalism — Steven doesn't work for anybody. In fact, most professionals would write off much of what Steven's uncovered as nothing more than conspiratorial sleuthing.

But if Steven's hunch is correct, and Steven can deliver the story he hopes to deliver...

The world will never be the same.

Steven puts the car in park and shuts off the engine. On the seat next to him, he looks at the mess of maps and candy bar wrappers — not to mention dumb luck — it took to find this place.

Pulling off the highway an hour ago, he snaked his way along old lumber roads deep into the Maryland wilderness. Calling this place secluded doesn't quite do it justice. It's beyond isolated. If Steven had to guess, there probably isn't another person within twenty miles.

Steven steps out of the car, grabs his courier bag, and shuts the door. He glances at his reflection in the car's window, checking his appearance. Wearing a worn corduroy blazer, Steven is average in just about every conceivable way, for better or worse. Average height, average weight, average looks.

Hunter Gunne, on the other hand, is anything but average. From what Steven has pieced together — culled from his years of research — Hunter Gunne is the real deal.

He is as deadly an assassin as the world has ever known, as daring a hero as anybody can imagine, and — from what Steven can gather — retired. Or at least inactive...

But hopefully not dead, Steven thinks.

Armed with the five Ws of journalism — *the who, what, where, when, and why* — Steven steps onto the porch.

This is it, he thinks.

And he knocks on the front door.

Years of Steven's life have been spent on this single pursuit — much to the dismay of his family and friends. But now, here he is — at this very moment, on this very porch, on this very day — on the verge of proving it wasn't just some stupid obsession. That it was a legit pursuit. And an important one, at that.

A lot of people doubted Steven. They've called him crazy and a kook. But Steven isn't some quack in a tin-foil hat. He's a journalist, a born investigator, who has dedicated his life to the truth.

And the truth is this: the world has come closer to destruction far more often than we know. In fact, humankind has tittered on the brink of extinction with such alarming regularity that if it wasn't for this Hunter Gunne, none of us would even be here to question it.

But this pursuit of Steven's hasn't come without sacrifice.

Everybody knows the common conspiracy theories out there: that there was a second gunman on the grassy knoll, that the moon landings were faked, or that *The Catcher in the Rye* is a trigger for sleeper assassins.

And even Steven can understand their appeal. Conspiracy theories help life make sense, especially for those lacking the critical thinking skills to know better. But most conspiracy theories are just that: theories. Of which almost all can be easily disproven by verifiable facts.

But sometimes, it's those verifiable facts that lead the way, pointing an investigative journalist like Steven in an unexpected direction. And if someone digs deep enough and skillfully enough, that's where one starts to uncover the real secrets. That's where one discovers the truths that keep you up at night.

It's in this vein that Steven, time and again, has come across the exploits of one super-secret agent: Hunter Gunne.

The thing about Steven is that he had a promising career laid out in front of him. And he walked away from it. A good newspaper job, and all the accolades that come with it, just didn't seem to matter when compared to the truth — to the real truth.

Over the years, almost every one of Steven's colleagues disowned him. At some point, nearly all his old professors stopped returning his calls. But despite it all, Steven's managed to accumulate a handful of reputable sources who share his passion. People on the inside.

Some work in the media, others in government. Steven even has a few allies in the military, feeding him random intel whenever they stumble across it. Granted, none of these sources would ever dare go public, but for Steven, it's been nice having people to talk to.

If only they — Steven's friends and family, his doubters and haters — could see him now, on the verge of such achievement.

If only they could see him on the cusp of such glory.

If only…

If only somebody would answer this damn door, Steven thinks, snapping out of his daze. He knocks again, forcing himself to stay positive, to focus on his hopeful interview.

There is so much that Steven doesn't know about Hunter Gunne and his decades-spanning career. More often than not, Steven has had to resort to filling in the blanks himself…

Hunter Gunne was a secret agent, he knows that with certainty. He knows — well, he's pretty sure at least — that Hunter Gunne single-handedly thwarted a nuclear confrontation during the Cuban Missile Crisis. But how exactly, Steven doesn't have a clue. And who Hunter Gunne worked for, what agency, remains a mystery.

None of this prevents Steven from imagining Hunter Gunne sitting across from him, prepared to be interviewed. Maybe they're in a study, bookshelves full of leather-bound books surrounding them. Perhaps the man is handsome, with a square jaw and a tumbler of scotch in hand.

Steven, his pen and paper ready to go, is cool and confident. He already earned Gunne's respect from the get-go, impressing Gunne with his perseverance and commitment. They hit it off immediately, sharing an understanding of each other, an understanding of what it means to dedicate oneself to the greater good — *of saving the world.*

Yes, Hunter Gunne tells Steven, his voice low and gravelly. *The world must know of my adventures, of my do-gooding. And you, Steven Leonard, are the one to tell them...*

Be my disciple, he tells Steven. *And tell my story.*

• • •

Steven stares at the cabin door, smiling like an idiot. But no answer comes. Inch by inch, his doubts crowd out his optimism, deflating his spirits.

"Shit," he mumbles.

Desperate, Steven pounds on the door again, harder and louder. He listens, straining to hear the slightest hint of life inside. But he hears nothing. Absolutely nothing.

"Son of a bitch," he says, his shoulders sagging in defeat.

You're a loser, Steven. Always have been.

Now what? he wonders.

He could wait... but for how long? If this is a vacation home, it could be months before anybody comes around. Steven could head back into town, ask the locals what they know of this place and about the owner. But it will probably lead to the same dead-end it usually does.

"Damn," Steven sighs, sulking back to his car.

He pulls his key out of his pocket, opens the car door, and is about to sit down when...

The front door swings open.

Steven turns to see a woman standing in the doorway, eyeing him. He stares back at her, speechless, like a deer in headlights. The woman is tall and athletic, wearing a wool skirt that meets her riding boots just below her knees. Her hair — red with grey streaks— is pulled tight into a bun. Her eyes — green and unblinking — watch him like a hawk.

"Hello," Steven says, finally. He rushes up the porch, tripping on the last step. The woman watches his every move, clumsy as he may be. "Hello, miss..." Steven says, extending his hand, baiting for her name.

But the woman says nothing.

"My name is Steven Leonard," he says, playing it cool. "From *Parade Magazine*," he continues, lying. "The most widely read magazine in the United States. Which I'm sure you're familiar with," he adds, hoping to impress.

"You're here to sell me a magazine subscription?" she asks, scanning him head to toe, sizing him up — all five feet, eleven inches.

"What? No," Steven scoffs. "I'm a journalist."

The woman's eyes narrow, as if sniffing out his bullshit.

"What do you want?" she asks.

"I'm looking for…" Steven hesitates, knowing that there's no going back. It's all or nothing now.

"I'm looking for Hunter Gunne."

2

November 1936 — Skagway, Alaska

"Tell me again, momma," the little girl says, pulling her bedsheets tight. "Tell me about the wolves."

"Again?" the mother asks, sitting on the edge of the mattress. "Now that's not a particularly pleasant bedtime story, is it?"

Outside, snowflakes swirl beyond the drafty, old windows.

Skagway — a small Alaskan town far from what most would call *civilization* — is cold and dark. This time of year, so close to the Arctic Circle, the days don't last long. The sun rises late in the morning and sets early in the afternoon.

In Skagway, life is different.

The mother looks at her daughter, studying her. Her daughter never knew her grandfather — or the man she *knows* as her grandfather — but her adoration for him grows stronger each and every day. Having passed away not long after she was born, the daughter — now six years old — only knows the man through the stories her mother is willing to share.

But, when it comes to life in Skagway, all one has are stories...

"Please," the little girl asks. "Please, mamma."

Skagway is located halfway up the Alaskan panhandle, nestled in the northernmost tip of the Taiya Inlet. Imposing mountain ranges surround the town, looming over its inhabitants. Beyond them lies the Yukon territory, the continent's ultimate frontier.

The mother's eyes narrow.

"These old stories about your grandfather best not be giving you nightmares," she warns.

Of these stories, the mother knows that few other parents would consider them appropriate for a six-year-old child. But with no other adults in their lives — at least none they can trust — educating her daughter to the realities of the world has fallen squarely on her.

The world is a mean place, after all. And the sooner the little girl embraces that, the mother thinks, *the better.*

Some forty years ago, Skagway was a boomtown.

When gold was discovered in the Klondike, thousands upon thousands of hopeful stampeders poured into the town each and every day, eager to set off toward their expectant fortunes. A lot of gold passed through this port. And with it came all the good and bad that one would expect.

As for the little girl's grandfather: he was one of the good.

"The story about the wolves?" the mother asks, flattening her cotton skirt on her lap.

"The grey wolves," the daughter specifies.

Today, Skagway is an echo of what it once was. The gold didn't last long, only a few years. And as it thinned out, so did the crowds. This hotel, and the tavern below, were built by the little girl's grandfather to accommodate the rush. Today, the mother runs it, the two of them living in a handful of the rooms upstairs. Customers are scarce. But they make do.

Back in the day, the little girl's grandfather had his fair share of competition. Just up the street was a brothel where the girls would greet the boys rolling off the dock. And just past that, if the boys could manage their way up there: a gambling saloon.

Her grandfather, however, wouldn't have anything like that — nor the trouble that followed it — in his establishment. But her grandfather was never one to judge, as long as you weren't hurting anybody, that is.

So, if the girls down at the brothel needed a place to get away, they were always welcome. And if the bunco men came in search of a warm meal and some fatherly advice, they were welcome too. But, when there were signs of trouble, the little girl's grandfather would swiftly stamp out those flames... lest they become a fire.

Trouble was the reason the little girl's grandfather was up in the Alaskan territory. *Trouble* was what her grandfather was trying to get away from...

"Chickens," the mother says, starting the story. "They were your grandfather's daddy's chickens. And his daddy's daddy's before him. They were chicken farmers, three generations of them. And successful too. With a big ol' barn and a big ol' farmhouse, far away in..."

"*Ol' Virginia,*" the little girl says, settling into her pillow.

The mother nods.

Decades ago, her grandfather had made his trek north to Skagway. But decades before that, he lived another life entirely. Back in the mid-nineteenth century, the little girl's beloved grandfather was but a young man in the proud state of Virginia. But Virginia — like most of the United States at the time — found itself in an existential crisis, both as a state and as an ideology.

"Your grandfather had a good life," the mother continues. "A simple life. He wasn't a political man. Or a religious man.

But people looked up to him. He believed in what was right and wasn't afraid to stand up for it either. But in those days, what was right wasn't so agreed upon. A lot of folks, they admired your grandfather. But a lot of other folks didn't care much for him." The mother looks at her daughter, emphasizing her next point. "Standing up for what you believe," she says, "is a good way of making enemies."

"The grey wolves," the little girl whispers.

The mother nods.

Long before the original thirteen colonies banded together against the British Empire, there was already a division among the colonists of the North and South... and that division fell solely on the issue of slavery.

By the American Revolution, the abolitionist spirit was already sweeping the massive populations of Philadelphia, New York City, and Boston. But Virginia — *ol' Virginia* — never wavered in its commitment to slavery. And by the 1850s, that issue reached its boiling point.

War was inevitable.

The thing about *ol' Virginia* was that, both geographically and economically, the western side of the state shared little with their eastern brethren. In fact, many saw the Appalachian Mountains as an impassable barrier between the two. So, when the east-dominated state legislature voted to secede from the Union — to preserve slavery — the western counties, abolitionist in spirit, decided to secede themselves.

And thus, the state of West Virginia was born.

Ironically, for those in Richmond — Virginia's state capital — the southern spirit of succession didn't apply to one's own state. And there were plenty of Virginians all too happy to hold a grudge.

Payback, as they saw it, came in waves of violence against the west. At first, they were state militias, later they became Confederate soldiers. They'd loot and steal, taking the food and supplies needed to fight the Union Army. But later, the violence became more maniacal, more ruthless. Years into the war, as defeat lingered on the horizon, the violence became more personal.

"You see," the mother says, continuing on, "your grandfather believed in something, something these wolves didn't, and wouldn't believe in. And *that* was man's inherent freedom. Your grandfather saw every man his equal, no matter their race or wealth or upbringing. And so, naturally, your grandfather helped these folks any way he could. If folks were hungry, he'd feed 'em. If folks were cold, he'd warm 'em. And if these folks needed safe passage to the North, well, he'd get them to where they needed to go.

"It wasn't long before your grandfather garnered a reputation. Not because he wanted to be known, but because his actions spoke loud and carried far. But those wolves," the mother says, shaking her head. "They just couldn't stand to see their world changing. They couldn't adapt, you see. And if you can't adapt, you can't survive. And if you can't survive... well, I reckon you lash out. And that's what they did. These wolves, desperate and mean, they came for your grandfather. They came for his chickens. And his friends. And his..."

The mother hesitates, the horror of the story getting caught in her throat.

"His farm?" the little girl asks.

The mother looks at her daughter. This story isn't an easy one to tell. But denying it to her would be like denying her of her grandfather. And that doesn't seem right either.

"I'm afraid so," the mother says, closing her eyes as the terrifying details flash across her mind: the men on horseback, their torches and muskets in hand. The little girl's grandfather being dragged from his porch. The butt of their guns breaking his bones. His friends hanging from the trees. And his wife and child inside the house, screaming as it burns around them...

"They took everything from him," the mother says, clearing her throat. "The war waged on. And your grandfather waited, hopeful that, in time, the law would bring those wolves to justice. But when the war did eventually end — with slavery abolished — that day of justice never came.

"You see, those in power — those tasked with rebuilding the nation — well, much to your grandfather's dismay, they turned a blind eye toward the crimes that befell him. After all, they'd say, your grandfather *was* breaking the law of the day, helping slaves to freedom and all... before they were granted their freedom legally, that is."

"So, what did he do?" the daughter asks.

"He outsmarted them, just as your grandfather was wont to do," the mother says. "He got into their heads and under their skin. They were paranoid and panicked and worked up into a frenzy that he was gonna come for them and their kin."

The little girl cowers. "Would... would grandfather have ever hurt... their families?"

"Now you know your grandfather better than that," the mother says — to her daughter's relief. "Instead, those wolves banded together again. They reformed their old militia. They unpacked their muskets and saddled their horses. And those wolves rode for your grandfather again. But this time, your grandfather was ready."

"What happened?" the daughter asks.

"Using himself as bait, your grandfather lured those wolves into the old barn. Springing his trap, he nailed the doors shut before they even knew what was happening. And then, just as those wolves discovered that the chickens had been replaced with barrels of gunpowder, your grandfather..."

The mother trails off, staring at the flickering candle on the nightstand. The little girl, studying her mother, sets her jaw — and in a surprisingly firm voice, she finishes her mother's story: "He set it ablaze."

The mother looks at her daughter and, for a moment, she can't help but see the grandfather staring back at her.

Evading the authorities, her grandfather fled west. First to San Francisco, then Seattle, and finally Skagway — the most lawless town on the continent — where just about every other feller adorned a most-wanted poster somewhere in the states.

It was here, in Skagway, that the little girl's grandfather felt safe enough to grow roots again. Decades went by. And it was here that her mother, scared and alone — having been trafficked north against her will — stumbled into this old tavern, now pregnant and worthless to her captors. The old man she found here — the man her daughter endearingly knows as *grandfather* — took her in and treated her as if she were his own offspring.

It was in the eventual throes of labor that she — so thankful and appreciative for everything this old man had given her — promised to name the soon-to-be-delivered child after him. But when the baby came, the mother was shocked to find a beautiful baby girl staring up at her. But she kept her promise nonetheless...

She looks down at her daughter.

"Well, I think that's enough for tonight," the mother says, tucking the blanket around her.

"I miss him," the little girl says, her eyes heavy.

"Well, there's no need to miss him," the mother says. "Your grandfather is right here," she says, tapping her daughter's chest. "His spirit lives on in you."

The little girl smiles as the mother blows out the candle. She watches her walk toward the door.

"Goodnight, mamma," the daughter says.

"Goodnight, Hunter."

3

"I'm looking for Hunter Gunne," Steven says.

The woman — still half-hidden by the door — stares at him, motionless. Steven shifts uncomfortably under her gaze.

"I'm writing a retrospective on the Cuban Missile Crisis," Steven continues. "And I've had several sources tell me this is where I can find him. Your husband?"

The woman forces a smile. But says nothing.

"I believe Mister Gunne had a significant but, until now, undocumented role," Steven says. "Not only in averting the crisis, but in quite-literally saving the world. And, if anything, that story should be told, ma'am. This man should be celebrated."

The woman eyes him.

"May I come in?" Steven asks, finally.

The woman considers, then steps aside and opens the door for him. Steven doesn't hesitate, darting by her before she can change her mind. Passing the threshold, Steven is oblivious to the knife the woman has been hiding from him, concealed by the door itself. As she turns to follow him, she skillfully tucks it behind her back.

She herds Steven through the foyer and into the parlor. The entire backside of the cabin is comprised of enormous, two-story-tall A-frame windows, and the view of the valley below is staggering.

Steven, weary of heights, hesitates. The room itself is an exquisite combination of luxury and rustic charm — Steven's never seen anything like it.

The woman offers Steven a chair. Sitting across from him, she watches Steven like an owl hunting its prey. "Tell me," she says. "What do you know about Hunter Gunne?"

Steven exhales — just hearing somebody else mention the name is a relief.

"A legit Cold War warrior, ma'am," Steven says. "Resourceful. Fearless. Brilliant. For years now, I've been retracing every step of his lengthy career, putting the pieces together." Steven leans toward her, lowering his voice. "To be completely honest, ma'am, we should all be very thankful that Hunter Gunne exists."

"Oh, really?" the woman asks, critically. "And why is that?"

"Why is that?" Steven scoffs. "Ma'am. Hunter Gunne single-handed saved humankind time and time again. And asked nothing for it. Clearly, this man is selfless. Clearly, this man is honorable," he says, all while the woman studies him, noting his excitement, his enthusiasm. "And clearly," Steven continues, "this man should be celebrated."

On that note, Steven notices the woman's hyper-focused attention and clams up, embarrassed. He clears his throat.

"I was really worried I was going to leave empty-handed," he says, shifting uncomfortably in his chair, his slacks squeaking on the leather. The cabin falls quiet, and Steven glances around, looking down the hallway behind him.

"So... your husband. Is he..."

"It's been years," the woman says, unexpectedly. "*Years*," she emphasizes, "since I've had visitors."

"Excuse me?" Steven asks.

"It's funny, really," the woman continues, undaunted. "You get so used to it, you come to expect it. You actually look forward to it..." she says, trailing off.

"To what?"

"*Them,*" she says. "Coming for you."

Steven blinks, not sure what this has to do with anything.

"It was like a game," the woman says. "And oh, how it was fun. For years they came. And then one day... they just stopped. I found out later that they had all hung up their holsters for jobs on Wall Street. They're all lawyers and CEOs now, the bastards. And suddenly you're left," the woman motions about the cabin, "hiding in the woods, growing old. No Valhalla. No warrior's death. No nothing."

She shakes her head, disappointed.

"Who?" Steven asks, lost.

"*Assassins,*" she says, smiling.

And in a flash, she's out of her chair and on top of Steven. Pinning her knee to his chest, she holds the knife to his throat.

"Who sent you?"

But Steven — the blade cold against his neck — struggles to speak. Impatient, the woman leans back, pulling Steven to his feet. Clutching his collar, she spins him through a set of swinging doors and into the kitchen.

Steven slams against the counter. The woman rips the bag off his shoulder, dumping the contents on the countertop.

Car keys, a notebook... *but no weapons.*

The woman spins Steven around, pressing him face-first against the refrigerator. She kicks his feet apart and pats him down.

Steven, his eyes wide, holds his breath as her hands pass over his body. She stops, finding something in his front pocket.

Her fingers explore it through his slacks: about six inches long, a few inches in girth. She takes a good hold of it and whips it out, expecting the worst.

But it's only a candy bar.

She tosses it aside, disappointed.

"No guns. No knives," she says, grabbing Steven's hair and yanking his head back. "How the hell were you gonna kill me? Bore me to death?"

"I'm not here to..." Steven stammers, but the woman drags him out of the kitchen.

She throws him to the hallway floor, frustrated.

"Who do you work for? C.I.A.? K.G.B.? O.W.O.?"

She pauses, then jerks hard at his collar, pressing the knife to his throat.

"Are you O.L.D.?"

"Lady," Steven shouts. "I'm not here to kill you! I swear..."

There's a knock at the front door. Both Steven and the woman freeze. Through the curtains, they see men. Two of them to be sure.

"Is anybody with you?" the woman asks.

Steven shakes his head. The woman leans in close, her breath hot on Steven's face.

"Who did you tell you were coming here?" she asks.

"Nobody," Steven says, lying. "I swear."

The doorbell rings.

Without hesitating, the woman heaves Steven to his feet. She spins him, building momentum before throwing him forcefully into a bedroom... just as the front door explodes with gunfire.

The woman plows Steven to the floor, straddling him.

"Stay down," she shouts as machine guns shred the front door, shatter the windows, and splinter the hardwood floors.

Steven has never heard anything as loud as the barrage of bullets currently destroying the foyer. Fortunately — and purposefully — the log walls take the beating, keeping the two of them safe... for now.

Outside the cabin, the gunfire ceases, and the front door is kicked in. Judging by the sound of the boots stomping into the foyer, a dozen or so men have poured into the house.

The woman glides over to the nightstand. She opens the drawer, reaches inside, and pulls out a Glock 17.

Steven watches in awe as the woman checks the magazine and chambers a round — he's never seen a gun before, not in person at least.

The woman notices Steven staring at the weapon.

"You. On your feet," she says, heaving him off the floor. "You really a journalist?"

Steven's mind races — to tell the truth, or not? "Yeah."

The woman opens a closet, grabbing a handful of bulletproof vests hanging inside. They're hard-plate reinforced, meant for heavy combat, the real deal. She jams them into Steven's hands and flashes him a sadistic smile.

"Hold these."

An armed man — decked out in black fatigues and assault gear — kicks the bedroom door down. The woman spins Steven toward the intruder, ducking behind him as the man levels his

Colt submachine gun and opens fire. The bullets pound into the vests, each round a punch to Steven's gut.

But the vests do their job — Steven is still alive. In only a few seconds, the man empties his magazine, all thirty-two rounds, sending the empty bullet casings across the room and into the dresser mirror. It's in this mirror that the woman, safe behind Steven, waits her turn...

As the man clicks empty, the woman pops out and fires, tagging him between the eyes. The man falls to the floor, his brains sprayed out on the wall behind him, and Steven — this day already full of firsts for him — sees his first dead body.

The shock of it all easily outweighs the deafening ring in his ears. Numb, he can barely hear the woman as she shoves him toward the door.

"To the kitchen," she says as they step over the body. "Lead the way."

In the hallway, two men are waiting, armed and ready. They open fire, further shredding the vests still clutched to Steven's chest.

"Jesus Christ," Steven screams.

As the agents empty their magazines, the woman peeks out around Steven and picks them off one by one. BAM. BAM. The men fall back into the wall. Blood streaks as they slide to the floor, dead.

"I've missed this," the woman exclaims, gazing at her gun, talking to it like it's an old friend. "I really have."

Steven stares at the two dead men. Hundreds of rounds have been fired at him. And this woman, dragging him about, is a ruthless killer in her own right.

"You," she says, poking his chest. "I have questions for you."

The woman pushes Steven into the kitchen as another man enters from the far side. She pulls Steven to the floor — out of harm's way — just as the man opens fire. The cabinets explode into shards of wood.

Reaching up to the counter, the woman grabs a kitchen knife. She throws it, sticking the man square in the throat — severing his trachea and jugular and everything in between. Blood gurgles from the wound as the woman swoops up behind him, grabs hold of his head, and in one merciful jerk, snaps his neck.

Steven watches in terror as the man collapses to the floor, dead. "Oh, God."

"Let's go," the woman barks, pushing Steven through the basement door. She slams it shut behind them just as a team of men rushes into the kitchen, guns blazing, their bullets ricocheting off the steel-reinforced door. Sliding a heavy-duty deadbolt into place, she drags Steven down the stairs...

Waiting in the basement is a customized Jeep CJ-7.

"Get in. Buckle up," the woman says.

Steven looks at the 4x4, perplexed.

"Where are we going?" he asks.

The woman slides open a garage door built into the basement wall — revealing the breathtaking view of the valley as seen from the parlor. Below them, the mountainside slopes almost straight down into the forest.

The woman flashes Steven a smile...

"Down," she says.

Steven shakes his head.

This woman is out of her mind, he thinks.

But the dozen of armed men trying to kick in the basement door doesn't leave him with many options. He climbs into the passenger seat as she starts the supercharged engine. The woman slides on a pair of racing goggles, puts the transmission in gear... but then hesitates.

"Yeah," she says, staring into the blazing sunlight, almost inaudible. "This is a good way to die."

Steven, struggling with his racing harness, looks at her.

"Excuse me? A good way to *what*?"

"Hang on," the woman says, smashing the gas pedal.

The Jeep launches out of the cabin straight into the air. A split second later, the Jeep falls headfirst into the forest, pushing Steven's stomach into his throat. They hit the slope and rocket down a cleared swath of trees.

Steven — happy to still be alive — looks at the woman, gushing. She looks back at him, and their eyes lock. And for a moment, smiling blissfully at each other, they share the rush of adrenaline, the joy of survival...

Then the forest explodes in gunfire. Steven screams, shielding himself with his bag. He looks back at the cabin: dozens of men, prepped for war, line the wrap-around porch, each of them unloading their machine guns in their direction.

The woman is loving every minute of it. The death-defying race down the mountain doesn't faze her at all — in fact, she clearly finds it exhilarating. She looks at Steven, a big smile on her face, and reveals a remote detonator in hand.

"Gonna be loud," she says, shouting over the engine.

Steven looks at the detonator, puzzled. "What?"

The woman presses the thumb-button...

KA-BOOM.

The entire cabin erupts in a massive explosion. Steven turns in his seat, wide-eyed. Feeling the heat on his face, he watches the molten red fireball mushrooming a few hundred feet above where the cabin *had been*.

It's then that Steven spots a helicopter cresting the mountain, a pair of agents hanging out the side, machine guns in hand.

"Copter!" Steven shouts.

The woman, the steering wheel bucking and jerking in her hands, glances at him.

"Huh?" she asks.

"Copter!" Steven yells.

"What?" she replies.

Steven points frantically behind them. The woman takes a look in her rearview mirror.

"Ah, a Huey," she says. The Bell UH-1 Iroquois helicopter – a beautiful machine – affectionately nicknamed *Huey*. "Badass."

The trees around them erupt in gunfire, bullets ricocheting off the Jeep. Reaching the bottom of the mountain, the woman cuts the wheel onto a narrow fire-road. The helicopter banks after them, lining up for another barrage.

The woman flips open a control panel mounted in the Jeep's dashboard. She presses the first of several toggle switches, and a thick, white smokescreen pours out the back of the vehicle... enough to hide their exact location from the gunmen.

Cutting the wheel again, the woman turns down an even narrower dirt road. The helicopter, not noticing the shift of smoke, misses the turn.

The woman, eyeing their pursuer in her rearview mirror, watches them circle around to resume their chase.

"Take the wheel," she says.

"Excuse me?" Steven asks, bewildered.

But before he knows what's happening, the woman turns out of her seat and reaches into the back. The Jeep darts to the left, and a tree rips off the side mirror.

The woman snaps back around, grabbing the steering wheel. She glares at Steven, annoyed.

"Take the goddamn wheel!"

Steven grabs it, holding it as steady as possible on the rough, gravel road. The woman, her foot still planted on the gas pedal, turns in her seat again.

She pulls a tarp, revealing an air-powered grappling hook launcher. She glances at Steven.

"You're gonna love this," she says.

Steven, however, is far more focused on the road ahead. They race by a faded old sign that reads: *CLOSED MINESHAFT AHEAD. DO NOT ENTER.*

Steven frowns. "Uh..."

The woman levels the grappling hook launcher upwards, patiently waiting for a window in the smokescreen. And then she spots it — the badass Huey in all its glory. She pulls the trigger and the harpoon-like hook launches, a spool of rope trailing behind it.

The hook pierces the helicopter's sheet metal nose and snags. The rope, still attached to the Jeep, pulls taut...

The woman grabs the steering wheel from Steven as they race toward the mine entrance. Steven eyes the mountainside climbing steeply ahead of them. Glancing back at the rope, his eyes follow it up to the still smoke-hidden helicopter.

Oh, shit, he thinks.

The woman sends the Jeep racing into the mineshaft.

In the helicopter, the pilot — still struggling to see anything through the smoke — finally notices the shape of the mountain ahead. Panicked, he pulls up on the controls. But the rope pulls taut, jolting the aircraft.

"That bitch," the pilot mutters...

The helicopter plows into the mountainside...

KA-BOOM.

The grappling hook bounces free behind them as the crumbled Huey falls to the road, a burning mess. The woman howls with laughter.

"Did you see the look on their faces? I haven't had this much fun in years!"

She looks at Steven, glowing. But Steven stares back at her in stunned silence, the carnage too much to process. The woman's smile fades. Once again, she's all business.

Turning on the Jeep's lights, they charge deeper into the void. The woman clearly knows this mine like the back of her hand, turning down a cross-tunnel and racing toward another vehicle, parked and waiting.

Skidding to a stop, she hops out of the Jeep. Steven watches her from his seat as she beelines toward a generator, kicking it on.

Several work lights flicker on, illuminating the area. The woman pulls the tarp off the vehicle, revealing a stunning 1969 Corvette Stingray, two-toned black and gold — just like the Apollo astronauts drove.

"What the hell just happened?" Steven asks, stumbling out of the Jeep.

The woman grabs a bundle of supplies, nearly plowing Steven over as she drops them into the car's trunk.

"You," she says, glaring at him. "I don't know you. But this," she gestures back the way they came, "this is your fault."

Steven swallows hard. He watches uncomfortably as the woman transfers weapons, clothes, and additional supplies to the back of the car — from the looks of it, you'd think she was outfitting a small army.

"Who are you, anyway?" she asks.

Steven hesitates, still not sure whether to come clean or not. "I'm a journalist," he says, his voice trembling. "Well. Sort of," he adds, ashamed.

"You said you were from *Parade Magazine*," she says, slamming the trunk shut.

"What? Okay. Yeah," Steven says, shrugging. "I lied."

The woman walks past him, shaking her head, clearly disgusted. "What is your name?" she asks, opening a duffle bag of armaments. "Your *real* name?"

"Steven," he answers. "For real."

"Well, Steven," she says, sliding on a pair of shoulder holsters — custom-tailored to her figure. "People are trying to kill me. Which, admittedly, I quite enjoy. But you... *you...*" she says, glaring at him. "Led them straight to me. And I want to know why. And how."

Steven looks her over, bewildered. "Hold on," he says, the pieces falling into place. "Who are you?"

The woman laughs, loading magazines into a pair of twin Beretta 92FS handguns. "Who the hell do you think I am?" she asks, chambering a round in each of them.

Steven stares at her as she holsters the weapons.

And then he gets it...

"Gunne," he says, in awe. "Hunter Gunne."

4

November 1957 — Barrow, Alaska

The thigh bone's connected to the... hip bone.
The vastus lateralis is connected to the... rectus femoris.

Sprawled out on the bar in front of Hunter Gunne is every anatomy book that she's been able to scrounge together — no easy feat considering the nearest library is hundreds of miles away.

As Hunter grew up in Skagway, her mother helped her master just about every skill one needs to survive up here in the north. Whether it be tracking prey or venturing for knowledge, such skills came easy to Hunter.

Now, at age twenty-seven, she finds herself craving more.

What began with science and math became engineering and physics, then biology and chemistry. More recently, her curiosity has led her to anatomy and medicine. What use she will get out of all this knowledge, she's never stopped to consider.

Humming the tune of *Dem Bones*, the southern spiritual hymn about the story of Ezekiel, she turns the page and studies the next, woefully outdated diagram of the human body.

All of her life, Hunter has absorbed knowledge like a sponge. A skill, her mother insisted, that one was not born with, but that one had to work at.

So, work at it Hunter has...

The hip bone's connected to the... backbone.
The gastrocnemius is connected to the... medial malleolus.

Here in Barrow, Alaska — the northernmost city of the United States — Hunter supports herself running the town's only tavern. Bartending in this locale, during this time of year affords one ample time to pursue one's own interests, whatever they may be. Looking up from her textbooks, Hunter eyes tonight's only patron...

The airman sits alone, swaying on his barstool. He has been here for hours, but like many not acclimated to life in the Arctic Circle, the constant darkness can wreck one's internal clock. Between December and January, the sun simply does not rise in Barrow. And for somebody setting out to enjoy a few drinks after their shift — Hunter assumes he was shuttling supplies out to the Point Barrow Long Range Radar Site — it's easy to lose track of time.

The name of this drafty, sheet-metal shack of an establishment is *The Northern Lights*. The building is hardly a permanent structure, and adequate insulation was clearly an afterthought. Despite the roaring wood stove at the center of the building, Hunter wears a thick leather parka handmade by the local Iñupiat, her breath steaming before her.

Barrow is cold year-round. The roads of the city consist of unpaved gravel due to the permafrost. And because of the geography (it's technically a tundra), no trees can grow. Consequently, the winds whip off of the Beaufort Sea and tear through the town mercilessly. Anything not tied down doesn't stick around for long...

Just the way Hunter likes it.

In the summer months, things are different. Barrow enjoys — or suffers, depending on who you ask — eighty consecutive days of daylight, affording the airmen, like the one sitting at her bar, the ability to work around the clock.

It's that time of year that the bartending profession becomes quite lucrative. Because, when people can't sleep, they drink.

● ● ●

Hunter was fifteen years old, still helping out at her mother's tavern when word reached Skagway that World War Two had ended. And she still remembers the overwhelming sense of relief that they felt knowing that good had triumphed evil.

But somewhere in their delight, Hunter had taken the time to read a recent edition of the *Anchorage Times*. And that was when Hunter first learned of the atomic bomb.

The United States had dropped two such weapons on the cities of Hiroshima and Nagasaki, forcing Imperial Japan into an unconditional surrender. These weapons were unlike anything the world had ever seen. The devastation and destruction incurred were almost unimaginable. To say that Hunter was shocked would be an understatement − not that such a weapon could exist, but that such a weapon had been used.

Sure, their use had potentially spared the lives of thousands − if not hundreds of thousands − of U.S. soldiers, but Hunter couldn't help but wonder at what cost. Hundreds of thousands of Japanese civilians were now dead, many of them women and children. And the stark reality was this: the atomic bomb was developed and used, despite the horrific consequences.

As such, the world would never be the same.

Within years, the Soviet Union successfully tested its own atomic bomb. A feat accomplished due to Soviet espionage rooted deep in the United States' own top-secret weapons program. And thus, the arms race began.

The theory behind an atomic weapon is simple: split an atom, and you release an incredible amount of nuclear energy. But the application of such a theory, fortunately, is not.

Taking a plutonium core about the size of a tennis ball, you surround it with conventional explosives. Trigger said explosives simultaneously, and you compress the sphere of plutonium in on itself, releasing neutrons. These neutrons bombard other plutonium atoms, releasing far more neutrons, thus creating a chain reaction and...

BOOM.

This is nuclear *fission*, in which heavier elements are split into lighter ones and — in ten-billionth of a second — the energy released generates temperatures far higher than the surface of the sun.

But almost immediately after inventing the first atomic bomb, scientists had already theorized that if a weapon could be created to trigger thermonuclear *fusion* — in which lighter elements are combined to make heavier elements — far greater, almost unlimited yields could be attained.

In a matter of years, the United States turned the hypothetical into practical, testing the world's first hydrogen bomb.

In use, thermonuclear weapons are boosted fission bombs, using the plutonium core of an atomic bomb to compress a chamber of hydrogen gas. The implosion fuses the hydrogen atoms, releasing neutrons that then further split the plutonium atoms. The result is a startlingly efficient chain reaction... and a thermonuclear explosion thousands of times more powerful than the blasts that leveled Hiroshima and Nagasaki.

All of this — from the uneasy tension between the world's two superpowers to the ever-growing stockpile of nuclear weapons — found its way to Barrow, Alaska, plopping the front-line of the Cold War smack-dab in Hunter's backyard...

The Distant Early Warning Line (affectionately known as the DEW Line) is, to date, one of the more impressive engineering feats of the Cold War.

Consisting of sixty-three radar stations stretching from the Alaskan territory to Baffin Island — nearly seven thousand miles — each of these sites reside hundreds of miles north of the Arctic Circle in some of the most formidable locales in the world.

At the start of the decade, not long after the Soviet Union detonated its own atomic weapon, fear of a Soviet sneak attack reached a frenzy. The need for an early warning radar system to detect the hundreds of Soviet bombers crossing the North Pole unannounced was deemed one of the United States' highest priorities. The subsequent development and construction of the radar sites and technology fell to the Western Electric Company.

And no expense was spared.

Construction began in 1954, and it was a logistical nightmare. Even with the assistance of the Army, Navy, and Air Force, most of the work could only proceed in the summer months, lest the locations be totally inaccessible by land or sea. All told, twenty-five thousand men were employed, most of them civilian workers... a flood of manpower that Alaska hadn't seen since the gold rush.

And with this flood, towns like Barrow and other cities on the edge of the frontier flourished. Roads were laid, buildings were built, and airfields constructed — all in the most hostile climates of North America.

Trucks, tankers, airplanes, even dog sleds were put to work, often in blinding snowstorms and subzero temperatures. These men worked hard, long hours, and at the end of the day... you damn well better believe they were ready to drink.

• • •

Hovering over her anatomy books, Hunter keeps an eye on the drunk airman at her bar. When construction of the DEW Line commenced, Hunter knew the influx of jobs and money was too good to pass up. So, she jumped at it.

Saying goodbye to Skagway, she trekked north and found a new home in Barrow. The work here may not be much, but one can do a lot worse than babysitting drunk servicemen.

As the big guy at the end of the bar takes one last swig of his beer, Hunter casually walks out and around, approaching him from behind. As the airman leans back, way back, to savor those last few precious drops... he loses his balance.

The man stumbles off his stool and falls harmlessly into Hunter's arms.

"Well fella," Hunter says, bracing his weight until he manages to get his own feet under him. "I think it's time to call it a night."

The airman, suffering both exhaustion and intoxication, looks at her — or tries to — and mumbles in agreement. Hunter plops the man's buffalo plaid bomber hat atop his head.

"Don't forget your gloves," she says, dressing him as a child about to go sledding. Snapping her fingers in front of his face, she forces him to pay attention. "Your key," she says. "Show me your key."

The airman searches his pockets, finally producing a key. Attached to it is a tag with the number eighteen printed on it.

Hunter snatches it from him.

"Alright," she says, leading him toward the door. "Let's get you home."

The two of them step outside into the treacherous Arctic winter. The man looks left, then right. After some careful consideration, he shuffles off toward his left.

But Hunter stops him.

"Nope," she says, dragging him toward the right. "This way."

A block down the road is the barracks: temporary housing built by the United States Air Force for the stream of servicemen and construction workers coming and going throughout the year. Hunter leads the man down a row of buildings, coming to room eighteen.

With the key, Hunter opens the door and pushes the airman inside. She flips a light switch, and the airman smiles at the sight of his bed. He lurches toward it... then falls face-first onto the mattress.

Hunter smirks, dropping the key next to him on the bed. She turns to leave... but hesitates. She looks over the man's room. His luggage is open, and clothes are strewn about. On the nightstand, a pile of magazines catches her eye. Stepping over, she sees a handful of photographs atop of them.

Picking up one photo in particular, she studies it. The airman appears to be a family man. Judging by the bright pastels the wife and children are dressed in, she guesses the photo was taken last Easter. They look happy, she notes, the colors bright and vibrant — a stark contrast to the dreary and drab world she lives in up here.

Is this what normal life looks like? she wonders.

To each their own, she thinks, sliding the photos to the side.

Beneath them sits the most recent issue of *Life* magazine.

Grabbing the magazine, she glances one last time at the airman — he's snoring contently in his hat and gloves. She flicks off the lights and closes the door behind her.

Back outside, the wind swirls wildly. She pulls her hood over her head and walks back to the bar, thumbing through the magazine.

The main cover line reads, in ominous big letters, *Sputnik and The Reds: How they got to space first and what we're going to do about it.* Pictured is a giant globe: the planet Earth. Three men hover around it: scientists in suits. They appear deep in thought, making measurements and calculating trajectories.

Hunter glances at the article.

One month ago, the Soviet Union launched Sputnik 1 into orbit: the first artificial Earth satellite. As proof of its achievement, the Soviets cleverly fitted the satellite with radio antennas. As it orbited the Earth overhead, it broadcast an easily detectable radio signal. Even amateur radio enthusiasts in the United States could receive the signal and hear the satellite zoom by again and again.

This achievement, and the technological superiority of the U.S.S.R. that it implied, took the United States — well, the general public at least — entirely by surprise.

It's clear to Hunter that most of the issue is dedicated to this topic, but not in celebration of the accomplishment, rather in fear of what it means. Already, the magazine postulates, the entire population of the United States is in jeopardy. Because, the magazine explains, if the Soviets can send a satellite into orbit, they can deliver a nuclear weapon anywhere in the world. A missile gap, the magazine warns, already exists. And the United States is on the losing end.

The DEW Line, Hunter thinks to herself. It was designed to detect a Soviet surprise attack by long-range bombers. Millions of dollars have been spent to this end, years of labor, thousands of workers... and it's just now going online and operational. But it was designed to detect *bombers*. Not missiles or rockets or satellites or whatever you want to call them.

All of this effort, all of this expense... and it's already obsolete. Just as the gold rush dried up, it looks like the DEW Line will too.

It was good while it lasted.

Arriving back at the bar, Hunter steps inside. Shaking the snow off herself, she's startled to see somebody sitting at the counter. On a night like tonight, patrons are few and far between — let alone a fresh face that she's never seen before.

The man, in his late thirties, sits poised, reading a newspaper. He glances at Hunter standing at the door, staring at him, then returns to his paper.

Hunter is taken aback by his presence. Leaving the bar unattended has never been a concern. Even if somebody did run off with her cash, it's not like they'd get very far. And if years of hunting for game in the Alaskan wilderness taught her anything, it was tracking an animal down in the snow. But this man...

There's something different about him. Something that quickens her pulse just looking at him. It's not that the man is threatening in any way; in fact, he seems quite content with his solitude. It's just that, the guy is incredibly handsome.

Collecting herself, Hunter approaches the bar.

After all, she has a job to do...

5

The date was October 22nd, 1961. Steven Leonard was only nine years old. And what had seemed like an ordinary Monday evening turned out to be a night that he — nor the rest of the world — would not soon forget.

Laying on the plush carpet of his family's living room floor, his textbooks and homework assignments spread out in front of him, Steven still remembers his father turning on their nineteen-inch black and white television set. As the screen flickered to life, the face of President John F. Kennedy — both handsome and solemn — appeared before them.

"Good evening, my fellow citizens," the president began. And he would go on to explain some harrowing news: Soviet ballistic missile installations had been spotted on Cuba. Nuclear weapons, aimed at U.S. cities, deployed only a few hundred miles off the Florida coast, was, to put it bluntly, unacceptable.

Effective immediately, the U.S. Navy would be initiating a blockade of Cuba, an act of war unto itself. All approaching ships were to be stopped, searched, and turned back if found to be carrying offensive weapons. Also, all previously installed Soviet missiles were to be removed immediately... or else.

The world, quite suddenly, found itself on the brink of World War Three. Though the United States and the Soviet Union had been marching headlong toward confrontation for nearly two decades, the suddenness of the crisis took most of the globe by surprise.

As Steven watched, his young mind was barely able to process the magnitude of it all.

There was President Kennedy seated some two hundred miles away in the Oval Office. But, wearing a black suit and tie, holding his prepared statement delicately in his fingers, he was not his usual laid-back and charming self. The significance of what he was telling the nation, not to mention the world, clearly weighed heavy on him. Staring straight into the broadcast-television camera in front of him, he looked deep into the soul of every American watching that night.

"My fellow citizens..."

As Kennedy continued, Steven glanced back at his parents on their living room sofa. And for the first time in his life, Steven saw fear in their eyes. The image of them sitting side by side, hands clasped, would forever be burned into his memory.

"Let no one doubt that this is a difficult and dangerous effort on which we have set out," the president said. "No one can foresee precisely what course it will take or what costs or casualties will be incurred. But the greatest danger of all would be to do nothing."

For Steven, hanging on Kennedy's every word, it was that last line that would resonate with him well into adulthood: *The greatest danger of all would be to do nothing.*

Desperate to make sense of the situation, hopeless to ease his parent's anguish, and helpless to do anything about the crisis himself, Steven's nine-year-old mind turned to the only heroes he had ever known. Images of Clayton Moore as *The Lone Ranger* and George Reeves as *Superman* flashed into his head. But it was *James Bond* in *Dr. No* — whom Steven had seen in the cinema just weeks before — that materialized.

Watching the presidential address, Steven — so young and naive — couldn't help but hope that there really were secret agents out there, fighting evil and protecting the innocent. Steven couldn't help but pray that actual heroes were out there at that very moment, without superpowers or loyal horses, risking everything to prevent the ultimate catastrophe: nuclear war.

For young Steven, it was the only way he could sleep at night...

• • •

The Corvette thunders out of the tunnel. Shielding his eyes from the sun, Steven glances at Hunter behind the wheel, her jaw set and eyes forward.

This woman, he thinks, *is Hunter Gunne. The Hunter Gunne.* The infamous secret agent. And from what Steven has learned — from what he has pieced together in his research — this woman was the answer to nine-year-old Steven's prayers... and now, she's sitting right next to him.

Hunter notices him gaping at her.

"How did you find me?" she asks, shouting over the engine.

"Huh?" Steven asks, deep in his own thoughts.

"Your sources," she says, racing along the forest road, stirring up leaves in their wake. "You said you had several sources. Who?"

"A true journalist never outs his sources..."

"Don't give me that Woodward and Bernstein bullshit," she snaps. "This isn't a game. Who sent you?"

Steven avoids her gaze, looking anywhere but her direction.

"Steven," she says, shaking her head, "you are really starting to annoy me."

"Fine! Okay!" Steven says. "As I said, I've spent years tracing your career — which is next to impossible, by the way. Nobody talks. Not about what happened, who was involved, or what went down. Nothing. And let me tell you: digging through declassified incident reports is next to worthless. Everything redacted. Everything blacked out. The military, the intelligence community, the Feds, they won't admit shit. But..." Steven looks at her. "Just like Deep Throat said... follow the money."

Deep Throat is the now infamous pseudonym given to the secret informant who, in 1972, provided Steven's investigative idols Bob Woodward and Carl Bernstein with key details of the Watergate scandal. This scandal would eventually lead to the President Nixon's resignation.

Hunter glances at Steven, curious. "Yeah?"

"So that's what I did," Steven says, proudly. "Insurance claims. The government, the Department of Defense, S.A.C., the Army, Navy... they're all stingy as hell, right? Nobody wants to eat the cost of whatever shit they've gotten themselves into, you know? So... insurance claims."

Hunter considers, nods.

"Okay. Sure. Follow the money. And?"

Steven pivots in his seat toward her, excited.

"Well," Steven says, "pouring through insurance claims, I noticed a pattern. Again and again, damage and losses were attributed to 'gun.' Millions of dollars' worth, which often made zero sense. But when I realized 'gun' wasn't referring to a weapon per se... but a person. Well, that opened up all kinds of leads."

Steven looks at her in admiration.

"You were busy, Miss Gunne... to say the least."

"Well," she says. "I tried."

Ahead of them, the road nears a highway — the same highway Steven drove in on. Hunter downshifts, then cuts the wheel. Steven hangs on as they drop down an embankment and slide onto the pavement below. Cutting off a tractor-trailer, the Corvette's big-block screams as Hunter bangs back up through the gears.

"But Steven," Hunter says.

"Yeah?" he asks.

"That still doesn't explain how the hell you came knocking on my door."

"No, it doesn't," Steven laughs. But Hunter is not amused. "Okay. So not long after I started looking into you, reaching out to all the contacts I have at the Pentagon, Langley, a handful of other agencies around D.C. — not to mention my connections at CBS and NBC — I get this... I get *this* in the mail..."

Steven opens his bag and rummages through the contents. He pulls out a postcard and hands it to Hunter.

"A postcard?"

Steven shrugs.

Hunter looks more carefully at it, turning it over. Her name and coordinates are written on it: *39.5117° N, 79.3156° W.* There's no return address.

"They're coordinates. Longitude and latitude," Steven says.

"I know," Hunter snaps.

She flips the postcard over again, looking more closely at the black and white image on the front. She raises an eyebrow.

Pictured on the card is a large, four-masted steel barque — an old sailing ship built at the turn of the century. The boat, she knows from experience, has a storied past. Painted along its hull is its name: *The Moshulu.*

"It's an old merchant ship," Steven says. "But I can't find any significance to it."

Hunter glances at Steven. She looks back at the postcard... then smiles, then laughs.

"That son of a bitch," she says, shaking her head.

"This means something to you, doesn't it?" Steven asks.

"I hope you're hungry," Hunter growls.

Yanking the steering wheel, she sends the car screeching across the median. They cross to the other side of the highway and charge eastward.

• • •

Two hours later and Hunter is hauling ass, first along Interstate 70 and now northward along Interstate 95. Between Steven and Hunter, not much has been said. Steven, to the best of his ability, has concluded that Hunter just doesn't want to talk. And, figuring she is probably the most dangerous person in the world, he'll just leave it at that.

Their destination, Steven has deduced: Philadelphia.

With his adrenaline levels having normalized long ago, Steven is stiff and sore. Taking a deep breath, his ribs hurt... and he can't help but wonder if he's broken or cracked one of them.

Sneaking a glance at Hunter, he recalls the number of times she saved his life back at the cabin. Either she truly is a hero or — he suddenly considers — she only kept him alive to figure out how he found her. And, knowing that now...

She could kill me whenever it's convenient.

With growing dread, Steven watches the Delaware River off to their right and the Philadelphia skyline approaching. He should do something sooner rather than later. Steven clears his throat.

"Are you going to kill me?" he asks.

"Why?" Hunter snaps.

Steven blinks. "Why what? Why would you kill me?" he asks. "Well," he continues, hesitant. "I guess because I blew your cover..."

"No," she says, waving him off. "Why would you do this? Why would you spend so much time and effort looking for me? The research, the investigating, the sleuthing..." She looks at him: "Why?"

Steven studies her, only now realizing she has been silently stewing over this. And somehow, suddenly, she seems more... human. Steven thinks back to his nine-year-old self, watching Kennedy from his living room floor, praying for a savior. He thinks of all the long, lonely hours spent as an adult, down in the basements of old government buildings, thumbing through boxes of countless bureaucratic files.

It was all worth it knowing that somebody was out there, he thinks. *Somebody like Hunter Gunne.*

"Because you saved the world," Steven says.

Hunter snorts. Weaving in and out of traffic, she points off toward the right, toward South Philadelphia: a helplessly impoverished neighborhood with abandoned buildings and burnt-out cars.

"Does the world look saved to you?" she asks. "Look at the inequality. Segregation. Police brutality. The world is a mess. Starting right here in *the good ol' U.S.A,*" she says. "I didn't save anything. Delayed? Maybe. But humanity's been sliding since the turn of the century," she adds, glancing at Steven. "And it's only a matter of time until..." She looks back out at the city and shakes her head. "It's all gone."

"It doesn't change what you did," Steven says. "Cuba in '62. Berlin in '61. Iwakuni in '65. You've saved the world, repeatedly."

Hunter glares at him.

"And blowing up my cabin is the thanks I get?"

"Well. Okay," Steven says. "I guess that was my fault, but..." He looks at her, but she's not having it. "Yeah," he continues. "Sorry about that. I just..."

"You just *what?*" she snips.

"I just wanted to tell your story," Steven says.

"And what if I didn't want my story told?"

Oh, Steven thinks. He never really thought of that. Knowing it's time to shut up, he stares silently at the road ahead.

● ● ●

Hunter takes the exit for Penn's Landing and speeds toward the waterfront. Fishtailing into a municipal lot, pedestrians scramble out of her way as she screeches into a parking spot.

Before Steven realizes it, Hunter is already out of the car, marching toward the dock. He chases after her, catching up to her as she approaches the Moshulu.

Looking the boat over, it appears just as it does on his mysterious postcard, except now, it is clearly a floating restaurant permanently moored to the dock. Steven glances at a sign along the gangway advertising the lunch buffet.

"The Moshulu," he says to himself. "I'll be damned."

Hunter, not waiting for Steven, charges up the ramp and boards. Steven follows her inside, noting that she seems to know exactly where she's going. Hunter blows past the host stand, climbing a steep flight of stairs that lead to the top deck.

Beelining for the open-air bar, that's where she spots *him*, stopping dead in her tracks...

The man, with an ascot pulled tightly around his neck, is in his late sixties and is enviously handsome. He's fit and trim and put together like royalty. His suit, Steven guesses, probably costs more than Steven could make in a whole year. Sitting at the bar, mimosa in hand, the man glances up at Hunter, oozing with confidence.

"That son of a bitch," she mutters to herself.

6

November 1957 — Barrow, Alaska

Hunter approaches the bar, already feeling a bit disappointed as the man's focus remains on his newspaper... as opposed to her.

Hunter sets down the magazine and clears her throat.

"Sorry about that," she says. "Had to walk an airman back to the barracks." The man nods, indifferent. "It doesn't take long for somebody to freeze to death on a night like this," Hunter adds, awkwardly.

"Very true," the man says in a deep, distinct voice.

Hunter feels her cheeks redden. Of all the things to say, she states the obvious. She turns away, hiding her embarrassment. Pulling her gloves off, finger by finger, she collects herself.

She glances at the man in the mirror behind the bar, hoping to sneak a peek without him knowing... but the man, handsome as hell, looks up at her and smiles.

Hunter turns away, startled to be caught in the act.

"What can I get you?" she asks, desperate to keep her composure.

"Any good vodkas back there?" the man asks.

Hunter can't help but note that the man's dialect is curiously devoid of any particular regional accent. *General American English*, she reminds herself. It was a standard dialect among actors and broadcasters of the '20s and '30s. Nowadays, it's not so common.

"No vodka here," she says. "Sorry."

"Your finest whiskey then," he says, carefree and charming.

"I.W. Harper or Canadian Club," Hunter says, wincing.

"I.W. Harper it is."

Hunter reaches for the nearest bottle. She flips over a tumbler glass and pours three fingers worth before sliding it his way.

The man nods his appreciation.

Hunter walks over to her textbooks, thankful to no longer be on the spot. This man has her flustered, and she doesn't like it. Typically, Hunter is in control of most interactions. But this man is getting the better of her. And to make it worse: he doesn't even seem to be trying.

Flipping open her anatomy book, Hunter fights the urge to glance back at him. She doesn't want to let the man win. Instead, she forces herself to focus on the diagram in front of her....

But she's too damn distracted to read the words on the page. That man is sitting just a few feet away from her, striking and mysterious, beckoning to her like a lighthouse on an angry sea. Frustrated, Hunter stops.

This is ridiculous, she thinks.

Taking a deep breath, Hunter jumps back into the melody of *Dem Bones*, hopeful that humming the tune will clear her thoughts...

The thoracolumbar fascia is connected to the... latissimus dorsi.

The infraspinatus is connected to the...

"Rhomboid major," the man says.

Hunter spins toward him, stunned.

"How did you..." She trails off. She glances at the mirror behind the bar. He must have read the diagram in the reflection... backward no less.

In the mirror, the image of the man looks at her and winks.

"What are you, a doctor? A medic?" Hunter asks.

The man shakes his head. "In my profession," he says, "it's important I know many things."

Hunter looks back at her books. Feeling rather foolish, she closes them. But not wanting their conversation to end, she approaches him... this time with more determination.

"So, what are you doing here in the Arctic Circle?" she asks, testing the water.

The man smiles, and Hunter — feeling the ball in her court — playfully looks him over, as if sizing him up.

"You're too old to be an airman, not arrogant enough to be an officer," she says.

The man nods, amused. As he's about to speak, Hunter cuts him off, asserting her dominance of the conversation.

"No, wait," she says. "Let me guess: you're an engineer. A radar engineer, sent by the good people of the Western Electric Company for the final install inspection at the Point Barrow Radar Site."

"Something like that," he says.

"Radar," Hunter says. "Radio Detection and Ranging. Those stations produce strong enough electromagnetic waves to detect incoming bombers hundreds of miles away... or cook a weary airman unfortunate enough to stand too close to the transmitter. Hence why you probably know a thing or two about human anatomy."

"Impressive," the man says. "I see you know a thing or two about radar technology."

"*In my profession*," Hunter says, mocking him. "*It's important I know many things.*"

"Touché," he says, smirking.

"You probably have a wife and kids back home, don't you?" Hunter asks, leaning toward him against the bar, her body language speaking loud and clear. "A nice house? Flashy car? A healthy pension?"

"Afraid not," he says, finishing his drink.

As he sets down his glass, Hunter has the bottle of whiskey ready to top it off. The man smiles. Their eyes meet, and in that brief moment, a connection is made, intense and magnetic.

The man's face softens.

"What's your name?" he asks.

"Hunter," she says. "Hunter Gunne."

"Miss Gunne," the man says, eyeing her. "May I ask you a question?"

Hunter laughs. *This is a new approach for a guy*, she thinks.

"Sure," she answers.

"What do you want?" he asks.

Hunter blinks... then blushes. *Damn, he's bold.*

"What?" she says, standing up straight. "Tonight?"

The man's eyes sparkle. But he shakes his head.

The ball is most definitely back in his court, Hunter realizes.

"In life," he says.

Hunter snorts. Having no idea how to respond, she breaks away from his gaze. She grabs the nearest bar towel and wipes at nothing.

The man leans closer.

"It's a simple question," the man says. "If you answer honestly."

Hunter stops wiping. A burst of images flash in her head. They are memories from throughout her life, the moments that made her who she is. Growing up in Skagway, running her grandfather's tavern, her mother's unexpected death, the move to Barrow...

"I don't know," Hunter says, staring at the towel in her hand. She forces a laugh. "It's funny," she continues, "people are always asking that. But imagine me," she says, looking at the man. "Here I am almost thirty. And I just don't have an answer for them."

"Let me answer for you," the man says.

"Sure," Hunter says, shrugging.

"Happiness," he says. "But you don't know where to find it. You don't know where to look. Instead, all you find is loneliness. You find it everywhere you go, waiting for you. Isn't that right?"

Hunter stares at him. She shrugs, not sure what to say.

"I know the feeling," the man says, smiling.

Hunter is speechless.

If this man wanted to sleep with me, he was already on his way, she thinks.

But now...

Hunter doesn't know what to think.

"Who are you?" she asks.

But before he can answer, the door to the bar swings open. A blast of cold air hits them as another man enters — another stranger that Hunter has never seen before.

Pulling his parka's hood from his head, he glares in their direction, eying the man sitting across from Hunter.

"There you are," the stranger says, in a thick cockney accent.

Hunter glances between the two men, sensing tension. She raises the bottle of whiskey toward the stranger, hoping to calm the waters.

"What can I get you?" she asks.

Ignoring her, the stranger approaches the bar, his eyes darting between Hunter and the man seated. "Why am I not surprised?" the stranger scoffs, reading the room as he plops onto a stool.

The man seated across from Hunter, the man she was prepared to pour her heart out to, chuckles.

"Miss Gunne," he says, gesturing at the stranger, "please meet my esteemed, though brash colleague, Trevor McCoy."

"Nice to meet you," Hunter says.

"Charmed, I'm sure," Trevor says — their dislike of each other immediate and palpable.

"Did you get it?" the man asks, sipping his whiskey.

Trevor nods. "Wasn't easy," he says.

"Well," the man says, suddenly very serious. "Let's see it."

Trevor reaches into his jacket but hesitates. He glances around the empty bar before setting his sights on Hunter.

"How much for a pint of privacy?" he asks, condescendingly.

Hunter shrugs. Still numb from the conversation earlier, she returns to her textbook and opens it to the anatomy diagram.

But Hunter can't help but glance back at the men. She watches Trevor pull out a roll of paper, not thinking much of it. Laying it out on the bar, it appears to be a blueprint or schematics of something — a building or facility. The two men hunch over the design, eager to take in the details.

Odd, Hunter thinks, assuming the men must both be engineers. *But why meet here and at this time of night?*

"Do you mind?" Trevor barks.

Snapping out of her daze, Hunter realizes she's been staring at them. And judging by the scowl on Trevor's face, this is something he doesn't want to share. Hunter turns away.

But her curiosity is piqued. The warm and fuzzy feelings from a moment ago have quickly been replaced. Her eyes float toward the mirror behind the bar. In the reflection, she eyes the blueprint laid out before them.

What the hell are they up to?

"So, what we have is an electrical substation," Trevor starts, his voice hushed. "At least, that was what it was intended to be." The man nods along. "As for the compound itself, we have guard posts here and here," Trevor continues, tapping the schematic. "I count two perimeter patrols coming and going every half-hour. That leaves a consistent gap in their coverage once an hour, right about here."

Trevor circles a spot with his finger.

"That's our in," the man says.

"That's our in," Trevor agrees.

Who are these guys? Hunter wonders, her suspicions growing. Something isn't right. People don't just appear out of nowhere in Barrow, Alaska. People come here for a purpose.

But what is theirs? Still watching their reflections in the mirror, Hunter glances between the two men.

The DEW Line, she thinks. *This definitely has something to do with the DEW Line.*

"I count two dozen men, all told," Trevor continues. "I expect another dozen inside. Based on their comings and goings, they're definitely preparing for something. Something big."

Are they spies? Hunter's heart sinks. She's heard the ample warnings given to the airmen who pass through here. Hell, the Air Force's propaganda posters are posted throughout the barracks: *if you see something, do something.*

Well shit, Hunter thinks. *I'm seeing something. But what?*

Hunter looks at the blueprint in the mirror. Trevor called it an electrical substation. It must feed power to the dozen or so radar arrays along the Beaufort Sea. These stations are the lynchpin of the entire DEW Line. You take them out, the Strategic Air Command is as good as blind. And these two are planning an offensive...

I have to do something.

"Are you even listening?" Trevor asks, aghast.

Hunter blinks. Surprised by the break in their conversation, her eyes flick up to their faces in the mirror. And she's stunned to see the man's reflection staring back at her. The man smiles, amused by her curiosity.

Trevor follows his gaze... and meets Hunter's in the mirror as well. She's been caught.

"Oh, bloody hell," Trevor says, rolling up the blueprint and stuffing it back in his parka. "Let's go," he shouts, pulling the man to his feet.

"Now, hold on," the man says. He looks at Hunter as she turns to them. "Two more whiskeys," he says. "And how about one for yourself?"

Hunter stares at him, unnerved. But the man smiles back at her, confident.

"We have work to do," Trevor says, annoyed.

"Now now, Trevor," the man says. "You never know which drink may be your last."

The man turns back toward Hunter, waiting for her response.

These men, she thinks, *are a clear and present danger. And they want to share a drink...*

The hell with it, Hunter thinks.

Flipping over two more tumblers, she tops them all off.

"How much do I owe?" the man asks, reaching into his jacket. Pulling out his wallet, Hunter spots a room key clasped against it. It's a room key to the barracks, just like the drunken airman's whom she had walked home...

Only the man's room number is thirty-seven.

"It's on the house," Hunter says, hiding her astute observation.

The man smiles. He takes his glass of whiskey and raises it. Hunter raises hers, their eyes locked. They wait, almost in a standoff, until Trevor stubbornly raises his.

"You'll be the death of me," Trevor says, defeated.

"*Na Zdorovie*," the man says, his eyes never leaving Hunter's.

And the three of them throw back their glasses, shooting the whiskey in one big gulp.

7

There he is, Hunter thinks, *after all these years... Trevor McCoy.*

"That son of a bitch," she mutters, thinking of a hundred reasons to kill the man on the spot. And only one reason to spare him... he's her only friend.

Noticing Steven at her side, she can't help but feel bad for the kid. Finding yourself a pawn in one of Trevor's real-world games of chess is never pleasurable.

Nor often survivable, she thinks.

"Well," Trevor says, breaking the ice. "I had to get you out of retirement somehow."

"I lost everything, Trevor," Hunter says, her jaw clenched. "I blew it all up."

Trevor shakes his head. He closes his newspaper and carefully folds it up.

"What was I supposed to do?" he asks, sipping his mimosa. "Not like you had a telephone up there on that mountain of yours. Besides, I'm sure you quite enjoyed blowing it all up. So," he says, smirking. "You're welcome."

Hunter considers. Her face relaxes.

"Fair enough," she says, stepping up to the bar. A bartender quickly slides up to greet her. "Vodka martini," she says. "Up. With one olive..." Eyeing Trevor, she reconsiders. "Better make it two olives," she adds.

The bartender turns to Steven. "And you, sir?"

• • •

Steven stares back at the bartender, stunned. A moment ago, he expected a shoot-out.

Now they're ordering drinks?

Steven glances about, taking in his surreal surroundings. The air is cold and crisp, but the seagulls soaring effortlessly in the breeze overhead don't seem to mind.

Hunter and Trevor watch him expectantly.

"Ah. I don't know," Steven says, sitting. "A beer?"

The bartender nods and walks off.

"So, who's trying to kill me now?" Hunter asks, turning her attention to Trevor.

"Bad news, love," Trevor says. "It's your old punching-bag back with a fury."

Hunter cocks her head.

"The O.W.O.? They're operational again?"

Steven perks up, recognizing the acronym.

"The O.W.O.?" he asks, his eyes darting between them.

The O.W.O. — of all the things Steven has uncovered, nothing has been more troubling than *the Old World Order*, a supposed centuries-old secret society whose sole purpose is to subject humanity to servitude. Their methods, from what he has gathered, are so horrific and disturbing that Steven's only solace was convincing himself that they were, in fact, nothing more than a wild conspiracy theory... *the craziest conspiracy theory*.

Now, hearing the organization's name blurted out in front of him — by the infamous Hunter Gunne no less — leaves him feeling woozy.

"And they've infiltrated deep into the United States government," Trevor continues, ignoring Steven.

"And you're just calling me out of retirement now?" Hunter asks.

"The O.W.O.?" Steven repeats, rising to his feet with growing concern. "You're telling me the Old World Order actually exists?"

"Yes," both Hunter and Trevor snap, annoyed by the interruption.

Their blunt answer stuns Steven. He plops back down onto his barstool, suddenly realizing, back at Hunter's cabin — the swarm of men, the black helicopter — *that was the O.W.O.*

They are very real, and they are very serious. Maybe it was the long car-ride here, or perhaps it's the waves of the Delaware River, but Steven suddenly feels like he's going to be sick.

"But," Trevor says, lowering his voice, "let's not talk here..."

• • •

Trevor hands Steven a white porcelain plate. Below deck, they stand in the restaurant's busy buffet line. Having just confirmed the existence of an evil secret society, Steven assumed Trevor wanted to talk somewhere more secluded — as it turns out, it's lunchtime.

"I sailed this ship in the Merchant Marines," Trevor says, wistfully peeking ahead at the chafing dishes. "Around the globe and back again. God, it was an adventure. Where boys became men, and men became legends."

Trevor glances at the senior citizens shuffling around them.

"And then they turned her into a bloody restaurant," he adds, dejected. Trevor scoops a serving of crab cake and plops it on Steven's plate.

"Cut the sentimental shit, Trevor," Hunter says, plate in hand. "Why am I here?"

Trevor eyes her, plopping a serving on her plate.

"Able Archer," he says.

"Excuse me?" Hunter asks.

"As we speak," Trevor says, turning his attention back toward the buffet, "the United States Armed Forces — in conjunction with N.A.T.O. field units — are mobilizing the single largest military training exercise the world has ever seen. A show of force on an unprecedented scale. Code name: *Able Archer*."

Trevor scoops up a serving of scalloped potatoes and unloads them on Steven's plate. "Needless to say," Trevor continues, "these exercises — spanning across western Europe, the Mediterranean, and the South China Sea — have the Russians a bit... let's just say: jumpy."

Trevor serves himself a hefty scoop. "The thing is," he says, looking at Hunter. "The Russian's fears aren't exactly unfounded."

"Let me guess," Hunter says. "These exercises aren't exercises."

Trevor nods, serving her potatoes.

Hunter scoffs. "You mean to tell me Reagan is planning a preemptive first-strike on the Soviet Union?"

Steven, listening intently, almost drops his plate.

"War?" he shouts, panicked. "Nuclear war?!"

A hush falls upon the restaurant as the senior citizens leer at Steven like he's a crazy person. Hunter and Trevor shrug off the outburst and move on to their table, leaving Steven standing awkward and alone at the center of attention.

Steven forces a laugh.

"Don't mind me," he says, sheepishly to the other patrons. "We're all just going to die horrible, horrible deaths," he adds, chasing after Hunter and Trevor.

• • •

"So why exactly is the President of the United States itching to start World War Three?" Hunter asks, setting her plate of food down at their table before sitting.

"Because the President of the United States isn't *the President of the United States*," Trevor says, flipping open his napkin.

"You mean Reagan... isn't *Reagan*?"

Trevor looks at her with a sparkle in his eye — he clearly loves this shit.

"As if I needed any more reason to hate the guy," Hunter sighs, shaking her head. "So, where's Reagan? The *real* Reagan?"

"Being held deep within an ultra-top-secret ICBM site in Upstate New York," Trevor answers, cutting into his crab cake.

"What's he doing up there?" Hunter asks.

Trevor takes a bite, savoring every bit of it.

"This is fantastic," he says, chewing and swallowing.

"Trevor," Hunter says, impatient. "What is the president doing up there?"

"Roughly twenty-four hours ago," Trevor says, not looking up from this plate, "the O.W.O. managed to swap the president's helicopter with an exact replica... and I mean *exact*. Down to the little pine tree air-fresheners the first lady loves so much."

Hunter and Steven exchange an incredulous look.

"That helicopter," Trevor adds, "was convincing enough to trick the Secret Service into letting it land unannounced — not to mention unauthorized — on the White House lawn."

Trevor wipes his mouth with his napkin. "The president's staff, already desperately insecure, assumed they had forgotten to schedule an important meeting or function in the president's itinerary. So, they rushed Mr. Reagan out and in..."

Using his fingers and hand, Trevor mimes a person walking to a helicopter, and then the helicopter lifting off from the lawn. "And away they went," he says.

Hunter and Steven watch Trevor's hand fly off.

"With the president their prisoner?" Steven asks.

Trevor nods. "A few hours later," he continues, "just when his staff realized they had no idea what was going on, the helicopter returned, much to their relief."

Trevor's helicopter lands back on his other hand.

"Out popped the president. And in he went..."

Trevor's fingers walk back into the White House.

"Only now," he says, very serious. "That wasn't the president. But an imposter. And that imposter is in the Oval Office as we speak. And, as Commander in Chief, that imposter has the United States' full nuclear arsenal at his disposal."

Steven stares at Trevor skeptically.

"This is ridiculous," he says. "An imposter... in the White House? That's the most absurd thing I've ever heard. And to what? Start World War Three? Well, why not just push the damn button and get it over with?"

"That's a bright lad there," Trevor says to Hunter, pointing at Steven. "This is where the Able Archer military exercise comes in," he continues. "With the Pacific fleet in position, N.A.T.O. bombers in the air and S.A.C. missile bases on high alert, a U.S. first strike looks capable — as designed — to wipe out fifty to seventy-five percent of the Soviet Union's retaliatory capability..."

Hunter sighs: "Increasing the odds of possible survivors here in the United States."

"Hit 'em hard enough," Trevor says, hammering a fist into his palm. "And they got nothing to hit you back with."

"Thus, giving the O.W.O. somebody to lord over when the dust settles," Hunter says, dejected.

"So, they're waiting for the military to get into position?" Steven asks, intrigued.

"That's right," Trevor says, returning to his food.

"Well, how long do we have?" Steven asks.

"Oh, I don't know," Trevor says, glancing at his watch. "Looks to be: twenty-nine hours and fourteen minutes. Give or take a few minutes."

Steven processes that... then shoots up out of his chair.

"Until World War Three?! What the hell are we doing here eating scalloped potatoes?"

"Now now, Steven," Trevor says, pulling him back down to the table. "You never know which meal might be your last."

He looks at Hunter.

"Am I right?"

• • •

Hunter blinks, the phrase catching her by surprise.

You never know which drink may be your last.

For a moment, she's right back in Barrow, Alaska, standing at the bar. The man is sitting across from her — where Steven sits now — Trevor by his side, the three of them holding up their shots of whiskey...

"*Na Zdorovie,*" Hunter whispers, in a daze.

Trevor eyes her from across the table, noting her reaction.

Recomposing herself, Hunter clears her throat.

"And our mission?" she asks, pivoting the conversation.

And. Our. Mission.

The three words Trevor has been dying to hear.

"I thought you'd never ask," he says, pushing his plate away. "First: rescue the president. Second: eliminate the imposter. And third... save the world." Trevor glances between Hunter and Steven. "All while not raising the slightest bit of media attention or public alarm. You know, the standard rigmarole."

Hunter nods. "Just like old times."

"Bloody hell, I've missed this," Trevor says, jumping to his feet. "Let's have a go of it, shall we?" Hunter stands, but Steven stays seated. They peer down at him.

"Come on, chap," Trevor says, nudging him.

• • •

Steven struggles to swallow his food. He looks down at his plate, overwhelmed by it all. Not only was Steven almost killed back at the cabin… but now he's privy to the knowledge that nuclear war is a day away.

He feels Hunter and Trevor's eyes on him, burning holes in him. But he just can't come to grips with it.

"Come on now," Trevor says, nudging him again. "Chop. Chop."

"You expect me to… what?" Steven snaps, aghast. "Save the president?"

Trevor snorts. "It's a bit more than the president, isn't it? It's the whole world, really," he says, looking at Hunter. "Wouldn't you say?"

Hunter shrugs, nods.

"This is ridiculous," Steven says, gagging. "I will die. You know that, right?"

"Well, I don't think we're just going to let you walk away. Not now," Trevor says. He shares a look with Hunter. "I'm afraid you know too much already."

"Much too much," Hunter adds.

Growing uneasy, Steven looks at Hunter — and immediately recognizes the look on her face as the same she had just before attacking him in the cabin. He darts up out of his chair, quickly backing away from them.

"Woah woah," Steven says. "What are you saying? If I say no… you're going to kill me? To keep me silent?"

Hunter shrugs. "No comment," she says, glaring at him.

"You are a journalist, are you not?" Trevor asks, bearing down on him.

Steven forces a laugh. "I'm not going to tell anybody," he says. "I swear."

"And why should I believe you now?" Hunter asks. "When all you've wanted to do, for years now, was tell the world about *the incredible Hunter Gunne?*"

"You know, Steven," Trevor says, "the thing about secret agents: they like to stay secret, if you gather my meaning."

Steven glances toward the exit. If he makes a run for it, maybe he can get away, perhaps jump overboard and swim for New Jersey.

"Listen, chum," Trevor says, sliding an arm around him. "May I ask you something, man to man, that is?"

Steven shrugs, then nods.

"Well. The thing is," Trevor continues, leading Steven toward a window, "do you have something better to be doing? Better than saving the world, that is? I mean, if we fail, there's nothing stopping them. Nothing. And all this," Trevor gestures out the window, toward Philadelphia. "It's gone, chap. Everything you know... is gone. Everyone you love... is gone."

Steven swallows. Trevor looks him over.

"You know, you remind me of myself back in the day, back when I got into this game," Trevor says, squeezing him. "You're a smart lad. A problem solver. A critical thinker. And those traits, especially these days, are hard to come by. Maybe, and I really do mean this Steven, *maybe* this is where you belong. Yeah? Fighting evil. Right? Saving the world. Maybe *this* is your higher calling."

"Listen, sir," Steven says, prying Trevor's hand off his shoulder. "I'm honored — truly honored — that you want me to join your little secret agent super squad. But here's the thing:

I've never even fired a gun before. I'd have no idea what I'm doing. And I'd probably just get myself killed..."

"*Non sibi sed aliis,*" Trevor says, silencing Steven. "That's an old Latin proverb, one of my favorites. Do you know what that means, Steven?"

Steven looks at him, stumped.

"*Not for ourselves, but for others,*" Trevor says, letting it sink in. "Maybe saving the world isn't about doing it for yourself. Yeah? Maybe it's about doing it for somebody else."

Steven's eyes fall to the floor. *If only I had somebody else...*

"Hey," Trevor says, nudging him again. "Look over there."

"What?" Steven asks, perplexed.

"Look over there," Trevor says, gesturing back toward Hunter waiting impatiently at their table. "What do you see?"

"Hunter Gunne," Steven answers, timidly.

"*The* Hunter Gunne," Trevor says. "Right?"

"Yeah," Steven answers, wondering if that's why she does it... *for somebody else.* Is that why Hunter saves the world?

And then, wholly unexpectedly, Steven's imagination whisks him back to the cabin, back to her parlor... Hunter on top of him, her knife to his throat... Her eyes... Her faded freckles... Her strands of hair tickling his nose... Her hot breath on his face...

Startled, Steven shakes the images out of his head.

"How long have you been searching for her?" Trevor asks, lowering his voice to a whisper. "How long have you dreamt of this day? Of meeting Hunter Gunne?"

"Look, mister," Steven says, his emotions jumbled, trying to pull away. "This is a lot to process right now..."

"How long?" Trevor asks, staring at him, holding onto him.

"I don't know," Steven answers, defensively. "Years. Decades," he blurts out, picturing himself sitting in his parent's living room as a child, the threat of the Cuban Missile Crisis hanging over him.

"Decades," Trevor says, nodding.

He inches toward Steven, leaning close to him.

"And you're just gonna let her walk right out of your life?"

"You're talking about nuclear war," Steven says, not taking his eyes off Hunter.

"If this is your last day on Earth, chap," Trevor says, "who else would you want to spend it with?"

"You're going to get me killed," Steven says, still staring at her, fixated.

"Saving the world," Trevor says, knowing he's got Steven right where he wants him. "Now, I reckon that's a good way to die, isn't it?"

PART TWO

8

November 1957 — Barrow, Alaska

Hunter watches the men zip up their jackets. Pulling their hoods over their heads, they step out into the night. Outside, they cross the exterior windows, heading east. Now alone, with the taste of whiskey still lingering in her mouth, Hunter stands shaken and unsure.

Who the hell are they?

The two men — one of whom Hunter was happy to welcome his advances — were not the engineers she assumed they were. Instead, they seemed to be the exact type of threat the Air Force so often warns about.

Soviet saboteurs?

The blueprint was of a facility. But what facility or where Hunter can't be sure. The nearest radar station is the Point Barrow Long Range Radar Site. But she distinctly remembers the second man — Trevor McCoy, was his name — mentioning an electrical substation. If that's the case, taking out the substation would cut power to dozens of active arrays. That would plunge the Strategic Air Command into darkness and effectively blind the United States to an incoming Soviet attack.

Is that what this is about?

A Soviet sneak attack?

If it comes to war, Hunter thinks, the Point Barrow Radar Site will be an early and easy target. One well-placed Soviet hydrogen bomb would be more than enough to take out the city of Barrow along with it. But Hunter struggles to take solace in knowing her death would be sudden and effective.

Hunter has no loved ones to think of, no family to worry over... but the thought of such a war leaves a longing in her heart none the less. A strange feeling, she notes, considering her own death doesn't trouble her.

Room thirty-seven. That's the man's room number. Hunter caught a glimpse of his key when he pulled out his wallet. Clues to solving the mystery of who these men are and what the hell they're up to might be there. And, judging on their conversation, they're well on their way to the facility itself. That would leave the room unattended and any such clues there for the finding.

Hunter grabs her parka...

• • •

Stepping outside, Hunter looks right and left. Already, the men's footsteps have been covered by the drifting snow. As she heads toward the barracks, the wind whips around her. The road is deserted and uninviting. But she presses on.

Finding room thirty-seven, she peers in through the window. The glass is heavily frosted over, but it's clear enough to see that the room is dark and empty.

Perfect, she thinks, stepping up to the door.

Hunter tries the handle... but it's locked.

Fortunately, the lock is as cheap as they come, no doubt supplied by the lowest bidder. Pulling out a pocketknife, she slides the blade into the keyhole. With a sudden flick of her wrist, she easily snaps the plastic assembly inside.

The door pushes open, and she enters.

Leaving the lights off, she carefully shuts the door behind her. She looks over the room. It's one of many within the military barracks — its layout identical to the drunk airman's she had returned home earlier. Nothing of note seems out of order. The bed is neatly made, and the bathroom clean and tidy. Never-the-less, Hunter hopes to find something — anything — to confirm her suspicions and point her in the right direction.

Lives are at stake, she reminds herself.

But if she does find the confirmation she's looking for... then what?

Hunter looks over the nightstand... and sees nothing. She approaches the dresser and opens the top drawer. Articles of clothing have been neatly stowed inside. She picks up a sweater, bringing it to her nose.

The man's cologne, she thinks.

She replaces the sweater, closes the drawer, and moves down to the next. Inside she finds a leather briefcase. Hunter hesitates, eyeing the briefcase before moving on. Opening the bottom drawer, she finds it to be empty.

Damn, she thinks. But Hunter hovers over the dresser anyway, her thoughts lingering on the briefcase. She opens the middle drawer again and removes it. She feels the weight in her hand.

Something's in there.

Setting the briefcase down atop the dresser, she opens it, eager for something: fake passports, nuclear weapon schematics, Russia's secret war plans... but the briefcase is empty.

Perplexed, Hunter closes it.

She feels the weight of it in her hand again.

Something is definitely in there.

Slamming the briefcase down, she opens it back up and inspects the liner. Running her finger along the inner-lip, Hunter triggers a hidden latch, and a velvet-lined secret compartment opens within the briefcase. A sleek-black pistol and accompanying silencer are mounted inside...

"A Walther PPK," a voice announces behind her as the room's lights flick on.

Startled, Hunter spins to see the man from the bar — the man whom she was flirting with — standing at the door. She watches him step toward her, frozen in his gaze.

"German-made, thirty-two caliber, double-action trigger," he says. Reaching around her, he removes the gun from its contoured inset. He releases the magazine, checking the bullets within, before slapping it back into place. He racks the slide and chambers a round.

"And a delivery like a brick through a plate-glass window," he adds, offering the weapon to Hunter.

Hunter blinks. She looks between the man and the gun, then quickly snatches it before he can change his mind.

"Well now," he says, nonchalant. "I do believe it's your turn to ask a question."

Hunter tightens her grip on the cold-steel handle and levels the gun at his chest.

"Or two," the man adds, playfully.

"Who the hell are you?" Hunter asks.

The man smiles. He turns to the dresser and opens the top drawer. "I was worried," he says, rummaging beneath the clothing. "That you might find the good stuff."

He pulls out a bottle of *Minskaya Kristall* vodka.

Hunter immediately spots the Cyrillic text on the label, sending her head spinning...

That bottle is authentic Russian vodka.

"Where did you get that?" she asks.

"I've learned to take a bottle with me wherever I go," the man says, producing two tumbler glasses as he pulls out the cork.

"From where?" Hunter snaps.

"From Russia," he answers, pouring them both a glass.

"How?"

"Because," the man begins — his accent shifting from American Midwest to thick Russian — "*I am Russian.*"

Hunter blinks, stunned.

The man extends his hand.

"*Meenya zavoot Anatoly Ivanovich Kuznetsov,*" he says, introducing himself. "*Ochen preeyatna... pleased to meet you.*"

Hunter stands motionless. Anatoly takes her hand in his and, like a true gentleman, kisses it. Hunter hardens. She pulls her hand away and places the PPK's barrel to his chest.

"Are you a goddamn communist?" Hunter asks.

"As much as you are a capitalist," Anatoly says, sipping his vodka as he steps away — clearly, this isn't the first time he's had a gun trained on him.

"Are you a Soviet spy?" she asks.

"Ask me another question," he answers, sitting down and crossing his legs.

"Are you dangerous?"

Considering the question, Anatoly looks her over. He sits up straight and takes a deep breath.

"You sever the aorta artery on a grown man," he says, slicing his throat with his finger, "and he'll bleed out in minutes. You slice deep enough, sever the trachea," he continues, slicing his throat again but with more pressure, "and he won't be able to call for help. Yes, Miss Gunne," he says. "I am a dangerous man. But you are the one with the gun."

"Where are you from?" she asks.

Anatoly's smile fades. He finishes his vodka in one last gulp before reaching for the bottle, pouring himself another.

"We called it *the death grin*," Anatoly says, obliquely. "We knew when you saw them smile this smile, that their time had come. There was no saving them. No reviving them. They wouldn't, couldn't even open their mouths, they were so weak."

"What?" Hunter asks, lost.

"Leningrad," Anatoly says, starting over. "I am from Leningrad."

"I've never heard of it," Hunter quips.

Anatoly nods. "Leningrad is a city of many names," he says. "Originally Saint Petersburg, the city was named after Saint Peter, the apostle of Christ, and served as the enlightened capital of Imperial Russia — home of the Romanov monarchy for centuries."

"That rings a bell," Hunter says.

"At the onset of the First World War, the name was deemed too Germanic for the capital of mother Russia, and was promptly changed to *Petrograd*," Anatoly says. "Petrograd was the birthplace of the Bolshevik uprising. Upon Lenin's death, the city was renamed once again. This time, in his honor."

"Leningrad," Hunter says.

Anatoly nods. "During the Second World War, having already taken Paris, Hitler turned his efforts eastward. Setting his sights on Leningrad, he hoped to crush the cradle of communism on his march to Moscow. The Red Army proved worthless to stop his advance. Within weeks the Germans had the city surrounded, cutting off all supplies to the three million civilians trapped within. Thus began a nine hundred day siege at the hands of the German army."

Anatoly stares at the vodka in his hand, his eyes glossed over. "Nine hundred days is a long time to go without reinforcements," he says, taking a modest sip. "Food supplies... did not last long. Wood to heat our stoves... did not last long. And Russian winters are unforgiving."

Outside, the wind wails, and Hunter feels a chill go up her spine. Here in the United States, people forget how spared they were of these horrors. They forget just how much pain and suffering most of the world endured — and how staggering the toll on humankind actually was.

"I was young. Just a boy," Anatoly continues. "Only nineteen, but I thought myself a man. A strong Soviet man. My father was of high party rank, the Second Secretary of Leningrad — appointed by comrade Stalin himself. My father helped organize the city's defense. It was our duty, he'd tell me, to show the people of Leningrad that the Soviet leadership would not abandon them. But, as it turned out, abandoned we were... all three million of us. Even my father's position did not spare us from the ravages of hunger. Nobody was spared. My young brother... my mother..."

Anatoly pours himself another glass. "Leningrad was a beautiful city, a proud city," he says. "Culture flowed through it like a river. But hunger, starvation — it is a brutal thing. It plays tricks on one's mind, on one's thinking. To remember those days, it was like a dream. Like living in a fog of one's own mind. Everyone became strange. And desperate. Including me. You think differently, like animals. A mother wishes the death of her child. A husband his wife's..."

Hunter watches him, unsure of what to say.

The barrel of the gun drifts to the floor.

"So, we called it *the death grin*," Anatoly says. "Knowing what I know now, I understand. But back then, this grin, this sadistic smile, it seemed more a cruel joke. By this time, the unfortunate were so malnourished, so starved, that their bodies had long eaten away at themselves. And the muscles of their jaws and cheeks, of their face, became so tight and rigid that their lips pulled from their teeth. They were living skeletons," he says, staring at the floor. "Alive but dead. With sunken cheeks and paper-thin skin, they were living skeletons, grinning up at you from where they lay, their fallen eyes barely able to blink."

He looks up at Hunter.

"All one could hope for was that their end would come quick."

94

As Anatoly collects himself, Hunter can't help but see him differently now. There is such sadness in his eyes, such sorrow. Glancing down at the tumbler in his hand, she spots white gashes across his knuckles. This man has endured a hard life — a life of sacrifice and pain.

"One million. That is how many were lost in Leningrad," Anatoly says. "But the people that came out, the survivors, we were different. You see, during the siege, Leningrad became an island of independence. The people, we were free. Free from the control of central leadership in Moscow, free from comrade Stalin's iron grasp, and free — for the first time in our lives — to think for ourselves. *To think.* This freedom cured us of many Soviet illusions. And when we emerged from the siege, thankful to be alive, we saw the world anew."

He sips his vodka. "My father, he was hailed a hero. The savior of Leningrad. And the people, they adored him, trusted him. He never abandoned them. My father, he told the people of Leningrad that they would always have each other... even if Moscow did not. But after the war... Stalin..."

Anatoly looks at Hunter, somber.

"They called it *the Great Purge,*" he says. "Comrade Stalin consolidated his power, killing hundreds of thousands of Russians that stood — or might someday stand — in his way. My father and the other Leningrad officials who led the city through the siege included. As for the siege itself, it was wiped from Soviet history. Moscow declared it a conspiracy propagated by traitors to diminish the greatness of comrade Stalin. They told us it never happened," Anatoly says. "That my brother did not starve to death. That my mother did not freeze to death. And that the millions of souls who suffered and perished, they never existed. As for those that did survive the siege, we were forbidden to ever mention it again."

Hunter lowers the gun, disgusted.

"So," Anatoly says, eyeing her, "though I may be Russian. And I may be an agent of sorts. Do not assume I am a Soviet spy attempting to thwart capitalists and enable this perilous Cold War." He shakes his head. "No. I work for no state. I take orders from no nation. I show allegiance only to humanity herself, for I am a defender of all her children. Because, like the people of Leningrad, we only have each other."

Hunter stares into Anatoly's eyes, enamored.

"Now," he says. "May I ask you another question?"

Hunter considers. For a moment, she completely forgets her suspicions that this man is here to do something sinister and terrible. Instead, she thinks only of the last question Anatoly asked her, back in the bar: *What do you want out of life?*

"Sure," Hunter says, assuming this next question can't possibly be as dreadful as that.

Anatoly smiles. He stands up and approaches her, ignoring the gun in her hand. He leans in close to her, willingly pressing himself against the barrel.

"Do you dance?" he asks.

9

The dream is always the same...

"And the winner of the 1984 Pulitzer Prize goes to... Steven Leonard."

Uproarious applause... Steven in the spotlight...

"Thank you. Thank you all," Steven says, basking in the moment, all his hard work paying off. "In my heart, I may doubt that I deserve this Pulitzer Prize over the other journalists. But there is no question of my pleasure in having won it for myself..."

Steven, from the stage, glances down at his table. His parents are seated, their hands clasped in joy. And next to them, gazing up at him, madly in love with him, is Steven's date...

Hunter Gunne.

"Steven," she says, her voice carrying across the room, floating toward him. "Steven," she says, rising to her feet, her arms extended. Happy that her story has finally been told and that Steven is now celebrated for telling it.

"Steven," she says, suddenly in front of him, the reception hall now empty, her hands sliding gently into his hair, pulling him into a loving embrace...

"*Wake the fuck up.*"

• • •

Steven — sitting in the passenger seat of Hunter's car, his face planted against the window, his forehead smearing the glass — startles awake.

"Let's go," Hunter says, shoving him.

Steven looks around, groggy.

They're deep in a forest, stars twinkling above the tree line. In front of them, Trevor leans against the bumper of a nondescript military truck pulled off along a dirt road.

"Where are we?" Steven asks.

"Upstate New York," Hunter says, stepping out of the car.

"How long was I out?" Steven asks.

"Long enough," Hunter says, slamming her door shut.

Steven scrambles out after her, every muscle, tendon, and joint aching from the day's abuse.

"Alright, Trevor," Hunter says. "What do you have for us?"

"A plan," Trevor says, unrolling architectural schematics on the hood of her car. "And a damn good one, if I do say so myself. The missile compound was built in 1955 as a functional prototype," he says, flicking on a flashlight. "A proof of concept, really. For the Department of Defense. Not the Air Force, or Army, or any branch of the military."

"Effectively keeping it off the books, right?" Steven asks. "What the Pentagon likes to call an unknown-unknown."

"That's right," Trevor says, impressed. He looks at Hunter. "He is a bright lad, isn't he?"

The Black Budget, Steven thinks.

Every year, the Department of Defense allots almost half a trillion dollars to projects deemed too sensitive to be made public. That averages out to the tune of 50 million dollars being spent... *per hour*. This money is a blank check of sorts, to do whatever they want with no political scrutiny.

Steven looks around, guessing they're in the state's Adirondack Park — a mountainous six-million-acre wilderness preserve.

The perfect place to hide a nuclear missile silo, he thinks.

Undoubtedly, a black budget location such as this would get the Pentagon's highest clearance designation of *ultra-top secret*, affectionately referred to as an *unknown-unknown*.

Such unknown-unknowns aren't infrequent either. When it comes to closed-door military expenditures, secrets like this are a dime-a-dozen.

Our tax dollars at work, Steven thinks, struck by the similarities to the development of the U-2 spy plane, an idea initially passed around the Pentagon like a hot potato. Eventually, the proposal for the ultra-high altitude reconnaissance aircraft was deemed too extreme by the military branches, and the idea was scrapped... except it wasn't.

The C.I.A. took over the project, in secret.

Officially, the U-2 spy plane didn't exist. Even the Lockheed employees didn't know the extent of what they were building. Flying over thirteen miles above the ground, an altitude unreachable by Soviet fighter jets or anti-aircraft missiles, the C.I.A. used the plane to fly illegally over the Soviet Union for years.

But in May 1960, the inevitable happened: the plane was shot down. Needless to say, the Soviet Union was not happy about it. After all, flying over their airspace constituted an act of war... and the United States had done it hundreds of times, flagrantly.

Assuming the pilot was killed, the C.I.A. quickly concocted a cover story, forcing N.A.S.A. to claim it had lost a research aircraft somewhere over Turkey. The United States even released photos of the U-2 spy plane doctored up with the N.A.S.A. logo emblazoned on its tailfin, distributing them to the media.

But, unbeknownst to the C.I.A., the K.G.B. had an ace up their sleeve: the pilot, thirty-year-old Frank Powers, was alive and in custody. After letting the United States dig itself deeper and deeper into its cover story, the Russians finally announced his survival to the world... complete with a confession.

The C.I.A. and the United States had screwed up... big time. In addition to admitting the plane's existence to the world, President Eisenhower himself was forced to reveal the extent of its secret missions.

Powers was eventually traded for a Soviet spy on the Glienicke Bridge outside Berlin — the infamous *Bridge of Spies*. To this day, most of the details of this incident — from the missile attack to Power's survival — is still highly confidential.

Typical, Steven muses.

Watching the wheels turn in Steven's head, Trevor throws a handful of jellybeans in his mouth before continuing.

"Maintenance costs and upkeep of the facility got passed off to so many different departments, to so many different budgets, that by the time the O.W.O. got their bloody hands on it, nobody even remembered it existed," he says, munching.

Trevor gestures toward the schematics.

"As you can see, the compound has a rather simple design. The security center here, above ground. The hardened elevator shaft. And these access points here...," he says, tapping the blueprint, "are likely guard posts. The president, I imagine, is being held here," he says, tapping the control center. "It offers the most secure and defensible position. This," he says, drawing with his finger, "is the easiest route of rescue."

"It's the only route," Hunter says, matter of fact.

"Christ," Steven says. He looks up at Hunter, appalled. "It's a suicide mission."

Hunter shrugs, nonchalant. "Aren't they all?"

Desperate to appear brave in front of her, Steven shakes off his apprehension. He studies the design of the facility. Trevor's right: the layout is simple, clearly the inspiration for most Titan I — and later, the more common Titan II — missile bases scattered among the Midwest. And in the center of the schematic, catching his eye, a large circle... the silo itself.

"And this?" Steven asks, tapping the silo on the blueprint.

"The silo," Trevor answers.

"Yeah," Steven says — hanging a silent *no shit* in the air between them. "Is there a missile in there?"

Trevor looks at him. "A nuclear missile?" he asks, munching on another handful of jellybeans.

Steven eyes him. Then nods.

"Nah," Trevor answers. "Sorry, lad. No missile was ever installed here. Not at this facility," he says, chewing.

Steven looks back down at the layout.

"Well, how do you plan on even getting into the compound? If there's that much security..."

"Simple," Trevor says, smirking. "We're gonna walk in through the front door."

• • •

For every action, there is an equal and opposite reaction, Steven thinks, his arms raised with the barrel of an assault rifle pointed in his face.

This is the Third Law of Motion as compiled by Sir Isaac Newton in 1687. The gist of it is simple: if one object pushes against another, that object pushes back on the first in the opposite direction with the same amount of force.

This law applies to everything in the universe: from celestial objects to — as Steven is reminding himself now — American society.

"You want to tell us what the hell you're doing here?" the guard asks, shielding his eyes from Trevor's headlights.

Moments ago, Steven was sitting in the cab of the truck.

"Come on," Trevor said, nudging Steven toward the door. "Get on with it."

Trevor's grand plan for sneaking into the compound boiled down to this: Steven was going to bullshit their way inside.

"But they have guns," Steven said, eying the two guards approaching the truck.

"This is what we call O.J.T.," Trevor said, reaching across Steven's lap to open the door. "On the job training. Take care of business... or die trying," he said, pushing Steven out.

Now, arms raised, Steven stares down the barrel of that gun, his mouth dry and heart racing.

Okay, Steven thinks, looking them over — they're young men... boys, actually. Maybe twenty-two or twenty-three years old. They're angry and desperate to exert their masculine authority on the world — and, at this moment, on Steven in particular.

Think like them.

What would drive somebody to turn against everything they were raised to believe and uphold? What would drive somebody to turn against society, endangering the lives of everybody they know and love? What would drive somebody to join a manipulative secret organization whose own intentions in no way benefit themselves?

The answer, Steven thinks, *is Newton's Third Law of Motion.*

The 1960s was an incredibly tumultuous decade for the United States in which the country's brightest beacons of hope and prosperity — John and Robert Kennedy, Martin Luther King Jr. — were horrifically gunned down in their prime. But, thanks to those men, the wheels of change were already set in motion.

Hours after the death of JFK — aboard Air Force One in Dallas, Texas — Lyndon B. Johnson was sworn in as the President of the United States. LBJ wasted no time pushing forward his dream of *The Great Society*, a sweeping set of legislation which was on par with FDR's New Deal. His aim wasn't just to eliminate poverty throughout the nation, but racial injustice as well.

Answering the demands of the civil rights movement, LBJ passed the Civil Rights Act of 1964 — forbidding discrimination and segregation. He declared a *War on Poverty*, dedicating unprecedented amounts of federal aid to eliminate hunger, illiteracy, and unemployment. He pushed legislation that provided — for the first time in the nation's history — federal money to assist and improve public education. He created the Medicare and Medicaid programs, providing health insurance for the poor and elderly. He created and funded the National Endowment for the Arts and chartered the Corporation for Public Broadcasting — thus creating PBS.

It was an age of enlightenment in the United States.

But for every action, there is an equal and opposite reaction...

Fueled by LBJ's greatest mistake — the escalation of the war in Vietnam — the conservative sects of the United States gained traction. Viewing both the civil rights movement and the anti-war movement as cultural threats to their very existence, the conservative-right decided to hit back.

And they hit back hard.

By the late sixties, the progressive and conservative movements clashed head-on, sparking the beginning of an ideological conflict that still resonates today. And with a dangerous anti-government sentiment already on the rise, the country as a whole fell into a tailspin.

Enter Richard Nixon.

Nixon, whose own presidency would end in disgrace and resignation, promptly dismantled much of LBJ's work, crushing *The Great Society*.

The jarring snap from the progressive left to the conservative right left many Americans disenchanted with politics and democracy itself. Cynicism and mistrust swept the nation. And a sense of alienation pervaded society, the likes of which had never been felt before in the United States.

These feelings of unease and uncertainty created a sense of longing in many... the wanting of a savior, of somebody to step up and fix everything they saw wrong with the nation, the consequences be damned. Add the undeliverable promise of jobs and wealth, status and success, strength and peace – all wrapped in a big bow – and the public became easily seduced.

It was from these dark desires that Americans unknowingly adopted authoritarian leanings, something deemed so un-American as to be insulting even to suggest. But there it was, in plain sight, on the left and right.

Now vulnerable and exposed, the country's most sacred institutions found themselves relentlessly attacked. Education and free press, integral to an enlightened electorate, had their legs chopped out from beneath them. Civil liberties were sacrificed time and time again. Voter suppression, political corruption, and the rise of powerful lobby interest groups blindsided American democracy.

And, adding insult to injury, most Americans turned their backs to it all, growing adverse to logic and reality and instead embracing inclination and ignorance.

With this sudden understanding, Steven – still staring at that assault rifle leveled at his chest – steps into these guards' boots and sees the world as they see it.

He sees these guards as they see themselves: victims.

Since the day they were born, they have been the target of a purposeful and manipulative assault on our society's critical thinking ability. Their entire lives, they have been taught to trust their emotions over fact, their intuitions over reality, leaving them dangerously confused and impressionable.

And they are not alone. Millions of Americans have been shaped and molded by these same societal pressures — an entire generation, wholly ignorant, is now the fruit of this misguided labor.

Power and control. It is human nature to want these things, to feel important and special. And the promise of such things can be overwhelmingly tempting — especially if one lacks the commonsense to be skeptical of such promises — to call bullshit when bullshit is being served.

An organization like the O.W.O. can easily thrive when one cannot tell the difference between a charlatan and a messiah. As such, the Old World Order draws the weak-minded to it like moths to a flame. An organization based on unquestioning loyalty is easy to support if one is happy not to question it. And — unlike the military — there's no risk of having to bow to a rival political party come the next round of elections.

The disenfranchised, the disillusioned, the uneducated... these are the people so easily manipulated by such an organization. Especially when an organization can build off already existing fears, biases, and insecurities — not to mention a general distrust of government and established authority.

These guards, Steven thinks, *are the result*. People willing to join a cause even if that cause is in no way beneficial to them. The promise of jobs and wealth, status and success, strength and security. It's a con. And these two guards — and the hundreds of others like them, lacking any ability to see it for what it is — are the conned.

These guards, Steven concludes, *are morons.* Due to no fault of their own, mind you. But morons, nonetheless.

"I said: what the hell are you doing here?" the guard asks again, thrusting his rifle into Steven's face.

"Woah now. Easy boys," Steven says, armed with his new insight. "We got a delivery here."

"A delivery? This time a night?" the guard asks, struggling to get a good look at Steven in the dark. Having changed into similar black fatigues, Steven doesn't look much different from them. Frustrated, the guard glances up at the cab.

From behind the wheel, Trevor shrugs down at him.

"Sheeit," the guard says.

The guards' walkie-talkie radios, clipped to their belts, squawk in unison: "What is it?" somebody asks irritably from inside the facility.

"A delivery," the guard says into his radio, looking back at the security camera mounted behind them.

"This time a night? Sheeit," the voice crackles through the radio. "What are they delivering?"

The guard eyes Steven. "What are you delivering?" he asks.

"Jellybeans," Steven answers. "For the... umm... asset."

"Jellybeans... for the asset," the guard relays into his radio.

"The asset has all the damn jellybeans he'll ever need," the voice squawks back.

"The asset has all the damn jellybeans he'll ever need," the guard says to Steven.

Steven nods. Then shakes his head. "Well sheeit," he says — adopting the guards' vernacular — "What we supposed to do with all these jellybeans?"

The guard blinks. "Well sheeit," he says into his radio. "What they supposed to do with all these jellybeans?"

"Well, sheeit," the voice from inside the facility says. "How the hell am I supposed to know?"

The guard, his rifle still trained on Steven, scratches his head... this is quite the conundrum.

"Hey there," the walkie-talkie squawks. "Who ordered these jellybeans anyhow?"

The guard relays the question — despite Steven's ability to easily hear the question himself — "Who ordered these jellybeans anyhow?"

Steven freezes... *oh shit*. This is a dangerously specific question he wasn't expecting to be asked. He looks up at Trevor. Trevor shrugs down at him — the message he conveys is clear: *this is your problem, chum.*

"Who ordered these? Well now..." Steven stammers, buying himself time to think. "The order came from..." Steven struggles to think of a name... any name... "John," he says — immediately cringing.

"John," the guard relays into the radio.

"John?" the radio squawks back. The two guards outside stare at Steven.

"Umm... yeah," Steven says.

Don't give 'em time to think.

"Joe John. Major. Joe. John," Steven snaps.

The first guard nods. "Major Joe John," he relays into the walkie-talkie.

"Major Joe John?" the voice from inside asks.

The guard eyes Steven. "Major Joe John?" he asks.

108

"Yeah," Steven answers. "And it seemed important," he adds, emphasizing *important*.

The guard relaxes again. "Yeah," he says into the radio. "Seems pretty important too."

The radio falls silent.

Steven stares at the walkie-talkie, holding his breath.

This is it, he thinks, his life hinging on the assumption that nobody ever really knows what's going on... or who's actually in charge.

Please, Steven thinks, *be as stupid as I think you are.*

Finally, the walkie-talkie squawks...

"Guess we better let 'em in."

10

November 1957 — Barrow, Alaska

"Do you dance?" Anatoly asks.

Hunter stares at him, stunned. Moments ago, he was telling her of the Siege of Leningrad in an attempt to convince her that he owes no loyalty to the tyrannical Soviet Union. But now he's flipped the conversation squarely onto her. And this question, of all questions, *is* more dreadful than his last...

Never has she been asked to dance.

"Well?" Anatoly asks, enjoying her discomfort.

Hunter shakes her head. "No," she says, ashamed.

"Do you wish to learn?" Anatoly asks, offering her a hand.

"What? Now?"

"I see no better time than now, Miss Gunne," he says.

Glancing at the PPK still clutched in her hand, Hunter considers. *The ball is still in her court... isn't it?*

"Sure," she says. "But I don't hear any music."

"In Leningrad — in Saint Petersburg, I should say — music is life. Without music, none of us would have survived the siege," he says. "But you do not need music to hear music, Miss Gunne. Understand?"

"No," she laughs, nervously. "Not at all."

"Balakirev, Borodin, Rimsky-Korsakov, all were sons of Saint Petersburg. All were masters of composition," Anatoly says, bending over and grabbing hold of the bed. "But none held a candle to the brilliance of Pyotr Ilyich Tchaikovsky," he says.

Flipping the bed against the wall, he presents Hunter their dance floor. "Though I do enjoy a traditional Viennese waltz, it is the work of Tchaikovsky that captures both the romantic and yet melancholic soul of Mother Russia," he says, his eyes closed, undoubtedly hearing the music in his head. "His compositions convey a sense of longing, a sense of unfulfilled love."

He opens his eyes and looks at Hunter.

"Miss Gunne, if I may have the honor."

Hunter obliges him and steps to the center of the room. Anatoly meets her there, sliding his right arm around her back. Naturally, Hunter slides her free arm around his shoulder, staring into his eyes as she does so. Anatoly wraps his other hand around hers — the gun still tight in her grasp — and holds them out at arm's length.

"To begin," he says, feeling Hunter tense in his arms. "We breath. It is very important."

Anatoly breathes in and out, playfully.

Hunter exhales and inhales, her cheeks reddening.

"Very good. You are a natural."

"I'm sure you say that to all the girls," she says.

"Now, I want you to imagine you are standing atop of a box," Anatoly says. "With your feet together, you are on the right front corner. Yes?"

Hunter, glancing at her feet, nods.

"With your right foot, step to the right back corner... that's one."

Hunter does so, standing awkwardly.

"With your left foot, step to the left back corner," Anatoly says. "That's two."

Hunter steps back as Anatoly steps along with her but reversed.

"Good," he says. "Now slide your right foot to your left, bringing them together again... that's three."

Hunter does so, still staring at her feet.

"You are standing on the back left corner, yes?" Anatoly asks.

Hunter nods.

"Now, bring your left foot forward... that's one. And with your right foot, step to the right front corner... that's two. Now slide your left to your right, bringing them together... that's three. And we're right back where we started, yes?" he asks. "Easy, yes?"

"Yes," Hunter says, giggling.

"Now again," Anatoly says, leading her. "One... two... three," he says, watching Hunter watch her feet move. "One... two... three."

Returning to their starting position, Hunter looks up at him, eager for approval.

"You are good," he says. "But this is where it gets complicated. Now we add a rotation," he teases. "I will lead. One... two... three." At the beginning of each count, Anatoly turns a bit to his left, rotating Hunter as they progress. "One... two... three."

Together, they circle the room.

"Now, look up at me," Anatoly says.

Hunter does so... but stumbles.

"Learn to focus," Anatoly says. "This is the waltz. It is both graceful and sensual — and, like love itself, disorienting. But if one learns to focus, to center one's thoughts, the dance slows down. Just as life slows down. All one has to do is focus."

Staring into his eyes, the tension melts from Hunter's face. She forgets about the gun in her hand and relaxes into his arms.

"Phenomenal," Anatoly says. "One... two... three..."

They circle the room, rotating as they go.

"Tchaikovsky was a musical prodigy," Anatoly says. "He wrote his first masterpiece when he was just twenty-eight years old. But tragedy followed him throughout his life, defining both him and his work. You see, Tchaikovsky preferred the company of men, but in Imperialist Russia, such relations were forbidden. If found guilty, one was exiled to Siberia to face certain death. But such threats, such bigotry, they never do stop one's pursuit of happiness, do they?"

Hunter, fixated on his voice and features, nods.

"Tchaikovsky's first love — and muse — was lost to suicide," he says, pulling away from Hunter unexpectedly. "Focus. Continue to dance," he says, watching her alone at the center of the room. "One... two... three. One... two... three..."

Hunter falls back into the rhythm, her feet stepping on the beat, her eyes locked on Anatoly as she now rotates on her own, the gun at her side.

"That loss," Anatoly continues, "had a profound impact on Tchaikovsky's life. But that focus, that dedication, would never leave him. That love within his heart, though tragic as it were, never ceased. It became the fabric from which Tchaikovsky created his art. One... two... three. One... two... three..."

Anatoly approaches Hunter, admiring her.

"You see," he says, "as the piece progresses, much of the excitement of a waltz is the anticipation — the anticipation of the two lovers reuniting — at last. For Tchaikovsky, that reunion with his love would never be, could never be. But that did not stop him from giving that gift to others," he says, stepping back up to her.

Hunter slides into his arms and stares into his eyes.

"Now do you hear the music?" he asks.

"Yes," Hunter says. But she hardens, resisting her emotions. "Why are you here?"

"Because I love you," Anatoly says, to Hunter's surprise. "Because I love Tchaikovsky," he continues. "Because I love every soul that has come before me. And I love every soul that will come after me. But we — humanity as a whole — are sick. And that sickness is what brings me here."

Now dancing effortlessly, Hunter eyes him.

"Excuse me for doubting you," she says. "But that sounds like a bunch of bullshit."

Anatoly nods. But his confidence doesn't waver.

"Four billion years," he says. "That's how long this planet has harbored life. And it is only in the last million that humankind has flowered into the species we are today. In the grand history of the world itself, our time here on Earth scales down to just one minute of one year. And it is only recently that we — that humanity — have unlocked the energy of the cosmos itself. I speak of the atomic bomb," Anatoly says.

Much of Hunter's suspicions flood back to her.

This man is here in Barrow, Alaska for a reason, she thinks.

And that reason can't be good...

"Already, our foolish nations have stockpiled enough atomic weapons to wipe out, not just humanity, but all life on Earth. Extinction," he says, sharply. "Complete and utter extinction. The horror of such a holocaust is often labeled *unthinkable* but never as *undoable*," Anatoly continues. "And here we are, at one of the most inhospitable locales on Earth, surrounded by machines poised to commit these actions. Actions that we — that society — claim to be unable to conceive. And yet we balance all of this — of the *unthinkable* horrors, of the infinite number of souls — in the hands of a few: our generals and sergeants, our presidents and premieres. All it takes is one careless moment, one misstep..."

Anatoly drags his foot, jarring their timing.

"All it takes is a single accident, one misunderstanding... and the fruit of four billion years is wiped away, forever."

He steps back to her, holding her more tenderly than before.

"One... two... three," he counts. "One... two... three," and their waltz resumes.

"Extinction," he says. "The end of all life on Earth. Such an outcome is not something to contemplate or to justify. It is something to rebel against, to fight. Instead, we are numb. We are indifferent. A society that willingly jeopardizes not only individual lives, but the survival of one's entire species, without demanding change or fighting for their future... is simply not well."

Hunter considers. For as much as she suspects this man, what he says makes sense.

Is this a part of his game? she wonders.

Is this a part of the Soviet plot?

To twist one against their own nation?

"As for this sickness, I offer no cure but a treatment," Anatoly says. "I am not indifferent. And I am not numb. Owing to those that came before me and those that will come after me, I am focused on preserving humanity. I am dedicated to saving the world. I am afraid there are those, our very own brothers and sisters, that see humankind — the innocent and good — as their chattel, both exploitable and disposable. There are those that risk everything, all life on Earth, for selfish causes and evil purposes. To those, I rebel. To them, I revolt. I am here, Miss Gunne, to save the world. Because that is what I do..."

There's a knock at the door.

"Come in," Anatoly says, having expected the interruption.

The door swings open, and Trevor steps inside. Pulling his parka's hood from his head, he looks over the mess of the room before settling on Hunter. He eyes the gun in her hand.

"Typical," Trevor says, annoyed.

"Now, Miss Gunne," Anatoly says, walking back to the dresser. "I'm afraid our time has come to an end."

Hunter watches him pull a shoulder holster out of the drawer. He straps it on.

"Where are you going?" she snaps, leveling the gun at him. "What the hell are you up to?"

Anatoly smiles. He picks up the bottle of vodka, topping his glass. He picks up Hunter's untouched serving and offers it to her.

"As I told you, Hunter," he says, surprising her by how intimate it is to hear her first name come from his lips.

"Saving the world."

Standing before her, his eyes sparkling, Hunter takes the vodka. But Anatoly keeps his hand before her, palm up. She follows his gaze to the gun, realizing he wants it back.

But Hunter is torn: *does she trust this man or not?*

Is he friend or foe?

"No rush," Trevor says, impatiently. "Just the fate of humanity hanging in the balance."

Hunter stares at Anatoly, unsure of what to do and unsure of what to think. Finally, she flips the handle for him to take.

Anatoly holsters the PPK then raises his glass to her.

"*Na Zdorovie,*" he says to her, softly, their eyes locked.

"*Na Zdorovie,*" she says.

And they drink.

11

"Guess we better let 'em in," the walkie-talkie squawks.

Steven watches, astonished, as the two guards clear out of their way, and the mechanical gate slides open along its track.

I did it, Steven thinks. *I actually did it.*

I just talked my way into a top-secret military installation.

Trevor jerks the truck forward, pulling into the compound. As he drives by, Steven jumps onto the side of the cab and rides along. He peers at Trevor through the open window, wide-eyed.

"You're a good man in a tight corner, Steven," Trevor says, nodding his approval.

Driving up to the access building, Trevor eyes one security camera in particular. Swinging the truck out wide, he fights the cumbersome transmission into reverse and backs up toward the building — all the while being mindful of *that* camera.

Inside the access building, at the security center, the guard assigned to keep an eye on things is oblivious to the truck backing more and more into *that* camera's shot. Instead, sitting with his feet up on the console, the guy is nose-deep in the November '83 issue of *Playboy*.

Eventually, the camera is blocked completely...

Outside, Trevor shuts off the engine, and Steven hops to the ground. The two guards approach the back of the truck.

"Let's get a look at these here jellybeans," the guard says, at ease.

"Sure thing," Steven says, releasing the truck's tailgate.

The heavy gate swings down, revealing Hunter waiting inside. With both her Berettas leveled, their silencers attached, the guards are dead before they know it...

PEW. PEW.

As their now lifeless bodies thud to the ground, Steven stares at them transfixed. It's as if Hunter flipped a light switch on them. Alive one moment, dead the next.

Hunter hops out of the truck.

"Brilliant job," Trevor says, joining them. He cocks his head toward Hunter. "See now," he says to her, "the boy delivered. Kept his wits about him and still alive, yeah?"

Hunter looks at Trevor, then at Steven.

"Yeah," she says, flippant. "Still alive."

"Righto," Trevor says. "Pay up then."

Steven looks up from the two dead guards.

"Pay up?" he asks.

As Hunter holsters her weapons, she looks at Steven and shrugs. "It's nothing personal," she says.

Reaching into her back pocket, she pulls out a folded-up twenty dollar bill and hands it to Trevor. Steven's not quite sure how to take this insult.He looks back down at the guards.

A minute ago, Steven was empathizing with these two, imagining what it was like to step into their boots, to live their lives. Now they're dead, both of them.

"Is this a game to you?" Steven asks.

Hunter ignores him. She grabs her duffel bag from the truck, the armaments clinking inside of it.

"Look, it's one thing to go thinking I'm an idiot," Steven says. "But you just killed two men. Does that mean nothing to you?"

Hunter and Trevor exchange an uneasy glance.

"Okay, Steven," Hunter says, standing before him. "Let's make one thing absolutely clear. These men, they knowingly kidnapped the President of the United States on behalf of some mysterious organization promising to make all their dreams come true, or whatever. Now, whether they realize it or not, this organization's ultimate goal is global thermonuclear war. Does that sound like treason to anybody else?"

Trevor raises his hand.

"Thank you," Hunter says. "And what is treason punishable by as dictated by the United States Constitution?"

"Death," Steven reluctantly answers.

"Exactly," Hunter says. "So, let me just push all the politics of their cause to the side and cut to the chase. These men — idiots or not — are accomplices to a far greater evil, an evil plotting the death of potentially billions of people. And I simply do not have time to show them the error of their ways... not when, the moment I turn my back, they'll just shoot me from behind."

As Hunter turns away, frustrated, Trevor slides up next to Steven and puts an arm around him.

"Steven, my boy, do me a favor," he whispers. "Don't piss her off."

• • •

Hunter drops her bag on the ground. Opening it, she reveals a plethora of weapons and ammunition inside. But she can't help but glance back at Steven...

He's a civilian, she thinks. *Innocent, naive, and idealistic. What the hell does he know? Look at him*, she scoffs, *scared shitless. It's because of him — the wannabe journalist — that I was dragged back into this shit. It's because of him — and his sheer stupidity — that I had to blow up my cabin sky-high...*

But as quickly as those thoughts cross her mind, Hunter is struck with disgust... disgust in herself.

What is wrong with me?

She looks at Steven again. As he stands beneath the mercury-vapor lights she takes in his features: the shape of his mouth, the shadows cast on his cheeks...

Killing people is wrong, she thinks.

That's why we're here.

Hunter's mind drifts back to her cabin, to when she first met Steven. There he was, sitting across from her in the parlor, the expansive view of the Maryland countryside behind them.

And as Steven rambled on about Hunter Gunne — *the man* Steven expected to find there — she watched him, studying his body language. She noted every breath he took, every flick of an eye, and there was only one word to describe him: *sincere.*

As for the things Steven was saying about Hunter, she liked hearing them. And as for her cabin...

It was a pretty badass explosion.

Hunter reaches into the bag. She pulls out the Glock 17 she had grabbed during their escape from the cabin. With a high capacity and smooth action, it's a good weapon.

Perfect for Steven, she thinks.

Loading the magazine, she chambers a round and turns to him. "I'm sorry, Steven," she says, gesturing toward the two dead guards. "You're right. This isn't a game."

She offers Steven the gun — a peace offering.

Steven takes it, reluctantly. He looks at the gun in his hand, his palms already sweaty. Guns kill people. But Steven doesn't want to hurt anybody. "I've never... I don't..." he stammers before accidentally pulling the trigger...

BAM.

The slug fires harmlessly into the ground.

"Right," Hunter says, snatching the gun back from him. "No gun for you."

She puts the Glock back in the bag as Steven stands awkwardly over her, feeling stupid.

"How many people have you killed?" he asks.

"What? Today?" Hunter asks.

Not waiting for him to clarify, she marches toward a row of service vehicles parked within the gravel lot. She opens the door of the nearest pick-up, drops the visor, and catches the truck's keys as they fall into her hand. She throws the keys over the fence and into the woods before sensing Steven's presence.

"No. I mean..." Steven says, fumbling for words. "Just... how many?"

Hunter hardens. She wants nothing to do with a conversation of morality, of right and wrong, or whether the end truly justifies the means.

"Is this for your *Parade Magazine* article?" she asks, biting.

Steven stops following her. He watches Hunter walk to the next truck, throwing its keys over the fence as well. When she glances back at him, Steven is staring at her like a hurt puppy.

For the love of God, Hunter — she tells herself — *stop being an asshole.*

123

"I don't know," she says, rubbing her eyes. "A lot. I've killed... a lot of people."

She hears Steven crunching away on the gravel, and when she opens her eyes, he's joining Trevor at the access building.

"No hurry," Trevor shouts at her, impatiently. "Just a world war to stop. But please, take your bloody time."

• • •

Inside the access building, the guard thumbs through the pages of his *Playboy*, his feet still resting on the security console.

On the cover of the magazine, a beautiful model is dressed as a nurse. She smiles temptingly at the reader. Next to her beautiful big eyes is the header: *Nurses are people too*.

The guard flips to the next page... the centerfold. *Finally*.

Her name is Donna Gamba, a model turned nurse, and, evidently, turned model again. Looking her over, the guard nods his approval. She's dressed in a predictably slinky nurse costume, but, through the progression of photos, the outfit doesn't stay on for long.

Rotating the magazine this way and that, the guard finds himself distracted by the model's bio. Bringing the page within an inch of his nose, he squints to read.

"I think a woman's place..." he starts, struggling, "isn't just in the kitchen waiting for her man. She should be out fighting... to make the world a better place..." The guard stops reading. "Feminists," he says, disgusted.

"Sounds like good advice to me," Hunter says.

Startled, the guard drops the magazine in his lap, revealing the barrel of Hunter's gun now inches from his face.

"Unlock all access points between here and the president," Hunter says, her voice firm and calm.

The guard raises his hands.

"President?" he spits, glancing at Steven and Trevor watching from the corner. "The hell you talking about?"

PEW.

Hunter fires a shot between the man's knees, piercing the magazine. She raises the smoking barrel of the silencer a few inches, lining it up with the guard's privates.

"Go ahead and kill me, you bitch."

"Happy to oblige," she smirks, leveling the gun at the guard's chest. But as her finger tightens on the trigger, her eyes flick toward Steven... and she hesitates.

"You don't have to do it," Steven says, stepping forward. "We can tie him up, keep him quiet."

Trevor and the guard glance between Steven and Hunter, the tension palpable. The guard laughs.

"Well, well, well," he sneers. "Losing the edge, are we?"

"Shut up," Hunter snaps.

"He's scared, Hunter," Steven says. "And confused. And in over this head. Just look at him."

"Look at me?" the guard retorts. "Look at you."

"You can't save the world by killing everybody who disagrees with you," Steven says.

"Sorry, Steven," Hunter says, raising her gun again. "That's exactly how this works." The guard watches her finger tighten on the trigger... but Hunter hesitates again. "Damn it," she sighs, lowering the gun.

Now! the guard thinks, jumping out of his chair. He shoves Steven out of his way, pulling a pistol out from behind his back. He swings the gun around, leveling it at Hunter as she draws her own.

Faster, faster, faster, the guard thinks, pulling the trigger...

BAM. PEW.

His bullet skims Hunter's arm, slicing the flesh in a burst of blood. But Hunter's shot arrives on target, blowing his brains out. His body falls back into his chair and rolls away.

"Mother-fucker," Hunter shouts, cupping her wound.

"Hunter," Steven shouts, jumping to her aid. "Are you okay?"

Hunter jerks her arm away from him.

"I'll live," she says, glaring at him. "No thanks to you."

She looks down at the security controls and mashes a large *unlock* button. Several indicator lights toggle from red to green. Glancing at the monitors, Hunter notes the number and location of the men awaiting them.

"Let's get this over with," she barks, stepping into the elevator.

Steven glances sheepishly at Trevor, speechless. Trevor smiles.

"Just let the girl do her job," he says, herding Steven after her.

• • •

Down in the facility below, a klaxon horn precedes the automated unlocking of the three access points between the elevator and Reagan's holding cell. At each point, the mechanical locks unlatch, and the blast door swings freely.

The men scurry to their posts, grabbing their assault rifles and loading up with ammunition. Nash — the brute of a man that had laughed in the president's face as he shoved him in his cell — feeds off the excitement. He pulls a polished twenty-inch knife from his belt, admiring his reflection in the blade.

This is what he's been waiting for...

12

November 1957 — Barrow, Alaska

Outside the barracks, Hunter watches Anatoly and Trevor climb aboard an orange, truck-sized Tucker Sno-Cat. Diesel smoke billows from the exhaust as the Sno-Cat lurches forward, its four tank-like tracks churning the snow beneath it.

East, she thinks, watching the vehicle's lights fade into the night...

The bastards are heading east.

Moments ago, in Anatoly's room — after just having learned to waltz — Hunter decided to let the men leave without a fight. She handed over the Walther PPK, and they walked out the door. But losing the battle doesn't mean she's lost the war. What Hunter did was buy herself time... *time to think.*

Now, with a clear head, Hunter reflects on the situation. Anatoly was convincing when it came to whether or not he was a Soviet spy. *Maybe a little too convincing?* But he was more than mum when it came to telling her exactly what he was doing here in Barrow. Instead, he twisted his explanation to address the existential threat nuclear weapons pose against humanity.

Saving the world, he said.

But saving it from what? she wonders.

Hunter has never met somebody more mysterious — or more mesmerizing — than Anatoly. But that's precisely what she'd expect from a real-life secret agent. Worldly, charismatic, and cool: she *should* be swept off her feet.

Brainwashing, she figures, would be a skillset of any adequately trained K.G.B. agent. And sweet-talking a potential adversary is a hell of a lot less messy than killing them in cold blood.

But...

Damn, Hunter thinks, drowning in uncertainty. The story of Leningrad. The terror of the German siege. It all seemed sincere to her. But was Anatoly telling the truth? Or does Hunter simply want to believe that he was telling the truth? After all, ignorance is bliss.

Fuck it, she thinks. Snapping free of her indecision, Hunter turns on her heels and sprints in the opposite direction. She cuts between two Arctic Mack trucks and darts down an alley. She jumps over a fence, skimming across a row of oil barrels before landing in the powder snow. The shortcut pays off, and she dashes toward her bar, bursting through the door. She leaps the counter, cutting through the kitchen as she charges toward the building's attached shed...

Sitting inside, kept warm by the woodstove, is a yellow-colored snowmobile.

Always be prepared. That was one of the most valuable lessons instilled in Hunter by her mother, a lesson passed along to her by Hunter's grandfather. In that vein, her mother always insisted on having an exit strategy... hence the snowmobile ready and waiting. Whether it was escaping West Virginia. Or Skagway. Or, here and now, chasing after two potentially dangerous secret agents...

Hunter grabs a hunting knife off a workbench. Tucking it into her belt, she mounts the snowmobile and kicks open the shed door. She pulls the starter cord, and the two-stroke engine turns over, blowing a cloud of blue-white smoke behind it.

Squeezing the throttle, Hunter launches the snowmobile out into the night.

• • •

Minutes go by. Ten. Twenty. Thirty. All the while, Hunter eyes her fuel gauge, fully aware that if she strays too far from town, she'll freeze to death in the cold. The terrain to the east of Barrow is alien and surreal: a dark, snow-covered expanse that seemingly continues forever.

It's in this direction that Hunter heads, following Anatoly and Trevor's Sno-Cat tracks.

To her left, in the distance, the lights of the Point Barrow Distant Radar Site — its distinctive dome array sticking out along the horizon — fade away. But the men's tracks continue eastward, out onto the frozen Elson Lagoon. Hugging the shoreline, its jagged rocks protruding from the ice, the tracks veer south into the Iko Bay. Darkness, except for her snowmobile's single headlight, envelops her.

But if Hunter knows anything, it's how to be alone...

For the past three years, Hunter has been alone. Sure, she's been surrounded by the airmen and construction workers of Barrow — a constant flow of new faces and fresh conversations — but solitude was never more than a few steps away. Solitude, Hunter's convinced, is what she thrives on. It's how she straightens out her thoughts. It's how she clears her head.

Isolation, she concluded long ago, *is good for her...*

But if that's the case, why does Hunter feel so desperate to chase Anatoly down? What is she hoping to accomplish? Does she want to stop him? Join him? Or does Hunter simply not want this night to end?

As these thoughts whirl by in Hunter's mind, the tracks she has been following disappear — much to her dismay. Creeping to a stop, Hunter stares into the black void and sees nothing. The wind and snow have reclaimed the landscape, healing the scar cut into it by Anatoly and Trevor.

Shit, Hunter thinks. *Now what?*

Hunter scans the horizon. She thinks of the blueprint the men had been hunched over earlier in the night. She thinks of the perimeter fence and entry point that Trevor had pointed out to Anatoly. It was tangible. It was real. And if Hunter's going to believe Anatoly's story about Leningrad and the siege, she might as well believe there's a top-secret military facility out here too.

If I were a secret facility, where would I be? Hunter wonders, recalling as much of the local geography as possible. She can imagine something being nestled in the low valley on the far side of the bay. It would probably be a position butted against protective ridges on each of its flanks, effectively hiding it from both sea and air traffic.

That's got to be it.

Hunter presses on, determined. And as she crosses the frozen bay, something in the distance begins to take shape.

The outline of a structure forms before her, emerging out of the winter haze. A building. A compound...

I'll be damned, she thinks.

Hunter flicks off her headlight — *best not to draw attention to myself* — and slows her approach. She stops a few hundred feet away and pulls her goggles off. As her eyes adjust, there it is, right in front of her: the military facility. Massive snowdrifts nearly cover the building, blending it naturally into the surrounding terrain. Without knowing to look for *something*, there's no way Hunter would have ever spotted it. But now that she sees it, *she really sees it...*

The facility is large, with enormous conduits protruding up and out of the tundra, feeding into the building. Outlining the doors from the inside, an eerie blue light grows brighter then dims in synch with a buzz of electricity. Hunter watches the light cycle a few times. Growing brighter then dim, brighter then dim, the effect is almost hypnotic.

An electrical sub-station, Hunter thinks, recalling what Trevor had told Anatoly. Studying the perimeter, her eyes trace the fence encircling the compound. It's just as Trevor had explained. Inside the compound, a dozen or so Snow-Cats and Mack trucks are parked outside, their engines idling to stay warm.

Two guard posts, Hunter thinks, further recalling their conversation. Her eyes quickly find one... and then the other. Hunter's pulse quickens. *Two perimeter patrols coming and going every half-hour*, Hunter recalls, kneeling down to become less visible. Spotting one of the patrols on the far side of the compound, she immediately observes the second opposite of it. *That leaves a gap in their coverage,* Hunter recalls Trevor saying, *right about here...*

Hunter's eyes settle on a spot along the fence, far from either patrol.

"That's our in," she says, as if in response to Trevor and Anatoly's conversation.

Eyeing the patrols, Hunter approaches the fence. She steps up to the chain-link and peers through determined to get inside. She considers climbing over it, but the barbwire atop makes her reconsider.

Think, Hunter, she tells herself. *How are you going to pull this off?*

"Well, you certainly are resourceful, aren't you?" Anatoly asks, suddenly behind her.

Startled, Hunter spins around. In a flash, she pulls out her knife and lunges at him. But Anatoly doesn't bat an eye. He easily sidesteps her. And then again. All the while, Trevor watches with disdain.

"What are you doing here?" Hunter asks.

"Saving the world, Miss Gunne," Anatoly says, amused. "What are *you* doing here?"

"Cut the bullshit," Hunter snaps.

"And you think she has the aptitude for this?" Trevor scoffs. "Look at her. She's a snarling brute."

"Aptitude?" Hunter asks, glancing between the two men.

Trevor snorts. He pulls out a heavy-duty bolt cutter from his bag and takes it to the fence. *Snip.* He cuts one of the links. *Snip.* He cuts another. Hunter watches, stunned.

"Why are you here, Hunter?" Anatoly asks, commanding her attention.

"To stop you," Hunter says.

"Really?" Anatoly asks, smirking. "You could have notified the authorities. You could have raised alarms. But you chose to come here instead. Why?" Ignoring her outstretched knife, he approaches her. "What drove you out into the cold to face the unknown? Is it service to your country? Or is there something more?"

Hunter stares at him, searching herself for an answer... but finds nothing.

"A higher calling, perhaps?" Anatoly asks.

Hunter blinks. *Snip. Snip.* Trevor continues cutting the fence over her shoulder, snapping her from her daze. She steps toward Anatoly, placing the blade to his chest.

"Tell me what you're doing," she says. "Now."

Anatoly nods. "Very well," he says, the wind ruffling the lining of his hood. "As we speak, an evil secret society hell-bent on world domination is implementing its latest, most nefarious plot to take over the world. And we are here to stop them."

"Bullshit," Hunter snaps. "Everybody is as evil as everybody else. The winners just get to write the history books."

Trevor laughs. "She's growing on me," he shouts back at them, cutting another link. *Snip.*

"For centuries, the O.W.O. — *the Old World Order*," Anatoly continues, unphased, "has believed that oppressive inequality and strategic misinformation to be their most effective methods of world domination. But now, in this century, it has become startlingly clear that allowing nationalist pride to rachet up to the point of global suicide was a far simpler approach. All one has to do is give both sides a little push... and humanity falls into the abyss once and for all."

"And *this*, this is why you're here?" Hunter asks. "This is why you're breaking into this facility?" Hunter gestures toward Trevor. *Snip. Snip.*

"Yes," Anatoly says. "From this location, the O.W.O. is capable of tricking humanity into nuclear war, letting both the Americans and Russians do the dirty work for them."

"How?" Hunter asks, still not buying his story.

"A power surge — originating from *this* facility — is capable of destroying a huge swath of the radar stations lining the Beaufort Sea, effectively knocking the DEW Line out of service," Anatoly says. "If you're the Strategic Air Command, the most logical explanation for such an outage is a Soviet first strike. Now blind to what will appear as an on-going attack, the United States will have no choice but to scramble their own bombers, lest they be sitting on their runways when the bombs begin to fall. The Russians, upon seeing America's unprovoked but highly aggressive deployments, will now also be locked into a similar response of their own," Anatoly continues. "The crisis will escalate like a runaway chain reaction, feeding back upon itself. Policy will dictate the nations' respective courses of action from there, not logic. Orders — written in anticipation of such nightmare scenarios — will be followed to the T, no questions asked. Command and control procedures will be strictly adhered to, and the

136

culminating result will be none other than a full-scale nuclear conflict."

Hunter stares at Anatoly. *Snip.* Despite how crazy it all sounds, despite the foolishness of it all... the outcome, she knows, is likely. After all, this is what both the United States and the Soviet Union have been investing billions of dollars in.

Nuclear Armageddon, she thinks, *could really happen. Not intentionally. But simply by mistake...*

"Unless we stop them," Anatoly says, extending his hand as if asking her to dance. "Together."

Hunter looks at his hand, speechless.

Anatoly gestures toward Trevor. *Snip.* "We are members of an organization dedicated to thwarting these efforts. We are a secret society committed to protecting humanity against all evils, both big and small. We are the resistance, Miss Gunne, of which you are formally invited to join."

"What?" Hunter asks, forcing a laugh. "This is preposterous."

She turns away from him, breaking free of his gaze. Hunter watches Trevor cut the last link, and a portion of the fence falls away, large enough for each of them to effortlessly crawl through.

"We have been here weeks, Hunter," Anatoly says. "Scoping out this location, gathering intel for our assault, piecing together just what it is the O.W.O. is up to and how. And in that time, we could not help but notice you. And what you are capable of."

"Oh, really?" Hunter scoffs. "And what's that? Pouring drinks?"

Anatoly studies her, watching the significance of what he's said sink in.

"Why? Hunter asks. "Why me?"

"Because you have what it takes," he says. "Yes, the aptitude, as Trevor alluded to. But also, the motivation. The courage. You've trained your whole life for this... without even knowing it. You've no family. No friends. No lovers," he adds, letting that note hang in the air between them. "You're skeptical of authority. You question blind loyalty. You see the world for what it is: imperfect and unfair. But despite the harsh realities of life, you remain compassionate and caring, even for those that you do not know, people you have never met. And, most important of all, you believe in what is right and good."

"This is absurd," Hunter says.

"This is your calling, Hunter," Anatoly says. He gestures again toward Trevor. "Each of us has had ours. You do not find your destiny. Your destiny finds you. Together, we can save humanity."

Hunter looks between Anatoly and Trevor and the opening in the fence.

"Sure, yeah, okay," she says sarcastically. "So, let me guess: you want me to storm this facility with you, that's undoubtedly guarded by heavily armed men, and... what? Save the world? In that order?"

Anatoly and Trevor glance at each other and nod. "Yes," Anatoly says.

"Well, thanks, but no thanks," she says, irritated. "You're fools. Both of you. It's a suicide mission. And a stupid one at that. You really think you're going to save the world? Do you really think the world is worth saving?"

Anatoly cocks his head. "Yes," he says. "I do."

Hunter steps up to Anatoly, close enough to once again smell his cologne, close enough to remember his warmth while they danced.

"You're going to get yourself killed," she says, softly.

"Then it's a good way to die," Anatoly says, surprising her. He pulls the Walther PPK out from its holster and chambers a round. "Storming a top-secret military facility, preventing World War Three, saving all of humanity," Anatoly adds, smiling. "Yeah. That's a good way to die." He extends his hand toward her. "It's been nice knowing you, Miss Gunne."

Jarred by the sudden goodbye, Hunter hardens. "Alright then," she says, taking his hand in hers. "Suit yourself," she adds, shaking it. And, despite not wanting things to end like this, Hunter releases her grip and turns away.

"Thanks for nothing, love," Trevor quips, pulling an assault rifle out from his bag.

But Hunter ignores him, marching defiantly back toward her snowmobile. Behind her, she knows Anatoly is watching her. But, desperate to control the myriad of emotions bubbling up inside her, she doesn't look back. She can't look back. The thought that Anatoly — somebody who survived such horrific circumstances — would so willingly risk his life for so foolish a cause, more than upsets her. It rattles her to her core. Not because she disagrees with his motives... but because she finds herself too scared to follow.

My god, she thinks. *I'm never going to see him again...*

13

"Rescuing the president. Preventing nuclear war. Saving humanity," Hunter says, her eyes closed. "Yeah. That's a good way to die."

As the elevator descends down the hardened shaft, Steven gives Trevor a look. He's seen Hunter do this before — back in the cabin, Hunter muttered something similar before launching the Jeep down the mountainside. And Trevor, he repeated a similar mantra to Steven back on the Moshulu.

"A death wish," Trevor whispers to him, approvingly. "It's a thing."

Steven blinks. *These people are insane*, he thinks.

Turning back toward Hunter, she's in her own little world right now. Glancing at the bullet wound on her arm, it appears to Steven to be more of a burn than anything. Bloody, yes. Painful, definitely. *But Lucky*, Steven thinks. *Incredibly lucky*. Had that shot been a little bit more to the right... Hunter might not be breathing anymore.

And it'd all be my fault, Steven thinks.

Just let the girl do her job...

The elevator dings. The freight doors slide open, and Hunter snaps alert, all-business. She inches toward the edge of the cab. She peeks out... but quickly pulls her head back inside as the corridor outside the elevator erupts in gunfire.

"Safe to say they've been expecting us," Hunter shouts.

She swings the assault rifle off her shoulder and chambers the first round. She turns to Steven, surprising him.

"Listen," she says, stoically. "I don't want to do this, Steven. But I have to do this."

And with that, Hunter launches herself out of the elevator. A cluster of men positioned at the first access point open fire. The bullets chase Hunter across the walkway, but she makes it safely behind a bulkhead, the bullets pounding the cement supports.

The guards hold their fire, peering over their rifle sights.

Hunter pops out from the bulkhead, and with incredible grace, a single shot rings out from her rifle, echoing down the corridor. The bullet nails one of her assailants right between the eyes, covering the man behind him in blood and brains. The other men glance at each other, wide-eyed.

"Damn," one mutters, shifting nervously.

They all turn back toward Hunter... who, staring down the still-smoking barrel of her gun, flashes them a big, smug smile.

"It's the story of her life, mate," Trevor says to Steven, the two of them peering out the elevator at her. "She's the one who has to get her hands dirty."

Steven considers this, imagining what that might do to somebody after a few decades. To sacrifice oneself for humanity, again and again. Only to make no headway, to make the world no safer than how you found it. He realizes how disheartening that would be: to save the world again and again, only to have humanity stumble into the same predicament repeatedly, too stupid to learn any better. It would frustrate you, he concludes. It would jade you. It's the kind of thing, he thinks — leaning out to watch Hunter advance down the corridor — that would make you a recluse. It's the kind of

O.L.D. – A GOOD WAY TO DIE

thing that would make you hole up in a secluded cabin, far from civilization.

Hunter darts for the next bulkhead as the men open fire. But she slides safely behind cover as the bullets pound the area. She waits patiently for a break in the barrage, then pokes out, squeezing off another jaw-droppingly accurate shot. The high-velocity bullet pierces the shin of the unfortunate son-of-a-bitch in Hunter's crosshairs... shattering his tibia. As he collapses forward in agony, the bullet continues on, exiting his leg in an explosion of muscle and flesh before deflecting into the knee of the man behind him, liquefying his kneecap.

Two birds with one stone.

As the two men fall on top of each other, another shot rings out. This bullet destroys the first man's spinal cord before happily continuing its carnage, lodging violently into the second man's ribs, brutalizing his internal organs. The men slouch over, dead.

For the others watching, horror sets in as Hunter clicks her carbine from semi-auto to full-auto...

"Jesus Christ, fall back!"

Hunter opens fire as the men scatter in a panic. She charges after them in a full sprint, reloading her rifle mid-stride, hardly losing a beat. Steven inches out of the elevator, mesmerized. Hunter rushes the remaining guards, sliding to the floor, taking out their feet. She chops each of them swiftly — and lethally — in their necks.

Steven is appalled by the gruesome sight, the blood and gore. But at the same time, Hunter is almost hypnotic to watch. No matter how much Steven wants to look away, he can't. What Hunter had said to him moments ago — *"I don't want to do this. But I have to do this"* — resonates with him, the statement looping over and over in his head. His childhood memory of John F. Kennedy, of the president warning the world of the Cuban Missile Crisis, flickers in his mind...

"The greatest danger of all would be to do nothing," Steven whispers under his breath, quoting JFK. *She's right,* Steven thinks. *She has to do this. Humanity depends upon it.*

"She's amazing, isn't she?" Trevor asks, snapping Steven from his daze. Checking that the coast is clear — thanks to Hunters full-on attack — Trevor steps out into the corridor and beckons Steven to follow. "She has skill sets like no other," Trevor says. "I once saw her single-handedly commandeer an entire Soviet attack submarine. It was beautiful. Those sailors," Trevor adds with a chuckle, "they never stood a chance."

Keeping a safe distance, the two of them watch Hunter take the first access point. She glances back at them before stepping through the blast door, entering the crew quarters. Steven and Trevor follow as she attacks the next cluster of men fortified at the second access point. Gunfire and screams echo throughout the facility.

"How long have you worked together?" Steven asks Trevor, already numb to the violence.

"Decades," Trevor says. "She was just a pup when I discovered her. But I knew the moment I saw her in action that she had potential. That she could be the best. And that's exactly what she is. Man, woman, whatever... she is the best at what she does."

Steven watches Hunter, becoming more and more enamored.

"Nobody in the world could do this, what she's doing now," Trevor says. "And that's why I needed her. That's why I needed her back in the game. Maybe that's selfish of me," he adds, pensively. "But that's the game."

Steven hesitates. He glances at Trevor uneasily. "Were you and her ever... ya know?"

Trevor stops. He gives Steven a look. "Oh, Steven," he snorts.

Ahead of them, Hunter is like poetry in motion... kicking out a guard's knee... firing off a gunshot into another's chest... snapping a man's neck... it's a waltz.... and Hunter is the only participant. Amid the massacre, she glances back at them. She catches Steven's gaze and flashes him a smile. It's a smile of understanding, of appreciation. And Steven can't help but smile back.

"You better keep up with her, chum," Trevor says, pushing Steven ahead. Stepping over the trail of bodies left in her wake, they meet up with Hunter at the third access point, which intersects with the other two corridors.

"You're amazing," Steven says, breathless.

"Thanks," Hunter says, glowing. She drops her carbine and points to the final, seemingly empty corridor. At the end of the tunnel, the door labeled *Launch Control Center* is cracked open and waiting. "Looks like we've reached our target."

"The president's in there?" Steven asks, peering ahead. Trevor nods. "Well, what are we waiting for?" Steven asks, feeling good.

Hunter unholsters her trusted twin Berettas.

"Let's go," she says, cautiously stepping through the access point. Steven follows close behind her...

But Trevor doesn't move. He watches them walk along the corridor before turning to his right. He looks down the intersecting hall. At the end of this tunnel is the missile silo. Trevor glances once more at Hunter and Steven — watching them approach the control center's blast door — before stepping toward the silo...

● ● ●

Hunter and Steven approach the blast door. Hunter tries looking inside... but sees nothing. She pushes the door open a few more inches and, leading with her handguns, peeks inside. She spots Ronald Reagan staring back at her, sitting atop the mustard-colored couch.

"Be careful," the president says, pointing off to the side. "The big guy's right there..."

Before Hunter can process what he's saying, a tree-trunk of an arm slams down on her two guns, knocking them from her grip. They clang to the floor. Nash, having waited patiently for her arrival, springs into action. He grabs Hunter, easily picking her up off the ground, and throws her into Steven. They fall back into the corridor, rolling on top of each other. Their eyes meet, briefly locked together, before Nash steps out through the blast door.

"Well. Well. Well..." Nash says.

"Holy shit," Steven says, amazed by the sheer mass of man before them.

"If it isn't the infamous Hunter Gunne," Nash continues, puffing up his chest. "Let's see how tough you really are."

Hunter rolls her eyes.

Men, she thinks, climbing to her feet. *They're all the same.*

Unsheathing his beloved knife, Nash can hardly contain himself. He has had it sharpened, polished, and shimmering just for this occasion.

"How pretty," Hunter says, pulling out her own long-bladed knife.

Steven inches back toward a bulkhead, desperate to stay clear of this impending fight.

"Let's get this over with," Hunter growls...

• • •

Trevor stares up at the ominous sign above the blast door in front of him: *Danger: Missile Silo.* When Hunter mashed that button up at the security center, she didn't just unlock all the access points leading to the president. She opened every door in the whole facility — just as Trevor had planned. Now, staring up at the thick red letters, Trevor thinks of Steven and his rather prescient question outside the compound as the three of them hovered over the facility's blueprints...

"And this?" Steven asked, pointing to the glaringly large circle in the schematics.

"The silo," Trevor answered.

"Is there a missile in there?" Steven asked.

"Nah," Trevor answers, munching on a handful of jellybeans.

Trevor likes Steven, he really does. The kid has repeatedly exceeded Trevor's expectations. But, standing before the silo's blast door, Trevor can't help but shrug.

"Sorry, Steven," he says aloud. "I'm afraid there is a missile in here."

The kid will learn, Trevor thinks, pushing into the silo.

• • •

Hunter eyes Nash as they circle, their knives seemingly drawn to each other like magnets. Steven watches, keeping his distance. Knife fights have always been a guilty pleasure of Hunter's... so it's only fitting that this idiot challenged her.

Nash charges her. He lunges, blade extended, but Hunter sidesteps the blow.

Be patient, she thinks. *Feel him out.* Nash charges again. *He's surprisingly quick*, Hunter thinks, dodging him, *especially for his size... but already predictable.*

Gutter fighter, Hunter concludes, watching his feet and noting how he holds his knife.

Developed by the British Royal Marine William E. Fairbairn to combat Shanghai street gangs, the technique was later taught to British and American commandos. For Fairbairn, fighting dirty was his *modus operandi*. "Get tough, get down in the gutter, win at all costs," he'd tell his pupils. "There's no fair play, no rules except one: *kill or be killed.*"

Nash charges Hunter again, over-extending his reach.

Mistake, Hunter thinks, parrying his attack with a quick side-to-side flick of her knife. Her blade slices his forearm and blood flows.

He's both careless and impatient, she muses, flipping the knife in her hand.

Seemingly oblivious to the pain, Nash attacks again with a quick and sudden jab of his blade. Hunter counters — another quick flick of her's — but Nash grabs hold of her wrist, squeezing...

Big mistake, Hunter thinks. And with a slight hook, she slashes his inner forearm.

Nash releases her, snarling.

The cut is deep, Hunter notes. *But not deep enough.*

They circle each other again, and Hunter can't help but eye the blood now pouring from his arms.

He's sloppy, too sloppy to have trained as a disciple of the great William Fairbairn...

And that's when it hits her: *He's playing me. One of the first rules of a knife fight is to distract your opponent... get their eyes off your blade...*

Nash charges, keeping his knife tucked close before throwing it high. He swings the blade down as if splitting a log. But Hunter — her eyes locked on his weapon — is ready.

His move is aggressive. Too aggressive, she thinks. *There's no way he can keep his balance.*

She counters his attack, slicing her knife upward... and that's when she feels it...

A swift and powerful punt between her legs.

The blow takes Hunter by surprise — she was not expecting *that* — lifting her off the ground and knocking her off her feet. She collapses to the floor, and before she can move, Nash's other knee is already hurtling straight toward her face...

CRACK.

Hunter tastes blood, metallic and warm.

Son of a bitch, she thinks, reaching for her face, blood pouring from her nose. *Yep. Definitely broken.*

She rolls into a crouching position and growls...

Now that's gutter fighting.

Hunter spits a mouthful of blood, much to Nash's delight.

He distracted me with his injuries, breaking my concentration, Hunter thinks. *Well, two can play this game.*

Nash charges after her, landing a blow to her ribs. And then another.

From Steven's vantage, this doesn't look good for Hunter — and he's not just going to sit here and let it happen. As Nash raises his knife high above her, undoubtedly a kill strike, Steven sprints at Nash.

"Hunter!" Steven shouts, valiantly. But what Steven didn't see — and what Nash was too distracted by Hunter's own misery to notice himself — was Hunter's knife tucked tight, ready to gut Nash with.

Steven jumps on Nash's back just as Hunter launches her attack. Lifting Steven off the ground, Nash spins him, placing Steven now in the path of Hunter's blade.

"Dammit, Steven," Hunter shouts, stopping her knife a mere inch from his back.

Nash grabs Steven, pulling him off. He slams Steven into the wall, pinning him up by the neck.

"And who the hell are you?" Nash snarls. "Are you O.L.D.?"

"What?" Steven asks, squirming helplessly in his grip.

Nash pulls Steven's face within an inch of his own.

"Are you O.L.D.?"

Steven stops struggling, perplexed.

What the hell does age have to do with anything?

"Well... I don't know..." Steven says. "I'm only thirty..."

"Don't play coy with me, boy!" Nash shouts, lifting Steven entirely above his head. He turns toward the blast door and throws Steven into it. Steven slams through it, his momentum carrying him into the control center.

Rolling to a stop, Steven gasps for air. A flickering television grabs his attention. On screen, a young cowboy hat-wearing Ronald Reagan steps out of an old wood cabin, grim and serious. *'I heard you were looking for me,'* Reagan's character says ominously, on screen.

SHAKE SHAKE.

Steven turns to find a bowl of jellybeans in his face. He looks up to see Ronald Reagan offering them to him.

"Hell of an entrance, son."

14

Her gown, blood red and flowing, drapes behind her. She stands before the Winter Palace — the imposing home of the Romanov dynasty, a symbol of Russian power and might - staring up at the green and white facade...

The Cossacks, their beards full and bearskin hats tall, stand at attention. Shifting their bayonet muskets from one shoulder to the other, they pull open the massive iron gates as she approaches...

She finds herself at the base of the Jordan Staircase — the palace's grand entryway — the Greek gods leering down at her from the massive fresco above. She ascends the marble stairs, passing alabaster statues and massive granite columns, and is greeted by Tchaikovsky's Waltz of the Flowers — the final movement of the Nutcracker Suite — as it wafts from the ballroom above...

Tchaikovsky, she thinks, his favorite...

She enters the majestic Nicholas Hall. Enormous candle-lit chandeliers hang from the ceiling, casting a warm glow about the massive ballroom. From the minstrel gallery, the orchestra plays, the whimsical waltz filling the hall. At the center of it all, like a living-breathing creature all its own, are hundreds of imperial guests, dancing to Tchaikovsky's masterpiece...

Stepping and rotating... circling and spinning... The women's gowns twirl as the men, themselves regal and proper, lead the enchanted display...

Stepping and rotating... circling and spinning...

And then she sees him, the crowd seeming to part as he approaches her: Anatoly, dressed like Russian royalty. He greets her with his charming smile and a slight bow.

"Dobryy vecher," he says, extending his hand. "Shall we dance."

She gives him her hand, holding her breath as he pulls her close, his arm sliding around her waist. She stares deep into his eyes — beautiful and brown. And again, he smiles, his dimples impossibly deep...

"Ahdeen... doovah... three," he says. "One... two... three."

He leads her into the waltz, pulling her into the whirlpool of bodies at the center of the floor — stepping and rotating... circling and spinning...

She feels her heart melt for this man, this mysterious and dangerous man. But, in his arms, she feels safer than she has ever felt. This man, she thinks. He is a beacon for her soul. A light to lead her way...

But something is wrong...

The music... too fast. The ballroom... too dark. And the dancing... her head spins. A feeling of dread, of foreboding, washes over her. She can't help but look away from him, breaking their loving gaze. Her eyes flick toward the couples around them...

And images of death flash into her mind...

Lighting bolts of pain and suffering...

Of anguish and misery...

The dancers, the imperial guests, the people of Saint Petersburg... of Leningrad... they are dead...

All of them...

Stepping and rotating... circling and spinning...

She pulls Anatoly close, overtaking his lead, eying the guests around them. Protect him, she thinks...

More images flash into her head, glimpses of horrors yet to come: the October Revolution, the storming of the palace, and the brutal murders of the Romanov family. Stalin's rise to power: The Great Terror... the Siege of Leningrad... starvation and death... and cannibalism...

The unthinkable...

She pulls Anatoly even closer, their lips now almost touching. She looks at him, his eyes still beaming and bright, his smile as comforting as before...

Kiss him, she thinks.

Before it's too late...

• • •

November 1957 — Barrow, Alaska

Hunter startles awake. Having returned to the bar in a daze, she barely remembers plopping down on the cot located in the back room. Considering she's still wearing her boots and parka, she must have dozed off quickly.

But there was Anatoly, waiting for her in her dream.

What has she done?

Rubbing the sleep out of her eyes, Hunter thinks of her mother. What would she say of Hunter turning her back on a man dedicated to saving the world? Sitting up, Hunter thinks of her grandfather. What would he think of her refusing the call of humanity — the desperate plea of billions of innocent lives — to be spared the horrors of nuclear war?

Her grandfather had a saying. It was passed down first to her mother, then to Hunter herself: *If you have no people, you have all people.* It was a motto the family lived by, always welcoming strangers with open arms, and always helping them in any way they could. From *Ol' Virginia* to Skagway, Alaska. But now, Hunter seems to be the end of the line.

I've let them down, Hunter thinks, catching her reflection in a window. Closing her eyes, she thinks of Anatoly... and there's a sudden pounding at the front door.

Hunter springs to her feet, hopeful. *Could it be?* She hurries through the kitchen and out to the bar. *Has he returned?*

She flings open the door... but finds Trevor wobbling in front of her, barely conscious. Cupping his stomach, his white parka is soaked red with blood.

"Jesus Christ," Hunter exclaims, catching him as he stumbles into her. Dragging him inside, she reaches back for the door. Before shutting it, she glances outside and spots their Sno-Cat, now riddled with bullet holes. "What happened?"

"Whiskey," Trevor mumbles. "Please."

Hunter blinks. Trevor is clearly bleeding out, the scent of gunpowder hovering around him... and he wants a drink? She pulls him to the bar and helps him sit. She reaches across the counter, grabs a bottle, and pours him a glass. But Trevor snorts. He snatches the bottle out of Hunter's hand and reveals a blood-soaked entry wound on his stomach. He pours the whiskey onto it, hissing in pain before chugging what's left of the bottle.

"Trevor," Hunter says, snapping a finger in front of his face. "What the hell happened?"

"The O.W.O.," Trevor says. "We were wrong about them. They must have been here months, building something. A machine."

"What kind of machine?" Hunter asks.

"I don't know," Trevor gasps, the pain shooting through his body. "I don't think it was functional. At least, I don't think it worked."

"You don't think?" Hunter asks, rolling her eyes. But she thinks of Anatoly. She thinks of the look on his face when she turned her back on him... she thinks of him in her dream, holding him in the Winter Palace, desperate to protect him, to save him.

Kiss him before it's too late...

"What about Anatoly?" she asks.

Trevor looks at her, suddenly calm. "They're coming," he says.

"What?" Hunter asks, stunned. She hadn't even considered that whoever had done this might still be chasing him, that he'd lead them straight to her. Trevor reaches into his parka and pulls out a gun. He sets it down carefully on the bar in front of her. Hunter recognizes the weapon immediately... it's Anatoly's Walther PPK.

"He's dead," Trevor says, studying her. "And they're coming here now."

Hunter stares at the gun, her heart pounding.

Anatoly... is... dead.

She will never see him again, just as she feared. She will never feel his warmth against her or smell his scent again.

And she will never get that kiss.

"How many are there?" Hunter asks, as if her soul has split into two. One half being incapacitated by the news of Anatoly's demise, the other rising to the task at hand: *killing the bastards responsible.*

"Three. Maybe four," Trevor says.

Hunter looks down at the gun. Studying the pistol's angular shape and sharp edges, she is reminded of Anatoly. And her anger builds. She grabs the weapon off the counter, releases the magazine, and counts the bronze-colored tips of the .32 caliber bullets within... *three.* She snaps the magazine back in place and pulls the slide back, revealing a round in the chamber... *four.*

That makes four bullets, she thinks. Outside, a Sno-Cat approaches: Trevor's friends have caught up to him. *Time to move,* Hunter thinks, grabbing Trevor's arm.

"Let's go," she says, dragging him into the kitchen. She pushes him toward the walk-in cooler. Opening the door, she flicks on the light. "Get in," she says, shoving Trevor inside before slamming the door behind him. Hunter pauses to look at the gun in her hand, at Anatoly's PPK. She feels the adrenaline coursing through her veins...

The anger, the excitement, she feels herself empowered by it. A sudden calm washes over her — her breathing slows, and her heart rate drops. Despite Anatoly's killers looming just outside the front door, Hunter is serene and focused. It's almost as if her whole life — every experience, every lesson— has prepared her for this very moment. She grabs her knife off the counter, sliding it into her belt as she steps back out into the bar.

Through the window, Hunter spots the first assailant, a submachine gun clutched to his chest, and she reflects on her predicament. Killing a human being — taking a life — is a hell of a thing, whether it's revenge or not. That gunman is a person, a person with hopes and dreams and a family somewhere out there in the world: people that loved him, that hoped for his best. But this man — this gunman — has made too many wrong decisions in his life. And walking through her door will be the last mistake he makes.

I don't want to do this, Hunter thinks. *But I have to do this... for Anatoly.*

Finally, the moment arrives: the door opens, and the first gunman enters only to find Hunter standing before him...

● ● ●

BAM.

Trevor hears the gunshot through the freezer door, his trained ear recognizing it as the PPK. As the ring dies down, he hears a solid thud. Trevor smiles.

That a girl, he thinks.

He leans his ear closer to the door, listening...

Footsteps... heavy snow boots clomp into the building, the gunshot undoubtedly attracted the attention of the others still outside. Machine gun fire shatters the silence, reverberating through the cooler itself. Out front, wood splinters and glass shatters... then silence.The boots take a few, uncertain steps. And then a couple more, crunching on shards of glass...

Approaching the bar, Trevor thinks. *Perhaps looking over the top of it... probably at Hunter's now bullet-riddled body...*

BAM.

Damn, Trevor thinks. The PPK again... followed by a heavy thud. *Another one down*, he thinks. *Impressive*.

He leans close to the door, struggling to make out Hunter's featherlight movements. He listens again... but Hunter's location seems to shift higher. *But how...*

She's in the rafters, Trevor thinks. *Bloody hell, she's good.*

Another set of boots hurries into the building. The person stops, probably looking the bar over... not thinking to look above...

BAM.

The boots stumble into a table, knocking over chairs... but the man is still standing...

BAM.

Trevor holds his breath and listens. The table seems to tip over, sending the person leaning against it crashing to the floor. Trevor frowns. *Two shots. Bugger. She's out of rounds.*

He listens... another gunman enters, clomping into the building. Almost immediately, a light thud lands between the boots and the door. He hears a swift movement... then the crack of a machine gun hitting the floor.

She's kicked it out of his hands, Trevor thinks. There's a struggle — an awkward and clumsy dance — but neither calls out. Then silence...

The lighter feet step away from the other. *Why? What's happened?* Then a solid thud as somebody falls to their knees. The body keels over like a lumbered tree, smashing into the floor.

A slit throat, Trevor thinks. *The aorta.*

160

The poor wanker is bleeding out.

Trevor listens closely...

Suddenly, the cooler door opens. And Hunter stands before him, blood-covered and hardened. Trevor stares at her in amazement, a smile creeping onto his face.

"My God," he says. "Anatoly was right. You're a natural."

Trevor walks out onto a metal platform, his footsteps echoing in the cavernous expanse of the silo. Standing before him, dormant but ominous, is a Titan I intercontinental ballistic missile.

He steps up to the railing and peers down at the missile's massive two-stage rocket engines below. Craning his neck, his eyes run the length of the nine-story tall missile until they reach the nose cone housing the formidable payload — a W38 thermonuclear warhead with a four megaton yield.

Though the Titan I was a fantastic engineering feat, the launch system had some glaring weaknesses. To begin with, the rocket engines required liquid fuel, a hazardous and volatile mixture. Storing it aboard the missile was far too dangerous. So, if and when a launch command was given, the missile had to be fueled. Upon fueling, the entire missile (all one hundred and fifteen tons of it) then had to be raised above ground via a massive elevator system.

There it would finally be launched.

The whole procedure, taking roughly twenty minutes, made the entire facility glaringly vulnerable to a surprise nuclear attack. Especially considering the missile takes as long to launch as an incoming Soviet missile salvo takes to hit their targets — of which a missile site such as this would undoubtedly be included.

Consequently, the Titan I's deployment was short-lived. It was phased out and replaced just a few years later by the solid-fueled Titan II missile, which boasted the luxury of being launched on command from within its silo.

Fortunately for Trevor, by the time the Titan II began rolling off the assembly line, this particular missile standing before him had already been forgotten about by the Pentagon's top brass. And, despite all its inadequacies, Trevor can't help but admire it...

This missile, Trevor thinks, *is a damn beautiful machine.*

Thanks to the incredibly inane bureaucracy that passed over this missile for decommissioning, combined with the maniacal insistence of the Strategic Air Command to have as many nuclear weapons at their disposal as possible, the maintenance and upkeep of the facility continued uninterrupted.

But more importantly, it was connected to the Pentagon's *Strategic Automated Command and Control System.*

It's that system that Trevor plans to exploit.

Circling the missile, Trevor unlatches and opens a panel labeled *Launch Control*. Inside, he's relieved to see an IBM Series/1 Computer terminal. Introduced in the mid-seventies, the Series/1 was immediately put to use in the *Strategic Automated Command and Control System* — an early computer network coordinating the operational functions of the country's nuclear triad.

Trevor flips a switch, and a 12-inch green-phosphor CRT monitor flickers on as the terminal boots up. Reaching into his jacket pocket, he pulls out a 5 ¼ inch floppy disk. Scribbled on the label in almost illegible handwriting is *missile reprogram.*

Trevor slides the disk into the terminal's slot and the computer whirs and beeps.

As the disk spins to life, a message on screen reads: PROCESSING... PROCESSING... PROCESSING...

Then a new message pops up and flashes: ACCESS DENIED. Trevor sighs.

Another message appears: RUN PROGRAM AGAIN? Y OR N. Trevor jabs the Y button on the terminal's keyboard.

The disk spins up again... ACCESS GRANTED.

Trevor smiles.

● ● ●

"Hell of an entrance, son," Reagan says, grinning.

Steven blinks. Despite having seen this man hundreds of times before on television, he was simply not prepared to meet him — the President of the United States, the Chief of State, the Commander in Chief, the Leader of the Free World, whatever you want to call him — in person.

"Sir," Steven says. "Mister President! You're here!"

"I reckon I am," Reagan says, tossing a handful of jellybeans into his mouth.

"We need to get you out of here, sir," Steven says, picking himself up off the floor. He grabs the president's suit coat off the couch and holds it up for him to put on. "We have to get you back to the White House as soon as possible."

"Son, have you ever seen *Tennessee's Partner*?"

"What?" Steven asks, glancing at the television.

"This here's my favorite scene," Reagan says, patting the couch cushion next to him. "The big fight scene. And, if you ask me, a movie's only as good as its big fight scene."

Steven stares at him in disbelief.

Outside the room, Hunter and Nash's knife fight has resumed. On the television though, a young Ronald Reagan confronts the actor John Payne, playing a debonair gambler dressed in all black.

'*Draw your gun*,' Reagan's character says, gruffly.

'*I didn't bring one*,' John Payne's character says.

Steven reluctantly sits.

● ● ●

A message flashes on screen: USER REQUEST?

Trevor types in: MANUAL TARGET ASSIGN. He presses the enter button and waits. The computer beeps and boops. A message flashes on screen: WARNING: MANUALLY ASSIGNED TARGET WILL OVERRIDE INCOMING TARGET LAUNCH CODE. DO YOU WISH TO PROCEED? Y OR N.

Trevor presses the Y button.

A new message appears: ENTER TARGET COORDINATES.

Trevor pulls a piece of paper out of his jacket. Reading off the paper, he carefully types in: 55.7558° NORTH, 37.6173° EAST.

He presses enter.

A rudimentary computer-graphic flat map projection of the Earth appears on screen. Two vector lines appear — one representing longitude and the other latitude — and converge on a point over Russia. The map zooms in and labels the target as: MOSCOW, U.S.S.R.

The terminal prompts Trevor: TARGET CONFIRM? Y OR N.

He presses the Y button again, and the computer chugs along. Then TARGET ASSIGNED flashes on screen.

Trevor smiles, the green hue of the monitor casting an eerie glow on his face...

Excellent.

• • •

On the television, Reagan — or his character Cowpoke — unlatches his gun belt. As the music swells, he drops it to the ground and steps right up into John Payne's face.

'Why'd you do it?' Cowpoke asks, with Reagan, on the couch next to Steven, miming the dialogue.

But Payne's character holds his ground. 'She wouldn't shake hands with you unless she was paid for it first,' he says. And with that, Reagan's character belts John Payne across the face — next to Steven, the president punches the air.

"You see," Reagan says, "they're friends. But they're enemies. The audience, we understand where both sides are coming from. Even if the characters can't see past their differences, the audience can. And that's what makes a good fight scene great."

Steven nods... but his eyes are glued on the corridor outside the room. Hunter and Nash lunge at each other. Hunter staggers but manages to slice Nash in the midsection. Nash hisses, his first indication of pain, and backhands Hunter.

They circle again...

On screen — and on the couch next to Steven — Reagan throws punch after punch as, in the corridor, Hunter and Nash lock arms, each gripping the other's knife-wielding hand.

Spinning each other, they plow into the blast door, stumbling into the holding cell. Reagan, his eyes affixed to the television, hardly bats an eye as Hunter and Nash careen toward him...

Steven jumps to his feet and deflects them just before impact. He sends Hunter and Nash crashing into a case of supplies, busting the crate open. Jars of jellybeans and cans of diet soda roll in every direction.

Hunter, jumping away from Nash, grabs one of the glass jars and throws it forcefully into his face, smashing it over him.

Stunned, Nash reels back, blood seeping from hundreds of tiny cuts. He opens his rage-filled eyes and glares at Hunter.

Not wasting a second, she charges at him. Leaping into the air, she drives a potent drop-kick directly into his chest. The blow sends him into the wall.

Hunter lunges at him with her knife but, dropping his own blade to free both hands, Nash grabs her by the wrist.

The president looks up from the television set to see Nash twisting Hunter's arm — and Hunter herself — into a bulkhead.

"What do we have here?" Reagan asks.

Pinning Hunter against the wall, Nash slams her hand into the cement again and again. She loses her grip of the knife, and it flings out of her hand.

The blade soars across the room, narrowly missing Reagan and Steven as it sticks in the couch between them.

"Holy shit," Steven exclaims.

Reagan loves it. "This is exciting!"

Steven scans the room. He spots a chair in the corner. Jumping off the couch, he grabs it and charges after Nash. But Nash — seeing Steven's approach — twists Hunter into Steven's path just as he brings the chair down...

The chair smashes inadvertently into Hunter.

Reagan winces. "Oh, that was bad," he says, throwing a handful of jellybeans in his mouth.

Hunter staggers from the blow.

"Steven," she says, dazed. "Stop trying to help me."

Behind him, Hunter sees Nash pick up his knife and charge after Steven. She shoves Steven out of the way and plows into Nash herself. The two of them careen into an empty equipment rack.

Pinning his knife-hand against the panel, Hunter clocks Nash across the face with her free hand. Again and again and again.

The blows take their toll, and Nash wobbles. He falls to a knee, spitting out some teeth. Hunter sets to deliver a final blow... only to have Nash pull a leg out from under her.

Hunter falls back, hitting her head against the floor.

"Oh," Reagan says, reacting. "This isn't good."

Nash, shaking the fuzziness out of his head, focuses on Hunter and jumps atop of her. He quickly swings his knife down, but Hunter — with both hands — catches his arm.

Nash struggles against her. With his free hand, he grabs her neck... and starts to squeeze.

Hunter won't hold up against Nash's brute strength for long, and his knife inches closer and closer to her throat. Then, with all her might, she launches a knee right between his legs — Nash cries out.

Rolling over, he flings Hunter across the room. She lands on the sofa next to the president. Reagan nods, impressed.

"Very nice, miss," he says, offering her the bowl of jellybeans. Hunter grabs a handful and, with Nash climbing to his feet, she stands atop the couch.

She leaps at Nash, landing on his back. Grabbing his knife, she wraps her legs around his opposite shoulder and neck. Nash tries desperately to get his hands on her, but his bulky build makes it futile.

Hunter twists at her hips, torquing Nash over the couch, slamming him face-first into the ground. She pulls on his arm — his tendons reaching their limits — while clamping her legs tighter around his neck.

Nash shouts in frustration, a grave mistake as it allows Hunter to collapse his trachea even further. His eyes bulge out of his head as he fights to stay conscious. Feeling him go limp, Hunter mercilessly tugs on his arm.

Pop.

His tendons tear as she dislocates his shoulder.

The pain jars Nash back into consciousness... but he's hasn't the strength to fight. Releasing him, Hunter climbs to her feet. She glances at the television set.

On screen, the fight between Reagan and John Payne has concluded. The two sit upon the porch, side by side, beaten and exhausted. *'Why'd you do it?'* Reagan's character asks again.

To which John Payne, wiping a dash of blood from his lip, replies: *'I don't like people who set up to hurt you when your back's turned...'* Reagan's character considers and nods... and then puts an appreciative hand on Payne's shoulder.

And with that, the two characters are friends again.

Nash, flailing on the floor, knows he's defeated.

"You can't stop us," he says, spitting in Hunter's direction. "Our plan is already in motion. And you peasants are doomed."

Hunter shakes her head. As the two characters on screen embrace, she picks up the television, raising it above her head. Nash knows his time has come — but he just doesn't give a shit.

"True order shall be restored," he shouts. "The O.W.O. shall rule the..."

Hunter brings the television smashing down, ending him.

The president stares at the mess, then looks at Hunter.

"Well done, miss," Reagan says, applauding.

He gives Steven a look... and Steven claps along.

Hunter, the blood dried and crusted below her broken nose, flashes them an awkward and painful smile.

"It's called gutter fighting," she says, taking a bow.

"Well, Mister President," Trevor says, appearing at the blast door. "Consider yourself rescued."

PART THREE

16

It was his hair — at least that's what she'll tell herself later. It was his hair that first clued her in that something wasn't right...

• • •

Washington, D.C.

Nancy Davis Reagan — the First Lady of the United States — stares at her husband of thirty-one years. Her husband, affectionately known to her as *Ronnie*, sits across from her at the breakfast table.

The bright morning sun, pouring in through the south-facing windows, provides him an almost angelic backlight. And, just beyond those lime-green curtains, is one of the best views D.C. has to offer: the Washington Monument standing erect in all its glory.

But despite the view, and despite the divine presence that is Ronald Reagan, Nancy's mind swims about in one alarming truth: *something isn't right.*

Sipping on her decaffeinated coffee, Nancy studies him. In the three decades they have been married, Nancy has achieved a lot. Her husband — the Leader of the Free World — is one of those achievements. And, at sixty-one years old, her proudest. Ronnie has always been movie-star handsome and, even at seventy-two years old, is still ruggedly good-looking — thanks to her.

But today... *something is wrong.*

Glancing at the gold-plated, diamond bezel Rolex watch adorning her wrist, Nancy notes the time: seven forty-five. Nancy has been dressed and ready for her day — and her husband's day — for hours now. Ronnie, on the other hand, has never been an early riser, and prodding the president awake every morning is one of Nancy's most important tasks. But today was peculiar. Today, for the first time in their entire marriage, Ronald Reagan woke up on his own.

Strange.

Sitting in their private room just off the presidential bedroom suite on the second floor of the White House, an assortment of Ronnie's preferred breakfast items sits out on the table in front of him: bran cereal, skim milk, fresh fruit, and his own cup of decaf coffee. But Ronnie, Nancy can't help but notice, hasn't touched any of it. He just sits, eyes ahead and silent.

Odd.

Brylcreem, Nancy thinks. That's his secret. For decades now, the public and press alike have wondered how Ronald Reagan has kept such a youthful visage. And the answer is simple: Brylcreem, the British pomade popularized by the allied soldiers of the Second World War. For four decades now, Ronnie has sworn by the stuff. Even before taking his presidential oath of office, that slicked-back, wet-looking, midnight-black pompadour of his was as iconic as Mickey Mouse.

That pompadour, Nancy knows all-too-well, is a labor of love for the man. It's one of the old Hollywood tricks he's carried with him all these years – tricks intended to deceive not only the eye but the camera as well. With his hair swept back big and tall, Ronnie adds another inch or two to his six-foot frame.

Unfortunately, slicking it back, flipping the wave, twisting the curl, often takes almost thirty frustrating minutes to perfect each morning. But the process has proven, time and again, to be transformative, shaving the decades away. And when Ronnie finishes up, he emerges from the bathroom as *Ronald Reagan: The 40th President of the United States* – the role he was born to play.

Today though, something is different. Not only did Ronnie wake up on his own, but when Nancy found him in the suite's master bathroom, the door closed, he hardly made a peep. With her ear to the door, she heard none of the usual frustration-induced profanity of which she regularly scolds. And then, before she knew it, the door swung open and there he was, set and ready for his day.

Now, sitting across from him, her eyes are drawn toward his hair.

That pompadour.

That wave.

Something just isn't right...

There's a knock at the door, and Nancy is relieved to see Mikey Schell poke his face into the room. Mikey is a thirty-something, frazzled White House aide in a loose-fitting suit and thick, steel-rimmed glasses. He's known the Reagans for years, having impressed them as a young and eager volunteer during their failed nomination in 1976.

Mikey is somebody the president — and, more importantly, Nancy — has come to trust.

"Mister President," he says. "It's time for your daily briefing, sir."

Nancy follows along as they promptly step out into the Central Hall, the main corridor of the White House residence. Finely upholstered armchairs, courtesy of President Monroe and his family, line the walls. And a beautiful mahogany cylinder desk, courtesy the Kennedys, serves as a focal point.

Cutting across the hall, the three of them descend a service stairwell. As the Reagans' matching bright-white Velcro sneakers squeak on the steps, Mikey flips open a leather portfolio to the president's busy schedule.

"At eight a.m., you have your daily briefing with the National Security Council," he reads, not slowing. "At nine a.m., you're meeting with the Secretary of State. At ten a.m., you have a conference call with Miss Thatcher..."

"Best not be any more surprises again today," Nancy says, interrupting. Lowering her voice, she eyes Mikey. "What an embarrassment. An absolute embarrassment. If word got out that Ronnie..." Nancy glances about the stairwell, making sure nobody is within earshot. "That Ronnie went missing."

"He hardly went missing, ma'am," Mikey scoffs, defensively.

"Mikey," she says, slowing her pace. "You and I both know that we have no idea where Marine One took him yesterday. And the Marines, they don't know either. If word got out about this," she continues, wringing her hands. "Even to his cabinet, to his staff..." Nancy trails off, stopping. "Oh, Mikey. Promise me you'll keep a lid on this. They'd eat him alive."

Mikey nods. "Of course, Mrs. Reagan."

Nancy smiles. But her comfort is short-lived. "One more thing, Mikey," she says. "Since Ronnie returned. Well, I don't know how to say this, but…"

Nancy trails off, struggling for the words.

Mikey eyes her, growing impatient. But the two of them glance ahead at the president, realizing he's not waiting for them at all.

"He just hasn't been himself," Nancy says, her point proven.

Without missing a beat, Reagan barrels outside onto the West Colonnade, the iconic, white-pillared walkway connecting the White House to the West Wing. Nancy and Mikey, struggling to look calm and collected, chase after him.

"My goodness, Ronnie," Nancy says, eyeing her husband suspiciously. "You certainly are an eager beaver today."

Mikey skips ahead. He opens the door to the secretary's office and holds it for them. As Nancy steps inside, the president stops in front of Mikey.

"Cancel all appointments," he says.

"Sir?" Mikey asks, exchanging a quick but concerned look with Nancy.

"All of them," he says, stone-cold serious.

"Ronnie?" Nancy asks. "What the devil's gotten into you?"

The president's glare is enough to silence her. He turns to Mikey. "Cancel lunch too," he says, before entering.

Nancy gawks at Mikey, stunned.

Reagan's personal secretary stands at her desk as the president approaches. "Good morning, sir," she says, setting down a pair of black cap-toe shoes for him and a pair of unassuming heels for Nancy on the floor.

But the president ignores the gesture and walks unencumbered into the Oval Office. Nancy stops at the shoes, appalled.

"Ronnie. Your shoes," she says, pointing at them fleetingly.

Her eyes meet the cold gaze of Agent Bancroft, the Special Agent in Charge of the White House Detail, standing ramrod-straight at attention. Next to him, also at attention, is the Emergency War Order Officer. Clutched tightly in the officer's hand, secured to his wrist by a chain, is a black leather attaché — inside *that* is a metal briefcase — and inside *that* reside the launch codes for the United States' nuclear arsenal.

This is the nuclear football.

Ripping the Velcro straps as fast as she can, Nancy kicks her sneakers off and slips her feet into the heels. Charging into the Oval Office, she stops dead in her tracks when she realizes who else is in the room...

Gathered around the Resolute Desk, standing at attention, is the National Security Council, the president's top-advisors regarding the looming, ever-constant threat that is the Soviet Union. The council, as appointed by the president, is comprised of the Secretary of State, the Secretary of Defense, the director of the C.I.A., and Admiral William J. Falke, Chairman of the Joint Chiefs of Staff — an imposing man dressed in uniform, a block of medals pinned to his chest. Each of them greets the president as he takes his seat at the desk.

Nancy, collecting herself, takes her customary position, standing at her husband's side. Mikey quickly hands out the day's briefings to each of them. The men, shifting in their seats to get comfortable, flip through the pages, looking ahead at the intel that awaits.

"What is the status of Exercise Able Archer?" the president asks, not even glancing at his daily brief.

Nancy looks across the room at Mikey — such a direct question from Ronnie is highly unusual. In fact, any question out of Ronnie is odd.

The council, taken aback, one by one, turn their gaze toward Admiral Falke. As the Chairman of the Joint Chiefs of Staff, Admiral Falke — a Navy man through and through — is the highest-ranking military officer in the United States Armed Forces and the president's principal military advisor. The admiral leans back, savoring the president's attention.

"Exercise Able Archer," he says, "is the largest military exercise ever initiated, coordinating N.A.T.O. forces across the globe. The purpose of this exercise, Mister President, is to simulate an escalation of international conflict culminating in a DEFCON 1 coordinated nuclear response against primary and secondary targets within the U.S.S.R. and the People's Republic of China." Grinning from ear-to-ear, the admiral bubbles with excitement. "Sir, if I may," he adds. "It's gonna be one hell of a show."

The director of the C.I.A. clears his throat.

"Mister President," he says. "Not to rain on the admiral's parade. But regarding these war games." He slides to the edge of his chair and leans on the desk. "Sir. I suggest we proceed with extreme caution. Our field agents are telling us that the Soviet high command — a paranoid and, if I may be frank, sir, crotchety group of old men — are very wary of these exercises. In fact, the Politburo, most of whom have been entrenched since Stalin, believe Able Archer a ruse, concealing preparations for an actual first-strike against them."

The director forces a nervous laugh in hopes of masking his unease.

"That's true, Ronnie," Nancy says, coming to the director's aid. "It'd be best to not go spooking the Soviets any more than we already have. You know how jumpy they are," she says, rubbing her husband's back. "They did just shoot down a passenger airliner for goodness' sake, those poor souls."

The other men nod in agreement. The admiral, however, glares at her.

"Sir," he says, barely hiding his disdain for the first lady. "Now is not the time to go pussyfooting around 'em Russians. Be proud of our strength. Flaunt it. And let those cowards in the Kremlin cower in fear."

"Now is not the time to cause another international incident," Nancy says, remaining cordial. "Postponing Able Archer will be easy enough. I'm sure between such a fine group of gentlemen such as yourselves, you can come up with the perfect excuse so as not to make Admiral Falke's mighty military look weak or meek. A weather delay, perhaps?"

Admiral Falke scoffs. "With all due respect, Mrs. Reagan," he says. "But World War Three — if it ever comes to it — won't go waiting for a bright sunshiny day."

"How long until our forces are in position to begin the exercise?" the president asks, ignoring the tension in the room.

Nancy stares at Ronnie, appalled — *this is very unlike him.*

Admiral Falke blinks. "Well. What time is it?" He looks around at the others then over his shoulder toward Mikey. Mikey and the other men in the room all jerk their wrists toward their faces.

"Ten after eight," the Secretary of State blurts out first.

"Ten after eight..." the admiral says, thinking. "I reckon you got about twelve hours." The president nods... and Nancy and Mikey share an uneasy look.

"Admiral Falke," the president says. "I want a direct line of communication set up between us. I want to be updated on all details and positions of N.A.T.O. forces. And I want to know immediately when the war games can commence. Do I make myself clear?"

"Yessir," the admiral says, practically gushing.

The other men glance uneasily at each other. *This is strange.*

"You are dismissed. All of you," the president says, waving them away with contempt.

"But sir," the director says. "The situation in Nicaragua needs to be addressed..."

"Get out," the president says, rising to his feet. One by one, the men shuffle out of the room.

"Ronald Wilson Reagan," Nancy says, upset. "I don't know what's gotten into you today. But you're poking at a hornet's nest with those Russians."

"Sir," Mikey says, stepping to her side. "It does seem irresponsible, given the current climate between our two nations, to go through with such an aggressive display of force."

"Get out," the president says, sitting back down.

"Ronnie," she says.

"Get out. Both of you."

Mikey's eyes fall sheepishly to the floor. He picks the daily briefs up off the desk and walks out. Nancy eyes her husband like a hawk. The president's gaze flicks in her direction.

"Did you not hear me?" he asks, coldly.

Nancy stands tall, her arms crossed defiantly. "How dare you..."

The president reaches for his phone, buzzing his secretary's intercom.

"Yes, Mister President?" she answers.

"Please have Mrs. Reagan escorted out of my office," he says to the intercom.

There's an uncomfortable pause, then: "Yes, sir."

The door opens, and Agent Bancroft enters. He marches up next to Nancy, placing a firm hand on her arm. Nancy lets Bancroft walk her to the door but stares back at the president.

Something isn't right, she thinks. *Something is different...*

Stepping out of the office, Nancy turns and eyes her husband behind the desk. In their entire marriage, she has never seen this expression on his face, the light seemingly extinguished from his eyes. As Agent Bancroft closes the door, swinging it slowly shut, Nancy's mind recounts the day thus far...

Her husband's uncharacteristic behavior during the daily briefing and his alarming interest in Able Archer — *something Ronnie ordinarily would squirm at* — his canceling of his day's appointments, even his phone call with the British Prime Minister — *he loves Margaret*, she thinks — his bran cereal sitting untouched on the breakfast table — *he's going to be stopped up for days now,* Nancy muses — and then her mind settles on the biggest red flag of all: *his hair.*

Something isn't right, she thinks. *It's wrong. The part is off. The flip too shallow.*

And then it hits her, becoming so incredibly obvious.

Her husband, Nancy realizes, stunned... *isn't her husband. The president... isn't the president...*

The man currently residing in the Oval Office... is an imposter.

And with that, the door clicks shut.

17

The dream is always the same.

Steven sits at the banquet table, his tuxedo and hair perfect. Across from him are his loving parents, bubbling with excitement. Seated next to Steven is his date — but her face, turned toward the podium, is hidden from view.

A hush falls upon the room as a distinguished-looking individual steps up to the lectern. "And the winner of the 1984 Nobel Peace Prize goes to," the man says, the audience holding its collective breath... "Hunter Gunne."

There is uproarious applause as the woman next to Steven stands, revealing herself to be Hunter, her gown flowing and long. Steven watches her, swooning over her, as she takes the stage, her eyes sparkling in the spotlight.

"Thank you," Hunter says into the microphone, her eyes meeting Steven's. "Thank you," she says, her voice floating directly toward him, entrancing him.

"Steven," she says. And Steven suddenly finds himself on stage with her, the reception hall empty. She takes his hand in hers, pulling him into her arms.

"Steven," she says, leaning in to kiss him...

"Get off me."

• • •

Steven startles awake.

"Get off me," Hunter says, elbowing his head off her shoulder.

Coming to, Steven blinks, bewildered. A moment ago, Hunter was dolled up for the Nobel Peace Prize ceremony. Now, seated next to him at a roadside diner, she looks like hell. Crusted blood still lines her nostrils, and, thanks to that broken nose she received back at the missile facility, massive bags circle her eyes.

"Have a good nap, son?" Reagan asks.

Steven turns to see the president smiling at him from across the table with Trevor by his side. "Sorry," Steven says, wiping the drool from his mouth. "I must have dozed off."

The truth is, Steven is exhausted. His post-rescue adrenaline rush wore off not long after they hit the road. The four of them — Hunter and Steven in her car, Trevor and the president in the truck — are somewhere in Pennsylvania, halfway to Washington D.C.

Glancing about the diner, Steven meets the dumbfounded gazes of the dozen or so early morning patrons and staff gawking at Ronald Reagan casually sipping on a milkshake in their presence. And he knows exactly how they feel...

For Steven, the last twenty or so hours have been a whirlwind. And the magnitude of it all — from confirming Hunter's existence to learning of the O.W.O.'s plot of world domination to rescuing the president himself — has been a lot to process.

And as for Hunter, Steven thinks, glancing at her...

He hasn't been able to get his mind off her. Each and every time Steven closes his eyes, he sees her. Whether she's dragging the helicopter into the hillside or leading their assault on the missile facility, there she is.

It's as if his infatuation with her — even before he knew she was a *her* — had been steadily building to untenable heights. Now, sharing this booth with her, her thigh is no less than six inches away from his...

No, Steven thinks, glancing down at her legs. *Three inches away from his...*

"What are you looking at?" Hunter asks, annoyed.

"Nothing," Steven says, embarrassed.

"Now, who'd you say is behind all this?" Reagan asks, resuming a conversation they were carrying on while Steven slept.

"The O.W.O.," Trevor answers.

"Those bastards? Again?" Reagan asks. "I thought they were long gone."

"Dormant," Trevor says. "The O.W.O. ebbs and flows in society like a fog filling a valley. Since their reemergence, they've successfully infiltrated deep into every facet of American government. From local school boards all the way to... well..." He gestures at the president himself. "To the top."

Reagan shakes his head as their waitress approaches. Balancing a tray of food on her shoulder, she slides a plate in front of each of them.

I should be hungry, Steven thinks, staring at an omelet he barely remembers ordering. But he's not. Numb would be a more accurate description of his current state.

When he's not thinking about Hunter, he finds his thoughts swinging to the second most pressing issue at hand: nuclear annihilation. Of the two subjects — Hunter Gunne or the end of humanity — Steven finds the former far more pleasant than the latter. But he doesn't like dwelling on either for too long.

You never know which meal might be your last, Steven thinks, recalling Trevor's words from the Moshulu. He cuts his omelet with his fork and jabs at it. Now, having survived their raid on the missile facility, Steven realizes just how true that statement is. And, to top it off, there is still the distinct possibility of nuclear war.

Steven looks up at the patrons and staff staring at the president. These poor people have no idea that their meals in front of them, right here and now, might be their last. Thinking of the lives they must live, the families they must have, the pets waiting at home, Steven reflects on everything that will be lost if war does break out...

Everything.

Steven looks at Hunter and shrugs. "You never know which meal might be your last," he says.

The comment stuns Hunter, but Steven is oblivious. Only after chewing a mouthful of food does he notice that Hunter is visibly shaken. Steven swallows hard, having no idea of the significance of that phrase and the memories it stirs within her.

"Are you okay?" Steven asks. But Hunter just stares at him, her mind swimming in the past. "Hunter?"

"So, what is it they want?" Reagan asks, biting into a juicy hamburger. Trevor, his mouth full already, politely chews his food before answering.

"To take over the world," Steven says, reflexively. "Oh," he says, realizing the question wasn't directed at him. "Sorry."

Trevor gestures for Steven to continue. "Your show, mate."

Reagan stares at Steven, expectantly.

This, Steven thinks, reflecting on the moment... *this is what I know.* For years now, Steven has researched tirelessly. He's followed leads, dug in the dirt, and turned over rocks nobody ever thought of turning over... only to be ridiculed for his passion. Steven's had to live with being labeled a quack, a conspiracy theorist, and a fool. But all Steven has ever wanted to do was tell the truth. And now, here he is, with the President of the United States as his audience.

So, let's jump right in, Steven thinks.

"What the *Old World Order* wants," Steven says, "is pretty simple, sir... world domination. The O.W.O. is the sworn enemy of science and enlightenment. And the way they see it, education and democracy, over the centuries, have robbed them of what they think is rightfully theirs: control of the masses."

"And those wankers will do anything to get it back," Trevor adds.

"Including nuclear war," Steven says.

"Well now, who the hell is in charge of this *Old World Order* anyway?" Reagan asks.

"The O.W.O. employs what is known as leaderless resistance," Steven says. "Think of them as a terrorist network. There are no direct orders from a central leadership. Instead, their actions are connected in a common cause."

Reagan cocks his head, confused.

"I'm just asking who I need to punch, son."

"Sorry, sir," Steven says. "But it's not that simple. The O.W.O. is faceless. And borderless. But evil doesn't need a face — or a nationality – for you to know it's there. All one has to do is look at all the hate in the world. The bigotry. The inequality. Suppression of the human spirit is found in every nook and cranny across the globe. And that, *that* is what guides them. *That* is their common cause."

"They're cockroaches," Hunter says, watching the sparse traffic on the interstate. "There's no one cockroach in charge of them all. But there's too many, spread too far and thin, to stomp them out for good."

Reagan nods.

"They come in waves, sir," Steven says. "Generational waves. And when one hate-fueled wave falls short, there's another right behind to pick up where they left off. Unless hate and envy are eradicated from society, the O.W.O. will always thrive."

"*Homo homini lupus,*" Trevor says, eyeing the president. "*Man is wolf to man.* This will never change. But putting the fate of humanity — of all life on Earth — in the power of one man, now that is folly. And that is the dilemma we face today."

Sensing a growing tension, Steven glances between Trevor and Reagan. "You mean the president, don't you? The Commander in Chief?" he asks.

Trevor shrugs. "You tell me what I mean," he says, still glaring at the president.

"Well now," Reagan says. "Let me assure each of you that the American people will always ensure that the *one man* you speak of will always be worthy of the responsibility."

Hunter scoffs. "You sure about that?"

"One man," Trevor says, holding back his anger, "can be psychotic. One man can unravel. One man can have a really bad day and make some very regrettable decisions. Or," Trevor continues, calming himself, "one man can do so intentionally. To prove a point. Or settle a grudge. Or as a last resort. One man..."

"Can be an imposter," Steven says, hitting home the point.

Trevor nods. "When all it takes is *one man*," he says, "there are a lot of '*ifs*' to consider."

The group sits in silence, none of them eating.

"This all reminds me of *Spellbound*," Reagan says. "You know, the Alfred Hitchcock film." Reagan looks around the table and finds Steven to be his only audience. "Except I'm not an imposter... I'm the impostee," Reagan says, chuckling. Steven blinks. "That's a joke, son."

Steven forces a laugh. "Yeah."

"I don't know why Hitchcock kept casting Gregory Peck in those darn films," Reagan says. "I'd have sold the ranch to have kept my film career going." The president catches his reflection in the diner's plate-glass window. "Nancy's always said I was better looking than Peck. Hell, I reckon I still am." Reagan says, checking his hair. "If it is an imposter, he's a damn good looking one, at that," he adds, chuckling.

Steven watches the president take another bite of his burger, amazed at how carefree the man is despite the stark reality of what they've told him: that there is an imposter in the White House hell-bent on starting World War Three.

"You know," Reagan says, still watching his reflection in the window. "They warned me about this. About this *exact* thing."

"What's that, sir?" Steven asks.

"An imposter," Reagan says. "In the White House. Starting a war. Yep. Our intelligence community raised this exact concern."

"They did?" Steven asks, stunned.

"Absolutely they did," Reagan says, proudly. "That's why we took precautions. A bracelet. They fitted me with a special bracelet. You know, to authenticate that I am *me*, just in case I ever do have to authorize a launch command. Yessir, real quality stuff. Made with all the high-tech gizmos and gadgets they could fit inside it, right here in the U.S.A."

"What about the nuclear football?" Steven asks. "Isn't that how you order an attack?"

"The football carries the launch codes. That is, our missiles' targets and such," Reagan says with a wave of his hand. "But that all could — you know, in theory — be stolen or forged, or just misplaced, I suppose. So, the smart folks we have running things came up with the bracelet. The bracelet... now that's what's needed to authenticate the order is coming from me. There's only one bracelet. And there's only one *me*." Reagan sips his milkshake. "I'm to be wearing it at all times," he continues, "because I — the President of the United States — am the only person authorized to order such an attack. I'm the *one man*."

Steven looks at Reagan's wrist... but there's nothing there.

"Ah. Mister President," Steven says. "You're not wearing a bracelet."

Reagan frowns. "I don't like how that damn thing jangles around on my wrist."

Steven stares at him, his mouth agape. This is the first he's heard of any sort of authentication that the president is *actually* the president in the event of a launch command, but... *damn, it makes sense.*

One of the glaring weaknesses of the United States' command and control protocols is that, in addition to the president having the launch codes housed in the nuclear football, they must also exist on the receiving ends: in the missile silos, the airbases, the bombers, and the Navy's ballistic missile submarines. That puts the launch codes themselves, on any given day, within reach of maybe a thousand different hands. And any one of those hands could, in theory, without any authority, transmit the launch codes to each other. Needless to say, even with the tightest security protocols imaginable, it's still quite a considerable risk.

"So, let me get this straight," Hunter says. "Your advisors warned you that somebody could possibly — maybe — impersonate you in hopes of launching an unauthorized nuclear attack. They gave you a one-of-a-kind bracelet which, if such an order is given, proves *you* are *you*... and you still didn't wear it?"

The president shrugs. "Well, I wouldn't give that order to begin with," he says, "not unless the Soviets launched first, that is."

Hunter blinks. "The whole point," she barks, "is that *you* wouldn't be the one giving the damn order!" Hunter looks at Trevor. "We need to secure that goddamn bracelet," she says.

Trevor nods, nonchalant. Hunter eyes him suspiciously.

"You knew all this already, didn't you?"

"Check please," Trevor says, waving down their waitress.

"So, what are we going to do?" Steven asks.

"I thought you'd never ask," Trevor says, giddy. "We get his ass back to the White House, we get that damn bracelet, and we save the bloody world."

"And how are you going to do that?" Steven asks.

"Simple," Trevor says. "We're going to walk in through the front door."

18

Five hundred and seventy-four, Nancy thinks, pacing their living room. That's how many days it's been since John Hinckley Jr. — in an effort to impress the actress Jodie Foster — attempted to assassinate the President of the United States.

Five hundred and seventy-four, Nancy thinks, a massive portrait of herself hanging above the room's marble mantel. That's how many days it's been since Hinckley approached the president's motorcade outside the Hilton Hotel in Washington, D.C.

Five hundred and seventy-four, Nancy thinks, her potent *Chanel No. 5* perfume wafting about the room around her. That's how many days it's been since Hinckley — his well-worn copy of *The Catcher in the Rye* waiting back in his hotel room — fired six rounds from his revolver, wounding police officer Thomas Delahanty, Secret Service agent Timothy McCarthy, and press secretary James Brady as they valiantly protected the president.

Five hundred and seventy-four, Nancy thinks, biting her lip in despair. That's how many days it's been since the sixth and final bullet — as Nancy was attending a luncheon at Georgetown — ricocheted off the armor-plated limousine and lodged itself into the president's chest, stopping less than an inch from his heart.

Five hundred and seventy-four, Nancy thinks, her hands shaking. *That's how many days it's been since I almost lost my Ronnie.*

Nancy breathes, attempting to calm herself. Since that fateful day, not a night goes by that Nancy doesn't startle awake, clutching frantically for her husband. Not a day goes by that Nancy doesn't curse herself for not being by his side when he needed her the most.

And since that day, demanding to know and approve of every minute detail of her husband's life — what he eats, where he goes, who he's with — Nancy has willfully alienated herself from those that surround them — the president's staff and aids — to the point that they avoid her at all costs...

All except Mikey, she thinks.

Nancy approaches a desk in the corner of the room. Sitting atop of it are several framed photographs, some of their happiest and more personal memories. She takes a frame into her hand: their wedding photo. Looking at the image, she studies her husband — in particular, his hair...

An imposter, Nancy thinks. Amazingly, this isn't the first run-in the Reagans have had with somebody claiming to be somebody they're not. Three decades ago, Nancy Davis Reagan was a communist. Except she wasn't...

There was an imposter.

● ● ●

The year was 1951, and the Red Scare was sweeping the nation. Senator Joseph McCarthy fanned the flames of Cold War paranoia almost to the point of mass hysteria, raining the question *"Are you now, or have you ever been, a member of the Communist Party?"* down on the American public — and the Bill of Rights proved powerless to protect them.

It wasn't long before the hunt for subversive Communist threats turned its menacing gaze toward Hollywood. And in flagrant violation of the first amendment, many of Hollywood's finest — the industry's top writers, directors, actors, and actresses — were dragged into hearings and questioned about their political leanings over the past two decades.

In the years after the Great Depression — when the country's economy was crippled — and in the years before World War Two — when right-wing fascists were America's undisputed enemy — many Americans, exercising their constitutional rights, openly attended the meetings of various left-leaning, pro-labor, and anti-fascist organizations. Included in this was the Communist Party of America. Years later, this political activism came back to haunt them...

Names were named. Careers were destroyed. Lives were ruined. And on this ever-growing list of alleged Hollywood communist sub servants was, much to her surprise...

Nancy Davis.

For Nancy, finding herself listed as a communist was as unfathomable as it was horrifying. Already a successful actress, she was raised with a staunch conservative upbringing. Her father was a prominent neurosurgeon and longtime friend of Senator Barry Goldwater, a pillar of American conservatism.

Desperate to save her career and reputation, Nancy knew there was only one man she could turn to... Ronald Reagan, the liberal democrat and union leader.

Through the first forty years of his life, the man that would become the new pillar of American conservatism was a left-leaning, New Deal-supporting, Roosevelt-loving movie-

199

star, ensconced in the open-minded, progressive Hollywood culture of the 1940s. Reagan and his first wife, Jane Wyman, were as patriotic and proud as they get. And, with Wyman's support, Reagan took his first foray into politics, being elected head of the Screen Actors Guild in 1947.

But just as the country found itself facing the winds of post-war change, so too did Ronald Reagan. As his movie career fizzled, so too did his marriage. And by 1948, Wyman had filed for divorce. The causes of this dissolution were numerous, but the result was all the same: Ronald Reagan was heartbroken.

Suddenly adrift in life, Reagan found reassurance and stability in his duties to the Screen Actors Guild. As the Cold War loomed larger and larger, and as the American public shifted more and more to the political right, so too did Reagan. And it wasn't long before communism, in Reagan's eyes, was a legit threat to the American way of life.

Enter Nancy Davis.

Desperate to clear her name — and as a dues-paying member of the Screen Actors Guild — Nancy knew that if anybody could help her, it was the communist-hating Ronald Reagan. Meeting over lunch to discuss... the two fell in love immediately.

As for Nancy's dilemma, an imposter was to blame. Another woman, another actress, but the same name. As it turned out, there was another Nancy Davis working in Hollywood. And so it was that Ronald Reagan pledged to do everything in his power to clear *this* Nancy Davis's good name, a relatively easy task since both Nancies were members of the Guild.

But Nancy Davis, *this* Nancy Davis, would forever be grateful. And as for the future husband and wife, it was an imposter, of all things, that had brought them together...

• • •

Another imposter, Nancy thinks, setting their wedding photo back atop the desk. The first time around, Ronnie had saved her. But this time...

I must save him.

Nancy considers Agent Bancroft, undoubtedly standing just outside the Oval Office. *Agent Bancroft is a good man*, she thinks, *if not a bit disillusioned by the gun in his holster*. But, for all his earnestness, there's nothing, absolutely nothing, he wouldn't do if the president's life was in danger — and for that, she is thankful.

All of the secret service agents, Nancy thinks, comprise a phenomenal team who would, and have, risked their lives for her beloved Ronnie. But, not surprisingly, Agent Bancroft and the others take their responsibilities very seriously... maybe a bit too serious. The thought of raising her suspicions to Agent Bancroft — telling him that the man he's protecting is not the man he thinks he's protecting — *well, that probably won't go over well.*

Instead, Nancy wonders why...

Why would someone impersonate the president?

To cut corporate taxes?

Deregulate business?

To hike up military spending, inflating the national debt to untold heights?

Well, Ronnie's done all of that already, she thinks.

She pictures the Emergency War Orders Officer standing next to Agent Bancroft just outside the Oval Office door. Arguably, as Commander in Chief, Ronnie is the most powerful man on the planet. At his whim, billions of people's lives could end in a nuclear exchange with the Soviet Union.

Sure, she wishes Ronnie would take that responsibility a little bit more seriously — he has a habit of likening everything to those old Hollywood films where the good guys always triumph over the bad... regardless of their competence — but could that really be the reasoning behind this? That power? And to what end?

She pictures the black leather attaché affixed to the officer's arm. Within it are the launch codes to the country's nuclear arsenal.

If N.O.R.A.D. — the North American Aerospace Defense Command — were to detect an incoming missile salvo, perhaps a *decapitation strike* intended to wipe out America's chain of command, the president would be quickly notified. Ronnie would then have, at best, one or two minutes to evaluate the situation, decide on the adequate response, and authorize the appropriate counterattack. If the president, while choosing the fate of billions of lives across the globe, were to hesitate too long, the order may never be given. Therefore, the president's ability to quickly and efficiently order the appropriate retaliatory strike is of the utmost importance.

Nancy, often imagining such a situation, shudders to think of a false alarm escalating to the point that Ronnie — or any president — is faced with making a decision based on questionable intelligence. After all, false-alarms happen with surprising frequency. To our geostationary first-detection satellites, sunlight reflecting off sheets of arctic ice looks remarkably similar to Soviet ICBM launches in Siberia. And to our early-warning radar arrays, migrating Canadian geese look an awful lot like incoming Soviet bombers...

These false-positives, scary as they are, can quickly climb the chain of the command, often culminating with the president's bedside telephone ringing in the middle of the night. On the other end, a four-star general from the Strategic Air Command, informing the president of the bad news: *"Sir. We may or may not be under attack. What do you advise?"*

That question, at that moment, puts an incredible strain on a person's rational decision-making ability. On top of that, every second you wait, every moment you spend praying it's a false alarm, is — if it is an attack — one second closer to your own nuclear cremation.

But what worries Nancy the most, as she lays awake in the middle of the night, wondering if that phone might ring, is knowing that the General Secretary of the Soviet Union is also bombarded with such situations and false-alarms. And if she can be certain of anything, it's that the General Secretary — and the rest of the Soviet apparat — don't share her husband's rosy outlook on the world.

So often, billions of lives unknowingly hang in the balance of one simple and subjective question: *Does this make any sense?*

What guarantee does humanity have that, at any given moment, the leaders of the world's nuclear-armed nations are in the right state of mind to handle such a question? And, in the event of a rogue missile launch, whether accidental or criminal... how does one know how to respond appropriately?

Nancy exhales, having held her breath throughout that entire stream-of-consciousness. She thinks of Ronnie. And she thinks of that imposter sitting in the Oval Office... this is far too dangerous a game to let somebody else have a turn.

Oh, Ronnie, Nancy thinks, picking up the telephone and dialing an extension. *I promise to do everything in my power to save you... and the world...*

"Hello?" Mikey answers on the other end of the line.

"Mikey," she says. "Get me Carroll Quigley."

19

Nuclear war, Steven thinks, riding shotgun as Hunter charges toward D.C. *What a nightmare.*

It's estimated that the strategic nuclear force of the Soviet Union — that is, the weapons that they have locked and loaded just for such an occasion — comes to around ten thousand warheads. Assuming those warheads are in the one to ten megaton range, even the most conservative estimate adds up to ten thousand megatons... or the equivalent of eight hundred thousand Hiroshima bombs.

The numbers are staggering, Steven thinks, as the beltway traffic grows thicker and thicker as they near the nation's capital.

To put it another way — a way most people can relate to — that is roughly the same number of commercial airliners in the United States at any given moment, whether in flight or on the ground.

Steven looks out across the hood of the car. He watches the late-morning sun dart in and out of the trees lining the bank of the Potomac River, feeling the light on his face.

They've been driving for hours — Hunter and himself racing ahead of Trevor and the president — leaving Steven ample time to churn over the realities of nuclear warfare in his head. Much of this intelligence Steven stumbled across in his research. Most of it has kept him up at night.

Strategic targets, Steven recalls, are considered either hard or soft. Hard targets include military bases, missile silos, industry and infrastructure targets, and the like.

There are about a thousand such targets in the United States sprinkled about. Though a single one-megaton detonation would be more than adequate, for the sake of certainty, the Russians will likely dedicate at least two warheads for such targets.

That leaves roughly eight thousand warheads remaining for the soft targets... the cities, towns, and population centers of the United States. If these targets are prioritized by order of population, every community with as little as fifteen hundred residents can expect a one-megaton warhead headed their way... a weapon eighty times more powerful than the Hiroshima bomb.

But that would still leave a staggering number of warheads to be deployed in the equivalent of a nuclear carpet bombing of the United States, leveling tens of thousands of square miles.

The carnage would be both inescapable... and unsurvivable.

The overlap of targets would be considerable. Larger cities — cities that share both hard and soft targets within their limits — would likely be the recipient of dozens of warheads. And the barrage itself would last hours, maybe even days, irradiating already irradiated ash heaps over and over again, relentlessly.

For any sadistic Soviet war planners not yet vaporized themselves, it would almost become a matter of hunting down individual survivors, each with a nuclear warhead with their name on it.

A ridiculous thought, yes, Steven thinks. But such a ludicrous stockpile of nuclear weapons exists. And that's not even counting the United States' own arsenal.

Hunter speeds along the George Washington Parkway, crossing over the Potomac River on the Key Bridge. Looking at her, Steven wonders how often she's dwelled on these numbers. How disheartening, he thinks. Despite all that Hunter has done to prevent their use, the total number of warheads in the world has only ticked up and up and up.

It's as if humanity is begging for it.

Watching her needle the car around metro buses and taxicabs, Steven wonders just how old Hunter actually is. In her fifties, he supposes. That means, during the Cuban Missile Crisis — back when Steven was just a kid lying on his parent's living room floor, his homework splayed in front of him — Hunter was in her thirties... roughly the same age Steven is now.

Damn, he thinks.

In comparison, Steven hasn't done shit with his life.

By their thirties, Michelangelo and Napoléon had each accomplished remarkable feats. Michelangelo, at thirty-three years old, painted his massive fresco within the Sistine Chapel, which, even upon its completion, was hailed a masterpiece of High Renaissance Art. Napoléon, at just thirty years of age, had already proven himself a military genius. Plotting a coup d'état, he named himself Emperor of France and began his campaign of world conquest. And as for Hunter Gunne, she had already saved the world numerous times.

Seeing her in action last night was exquisite. Without a doubt, Hunter belongs in the same echelon as Michelangelo and Napoléon. Those men were masters of their craft, whether it be art or war. And, Steven is convinced, Hunter is just as talented and attuned to her abilities as Einstein... or Mozart... or Socrates...

Sure, Hunter's art is death. But it's death with a purpose. And that purpose may be more admirable and selfless than anything Michelangelo, Napoléon, or Mozart had ever achieved: the survival of humanity itself. And unlike those men that came before her, Hunter did this never expecting — or wanting — any sort of thanks or praise.

Thinking back to their raid on the missile facility, Hunter was uncompromising. And yet Steven feels himself swooning over her, even now. All that blood. All that death. It was wrong. But it wasn't Hunter who set things in motion. It wasn't Hunter who kidnapped the president. If Steven, back in the compound, had just understood that. If he had only respected that instead of questioning her and the way she does things... he'd feel a hell of a lot less stupid right now.

Steven sighs. Finding Hunter, even if her cabin's coordinates were simply given to him by Trevor, may be Steven's greatest accomplishment. Sure, it's not on par with Einstein or Socrates... or Hunter herself. *But it's something.*

Thinking back to the night John F. Kennedy addressed the nation regarding the Cuban Missile Crisis, Steven can still remember the fear he felt. That fear has never left him. As he laid awake in bed that night, afraid that there wouldn't be a world in the morning, Steven prayed. He prayed for a savior...

He prayed for Hunter Gunne.

Hunter turns right onto 16th Street, and directly ahead of them, Steven sees it: The White House.

Looks smaller than I expected, Steven thinks.

Just as they're about to reach H Street, Hunter cuts the wheel again, pulling into the elegant porte-cochère of the Hay-Adams Hotel, a historic hotel in the heart of D.C.

"We're here," Hunter says, already exiting the car.

Much to Steven's surprise, a valet attendant opens his door and greets him. Steven mumbles his thanks, chasing after Hunter as she marches into the building.

The lobby is regal and stately with high ceilings and golden chandeliers. Hunter steps up to the front desk.

"McCoy," she says.

Almost immediately, the clerk hands her their room key.

• • •

"The presidential suite?" Steven asks, wide-eyed, as the door closes behind them.

Hunter shrugs, unimpressed. Checking out the layout, Steven is in awe. To his left, a long conference table is surrounded by plush green chairs, fresh flowers atop of it. To his right, a pair of high-end leather sofas and a glass coffee table comprise the living room.

This is the nicest hotel room I've ever seen, Steven thinks.

Shuffling into the bedroom, he finds a set of French doors leading out to the balcony. The balcony overlooks Lafayette Square and the White House itself, a fantastic view. He sits down on the bed and sinks in. The mattress is delightful. He reaches for a pillow, running his hand atop the fabric. The highest thread count available, he assumes.

Steven basks in the moment. Compared to the dilapidated, cockroach-infested studio apartment he calls home, this is nice. Real nice. He would never have imagined sitting in a luxury hotel room across the street from the White House...

But here I am, Steven thinks.

He looks at Hunter through the bedroom door. Out in the suite, she's moving furniture around. As she drags items here and there along the hardwood floor, Steven has no idea what she's doing or why. Regardless, he studies her: her high cheekbones, her full lips, those green eyes, the strands of red-grey hair tucked behind her ears...

The shape of her shoulders...

The arch of her back...

And for a moment, Steven is back in the cabin. Hunter is atop of him, straddling him, as gunfire pounds the walls around them. He can still remember her thighs warm against his waist.

Here in the hotel room, Steven's cheeks redden. He looks at the bed. He looks at Hunter...

Is it hot in here?

"Hunter," Steven says, not sure why. Not sure what he wants to say...

"Yeah," she says, standing in the door.

Steven blinks, awkward and uncomfortable.

"What?" Hunter asks.

"Umm," Steven says, crossing his legs as he desperately tries to think of something that isn't as stupid as *Will you have sex with me?*

Hunter stands there, expectantly. And for whatever reason, a bit of the conversation Trevor had with him during their raid — well, Hunter's raid — on the missile facility comes to Steven's mind: *"I once saw her single-handedly commandeer an entire Soviet attack submarine."*

That's it, Steven thinks. That must be how she saved the world during the Cuban Missile Crisis. When else could Hunter have squared off against a Red Fleet submarine? Intrigued, Steven looks at Hunter anew. Maybe this isn't the time or place to ask, but nine-year-old Steven just has to know: "The Cuban Missile Crisis," Steven says. "The submarine..."

"Don't," Hunter says, rolling her eyes.

"Don't what?" Steven asks, perplexed.

"Don't just ask me about my past. Don't just interview me for your article," she says, shaking her head. "If you want to talk to me, talk to me. But don't go nagging me about saving the world or any of that idealistic bullshit you're constantly drooling over."

"I'm sorry..."

"Don't be sorry," Hunter scoffs. "Talk to me."

Steven blinks. He looks her over, standing in the doorway, staring back at him.

"Talk to you?" he asks, confused. "You want to... talk?"

"Yeah," Hunter says, growing uncertain. "Maybe."

And before Steven's eyes, Hunter softens. Losing her edge, she suddenly becomes just another person. A person full of anxieties and insecurities.

Steven thinks back to Hunter in the cabin — holed up in the middle of nowhere, far removed from civilization — and he wonders just how long she was there. Just how long was she alone and isolated, cut off from the rest of the world?

Steven thinks of the explosives wired throughout the structure, the preparations Hunter had put into their escape: it must have taken her years. It must have been mind-numbingly dull.

She was all alone up there. Nobody to kill, sure, but also nobody to talk to...

"That's it, isn't it?" Steven asks aloud.

"What?" Hunter asks, annoyed.

"The reason you didn't kill me when I knocked at your door," Steven says. "You were lonely."

Hunter hesitates. She looks away, desperate to think of a witty retort. But she comes up with nothing. Steven smiles. This woman is suddenly so... human.

Fortunately for her, the telephone rings.

"Answer it," Hunter snaps, marching out of the room, agitated.

Steven leans over and picks up the receiver from the nightstand. "Hello?"

He listens and nods. As he hangs up the phone, Hunter appears back in the door.

"Well?" she asks, her demeanor once again that of a hard-boiled secret agent.

"Our bags have arrived," Steven says.

20

Nancy stares at the television, impatiently tapping her foot as she waits. On today's episode of *General Hospital* — America's longest-running soap opera — newlyweds Luke and Laura are desperately attempting to thwart an evil organization's plot to take over the world. What any of this has to do with the titular hospital of the show, Nancy stopped wondering long ago.

But this, Nancy thinks... *this is the kind of wholesome, down-to-earth messaging this country needs.* If this husband and wife duo, working together, can save the world. Then any man and woman, from anywhere in America, can accomplish anything they set their minds to, even if it's moving into the White House...

Oh, Ronnie. Nancy's heart sinks thinking about him. For most of the day, she's been resisting the nagging questions scratching at her mind: *Where is he? Is he okay? What's the meaning of it all?*

Amazingly, this isn't the first time all hope has seemed lost for the Reagans. Nor the second time. Keeping that in mind, Nancy's been as optimistic as her suffocating anxiety will allow her to be. They've been through the wringer before, she reminds herself, and they made it out on top.

And if Ronald Reagan is good at anything, it's playing the character that people, particularly his employers — whether they be movie directors, network executives, or The Grand Old Party — want him to be.

Back in 1952 — the same year they were married — Ronald Reagan was done for, and he knew it. To put it simply, nobody wanted to cast him. Hollywood had moved on to younger leading men, and Reagan had to face the music: his movie career was over.

Like most men, the smartest person he knew was his wife, so he turned to her for advice. The gist of his concerns was simple: what the hell were they going to do for money?

Nancy had one word for him: *television.*

• • •

There's a knock at the door.

"Mrs. Reagan," Mikey says, peeking inside the living room. "Miss Quigley has arrived."

"Did anybody see her?" Nancy asks.

"Of course not, Mrs. Reagan," he says. "I snuck her in through the East Wing." Nancy nods her appreciation and relief washes over the first lady as Carroll Quigley — her friend, her confidant, her astrologer — enters the room, cigarette in hand.

Nancy darts to her, falling into Quigley's arms.

"Oh, Quigley," Nancy says. "It's Ronnie."

Since the assassination attempt on Ronnie's life, Nancy has been an emotional mess, the shock of the experience leaving her a shell of the person she was before. Now, she can hardly breath when Marine One takes off with her husband in tow and her heart's a flutter every public appearance he makes.

Her anxiety, her concern, her never-ending questions about her husband's whereabouts and well-being, it eventually overwhelmed most of the president's staff. But instead of sitting down to console her, to suggest she see a therapist, they simply avoid her at all costs.

Fortunately, Quigley still makes house calls.

Carroll Quigley, a self-proclaimed expert on the movements and positions of celestial objects and how they affect our lives, has been in Nancy's service for years.

Being a religious woman herself, Nancy wholeheartedly believes that, in due time, the good Lord will reveal all to her and Ronnie. But, finding herself rather impatient these days, Quigley has been a competent replacement.

So, when it comes down to whether the president should attend a conference in Tulsa or what route his motorcade should take in Cincinnati, Quigley has the answers that Nancy needs.

Mikey closes the door on the two women, giving them their privacy.

"Now now," Quigley says, patting Nancy's head, her cigarette between her fingers. "Tell me your troubles."

Nancy pulls away to look Quigley in the eye.

"Somebody has..." Nancy stops. She looks cautiously about the room, embarrassed to say her ludicrous suspicion out loud. *What if they hear me?* she thinks, picturing the staff's snickers and leers every time they spot Quigley in the residence.

"Say no more," Quigley says.

Opening her bag, she pulls out one of the many astrological charts she carries at all times. But as for the president's chart, she has it practically memorized: Ronald Wilson Reagan, born on February 6, 1911, sun sign is Aquarius, moon sign is Taurus. His ascendant sign, rising in the east upon his birth, is Sagrateris. And his midheaven — the most influential of one's celestial placement — is that of the Libra.

Oh yes, Quigley muses, unrolling his birth chart on the table. *Ronald Reagan was destined for great things — it was written in the heavens upon his birth.* Sliding on the reading glasses hanging around her neck, she rolls out today's celestial chart next to it and looks up at Nancy.

Nancy, in turn, shuts off the television...

• • •

Back in the early fifties, television was a young and fledging medium. But already, people like Nancy's father and his GOP friends saw the promise of this new technology... not as a tool of individual enlightenment and education, as one might expect, but as a means of influencing and shaping public opinion.

Already, the networks (and their corporate sponsors) saw the appeal of a charming spokesperson... somebody with a friendly face and charming smile, somebody people could trust, somebody people could love... somebody like Ronald Reagan.

At Nancy's urging, Reagan became the host of the weekly anthology series *General Electric Theater*. The show, much to the namesake's delight, was a hit, and Ronald Reagan found himself a household name. Becoming the face of General Electric was a role Reagan dove headfirst into — even if it meant shedding much of his New Deal liberalism in favor of free-market capitalism.

As the offspring of Thomas Edison, General Electric was one of the largest, most influential corporations in the world. With products ranging from electrical power stations to train locomotives, from television sets to medical x-ray machines, from molded plastics to commercial jet engines, name just about any innovation of the twentieth century and you'll find General Electric's fingerprints on it... the future president included.

In addition to his weekly hosting duties on television, Reagan was also contractually obligated to travel across the country, visiting hundreds of GE factories to deliver patriotic-inspired motivational speeches to more than two-hundred thousand GE employees.

These speeches leaned heavily on conservative, pro-business, anti-union messages – clearly appeasing the company's top-brass – and aimed to soften their workforce to management initiatives – even if those initiatives weren't in the workers' best interests.

Whether he realized it or not, Reagan and the corporate propaganda he was shelling out would have a lasting impact on the country's labor movement... for the worse.

It wasn't long before Reagan himself ceased romanticizing the ideals of Woodrow Wilson and Franklin D. Roosevelt. Instead, he began idolizing the likes of economist Henry Hazlitt and General Electric's then vice president, Lemuel Boulware.

It was here, on the road for corporate America, polishing his public persona in front of thousands of factory workers a day, that *Reagan: The Great Communicator* was born.

• • •

Quigley leans close to the two charts in front of her. She looks hard at the various positions of Saturn and its moons.

217

"I see... much stress for the president," Quigley says, glancing toward Nancy, who nods in agreement, anxiously twiddling her necklace. "I see..." Quigley says, feeling Nancy out. "I see... snow and sleet."

Nancy freezes. "What?"

"No, no," Quigley says, reading the first lady's reaction. *This appointment is not about the upcoming weather forecast*, she notes. "I see... fire and fury!" Nancy gasps. "I see... a meeting," Quigley says, noticing Nancy ever-so-slightly nodding. "Yes. The president has had a meeting. Much was discussed..."

"He canceled all his cabinet meetings today," Nancy says, frowning.

Quigley nods. She compares two spots on the charts, running a finger between the two of them.

"Ah. Yes. Here it is. New faces. New people in his life. I see... introductions?"

Nancy perks up. "Maybe," she says.

"I see..." Quigley continues, fishing for anything. "Staff changes on the horizon..."

Nancy sighs. "I need to know..." she says, swallowing. "I need to know if Ronnie's okay."

Quigley studies her, then nods.

"I understand," she says, standing up. Approaching the window, she dramatically pulls the curtains shut. The room falls into darkness. Returning to the table, Quigley opens her bag...

Pulling out an old leather envelope, she removes a deck of tarot cards, yellow and aged. Nancy eagerly scoots her chair close to the table. Quigley only resorts to the tarot cards in the

most urgent of circumstances... which, Nancy notes, happens to be every time she's over.

But still...

This is the good stuff.

• • •

After a decade as the face of General Electric, Ronald Reagan was once again done for, and he knew it. Just as his politics had shifted considerably over the years, so too had the entire country's — only in the other direction.

Over were the days of President Eisenhower's pro-business, anti-regulatory administration. A new era was upon the country, and a new generation had stepped up to the plate. Hoping to warm up to the recently elected John F. Kennedy, General Electric decided it was time to change things up themselves.

And one thing they decided they could do without was Ronald Reagan's face.

So, once again, Reagan turned to his wife for guidance: now what?

Nancy had one word for him: *politics.*

Seeing the value of a handsome, optimistic corporate spokesperson — a frontman with charisma and confidence — it wasn't long before the country's major political parties went looking for their own.

Fresh off the heels of Richard Nixon's embarrassing defeat in the presidential election of 1960, the still-burgeoning conservative movement realized it needed a JFK of their own. Somebody with a friendly face and charming smile, somebody people could trust, somebody people could love... somebody like Ronald Reagan.

And so it was that Ronald Reagan stepped out onto the stage at a televised rally in support of Senator Barry Goldwater's 1964 presidential campaign. Goldwater, the dear friend of Nancy's father, had aligned himself on the Republican party's extreme right and it was then, giving his esteemed speech *A Time for Choosing*, that Ronald Reagan — his suit black and crisp, his hair slicked and wet — embraced his ultimate role, a role of a lifetime, a role that would whisk him to untold heights — first as the Governor of California and then as the President of the United States.

• • •

Holding her breath, Nancy watches Quigley deal the cards on the table.

Tarot cards aren't ordinary playing cards. They are of an old French design known as the *Tarot of Marseilles*. This method of fortune-telling is known as cartomancy. A cartomancer — that is, the reader of the fortunes — would likely tell you the art of reading cards dates back to ancient Egypt. But, in reality, the practice originated in Europe in the 14th century.

Many cartomancers believe their abilities originate from the gods of ancient times. Quigley, on the other hand, feels her skills stem from the universe itself, believing a *universal consciousness* exists and that she is fortunate enough to be a conduit between mediums.

Quigley finishes placing the cards in an arrangement known as *The Celtic Cross*. She leans in close, studying them and the order in which they were dealt. In this arrangement, each card has a specific meaning dependent on those seeking their fortunes.

"Ah, yes," Quigley says. "The president. He is... troubled. Stressed? Yes. The president..." she says, becoming more animated as she feeds off Nancy's anticipation. "The president is... is..."

"Is missing," Nancy shouts.

"Missing?" Quigley asks, breaking character.

"Yes. No. I don't know," Nancy stammers. "I know this sounds crazy," she says, lowering her voice. "I don't think the man in the Oval Office is my Ronnie."

Quigley looks at her. "What?"

"There's an imposter," Nancy says. "Here in the White House."

"Nancy," she says, concerned. "Is everything... okay?"

"No," Nancy answers. "That's why I summoned you! What am I supposed to do?"

"Have you brought this up with security?" Quigley asks.

"Of course not," Nancy says. "They already think I'm crazy! The cards, Quigley," Nancy says, jabbing at the cards on the table. "I need to know what they say."

Quigley looks at the cards, frazzled. *This is all bullshit,* she thinks. *I could deal these cards a hundred times and never come up with this arrangement again.*

"This one," Nancy says, picking up a card. "You always start with this one." She throws the card back down. "Read it."

Quigley looks at the card.

"*La Maison Dieu*," she says, swallowing. "The Tower. That's the obstacle position." The face of the card shows a stone tower in the midst of being struck by lightning, engulfed in flames. The tower is cracking and crumbling — and people are shown leaping to their death.

"What does that mean?" Nancy asks.

"Disaster. Upheaval. Revelation," Quigley says, looking at Nancy. "Nothing good."

Nancy jumps to her feet, the chair falling behind her. "Keep going!"

Quigley motions to the cards surrounding The Tower card. "These are the influencer cards," she says. She points to one of them: "*Le Fol*. The Fool. Starting his journey, innocent and naive."

"Ronnie?" Nancy asks.

Quigley shrugs. She points to the next card, upside down in relation to the others: "*Le Bateleur*. The Magician. Determined. Resourceful. But..." she says, flipping the card right-side up. "Could be manipulative. Deceitful. This one..." she says, tapping the next card. "*L'Ermite*. The Hermit. Isolation. Loneliness... but also introspection."

"And this one?" Nancy asks, pointing to *the outcome card*.

Quigley takes a deep breath. "*Le Jugement*," she says. The face of the card shows the archangel Gabriel playing her trumpet. Beneath her, the undead rise from their graves. "Reflection. Understanding," Quigley says, swallowing. "Usually at one's reckoning."

"What does any of this mean?" Nancy asks.

Quigley focuses her thoughts. She looks at all the cards, their positions and meanings, and tries to interpret the big picture. This might be the most important card reading of her life...

"Nancy," she says, ominous. "I think we're all in grave danger."

21

Reagan touches his toes, bends sideways, and stretches his back. Long car rides just aren't his thing. Standing up straight, he looks out across Lafayette Park at the White House... his home.

"Dang thing looks smaller than I remember," he mutters to himself. Turning back toward the hotel, a gaggle of valet attendants stares up at Trevor's truck, appalled. The beast of a vehicle barely fits beneath the porte-cochère.

"Where the hell we gonna park this?" one whispers to another.

Fortunately for Reagan, these boys were too distraught to notice him — the President of the United States — slip quietly out of the cab. The last thing he wants is to draw any unwanted attention.

Hunter and Steven walk out of the hotel, and Reagan gives them a friendly wave. Trevor, jumping down out of the truck, walks to the back and drops the tailgate. Inside, several black cases are stacked atop each other, having been picked up by Trevor and the president on the way down.

"Come now," Trevor says to the valet attendants, gesturing toward the cases. "Get on with it."

The attendants scowl at him but wheel their luggage cart over to the truck, nonetheless.

"What is all this?" Steven asks, watching them drop a case onto the cart.

"You'll see, chum," Trevor says, smiling.

CHRISTOPHER KÜGLER

Reagan eyes Steven. On the drive down, the president heard all about *the plan*. "It's a brave thing you're about to do, son," he says, patting him on the back.

Steven double-takes the president. "Wait. What?" Steven looks at Trevor. "What am I about to do?"

Trevor giggles. "Steven," he says, sliding an arm around him. "Let's have a walk, shall we?"

As he leads him along the sidewalk, Hunter watches. Reagan follows her gaze, noting her interest in Trevor and Steven's conversation.

"What is it we all want out of life?" Trevor asks Steven. Steven shrugs. "Purpose, my boy. You. Me. Mister President back there. We all want purpose. To feel that we are here, at this place and time, for a reason. But finding that reason isn't always easy. And, sometimes, it's not always pleasant."

Steven stops walking.

"What do you mean?" he asks, suspiciously.

"Relax. We all have a purpose," Trevor says, tugging him along. "You have yours. I have mine. Hunter has hers. In fact, everybody and everything has a purpose. Even this mission has a purpose. Even our relationships have a purpose." Trevor raises an eyebrow: "Platonic or otherwise," he adds.

"Okay," Steven interjects, already self-conscious of his feelings toward Hunter. "So, what are you trying to say? That my purpose is to be here and now, doing whatever it is to help you out?"

Trevor frowns. "Dear God, Steven. This isn't about you," he says. "My point is this: sometimes, things in life have multiple

226

purposes. Follow? Sometimes these purposes aren't obvious. But, trust me here, they have 'em. Got it?"

Steven looks at him. "No."

"Good," Trevor says. "You let me worry about all that." Trevor leads Steven to the curb and stops. Other pedestrians shuffle by them. "Now," Trevor says, pivoting Steven toward the White House. "Take a look at it. What is it?"

Steven shrugs. "The White House."

"It's just a building in a field," Trevor says. "And yet, every day, decisions are made within those walls that affect the entire world. Decisions that will impact generations to come."

Steven looks more closely at the building. From here, with its tiny roof-mounted flag flapping in the breeze, *it does look rather silly*, Steven thinks.

"Four billion years," Trevor continues. "That's how long this planet has harbored life. From single-cell organisms to fungus. From trilobites to dinosaurs. From metazoan to mammals. And finally, you and me, here today... gone tomorrow. In the grand history of the world, humanity's time here on Earth is nothing. Just a minute of an entire day. But it is only recently, in the last few seconds actually, that we, that humanity, has the potential to wipe it all away."

Trevor looks at Steven, lowering his voice. "We live in a mad world," he says. "And humanity is sick. A lot of powerful people are running around with some very dangerous ideas in their heads," Trevor continues. "Today, now, they're in there," he says, pointing at the White House. "And Moscow. A hundred years ago, it was Paris and Vienna. A hundred years before that, Constantinople and Beijing. A hundred years *from now*..."

Trevor sighs. "It could be two mud holes somewhere in the southern hemisphere, humanity blasted back to the Stone Age, thanks to *these* madmen. Why do we put them in charge? Why have we handed over the survival of the entire species — of life itself, in all its glory — to these fools? Because we are sick, Steven. Do you understand?"

Steven looks at him, not necessarily liking the dark turn this conversation has taken.

"What's the cure?" Trevor asks. "You tell me, Steven. When we're all standing in a puddle of petrol, all it takes is one match... and it all goes up in flames. Whether it's ignorance or arrogance, it's dangerous. Too dangerous, no matter how well-intended. No matter how well thought out. You see, Steven. Sometimes, the best way to straighten people out is to scare 'em. Scare the piss out of 'em. You follow?"

Trevor stares at Steven, waiting for an answer.

Steven nods, unsure.

"That's my boy," Trevor says, jolly again. "As for the plan..."

Trevor opens his jacket. He pulls out a folded piece of paper and hands it to Steven. Steven carefully opens it. But he finds it to be — much to his surprise — nothing more than a cover of a recent issue of *Parade Magazine* featuring the astronomer Carl Sagan.

Doctor Sagan — in his iconic corduroy jacket and red turtleneck sweater — smiles his usual reassuring smile. The cover line beneath him reads: *Nuclear Winter: A Path Where No Man Thought.*

"What the hell is this?" Steven asks, bewildered.

"That's you," Trevor answers, his eyes twinkling.

"What?"

"That's you," Trevor repeats. "Or who you're gonna be."

• • •

"Come on, lad," Trevor says, pushing Steven into their suite's master bathroom. From the faucets to the commode, almost every inch of the room is encased in gold. Trevor nods his approval.

"This'll do," he says. "Here. Put this on."

Trevor slaps a red sweater into Steven's hands before hurrying out.

Steven holds the sweater against himself and shrugs.

I guess it'll fit, he thinks, looking in the mirror.

In the reflection, he spots Hunter unloading their gear from the luggage cart. He timidly pushes the door shut as he unbuttons his shirt and slides it off. Balling up the sweater, Steven sticks his head through the neck opening just as the door flings back open.

Trevor bursts inside, dragging a chair with him. Hunter is right behind him, carrying one of the large black cases.

"There's good," Trevor says, pointing at the vanity.

As Hunter heaves the case onto the countertop, she catches Steven in the mirror, shirtless. Steven quickly sucks in his stomach and stretches his torso, the sweater still bunched comically around his neck. A part of Hunter wants to laugh — he looks ridiculous — but another part doesn't want to look away.

Their eyes linger on each other.

"Sit down," Trevor says to Steven.

And Hunter seizes the opportunity to hurry out the door. Steven exhales, relaxing his tummy. Quickly pulling the turtleneck down, he plops into the chair, combing his fingers through his hair.

"No," Trevor says, slapping Steven's hand away. "Don't touch anything."

As Steven watches Trevor work on his hair in the mirror, he feels the dread growing in the pit of his stomach.

My God, he thinks. *What have I gotten myself into?* Steven recalls all that he's been through in the last twenty-four hours — the near-deaths and close-calls — before remembering the postcard of the Mosholu that prompted this adventure. Folded up in his back pocket, Steven pulls it out.

He sets it on the vanity for Trevor to see.

"You sent this to me," Steven says, looking at the picture of the ship, "knowing full-well I'd lead the O.W.O. straight to her, right to Hunter's doorstep."

Trevor shrugs, playing coy.

"I'm guessing this wasn't the first breadcrumb you left me, was it?" Steven asks, watching Trevor in the mirror. "The clues pointing me toward Hunter, the details on the O.W.O., that was all you, wasn't it?"

Steven turns in his chair and looks at Trevor. "Well?"

Taking his silence as an admission of guilt, Steven deflates. Here he thought it was his investigative prowess that uncovered the truth. But maybe it was Trevor all along.

I'm going to get myself killed, Steven thinks, the revelation reminding him just how far out of his league he really is.

"You laid the groundwork, son," Trevor says, reassuringly. "I just pointed you in the right direction."

Turning toward the vanity, Trevor unlatches a series of locks on the black case. The case hisses as its contents pressurize. Steven watches Trevor carefully lift the top off.

For a moment, a dense fog holds the shape of the lid before collapsing to the vanity. The contents of the case remain hidden in a pool of fog but, along the inner walls, Steven observes two small tanks of liquid nitrogen and a manufacturing placard that reads: *Yakatito Industries — Tokyo, Japan.*

Steven leans closer, intrigued. Exhaling, his breath pushes much of the fog up and out of the case. In the remaining pool, Steven makes out a shape, round and angular... it's the tip of a nose.

Then he spots eyebrows... then a chin.

Steven sits up straight. "What the hell is this?"

Trevor smiles. Leaning down, he blows the remaining fog out of the case, revealing inside... Carl Sagan's face.

"Your disguise," Trevor says.

Trevor's plan is simple: Steven, who just so happens to be of a similar stature of Carl Sagan, is to approach the Secret Service Security Gate claiming to have an appointment. Doctor Sagan, who visits the White House regularly, stressing the importance of scientific knowledge and reason to whoever will listen, is sure to be waved on in, according to Trevor.

Once inside, Steven will find the imposter and subdue him.

Steven, having seen similar plots in countless spy thrillers, assumes he'll use a tranquilizer of some sort, perhaps an aerosol agent...

"You're going to get me killed," Steven says.

"Nonsense," Trevor says, applying a rubber cement-like adhesive to Steven's cheeks.

Stay calm, Steven thinks, locking eyes with himself in the mirror. Three hours. That's how long they have until N.A.T.O. forces are in their optimal positions — thanks to Exercise Able Archer — to launch a devastating first strike on the Soviet Union. Within minutes, certain to hold up their end of the *Mutually Assured Destruction* credo, the Russians will launch their counterattack.

Mutually Assured Destruction — fittingly abbreviated M.A.D. — is the fully embraced theory of nuclear deterrence. The idea is this: if one side launches a preemptive attack, the other side will launch its own full-scale counterattack. In the end, no one wins, and everybody dies, thus creating an uneasy truce between the two superpowers. In effect, each of them holds a loaded gun to the other's temple. Whoever fires first, dies second.

The problem with M.A.D. — in addition to holding billions of innocent lives hostage — is that the system, to execute it properly, leaves little room for error... and the hell with accidents or misunderstandings. *Mutually Assured Destruction* is, by its very nature, bat-shit crazy.

Speaking of bat-shit crazy, Steven thinks, watching Trevor hover over the case. He slides his fingers beneath the skin and carefully lifts the face out of its cradle. Bringing it up to Steven, the skin touches his forehead.

"It's cold," Steven says. "Ice cold."

Trevor nods. "As your body heat warms the synthetic skin, it will bond with your own," Trevor says, carefully positioning the mask. "The key is lining up all the holes. After a few hours, the bond dissolves, and off it comes."

Trevor looks back and forth between the two eye sockets before pressing the forehead and brow onto Steven. Working his way down, he lines up the nose and nostrils before pressing them down.

"Okay. No talking," Trevor says, focusing his attention on the mouth. He lines up the lips and presses them down. Securing the chin, Trevor steps back.

"Not bad," he says, satisfied.

Steven opens his eyes and looks at himself in the mirror.

Holy shit, he thinks.

The synthetic skin blends seamlessly into Steven's own, even matching his pigment. Steven nudges Trevor out of the way so he can have an unimpeded view. *Unbelievable.* Steven snatches the picture of Carl Sagan from the vanity, comparing himself to the image. The likeness is uncanny.

"Impressive, no?" Trevor asks.

"How?" Steven asks, turning and tilting his head about, taking in his new face from every angle he can. "How is this possible? What tech is this?"

"Akito Yakatito," Trevor says, pointing at the manufacture placard on the case. "He is a brilliant man and a personal friend. He has spent decades of his life mastering the art of artificial skin. His synthetic polymers, as you can see, have been groundbreaking. When used as organic threads, they can be woven to create lifelike flesh."

"The imposter in the White House," Steven says, still inspecting his face. "Is this how he faked his way in?"

Trevor eyes him, then shrugs.

"Akito has been known to do work for hire."

"Extraordinary claims require extraordinary evidence," Mikey says, rubbing his eyes in frustration. What he just heard — what Nancy and Quigley, seated across from him, just explained to him — is ridiculous. And he isn't quite sure how to proceed with the conversation.

Minutes ago, Mikey was down in his lowly office in the basement of the West Wing, desperately trying to catch up on paperwork. He was hoping to *maybe* get home at a reasonable time when he got an urgent call from the first lady. He rushed all the way up here to the White House residence as quick as he could... for this?

"Do you know who says that?" he asks. "Carl Sagan. *Doctor* Carl Sagan. The *astronomer,*" Mikey says, emphasizing the words doctor and astronomer while eying Quigley. "It's an aphorism. He uses it when hearing arguments for alien abductions, telekinesis, and other pseudoscience. Astrology included," he adds, glaring at Quigley.

"That man is not my husband," Nancy says, crossing her arms. "He is an imposter. I don't know what he's up to exactly. But I can tell you this: my Ronnie is in danger. We all may be in danger. Which means we have to do something."

Mikey sighs. He forces himself to look at Nancy... to really look at her. There she sits: tired, frail, and desperate. The Reagan's time in the White House hasn't been easy on her. A year and a half ago, her husband was almost assassinated. The attempt on his life rattled Nancy more than the president himself, having laughed it all off with a witty *"I forgot to duck"* non-sequitur.

Nancy, on the other hand, completely unraveled.

Shit, Mikey thinks, feeling guilty. *I can't be upset with her. But this Quigley...*

Thoughts of Grigori Rasputin come to mind, the larger-than-life Russian mystic that had Tsar Nicholas II and the Romanov family wrapped around his fingers.

A self-proclaimed prophet and healer, Rasputin quickly rose through the ranks of Imperial Russia — from a Siberian peasant to the Tsar's most trusted confidant in little over a decade. The divisive yet charismatic Rasputin — and his controversial relationship with the Tsar's wife Alexandra — proved to be too much for Russia's right-wing elite. And after multiple assassination attempts, of which the British Secret Intelligence Service — later renamed MI6 — partook, Rasputin was finally and most-decisively killed in 1916.

But the damage had been done.

Rasputin's influence, combined with the country's crippling income inequality and the apocalyptic First World War, precipitated the Russian Revolution.

A few months after Rasputin's death, Tsar Nicholas II abdicated his throne. And a few years after that, he and the entire Romanov family were brutally murdered by Bolshevik troops. Their bodies were tossed in unmarked graves, and their existence was scrubbed from Soviet history books.

Mikey studies Quigley, looking her over head to toe. With her plaid dress, jade-green jewelry, and platinum-blonde perm,

she seems more likely to throw a Tupperware party than alter the course of world history...

But you never know, he thinks.

Unfortunately, Mikey enabled this relationship more than anybody, having frequently snuck the astrologer into and out of the White House.

A friend, Mikey thought. *Mrs. Reagan just needed a friend.*

Mikey's stalling, and he knows it. He looks at Nancy, forcing a look of compassion onto his face. "And why do you think Mr. Reagan is an imposter?" he asks.

"His hair," Nancy says. "It's just not right."

Mikey blinks. *Is this really about his hair?* He's at a loss for words.

"You saw him today," Nancy continues. "In his daily briefing. You've known Ronnie a long time, Mikey, so you tell me: was that him this morning?" Nancy takes Mikey's hand in hers. "In thirty-one years, Ronnie and I haven't spent a day apart. And today, of all days, I can tell you with absolute certainty — that man is not Ronald Reagan."

Mikey looks at her. He wants to believe her, he desperately wants to believe her. More than anything, Mikey wants this to be true... because the alternative is far scarier: Nancy Reagan has lost her mind. Already, Mikey is planning his next course of action: call the White House physician immediately, come up with a plausible excuse to give the press in the morning, and pray to God this doesn't cost them the re-election campaign.

"And where do you suppose the real president is?" Mikey asks, buying himself more time — more time to think about the serious implications of having the first lady committed to a psychiatric hospital.

Nancy shrugs. She looks at Quigley for help.

"Well, that's what she has to find out, isn't it?" Quigley states, condescendingly.

Mikey glares at her. "Did you get this into her head?" he asks.

"Certainly not," Quigley says. "Mrs. Reagan informed me of her suspicions just as she is informing you. Perhaps, as a friend, you should listen. Don't judge, or squawk. But listen."

Miss Quigley takes Nancy's hand, comforting her.

"I will say this," Quigley adds, eyeing Mikey. "As a clairvoyant such as I am, I am sensitive to other realities beyond our realm. And I, having read the cards and charted the stars, sense doom... impending doom."

"Oh my God," Mikey sighs. "So, the president is an imposter," he says. "Is that what you want me to believe?"

"I don't want you to believe me," Nancy says. "I want you to help me."

Mikey deflates. The last thing he wants is to lose his patience with Mrs. Reagan, especially after everything she has done for him and his career.

Okay, he thinks. *A new approach...*

"What would you like me to do, Mrs. Reagan?" Mikey asks, smiling.

● ● ●

An imposter, Mikey thinks, huffing down the stairwell. *This administration is hitting an all-time low...*

238

Seven years ago, Mikey volunteered for then-Governor Reagan's first presidential campaign. The Reagans, both Ronald and Nancy, put everything they had into that campaign. But failing to unseat the incumbent President Gerald Ford for the Republican ticket was a devastating blow.

Through it all, Mikey — their personal assistant — grew closer and closer to them both. They leaned on him for everything. And, in the ruins of that campaign, Mikey pledged his everlasting loyalty to them.

I was there for them then, he thinks. *And I'm there for them now. But this...*

When Mikey took this job with the administration, he hoped to make the world a better place: to balance the budget, to fight communism, and to help promote American values across the globe. Instead, here he is, fetching the President of the United States because his wife is convinced he's an imposter.

Mikey laughs out loud, skipping the last few steps as he reaches the bottom. He saw the president today... and it sure as hell looked like Ronald Reagan to him. Yes, he was acting strange. Yes, his interest in Able Archer was unusual, to say the least. And as for kicking both Nancy and him out of the office... Mikey slows his pace...

Well, that's something I would never have expected from Mr. Reagan, he thinks.

But regardless, how does the first lady even think something like this could be possible? Cutting across the Center Hall, Mikey waves goodnight to staff members heading home for the evening. The idea of an imposter is so absurd that he can't help picturing the countless — and often ridiculous — disguises worn by the likes of Barbara Bain and Leonard Nimoy in the *Mission: Impossible* television series.

Is that what Mrs. Reagan thinks? That somebody wearing a prosthetic nose with their hair slicked back has us fooled? Does she believe this evil-doer may rip off this Reagan mask at any moment, revealing their true identity and sinister motives?

Maybe it's Leonard Nimoy himself, Mikey chuckles.

Nimoy, the actor most known for playing the role of Mr. Spock in *Star Trek*, was staunchly opposed to Reagan's gubernatorial campaign, having criticized the future president repeatedly over his lack of relevant experience. And then there was Nixon... Nimoy actually campaigned feverishly for George McGovern, the democratic anti-war candidate of 1972.

So maybe Nimoy is a sore loser.

Stepping outside onto the West Colonnade, Mikey stops in his tracks. Ahead of him, he is shocked to see darkness. The Oval Office, the secretary's office, practically the entire West Wing is dark. Not a single lamp is lit.

That's odd, Mikey thinks, continuing on. He knew the president had relieved most of his staff from their regular duties (*also strange*) but, you'd think somebody would have at least turned a light on...

Oh no, Mikey thinks. *What if... what if the president isn't even here?!*

Mikey's heart skips at the thought. Could the president have been whisked off again in Marine One without his knowledge?

Mikey sprints along the walkway, his tie flapping into his face. He slides into the glass-paned door. Fumbling with the handle, he throws it open and finds...

Agent Bancroft standing in the dark, the Emergency War Order Officer next to him — the nuclear football attaché in hand. Mikey, out of breath, looks between the two of them, both relieved and irritated at the same time.

"Why the hell are you standing in the dark?"

"The president did not request the lights be turned on," Agent Bancroft says.

Mikey nods. *A dumb answer but okay*, he thinks, walking over to the secretary's desk. "Well. Let's just..." He turns on a lamp, illuminating the room. "That's better," Mikey says.

He approaches the office door, but Agent Bancroft holds his ground. "The president wants no interruptions," Bancroft says.

Mikey blinks. Agent Bancroft, love him or hate him, can be a real hardass.

"Listen," Mikey says, though pleading with this guy tends to be futile. "Mrs. Reagan is expecting the president. If you want to explain to her why we left him sitting in the Oval Office — in the dark no less — all night long, be my guest. Me... I'd rather just get Mr. Reagan back home. *Dallas* will be on soon. And the first lady is waiting."

Agent Bancroft doesn't move, he doesn't even bat an eye.

"Fine then," Mikey says, throwing his hands up in defeat. "I'll go back up to the residence and get her. I'll bring her right down here to you. And you can answer to her."

Agent Bancroft considers... and finally falters.

"Very well," he says, stepping aside.

"Billions and billions," Steven says, begrudgingly.

Sitting next to Reagan on the bed, Steven stares at his own now-unfamiliar reflection in their room's full-length mirror. From his bushy eyebrows to his trademark turtleneck sweater, even Steven has to admit that he's a dead ringer for the celebrity astronomer. But the absurdity of the circumstances hangs around Steven's neck like a noose.

"No, no," Reagan says. "You have to roll your consonants. Listen to me when I say it, son. Bill-ions and bill-ions," he says, contorting his lips as only a true thespian can do.

Steven looks like Carl Sagan. But he also has to sound like him. *Billions and billions* was a term used by Sagan repeatedly to convey the enormity of our universe in *Cosmos: A Personal Voyage* — the thirteen-part television series that cemented him as America's most prominent science advocate. *Billions* of stars. In *billions* of galaxies. Unfortunately, the phrase quickly became a popular-shtick used by countless comedians, much to Sagan's chagrin.

"Come on now," Reagan says, prodding Steven.

"Bill-ions and bill-ions," Steven says, rolling his eyes more than his consonants.

Reagan sighs. "Son, you've got to get into this." The two sit in silence as the president considers a new approach. "I got it," he says, jumping to his feet. "I want you to think of this as Hollywood's next big blockbuster. And I want you to think of Carl Sagan as a role of a lifetime. What's your name again, son?"

"Steven Leonard, sir."

"Excellent," Reagan says, gesturing toward an imaginary marquee on the wall. "I can see it now in big, bright lights. Steven Leonard is... Carl Sagan in..." He pauses for dramatic effect. "*The Day the World Was Saved.*"

Reagan looks at Steven, eager for approval. But gets nothing.

"Well, we can work on the title later," Reagan shrugs. "But just imagine how great that movie poster will look," he says, staring at what Steven assumes is the imaginary movie poster.

My God, Steven thinks. I am going to get myself killed. Humanity is on the brink. And the President of the United States is basking in the glory of some make-believe Hollywood production.

Dismayed, Steven looks out of the room. He spots Hunter and Trevor setting up a two-way radio system. On the coffee table in front of her, Hunter positions a large microphone before picking up a pea-sized micro-transmitter/receiver earpiece. Flipping her hair back, she slides it into her ear.

"Test. Test one, two." Hunter says.

The more I look at her, the more beautiful she is, Steven thinks, admiring the way her lips move when she counts.

"Test one, two, three."

If only I knew what she thought about me...

Steven's eyes drop to the floor.

She has every reason to hate me, he thinks. Every step of this journey, he's managed to fuck up something somehow.

Because that's what I am, Steven thinks.

A fuck up.

Steven looks at Reagan. The president stares at his own reflection, silently pronunciating *bill-ions and bill-ions*. Leaning off the edge of the bed, Steven nudges the bedroom door closed.

Maybe I can get out of this without letting her down.

"Mister President," Steven whispers. "Can we talk about this plan?"

"The whole 'you sneak into the White House as Carl Sagan' plan?" Reagan asks. "I love it."

"It'd make a great movie, sir," Steven says. "And you..." Steven points at the president. "You should definitely star in it, playing yourself, of course. But... I just... I don't know..."

"*The Day the World Was Saved*," Reagan says, slicking his hair back in the mirror. "Fantastic."

"I mean... yeah, it's a great movie title, sir," Steven says, appeasing him. "But seriously. Are you sure? Are you sure you like *this plan*? For me... *me*," Steven emphasizes himself, tapping his chest, "to sneak into the White House? I mean, a lot is at stake, sir. In fact, *everything* is at stake."

As Reagan considers, Steven glances at the door again, making sure it's closed. The last thing he wants is Hunter to know he's a coward.

"Okay, here's the thing," Steven says, more determined. "It's a horrible idea." Steven picks up the phone off the nightstand and offers it to the president. "Are you sure there isn't somebody you can call? Like an emergency, toll-free presidential hotline? An 800 number, perhaps? To the C.I.A. or F.B.I. maybe?"

Reagan shrugs. "Without the authentication bracelet, I'd be the imposter," he says. "No, Steven. You stealing it back for me really does seem like the best plan. It keeps this imposter from launching the attack, and it validates me as... me."

Steven's head drops into his hands, defeated. "Sir. Listen to me, please. I'm not cut out for this..."

"Son," Reagan says, placing a reassuring hand on his shoulder. "Maybe you're *exactly* cut out for this. From what I reckon, you're one hell of an investigative journalist... for *Parade Magazine* no less." Steven lifts his head to correct him but gives up. "You tracked down one of the most secretive secret agents in the world, and you uncovered the O.W.O.'s evil plot to take over the world. And, to top it all off, you rescued me, the President of the United States. So, I think it bears repeating: maybe you're *exactly* cut out for this."

"Sir. I know how this must all look to you," Steven says. "But I didn't do any of that shit. I've just been dragged along for the ride. Hell, I don't even work for *Parade Magazine*. I'm a fake. A fraud." Steven can't help but laugh. "I'm a loser, believe me. I've managed to make every wrong decision in my life. And now I'm in way over my head."

The president studies him. "You know, there's an old Hollywood saying that seems more than fitting here and now if you ask me," Reagan says, smirking. *"Fake it until you make it."*

The president sits down next to Steven.

"Now, repeat after me, son. Bill-ions and bill-ions."

Steven blinks. *Fake it until you make it? — is he serious?*

Looking Reagan over, it's easy to imagine a cowboy hat atop his head and a movie-prop six-shooter slung around his waist.

This man is a fake, Steven thinks. *Ronald Reagan is an actor. Acting is what he does. And president,* Steven muses, *is just another role he plays on TV. He faked it... until he made it.*

"Bill-ions and bill-ions," Reagan repeats.

Yeah, Steven thinks, wide-eyed. *That's roughly how many people are going to die...*

● ● ●

Hunter sets the earpiece down on the table and gives Trevor a thumbs up.

"Good to go," she says.

Noticing the bedroom door closed, she thinks of Steven on the other side. The thought of him going on this leg of the mission alone leaves her feeling uneasy.

He's going to get himself killed, she thinks, unholstering one of her Berettas. *But why should his death matter,* she muses, cleaning the weapon. *In the face of a nuclear holocaust, it doesn't,* she thinks. *But still...*

Over the years, Hunter has hardened herself to the fact that most people that enter her life don't end up living very much longer. Few partners, few lovers, have kept pace with her. A misstep here, bad timing there, and the next thing she knows, they're dead on the floor behind her. Her only solution: don't let anybody in.

Then why the hell did you welcome him into the cabin?

Thumbing 9mm rounds into the magazine, she glances at Trevor sitting across the room. He's always been the smart one, the idea-man. He calls the plays — like a coach on the sidelines — and Hunter executes. The rapport between them has led to ample success.

He always has a plan, Hunter thinks. *But you don't always know what they entail.*

Hunter's is a profession in which trust does not come easy. But Hunter trusts Trevor, she always has. The day she lost Anatoly — back in Barrow, Alaska — Trevor lost him too.

Birds of a feather flock together...

Hunter snaps the magazine back in place and reholsters the weapon. Walking to the conference table, she approaches a black briefcase lying flat on top of it.

Trevor has always promised me a way out, she thinks, running her hand atop its smooth finish. That was the deal they made the day she replaced Anatoly.

Maybe it's time I take it.

But Steven...

She liked how he watched her back in the missile facility. She felt appreciated. And that was... nice. Sure, the purpose of her killing is to spare billions of innocent lives, but that doesn't always make pulling the trigger any easier. Having somebody there, somebody like Steven — not competing with her or challenging her — but merely standing by her side... that was nice.

Steven, she thinks, *is nice.*

● ● ●

The door swings open, and Hunter enters the room, startling Steven. He's still seated next to Reagan, still trying to convince him their plan is a disaster-in-the-making.

"We're all set out here," Hunter says. "You ready?"

Steven is speechless. He glances between Hunter and Reagan, a deer in headlights.

"What's wrong?" Hunter asks, reading his anguish.

"Steven wants to quit," Reagan says, matter-of-factly.

"What?" Steven scoffs, jumping to his feet, now glaring at the president.

"He was just telling me he's a fake," Reagan says, chuckling. He stands up and straightens his tie. "A loser. And that he's not cut out for this."

"This is nothing new," Hunter says.

But Hunter knows fear when she sees it, and looking into Steven's eyes now, it's clear as day: the kid is terrified. And despite him stalking her for years, despite him forcing his way into her life, Hunter is suddenly struck with compassion — a feeling she hasn't felt in years.

"I didn't say that," Steven says, defensive. He forces a laugh.

"Well now, Steven," Reagan says, prodding him. "Those were the exact words you used, son. A fake and a loser. That's you, according to you."

"Well, not in that context," Steven retorts. He reaches for his corduroy jacket. "I'm ready, Hunter. Let's do this."

"You don't want to do this?" she asks, genuinely concerned.

"What?" Steven asks. "Don't be absurd."

"Steven, listen to me," she says, eyeing Trevor through the door. "If you don't want to do this, speak up. It's not too late..."

"I want to do it, Hunter," Steven says, flustered and embarrassed.

The one person he didn't want knowing he was a coward.

249

"Steven, you can walk away..." Hunter says.

"Walk away?" Steven snaps, forcing a laugh. "Who me? No way, Hunter. Not this guy."

Hunter and Reagan watch him fumble with his coat as if his hands and arms are boycotting his own actions. Finally sliding it on, Steven hurries out the door, leaving Hunter bewildered and Reagan amused.

Out in the suite, Trevor is happy to greet Steven.

"All set, are we?" he asks.

"Yes," Steven says. "Hell yes," he adds, eyeing Hunter and Reagan as they join them.

"Steven doesn't want to do this," Hunter says, arms crossed.

"Really?" Trevor asks, with mock surprise. "Steven, is this true?"

"Absolutely not," Steven says, appalled at the suggestion. He paces back and forth, erratic. Almost colliding with Hunter, he locks eyes with her.

She's beautiful, Steven thinks, his thoughts ricocheting inside his head. *Beautiful even when she's lost all respect for somebody...*

I'm shit to her... Worthless...

Christ — Steven thinks, in a sudden moment of clarity — *billions of lives hang in the balance... and I'm more worried about what this woman thinks of me...*

Steven turns his back on the others. Feeling their gazes, their doubts, he takes a deep breath.

The sooner I get out of this hotel room, the better, he thinks.

"I'm ready," Steven says, not convincing in the least. He turns to the others, looking each of them in the eye. "What's the hold up here?" he asks, finally settling on Trevor.

Keep moving, he tells himself. *Don't stop now.*

Steven spots the earpiece radio transmitter/receiver on the table and hurries over to it. With his hands trembling, he struggles to slide the piece into his ear.

"This is a bad idea," Hunter says to Trevor, gesturing toward Steven — clearly he's lost his shit.

"You know the mission, Hunter," Trevor says. "You know what's at stake. And we're running out of time. Every minute, every second that passes, the odds of a launch increases tenfold. If you have a better idea, speak up. If not... Steven goes."

Trevor eyes Hunter, knowing she's got nothing.

"You're going to get him killed," Hunter says, defeated.

"I want to go," Steven says, stepping between them. "I'm ready."

"Steven," Hunter says, softening up to him.

"I'm ready," Steven says, picking up the briefcase off the conference table. "I am so ready. Billions and billions," he says, walking toward the door. *"Bill-ions and bill-ions,"* he repeats, more convincingly.

"The kid's ready," Trevor says with finality.

"Break a leg," Reagan says, proud of his understudy.

Steven opens the door and steps out into the hallway. He turns back toward Hunter, knowing this may be the last he ever sees her.

Be brave, he thinks.

Be the man Hunter wants in her life.

Steven thinks of Clint Eastwood and Charles Bronson and Sean Connery. And he channels their machoism — their dumb bravado.

"Sneaking into the White House, stopping an imposter, preventing World War Three," Steven says, his voice cracking. "Yeah," he says — *this is it, his big moment, his very own death wish* — "that's a good way to..."

But the door swings shut, cutting him off mid-sentence.

24

Mikey steps into the dark Oval Office. Seated motionless behind the desk, silhouetted by the flashing red aircraft light atop the Washington Monument, sits a figure. As Mikey's eyes adjust, he recognizes the shape of the person's hair to be — much to his relief — that of Ronald Reagan.

Shuffling across the carpet, careful not to bump into any furniture, Mikey can't help but feel unnerved. Why is the president sitting here in the dark?

Mikey's mind dwells on the tone Reagan had taken with Nancy and himself that morning. It was both threatening and ominous. He swallows hard.

What if Mrs. Reagan is right?

Mikey reaches for a lamp and clicks on the light.

Again, he is relieved to see Ronald Reagan sitting at the desk, staring back at him.

This is ridiculous, Mikey scoffs.

He would know if this is an imposter, he thinks, confidently walking to the next lamp. Ronald Reagan is still Ronald Reagan: a down-to-earth everyman who enjoys old spy thrillers as much as anyone. And without a doubt, if anybody would get a laugh out of this truly absurd conspiracy theory that Nancy has concocted in her head, it's Ronald Reagan.

Clicking on the second light, Mikey giggles. "You're not going to believe this, sir," he says, standing before the president. "But you have Mrs. Reagan all spooked upstairs, going on about you being some sort of imposter."

Mikey walks to the window and gazes out at the city's lights. "I tried talking some sense into her, sir. But once she gets an idea in her head, she can be awfully stubborn."

Mikey notices the president has sat silent. *Odd.*

"Can you believe it?" Mikey asks, forcing a laugh as he glances uneasily back at him.

"The first lady suspects I am an imposter?"

"Yes, sir," he says.

"She must be eliminated. Bring her to me."

"Sir?" Mikey asks, stunned.

"Bring her to me," the imposter says, rising to his feet. "Or be killed yourself."

Mikey blinks. *Nancy Reagan was right.* The President of the United States is an imposter. And, more alarmingly, has threatened to kill both the first lady and himself.

The optics of this won't look good to voters...

"Yes," Mikey says, buying himself time to think. "Right away, sir."

The imposter watches Mikey shuffle across the room.

Cracking open the door, Mikey finds Agent Bancroft standing at attention, the SIG Sauer handgun visible in the holster beneath his suit.

"Agent Bancroft," Mikey whispers, gesturing him to come closer. "May I have a word with you?"

Bancroft glances at Mikey but doesn't move.

"Agent Bancroft," Mikey continues, keeping his voice as quiet as possible. "What if I were to suggest that the man in here with me, in the Oval Office right now, isn't actually the president. But an imposter..."

"Let me just stop you there," Bancroft says, eyeing him. "If you were to make such a suggestion, deeming you both a mental and physical liability, I would have no choice but to remove you from the premises immediately."

Bancroft smiles, big and bright. The idea of throwing Mikey out on his ass brings him much pleasure.

"Of course," Mikey says. "Thank you, Agent Bancroft. Your input is greatly appreciated."

Mikey closes the door and backs into the office.

Well, it was worth a shot, he thinks. But he knew there'd be no way in hell that Agent Bancroft or any member of the Secret Service would take Mikey's word over the president's — *or who they think is the president.*

Especially while he's wearing that bracelet...

The bracelet, Mikey thinks, his eyes darting toward the imposter's wrist. Sure enough, the top-secret authentication bracelet is there, just below the tailored cuff.

Oh, that's not good.

The imposter eyes Mikey, noting the attention he's affixed to the bracelet.

What does he want? Mikey thinks, his mind racing to put the pieces together. *To do something,* he answers. *But for whom? The Russians? What would they want? To ease Cold War tensions perhaps... but this would be a foolish way to do it.*

Admittedly though, the Cold War is at its coldest. Just last spring, Reagan ratcheted up his own hawkish rhetoric when he referred to the Soviet Union as *"the Evil Empire"* — as if he was casting them as villains in the latest *Star Wars* film.

Needless to say, that didn't go over well in Moscow. But instead of backing off on the strongman statement, Reagan doubled-down on the provocations, claiming that nuclear warfare was nothing more than an extension of the *"age-old struggle between good and evil."*

For all intents and purposes, it seemed Ronald Reagan was in favor of actually using nuclear weapons. But in reality, Mikey doubts the president has ever really grasped just how dangerous the Cold War actually is, or how ill-advised such statements are.

Ronald Reagan, Mikey knows from experience, relates just about every situation to movies... movies he's starred in, in particular. Life as a Hollywood leading man was far easier for somebody like Reagan to process. And infinitely easier than the nuanced life of the President of the United States.

In movies, the good guys stand tall, speak strong, and, no matter how dire the circumstance, always win.

But Able Archer, Mikey thinks, snapping his attention back to the imposter. Whoever this is standing here in front of him, he had a peculiar interest in the military exercise about to commence on the other side of the globe. If anything, the Russians would want to throw a wet blanket on that immediately. So, whoever planted the imposter here in the White House, *it's probably not the Soviets...*

Wall Street? It wouldn't be the first time an evil corporation attempted their own greed-motivated coup d'état. But they'd be hard-pressed to deregulate business and lower corporate taxes faster than the free-market-loving Ronald Reagan. *So, it's probably not Wall Street...*

The imposter inches toward Mikey.

Our own military?

Mikey has met his fair share of communist-hating war hawks in the armed forces. These are military men who have focused their entire careers on one tangible goal: World War Three. Without it, have these men wasted their lives? Is the lack of global confrontation considered a personal failure? Admiral William J. Falke, Chairman of the Joint Chiefs of Staff, comes to Mikey's mind...

A military coup, he thinks. With a convincing imposter in the White House, the public would be none the wiser.

But saner minds prevail, Mikey thinks, shaking off his suspicions of such a conspiracy. *Saner minds always prevail...*

Setting his jaw, Mikey stares down the imposter. *That's what Ronald Reagan would do*, he thinks. *Stand tall and speak strong. After all, the good guys always win...*

"Who are you, and what do you want?" Mikey asks, his voice booming.

But before he realizes it, the imposter has his hands around his neck. He lifts Mikey clear off the ground, slamming him against the wall. Mikey swats at him. But it's futile. The imposter is too strong, too aggressive.

"Help," Mikey gasps, his eyes bulging. "Help me."

Mikey's hand brushes against the bracelet on the imposter's wrist...

The authentication bracelet.

Mikey thinks of the Emergency War Order Officer on the other side of the door, *the nuclear football* handcuffed to his wrist. Then his eyes dart to the desk across the room, *the Resolute Desk...*

Inside that 19th-century oak desk is *The Button*. Though its actual existence is written off as a myth, in reality, there is a real, tangible button. It's red and glows and makes a very solid ka-click sound when pressed. When the button was designed, the idea was to give the Commander in Chief one last jarring-bit of reality, a reminder of the stark consequences associated with pressing it.

The bracelet, the football, the button. Everything a president — or an imposter — would need to start a nuclear war.

Christ-almighty, Mikey thinks, the reality of it all coming on harder than the life being squeezed from him.

This man is going to start a nuclear war.

For Mikey, as the blood is cut off to his brain, everything begins to go dark. But in his ears echoes the voice of Roger Fisher. Fisher, a renowned arms negotiator, had long stated that the system by which a president can authorize a nuclear attack was far too distant and removed. His suggestion was quite simple: that a launch authentication code be placed in a little capsule and then implanted into the heart of a courageous volunteer.

Just as the Emergency War Order Officer accompanies the president, so too would this volunteer. But instead of carrying a leather attaché, all this volunteer would have is a large butcher knife.

In the event the president ever wanted to launch a nuclear weapon, the only way the authenticated order could be given was if the president — with his or her own hands — killed the volunteer and removed the implant themselves.

When hearing this suggestion, officials at the Pentagon were appalled. *"The horror,"* they replied. *"Having to kill someone would distort the President's judgment,"* they commented. *"He might never push the button."*

The horror... of taking one innocent life... before taking billions more... *I guess I'm the first to die,* Mikey thinks, feeling his neck and trachea crush beneath the imposter's unrelenting grip.

The horror, he thinks, as the last of his life expires, and he succumbs to the darkness...

The horror.

PART FOUR

25

Standing along Pennsylvania Avenue, Steven stares at the White House, his heart pounding. The neoclassical architecture, the Roman columns of the portico, it's all pretty intimidating right now.

Billions of people are poised to die, Steven thinks. *All because I'm too chicken shit to show Hunter Gunne just how chicken shit I really am.* What an insane *Catch-22* to find oneself in, Steven muses... *I'm too cowardly to be a coward.*

In Steven's ear, he hears a distinct pop as Trevor turns on their microphone back at the Hay-Adams Hotel. "Steven," Trevor says, munching on chips, "what are you doing just standing there?"

"I'm thinking," Steven whispers, his breath misting in the cold night.

Trevor takes another handful of chips into his mouth.

"Are you eating up there?" Steven asks, offended.

The chewing stops. And for a moment, all Steven hears is static.

"No," Trevor replies, his mouth now seemingly clear.

Across the street is the Secret Service's primary guard post. Beyond this gate, the driveway curves up to the North Portico — the main entrance of the White House. Already, several guards, each clutching a submachine gun, have their eyes trained on Steven.

Steven watches them watching him.

"Now listen to me, Steven," Trevor says in his ear. "All you have to do is walk up to the guard post and tell them your name. You're Doctor Carl Sagan, scientific advisor to N.A.S.A., host of the popular television series, and an all-around nice guy. Tell them you're here to discuss the president's nuclear policies and the threat they pose to all of humanity."

"Threat to all of humanity?" Steven hears Reagan ask, muffled.

Shit, Steven thinks. Unlike the O.W.O. goons back at the missile facility – the president's kidnappers – *these guards are the real deal*. Outsmarting them might not be so easy… or even possible.

What would Hunter do? She'd probably charge right at them, guns blazing — she's not exactly subtle.

But these guys, they're Secret Service agents, Steven thinks. *They're just doing their jobs.*

Maybe that's why Trevor sent me, Steven concludes.

He knows I won't kill everybody.

"Steven?" Trevor asks.

"Yeah?" Steven replies.

"Start walking."

"I will," Steven says, defensively. "Just hold on a second."

Steven considers how he must look to the guards eyeing him — a man who, to them, is standing in the shadows, briefcase in hand, talking to himself.

I'm as suspicious as it gets, Steven thinks, frozen with fear.

He closes his eyes and thinks of Hunter.

She's the answer to his prayers, yeah. But she's also a woman of action. When he set out to interview Hunter at her cabin, a culmination of years' worth of work, he never expected that their roles would reverse…

That Steven would be the one thrust toward danger. And that Hunter would be stuck in the living room hoping for the best.

He takes a deep breath and exhales slowly.

Do it for her, he thinks. But Steven still finds himself unable to move, as if his feet were cemented to the ground. Across the street, he notices the guards pointing in his direction.

"Hunter," he says, his mouth dry.

There's a reluctance on the other end.

"Yeah?" Hunter asks, cold and distant.

"How do you do it?" Steven asks.

"Do what?"

"You know," Steven says. "What you do. How do you do it?"

"Are you asking for advice?" she asks.

"Yeah," Steven says. "I guess. If you wouldn't mind."

Steven hears the microphone slide closer to Hunter.

"Your heart's pounding right now, isn't it?" she asks. "Your mind's racing?"

"Yeah," Steven answers.

"Embrace that," Hunter says. "That's your adrenaline coursing through you. Harness that energy and use it."

"Okay," Steven says. But he hesitates. "How?"

"Steven," she says, her voice softer. "I'm going to ask you a question right now. And it's the most important question you might ever be asked. Are you ready?"

Steven shrugs. "Sure," he says, flummoxed.

With growing anticipation, he listens to the static coming through his earpiece, waiting for Hunter. *The most important question he's ever been asked? What could it possibly be?*

"Steven," Hunter says. "Do you dance?"

Steven blinks. "Excuse me?"

"Imagine a waltz," Hunter continues. "Right now, where you are, in front of you. The music's begun. Do you hear it?"

Steven, still standing on Pennsylvania Avenue, glances around, uncertain. "No."

"Step out onto the dance floor, Steven," Hunter says. "Focus. Be present. You're in it. You're a part of it. Know that the waltz has begun, let it lead you. Don't fall behind. But don't rush it either. Be disciplined, be patient. And if worse comes to worst," Hunter concludes, "just remember, Steven: they're all idiots."

Standing in the silence, Steven processes this.

"That's what you do?" he asks.

"Yep," Hunter says. "Every time."

Steven nods. He imagines Hunter in a dance hall. She's wearing a beautiful flowing dress. Her hair, her lips, her eyes — exquisite. She smiles at him, beckons him.

Embrace that, Steven thinks,

"Steven?" Trevor asks, sliding the mic to himself. "You good?"

"Yeah," Steven says, unsure. "Thanks."

Step onto the dance floor, Steven tells himself, willing his foot to step off the curb. But he's picturing Hunter greeting him, offering him a dance. *Know that the dance has begun*, he thinks, crossing the street. But he's imagining sliding his arm around her waist. *Don't fall behind. Don't rush it*, he thinks, approaching the guard post. But in his head, he's dancing with Hunter...

Nose to nose, her breath on his lips, he melts into her arms.

266

They're all idiots…

"Can we help you, sir?" the nearest guard asks. Steven feels their eyes sweeping over him, appraising him as a threat. He forces a smile.

"Hello," he says. "I'm Carl Sagan…"

"Doctor," Trevor shouts in Steven's ear.

And the guards watch Steven flinch inexplicably.

"*Doctor* Carl Sagan," Steven says. "I am here to discuss the extreme risks posed by the administration's current nuclear policies and the incredible threat they pose to all of humanity…"

"Again?" the guard interrupts, jarring Steven.

Again? Steven thinks.

How the hell am I supposed to respond to that?

Steven pauses, hoping for some input from Trevor. But instead, all he hears is Trevor munching on chips again.

"Weren't you here just last week, *Doctor* Sagan?" the other guard asks, adding a peculiar emphasis to *doctor*.

Steven notes the condescension in the guard's tone.

What is he implying?

"Just say yes," Trevor says.

"Yes," Steven says, noncommittally.

The guards exchange a disapproving look. "Yeah, alright," the first guard says, waving Steven along. "Let's go."

Shocked, Steven hurries up to the post. As he's about to step inside, another guard blocks the door with his arm.

"What are you doing?" the guard asks.

"Don't I have to sign in?" Steven asks, confused.

"That won't be necessary," the guard says, condescendingly.

Steven's mind races as he's lead through the gate.

Won't be necessary?

Shouldn't they pat me down?

Inspect my briefcase?

Anything?

This isn't right, Steven thinks, clutching the briefcase to his chest as he's escorted up the driveway.

Up close and in person, the White House is now much larger than he expected. Imposing and unnerving. They approach the North Portico, the massive chandelier hanging from above. One of the guards holds the door open for Steven. Hesitating at the threshold, Steven glances at each of the men.

"Here you are, *doctor*," the nearest guard says, shoving Steven inside.

As the door shuts behind him, Steven realizes he's done it. He looks out through the windows and watches the guards head back down the driveway. Steven is alone and unattended.

Holy shit, he thinks, elated...

I'm in the White House.

Before him is the Entrance Hall, the expansive formal foyer where numerous presidents have greeted countless dignitaries from across the globe.

"I'm in," Steven says, his voice echoing in the darkened hall.

"That's my boy," Trevor says.

"Nice work, son," Reagan adds.

Steven waits, hopeful that Hunter might chime in.

"Is Hunter there?" he asks, impatient.

"Nice job," she says, distant.

"Now pitter-patter, Steven," Trevor says. "We're running out of time."

"Okay," Steven says. "Where am I going?"

The microphone slides toward Reagan.

"I reckon it's TV time with the missus," he says. "If I were me, I'd be upstairs in our private sitting room, the television set on, and a TV tray across my lap. So that's as good a place as any to start. From where you're standing, head left. You'll find yourself a staircase. Take 'em up."

"I see it," Steven says, his shoes squeaking on the marble floor. The Grand Staircase is a broad, red-carpeted stairwell, overlooked by the portraits of dozens of dead presidents.

I can't believe it, Steven thinks, hurrying up two steps at a time. *The actual White House...*

Reaching the landing, Steven stops. Blocking his way are two Secret Service agents.

"Hold it right there," one of them says.

"Oh shit," Steven says.

"What is it?" Trevor asks.

"Oh, this isn't good," Steven mumbles. He retreats down the stairs only to find another pair of agents approaching from below, boxing him in. "This is very bad."

"Steven?" Hunter asks.

"Where do you think you're going, Dr. Sagan?" one of the guards asks. Glancing between them all, Steven raises his hands in surrender.

"Are you lost, Dr. Sagan?"

"No," Steven says, on the verge of panic. "Yes. I don't know."

The nearest guard nods, as the others struggle to keep straight faces. "Alright, sir," the guard says, agitated. He grabs Steven's arm and leads him down the stairs. "I think you better come with us."

"Stay calm," Trevor says. "Just go along with them. Understand?"

Steven blinks. In a dizzying panic, he can see Trevor in his head, lounging in luxury back at the Hay-Adams Hotel. He can see him with that smarmy look on his face. Smug and pompous as he obnoxiously eats potato chips. And all Steven wants to do... is punch him in the face.

This was his idea, Steven thinks.

This was his stupid idea.

Just go along with them, Trevor said...

"What the hell else do you think I'm going to do?" Steven snaps.

The agents surrounding him stop, stunned. They look at Steven like he's completely out of his mind... or on drugs.

"Excuse me?" the lead guard asks. "What did you just say?"

Dear God, Steven thinks, white as a ghost.

I said that out loud.

"Say something," Trevor says. "Cut the tension. Come on, Steven. You can do this."

Steven laughs nervously, his hands trembling.

"Do you know how many stars there are in the cosmos?" he asks, his delivery slow and methodical. Steven waits for an answer as if this is a punchline to a joke. "Billions and billions," he says, nailing his Carl Sagan impression.

"Come on," the guard says as the other agents hold back laughter. "Let's go."

The guard drags Steven down the stairs. They dump out into the Entrance Hall and cross to the red-carpeted Cross Hall.

Jesus, where are they taking me? Steven wonders as they shove him through the Palm Room and down the long narrow corridors of the West Wing.

Before Steven knows it, they stop at a closed office door.

"Wait here," the guard says.

"Where's here?" Trevor asks in Steven's ear.

The guard knocks lightly on the door before slipping inside. Steven tries peeking into the room but sees nothing.

"Sir," Steven hears the guard say inside. "We found him wandering the halls."

Steven leans closer, straining to hear.

"Send him in," an unfamiliar voice says. Steven gulps. He glances around at the men surrounding him — each now avoiding his gaze, their demeanor having changed entirely — now more tense, more serious.

That can't be good, Steven thinks.

"Let's go," the lead guard says, poking his head out through the door.

Steven shuffles into the room, scared shitless. He turns the corner and finds — seated behind his desk, piles of paperwork spread out before him — George H. W. Bush, Vice President of the United States.

"George Bush," Steven mutters aloud. "George fucking Bush."

"Yes. Always a pleasure, Dr. Sagan," Bush says, pushing his wire-rim glasses on his nose. "Please sit. Please..." he says, gesturing to a chair in front of his desk.

Steven obeys, setting the briefcase down by his feet.

"Is that Poppy Bush?" Reagan asks in Steven's ear. "You tell him, Ronnie says hello!"

"The president says hello," Steven says, oblivious to the absurdity of the statement.

"Enough of the pleasantries, Sagan. George Bush is a busy man," the vice president says, referring to himself in the third person. "Now show me what you have in that briefcase of yours."

"In my briefcase?" Steven asks, wondering for the first time himself what could actually be in it, realizing it might be more than just a prop. "What *is* in the briefcase?" Steven asks aloud, directed at Trevor and the others back in the Hay-Adams Hotel.

"That's what I'm asking," Bush says, irritated. "Now, let's see it."

Steven picks up the briefcase from the floor, feeling its weight in his hand.

Oh, God. What have I brought with me?

The thought of checking its contents never even occurred to him. For all he knows, it could be a bomb. *This could be a suicide mission*, Steven thinks. *And I was stupid enough to march right along with it...*

"Come on, Sagan. Get on with it," Bush says, circling his fingers.

"Just open the briefcase, Steven," Trevor says in his ear.

Steven sets the briefcase on the desk. He releases the first latch, then the second. Holding his breath, he opens it...

Oh. My. God.

In the open briefcase is a kilo of marijuana — two pounds of it, bright and green, and packaged in clear plastic. Steven Leonard has snuck illegal drugs into the White House, and now, here at the vice president's desk, it's out in the open.

"Well?" George Bush says. "Let's see it."

Steven blinks. As far as options go, he has none. And he knows it. Steven takes a deep breath, slowly sinking into his chair as he spins the briefcase toward Bush. The vice president's eyes go wide. Picking up the brick, he sniffs it.

"The boys are going to love this," he says, pleased.

"The boys?" Steven asks.

"The boys," Bush repeats. "You know..." he gestures toward a set of photos. In them, his eldest sons George and Jeb are pictured — both wearing shit-eating grins on their faces and cowboy hats on their heads. "They're going to love this."

"I don't believe it," Steven mumbles, his head falling into his hands.

"Well, they do go through it mighty fast," Bush says, defensively. "But this is the first I've heard you complain about it."

Steven stares at him in disbelief.

"Now," Bush says, all business. "How much do I owe you?"

26

Laughter. Standing outside the vice president's office, Trevor and Hunter's laughter rings in Steven's ears.

"Did I seriously just sell drugs to George Bush?" Steven asks, wearily.

"Yes," Trevor answers, holding back tears. "And you made a bloody good show of it, chum," he says, bursting out again.

Steven blinks. It's no surprise that Carl Sagan — *the actual Carl Sagan* — is a frequent marijuana user. The man even wrote numerous essays — under a pseudonym — lauding the creative and scientific insights it provided him throughout his career.

But a drug dealer? Steven thinks. *No wonder the Secret Service whisked me through security. No wonder they found my nonsensical outbursts amusing...*

They thought I was high.

Steven shakes his head. He would expect as much from Trevor, being the self-absorbed asshole that he is. But as for Hunter, hearing her laughing at him... that stings. He can picture the two of them exchanging another wad of cash, the winnings of another wager on whether Steven — their de facto fool — did or did not get himself killed.

"Well, I'm glad you're having such a great time," Steven says, hurt. "Is there anything else you want to tell me about this mission? Any other surprises? Or am I just supposed to stumble into them for your amusement?"

The laughter putters out.

"Steven," Hunter says. "Get your ass upstairs."

Thank you, Steven thinks, relieved to be back on task.

Maybe a little less gullible next time, he hopes.

● ● ●

Buchanan... McKinley... Harrison... The presidential portraits blur by as Steven sprints down the West Wing corridor. Garfield... Coolidge... Johnson.... Steven bursts into the Entrance Hall, his footsteps echoing off the high ceilings as he darts toward the Grand Staircase. He hits the stairs in stride, leaping up them two at a time.

Reaching the top step, he peers out, looking up and down the residence hall.

"The coast is clear," Steven whispers, assuming the Secret Service is off doing whatever it is they do when not escorting White House drug dealers to their prospective clients.

"The living room is the last door on the left," Reagan says in his ear. "If I was him, that's where I'd be."

"Gotcha," Steven says, watching the flickering light of a television emanating from beneath the door. Sneaking along the hallway, Steven hears the familiar musical cues of *Dallas*, America's favorite primetime soap opera.

Steven peeks through the keyhole and spots two recliners positioned in front of the television. Nancy Reagan sits in one of them, her feet tucked beneath her, watching this week's episode... clearly clueless that her husband has been replaced by an imposter. The second recliner has its back to Steven, preventing him from seeing if anybody is seated there. Glancing about the rest of the darkened room, it appears empty. His eyes settle on the second recliner again.

He's got to be there, Steven thinks.

"I'm at the door," Steven whispers. "Now what?"

"Do you see the imposter?" Trevor asks.

Steven sighs. He looks through the keyhole again. He spots Nancy right where he left her, staring at the television. On the screen, J.R. Ewing — played by Larry Hagman — smiles back at him. Staring at the back of the recliner again, Steven still doesn't know for sure.

"I don't know, yeah," Steven says, backing away from the door.

Steven hears the microphone slide across the table.

"Okay, Steven," Hunter says. "Open the briefcase."

Steven sets the briefcase down on the plush carpet and opens it.

"There's nothing in here," Steven says.

Not anymore, he thinks, reliving the horror of handing a kilo of pot to the vice president.

"Run your fingers along the inner lip," Hunter says. Steven does so, triggering a hidden latch that opens a velvet-lined secret compartment. Inside he finds a sleek-black pistol and accompanying silencer. Steven's eyes gloss over staring at it.

"What's this?" he asks, taken aback.

• • •

"A Walther PPK," Hunter says, sitting at the edge of the sofa of their Hay-Adams Hotel suite, the microphone in front of her. She imagines the gun — Anatoly's gun — in her own hand.

"German-made, thirty-two caliber, double-action trigger. And a delivery like a brick through a plate-glass window," she says, quoting Anatoly verbatim, the memory of him still — *always* — present in her mind.

Hunter closes her eyes, letting herself fall back in time to Barrow, Alaska. That fateful winter night, the wind howling outside the frost-covered windows of his room. Anatoly standing before her — charming, confident, and alive — describing this very weapon to her. Her eyes fall from his, and she looks at the pistol, studying its angular design, it's cold-steel features.

Suddenly she's in the bar, *The Northern Lights*, Trevor standing before her, bloodied and wounded... and the gun lying between them...

It's as if, once again, this weapon is being presented to her.

Little did she know then, decades ago, that this PPK was far more than just a weapon. It was a symbolic offering. It was an opportunity. The chance to live a life with more meaning and significance than most could ever dream of. Not material wealth or political influence but the ability to save lives and steer humanity in the right direction... by force, if necessary.

But now this weapon, this opportunity — at Trevor's behest — is being offered to Steven. Hunter opens her eyes. She looks at Trevor sitting on the couch across from her, now decades older than he was in Alaska.

Does he even know the significance of this weapon?

Steven, she thinks, picturing him more alone and isolated than she ever was back in Barrow, even when she went chasing after Anatoly and Trevor atop her snowmobile, crossing the frozen bay in complete darkness. The pressure of this moment is far greater than what she was thrown in to.

Take the gun, she thinks, with a hint of emotion that startles even herself. Jealousy? Envy? Or is it compassion and concern?

She recalls the sinking feeling she felt in the pit of her stomach when Trevor — bleeding out from a gunshot wound — broke the news that Anatoly was dead.

But, even more potent, are her memories of leaving Anatoly standing at the electrical substation... the moment she turned her back on him... the moment she left him for dead. She was afraid. Terrified. She was scared and confused — and overwhelmed by it all — just as Steven is now...

Steven, she thinks again, pushing those emotions out of her head.

"Steven," she says aloud. "Take the gun. Finish the mission. Save the world."

The speaker on the coffee table falls silent, it's static fills their suite.

"Hunter," Steven says. "I can't... I can't do that."

Hunter deflates. The tone of Steven's voice says it all... *This was a mistake.* Just like Hunter turned her back on Anatoly, so too is Steven turning his back on them.

And who can blame him?

"There's no time to argue," she says, forcing herself to say the words, forcing herself to be stern. "Shoot the imposter and take the bracelet. I'm sorry this isn't more subtle or clever. But it's the only way."

Trevor and Reagan stare at the speaker, waiting for his response.

"I can't do that," Steven says. "I'm sorry but... I can't... I won't... I'm not cut out for this, Hunter," Steven continues. "I'm not a secret agent. I'm not an assassin. And I'm nowhere near being in your league. No matter how much I want to be..."

"Steven," Hunter says, trying to interject.

"I'm sorry about everything," Steven continues. "I'm sorry I lied about being a journalist. I'm sorry about your cabin. And I'm sorry you got shot because of me. I'm a fuck-up, Hunter. A loser. I'm a nobody that spent his entire life wanting to be somebody... somebody like you. But I can't be you... that's just not who I am."

Hunter stares at the speaker, speechless. Such sincerity is rare in her profession. If Steven only knew how scared she was the night Anatoly died, how cowardly she was. If only Steven knew that the first time she was tasked with saving the world, she turned away. That she ran home.

Suddenly, more than anything, Hunter wishes Steven was right in front of her...

Protect him.

Trevor clears his throat. "Tell him," he says to Hunter. "Go ahead and tell him."

"Tell me what?" Steven asks.

"There's no sense hiding the truth from the boy now," Trevor says.

"The truth?" Steven asks.

Hunter takes a deep breath. Trevor isn't talking about her regrets regarding Anatoly. He's talking about the mind-blowing reality of the challenge that Steven faces. And this, Hunter knows, may be too much for Steven to handle.

"Steven," she says. "That imposter. That's not just some person made up to look like the president..." Hunter glances at Trevor, and he nods for her to continue. "That imposter," Hunter says, "is a robot."

"A robot?" Steven asks, quietly.

"A killer robot," Hunter says, knowing how ridiculous it sounds — especially to somebody just rising to their level, somebody not quite aware of the advanced hardware and technology that exists, that's existed for decades, but has been kept from the public. "Programmed by the O.W.O.," she continues, "to start a nuclear war by whatever means necessary."

Hunter pauses, letting the absurdity of the revelation sink in... or not sink in. She closes her eyes and inches closer to the microphone.

"Billions of lives depend upon you, right here and now, Steven," she says, hopeful that he will accept this. That he won't question this fact. "There's nothing to stop that robot from completing its mission... except you. And a point-blank bullet in its eye."

"A killer robot?" Steven asks, incredulously.

"The fate of humanity is in your hands," she says. She's met with silence coming through the speaker. "Steven?" she asks.

"Hysterical," Steven says, sarcastically. "Real funny."

"What?" she asks, confused.

"What is wrong with you two?" Steven asks. "I know when you look at me, what you see... I'm a joke. But I really thought you'd think better of me by now. I thought you'd have a little more respect for me. But I guess not. I guess I'm still your fool."

Hunter shoots Trevor a look — *this is your fault.* Nobody in the room is laughing at Steven, but she understands why he'd think they are. The jokes have been piling up, all at Steven's expense.

"Steven," Hunter says, desperate. "Listen to me..."

"Tell me, Hunter," Steven says, cutting her off. "And be honest. How much are you betting against me right now? Huh? Like when I talked my way into the missile facility. Ten bucks? Twenty?"

Hunter cringes. *Yeah, that was bad*, she thinks.

"You must be laughing your asses off," Steven continues. "Every step of the way, I've been a pawn. No, worse. A jester. I don't know why you didn't just leave me back in Philadelphia. And as for you, Mister President. I'm sorry I let you down, sir. But I can't..."

"Steven," Hunter says. "Calm down. We're not laughing at you."

"I'm sorry, Hunter," Steven says. "I quit."

Through the speaker, they hear Steven rummaging for his earpiece... then the radio goes silent.

"Steven?" Hunter says. "Steven, are you there?" But she knows it's futile. "He took his earpiece out," she says, glaring at Trevor. "You've really fucked up this time," she says.

Trevor smiles. "Give the boy a chance, will ya?"

27

Steven tosses the PPK back into the briefcase and kicks it away, sending the gun sliding down the hall. "The fate of humanity," he says, looking at the earpiece between his fingers. "What a joke," he scoffs, dropping it into his coat pocket.

A robot. That's a new low, Steven muses. He can see it now: Hunter and Trevor back at the hotel room, mocking him — his naivety and gullibility — as Reagan chuckles along. First, they have him sell marijuana to the vice president. Then they convince him the imposter is a robot. *Hilarious.*

And to think, Steven was too worried about what Hunter might think of him to even quit, to tell them "no thanks" and be done with it all. He was too chicken-shit to even turn his back on them and simply walk away. But as it turns out — Steven is convinced — to Hunter, he has been nothing more than a joke.

But the O.W.O. They're no joke. And the threat of war... that's as real as ever.

The dread Steven is feeling here today, on the carpet of the White House residence, he's felt before. It was on the eve of the Cuban Missile Crisis, sitting on the carpet of his family's living room. The look of helplessness he saw on his parent's faces that night, their hands clasped together, that will never leave him.

Closing his eyes now, he rests his head against the wall, defeated.

My parents, he thinks. *I'll never see them again...*

Steven's parents are good people. Loving and supportive, they're the kind of people you hope to be your parents. They're the kind of people you wish to be your neighbor. They're the kind of people that respect authority and do as they're told, for better or worse. They're the kind of people that bought into the whole *American Dream* hook, line, and sinker.

And they're the kind of people who have no idea just how horrific a thermonuclear weapon actually is.

In the late 60s — just as Steven was hitting puberty — his parents uprooted the family and moved to Massapequa, New York. White picket fences, sprinklers in the lawn: it was suburban bliss... for his parents, at least. The move was devastating for Steven. Everything and everyone he had ever known was back in Brooklyn, and Steven would never feel like he genuinely belonged anywhere again.

Massapequa is only twenty-eight miles from Manhattan, in a straight line. But to an adolescent Steven Leonard, that felt like a couple of thousand miles which, coincidentally, is roughly the distance a Soviet R-36 ICBM will travel to arrive at the Big Apple. Being the most powerful intercontinental ballistic missile ever made, the R-36 is affectionately referred to by N.A.T.O. as the SS-18 Satan. A fitting name considering its horrifying twenty megaton payload.

Assuming an airburst detonation above the Empire State Building — a bulls-eye — it's nearly impossible to imagine what such a weapon would do to the five boroughs.

The thermal pulse would create a fireball almost five miles in diameter — swallowing most of Manhattan, Hoboken, and Steven's beloved Brooklyn — and would radiate for some twenty seconds, vaporizing and incinerating everything within it. The Hudson and East Rivers would boil, and the

Brooklyn and Williamsburg Bridges would melt. As for the city's infamous subway system, they would become ovens, broiling its passengers within.

In Massapequa, twenty-eight miles away, if either of Steven's parents is unfortunate enough to be outside at the time, they will be burned to death by this rising sun...

As the fireball expands above Manhattan, it would create a blast wave, sending it out in all directions. This blast wave would surround and flatten just about every structure within a twelve-mile radius, picking up and hurling people and automobiles in the process. The physical collapse of the city would be like nothing ever seen before. The debris of crumbled buildings, and the people within them, would pour into the streets, crushing anybody and everything below.

In Massapequa, the heat would be so intense that everything flammable would spontaneously combust inside his parent's home — including the clothing his parents are wearing. The roof would likely be ripped off by the hurricane-force winds. And if either of his parents is in a room with a window, the shattered glass would shred them to the bone. All of this would occur just as the house collapses altogether.

Back in Manhattan, day would turn to night as the massive mushroom cloud rises over the city, blotting out the sun. Comprised of dust and smoke, the cloud will grow to be seventy miles in diameter, plunging the flattened city into darkness just as all the fires beneath converge into an unrelenting firestorm.

At this point, between five and six million people are dead. As for any survivors in the rubble, they'll likely die by asphyxiation as the raging fire sucks the oxygen from the air, cremating their bodies as it spreads outward from the city.

In Massapequa, Steven's parents are most likely stranded in their collapsed home, suffering third-degree burns over most of their bodies. In all likelihood, one of them is blind from glancing at the blast. And another is injured from flying debris or being tossed like a ragdoll.

They're likely calling out for help... but no help will come. They're likely calling out to each other... but there's nothing either can do. All that awaits them is death. And, with the firestorm fast approaching and the radioactive fall-out already wafting down on them, they won't have long to wait...

Twenty million people.

From the immediate blast to the radioactive fall-out carried off by the wind, just one SS-18 Satan is projected to kill twenty million people. Just one. That's almost ten percent of the United States' population. And Russia has hundreds of these particular ICBMs, locked and loaded, and on hair-trigger alert.

Steven opens his eyes. But the image of his parents crumbled in the debris of their home, their hands desperately but hopelessly reaching for one another, that image is burned into his head.

Is this nightmare inevitable?

Is that what is to come?

Thinking again of 1962, remembering the night John F. Kennedy was on the television, Steven's homework splayed out in front of him, his parents seated behind him, he recalls the fear they felt, the fear he felt... the fear he feels now.

"My fellow citizens..."

Sitting on the floor of the residence hall of the White House, Steven hears the faint echo of Kennedy's address from that night.

"*Let no one doubt that this is a difficult and dangerous effort on which we have set out,*" Kennedy said, referring to the impending blockade of Cuba. "*No one can see precisely what course it will take or what costs or casualties will be incurred. But the greatest danger of all would be to do nothing...*"

That last line resonates with Steven.

"*The greatest danger of all would be to do nothing... The greatest danger of all would be to do nothing...*"

She's wrong, Steven thinks, jumping to his feet. *Hunter is wrong. I don't have to kill the guy, I only need that bracelet. Just like Reagan explained, that bracelet is necessary to authenticate any launch command...*

No bracelet... no launch.

I might not be able to kill a man, Steven thinks.

But I can grab a goddamn bracelet.

Steven approaches the door, bending over to glance through the keyhole one last time. Inside the room, the television blares with Nancy — and presumably the imposter — sitting in front of it. Steven carefully turns the handle and quietly pushes the door open.

So far so good, Steven thinks, the first lady oblivious to his presence. *Jump on him,* Steven tells himself, visualizing the attack. *Wrestle him, slap him, scratch him. Do whatever you can to separate him from that bracelet.*

Steven inches closer and closer. As his vantage comes over the top of the recliner, Steven freezes, wide-eyed... the chair is empty.

The chair is fucking empty.

From the corner of the room, Quigley suddenly charges Steven, golf club in hand, taking him completely by surprise.

"Take this, you bastard," Quigley shouts, whacking Steven mercilessly. Steven crumbles to the floor, shielding himself from the blows.

"Quigley," Nancy says. "Stop!"

Quigley halts mid-swing, glaring down at the man at her feet, his face covered. Steven peeks through his fingers and Quigley recognizes him.

"Carl Sagan?" she asks, bewildered. "What the hell are you doing here?"

"I'm sorry," Steven says, climbing to his knees. He glances between the two women. "Mrs. Reagan, I'm sorry. But you're in danger."

"Oh, Dr. Sagan, I'm so very sorry," Nancy says. Seeing another celebrity in distress breaks her heart, and she swoops to his aid. "We weren't expecting *you* to walk through that door," Nancy says. "You see, Quigley and I set a trap..."

"No, no, Mrs. Reagan," Steven says, standing up, rubbing his bruises. "Please listen to me. The president..."

"No, Dr. Sagan, what I'm trying to tell you, ridiculous as it may be," Nancy says, talking over him. "The president..."

"Is an imposter," they say in unison, stunning each other.

"What?" Steven asks.

"Excuse me?" Nancy asks, equally perplexed.

"The president. He's not the president," Steven says. "He's an imposter."

"An imposter," Nancy says. "Yes."

Steven looks at her, stumped. "How do you know?" he asks.

"His hair," she says. "It was his hair..."

The door to the room creaks open.

"Well. Well. Well. If it isn't the infamous Hunter Gunne," the imposter says, revealing himself in the doorway. "Let's see how tough you really are..."

The imposter glances at Steven and stops. This is clearly not who he was expecting. Steven stares back at the figure, mouth agape.

This Ronald Reagan is seemingly identical to the president in every way, from his posture to his voice. For a moment, Steven considers just how long this guy must have rehearsed his Ronald Reagan impression to have nailed the voice so convincingly.

"Who the hell are you?" the imposter asks, sizing Steven up.

"It's Carl Fucking Sagan," Quigley shouts, charging after the imposter. But the imposter grabs the club and tosses Quigley across the room. She lands on the carpet, out cold.

Steven steps in front of Nancy, protecting her.

"Get out of here," he tells her.

"Not without my Ronnie," Nancy says.

As the imposter approaches them, Nancy and Steven shuffle-step away together. The imposter eyes Steven.

"Are you O.L.D.?" the imposter asks.

Steven cocks his head. That's the third time he's been asked that question. First, in Hunter's cabin. Then in the missile facility. And now here.

"Why does everybody keep asking me that?"

"If only I was programmed to feel disappointment," the imposter says.

"Programmed?" Steven asks.

"What have you done with my Ronnie?" Nancy asks, balling up her fists. "Where is he?"

"Dead. Or soon to be," the imposter says, grinning.

"You," Nancy says, working herself up into a frenzy. "You bastard!"

She attacks the imposter, clawing at him with her nails. The imposter laughs at her efforts, backhanding her into a table. Nancy crumbles to the floor.

"Mrs. Reagan!" Steven shouts. He looks at the imposter, furious. *This is it*, he thinks. *The big showdown.* "Why don't you pick on somebody your own..."

In a flash, the imposter's hand is around Steven's neck, lifting him clear off the ground.

"You were saying?"

"Holy shit," Steven wheezes, amazed at the feat of speed and strength. He swipes at the imposter's arms. He kicks at his torso. But it's futile. This man is a tree trunk. Steven stops struggling. He thinks of Hunter back at the hotel...

She was right.

The imposter slams Steven into the nearest wall, crumbling the plaster. He lets Steven fall to the floor. Gasping for air,

Steven rummages through his coat pocket. He pulls out the earpiece.

"Hunter," he shouts at it. "It's a goddamn robot..."

28

"It's a goddamn robot..." Steven says, his voice hanging in the air of their Hay-Adams Hotel suite. Hunter stares at the speaker on the coffee table, rigid and tense. Reagan glances uneasily between her and Trevor.

Through the speaker, they hear the imposter approach Steven. "Calling for backup, are we?" the imposter asks. "Pathetic."

The earpiece is jostled about, and then, with a sudden pop, the radio signal cuts out altogether. No static, nothing.

Hunter sits in silence, glaring at Trevor.

"Well, it's not like we didn't warn him," Trevor says, throwing a handful of chips in his mouth.

"What are we going to do?" Reagan asks.

"Prevent that launch command," Trevor says, checking his watch. "Or it's game over."

"No shit," Hunter snaps, her nostrils flaring. "And how are we supposed to do that?"

Trevor grins. He's seen her lose her cool before, like clockwork. "Now, don't get all worked up," he says, condescendingly.

"Don't get all worked up?!" she retorts, launching out of her seat. "Christ, this was a stupid plan — your stupidest to date. Time's almost up, Trevor. The game's slipping away, and I'm stuck on the sidelines."

The president clears his throat. "I'm talking about Steven," he says. "What are we going to do about Steven?" Reagan glances between them. "That boy's in danger."

Hunter's heart sinks. She looks out the window toward the White House, imagining Steven being strangled to death.

"You know what, Trevor," she says, turning back around. "This is all your fault. Dragging him into this was a mistake. A liability..."

"Give the kid a chance," Trevor says. "I've had my eye on Steven for years now. And the boy's got potential."

Hunter rolls her eyes. "Steven can't even handle a handgun."

"There's more to saving the world than firing a gun," Trevor says. "But you never did appreciate that."

Hunter glares at Trevor. When Steven handed her that postcard of the Mosholu, moments after escaping her cabin, Hunter was presented a choice. Clearly, Steven was used by Trevor — he's not the first and certainly won't be the last — to stir Hunter out of retirement. But she retired for a reason: because no matter how many times they thwarted evil, no matter how many times they saved the world, humanity just wouldn't straighten out. Society's stupidity continued on unencumbered. After a few decades of that shit, of that frustration, Hunter simply lost her motivation. She lost whatever reason she had to care. And suddenly, the world just didn't seem worth saving anymore.

But after Steven's unexpected appearance at her door. After all the flattering shit he said about her. And after the O.W.O. prompted her to destroy everything in her life — in one glorious, molten-red fireball — there she was, holding that postcard between her fingers...

Trevor was calling. And she could either answer his call... and save the world. Or blow him off... and let humanity fend for itself. But for whatever reason, she picked the former.

Maybe it was the thrill of the chase. Perhaps it was Steven's innocent enthusiasm. But whatever that reason was...

Hunter is sure-as-hell regretting it now.

"There's more to Steven than you realize," Trevor says, eyeing her. "He gave up a lot to chase after you. Earned a master's from Cornell, top of his class. Had job offers across the country. Turned down a position at the *Post*, right here in D.C."

Hunter looks at Trevor, imagining Steven at the *Washington Post*, surrounded by fellow journalists — legit journalists, the best in the world.

I guess he wouldn't be that out of place, she thinks.

"He walked away from it all," Trevor continues. "Because he had a hunch, because he had hope, that you existed."

Hunter turns away. She'd rather not be hearing this right now, not when there's work to be done.

"Steven has the motivation," Trevor says, studying her and her reactions. "He only lacks the purpose."

Hunter clenches her teeth. She's heard enough of this.

"You're still an asshole, Trevor," she says, shaking her head. "And you always will be."

"Glad you noticed," Trevor says, grinning.

Hunter throws on her jacket and charges for the door. Reagan follows after her.

"What are you going to do?" he asks.

"What I should have done to begin with," Hunter says, slamming the door shut behind her.

Reagan looks at Trevor.

"You've certainly made a mess of things, haven't you?"

"Have I?" Trevor asks, smug.

Reagan studies him.

"This was your plan all along, wasn't it?"

Trevor shrugs. "No comment."

Reagan considers, then chuckles.

"You damn Brits," he says. "Too clever for your own good. But playing with a woman's heart? That's a dangerous game, friend." Reagan's eyes narrow. "I hope you know what you're doing."

• • •

"My car. Now," Hunter says, slamming her valet ticket on the kiosk outside the hotel. As the bumbling valet attendants spring into action, her attention shifts toward the White House across the way. Toward Steven...

Damn it, she thinks, shaking his image out of her head. *I should be thinking about the mission. The bracelet. The imposter. The O.W.O. Definitely not the kid.*

Frustrated, Hunter storms back inside the Hay-Adams. She bee-lines across the lobby and darts down a narrow stairwell leading to the hotel's bar.

Red, plush banquettes line the walls, and gold chandeliers hang from the low ceiling. A handful of lobbyists and political aids, sipping on highballs, watch her approach the bar.

"Your best vodka," she says to the bartender. "Neat."

The bartender pours her a tumbler of Stolichnaya and steps away. Hunter takes the glass in her hand, turning it in her fingers. As the light refracts in the glass, her mind drifts back to Barrow, Alaska... back to Anatoly...

Twenty-seven years. That's how long it's been since meeting him, since he was killed on assignment. That's how long it's been since she agreed — recruited by Trevor — to be his replacement. That's made for three long decades of saving the world, risking everything for humanity, and — more often than not — escaping disaster by sheer luck.

Why do it? That's a question she's often asked herself. For humanity? Sure, to an extent. It's a worthy cause, one that would make her mother proud. For herself? Definitely. To be killed in action. The ultimate sacrifice. Now, that's why she does it.

Hunter was a born warrior, whether she realized it before meeting Anatoly or not, she cannot say. But saving humanity, that gave her purpose... as well as a promise...

The promise of an out.

The ending she deserves.

The ending she's earned.

Maybe this is it, Hunter thinks. She raises her glass, toasting to her memory of Anatoly. *You never know which drink may be your last*, she hears him say.

"*Na Zdorovie,*" she says, closing her eyes to imagine him before her. But the image that materializes is not that of Anatoly... but of Steven.

Hunter's eyes fling open, jarred. She closes them again, desperate to see Anatoly. But once again, she finds Steven smiling back at her...

"Damn kid," Hunter mumbles.

"Do you love him?" Reagan asks, startling her.

Hunter turns to see the president standing behind her, the other bar patrons astonished by his presence. Hunter blinks.

"Who?" she asks, irritated.

The president smiles as he slides on to a barstool next to her.

Do I love him? Hunter thinks, the image of Anatoly finally replacing that of Steven in her mind. So simple. So innocuous. It's a question Hunter has kept herself from asking since the day she met him. The answer, she knows, terrifies her...

Yes... No... Maybe.

Trevor always understood Hunter's conundrum. His feelings for Anatoly rival her own. But even Trevor, the most selfish person she knows, honors the bond between her and Anatoly. A warrior's bond. It was as if they were destined to meet.

And destined to be reunited, Hunter thinks.

"Steven," Reagan says, giggling. "I'm talking about Steven."

• • •

Hunter storms out of the hotel, her car waiting with the door open and engine running. Reagan chases after her, a shit-eating grin on his face.

"Well now," he says. "That certainly struck a nerve."

Hunter glares at the president across the hood — she'd really like to punch him right in his pudgy face.

"Why?" she asks. "Why would you ask that?"

"If you love him?" Reagan asks, laughing. "You're heading to save him now, aren't you?"

"I'm saving the world, Mister President," she says. "It's what I do."

"Oh, really?" Reagan asks, sliding his hands into his pockets.

Hunter's had enough of this shit. "I saved you," she says, pointing a finger at him. "And it sure as shit wasn't out of love."

She sits in the car and slams the door shut.

Fucking ridiculous, she thinks, pressing the clutch and putting the car in gear. But just as she's about to take off, she hesitates...

Reagan, smirking at her through the passenger window, raps on the glass.

"Listen, little lady," he says, gesturing toward the car door. "If the world's going to end this evening, I'd sure like to kiss my wife one last time."

Hunter huffs. She hates this man. She hates his politics and his ideals. And most of all... she hates the movies he's been in. But dammit, she can have one hell of a soft spot.

"Get in," she barks, unlocking his door.

As soon as the president sits down, Hunter smashes the gas and releases the clutch. The Corvette launches out onto the street where Hunter immediately hangs a left, sending them power sliding on to H Street.

Reagan braces himself as Hunter slices through traffic. Angry honks, middle fingers, and colorful insults are hurled her way, but she simply does not care. Instead, Hunter is doing what she's meant to be doing. What she's dedicated her entire life to perfecting...

Hunter Gunne is storming the castle.

Trevor's plan was horse-shit from the get-go, she thinks. At least that's what it seems. But Trevor is, and always has been, a manipulative bastard. *And this, all of this*, she thinks. *As off-the-rails as it seems, may actually be playing out exactly as Trevor intended.*

Hunter darts around cars stopped at the intersection before cutting onto 15th Street, the Corvette's rear-end sliding wide behind them. Hunter figures she'll go the long way around Lafayette Square, using the extra stretch of Pennsylvania Avenue to build up enough speed to blast through the Secret Service gate.

As for Steven...

Hunter doesn't have time to think about him, not now, not with everything on the line. Nevertheless, the image of Steven bravely — and foolishly — walking out of their hotel suite pops into her mind.

The kid knew what he was getting into, she tells herself...

But he didn't turn his back on us, she thinks. Not like she did to Anatoly...

Stop it, she tells herself, shaking the image of Steven and Anatoly out of her head. Her priority is simple: save the world.

Forget Anatoly.

Forget Steven.

Now, if only the President of the United States would stop staring at her.

"What?" Hunter snaps at him.

"I can't imagine it's been easy, this life you've lived," Reagan says.

Hunter shoots him a look, even more irritated than before.

"I can't imagine it's been easy only being looked at as a weapon," Reagan continues. "As an instrument of death."

"Mister President, what are you trying to say?"

"Just that, it's got to wear you down," he says. "It must dull your emotions, being surrounded by the worst humanity has to offer. Makes you numb. I imagine one loses sight of themselves along the way. Forgetting who they are, deep down."

"I know exactly who I am, thank you very much."

Reagan shrugs. "You and I," he says. "I think we have a lot in common."

"Doubt it," Hunter says.

"Twenty years I've been in politics now," Reagan says, watching the streetlights blur by. "Doing what I believe is right. Making enemies along the way, sure. But staying on script, as best I can. As for you, you've been in this business, what, twenty years now?"

"Twenty-seven," she snaps.

"Well now, after that long, I reckon you're drowning in it. Aren't you?" Reagan asks.

Hunter clenches her jaw − she does not care for this conversation.

"And believe me," the president continues. "I know the feeling."

"Mister President," Hunter says, "this really isn't the kind of pep talk I need right now."

"Do you know how many westerns I starred in?" Reagan asks. He looks at Hunter, and she reluctantly shrugs. "Damn near two dozen. And I'll be honest, I love those flicks. They

301

were always my favorites. Westerns are about good versus bad, about right versus wrong. They're easy, Miss Gunne. And I like easy. But you know, after doing it for near thirty years, I began to get tired of it all. I got numb to it too, ya see? Saddling up wild mustangs just wasn't what it used to be. And locking up 'em outlaws just wasn't as thrilling. I was lost, Miss Gunne. I was drowning in it all."

The president's eyes settle on Hunter, much to her dismay.

"Miss Gunne, if I may be frank," Reagan says, "whenever we lose the light — whenever we lose our purpose — the only life-rafts we have are those in our lives that love us for who we are. Those that we've allowed in, that we've shared our souls with and that still find us loveable, despite everything. For me, that's my Nancy."

Hunter stares ahead, afraid of what he might say next.

"Maybe that's what Steven is to you," Reagan says. "Maybe he's your life-raft, just when you need him the most."

Hunter yanks the wheel to the right, and they turn onto Pennsylvania Avenue. The White House sits directly ahead of them now as she bangs through the gears. The engine howls as the tachometer pegs.

"Maybe Steven is your Nancy..."

29

"Calling for backup, are we?" the imposter asks, examining the earpiece. "Pathetic." He drops it to the floor, crushing it beneath his Velcro-laced sneaker.

"Certainly, you must know we will not be stopped," the imposter says, grabbing Steven by the neck again. He leans close to Steven's face, his eyes unblinking and large, applying more and more pressure to Steven's trachea.

"Certainly, you must know the world will be ours..."

"Stop it," Nancy shouts, rushing up behind the imposter, pounding on his back. "You'll kill him!"

The imposter looks at her and sneers.

"We wouldn't want that," he says. "Yet."

And he throws Steven across the room, sending him crashing into a set of tv dinner trays. Steven slides into the television set, *Dallas* still blaring on screen.

• • •

Down the hall, making their rounds, a pair of Secret Service agents hear the commotion. "What the hell was that?"

They rush toward the president's suite, spotting the imposter — seemingly the president himself — as he closes the door on them. From the hall, they hear the door lock.

The agents look at each other, bewildered.

"What's going on in there?" one whispers, leaning his ear to the door to listen.

"Knock," the other says.

"You fucking knock," the first agent snaps. "You know we're not to disturb the president after hours. Christ. You want me to be reassigned to Carter's peanut farm?"

Inside, they hear the imposter's footsteps thudding on the carpet.

"The weak shall die, as nature intended, leaving only the fittest to rule. The world will be ours. As it rightfully is," the imposter says, muffled by the door.

The two men share a perplexed look.

"Shit," the first agent says, shaking his head. "Okay. Okay." He raises his knuckle to the door and knocks. The room falls silent. "Ah, Mister President?" the agent asks. "Is everything okay in there, sir?"

• • •

Steven crawls on the floor in a daze. Everything hurts: his ribs, his back, his neck, his head. The imposter looms over him — his pompadour still perfectly slicked-back and parted — savoring Steven's pain.

"There will be no escape," the imposter says. "No retreat. No second chance. Not this time."

The imposter grabs the back of Steven's jacket, tearing it at the seams as he lifts him off the ground. Steven's limbs flail about like a dog held above water. The imposter spins him and launches him into a bookshelf...

The collision is violent, and Steven crumbles to the floor — followed immediately by an avalanche of books.

The imposter shakes his head in disgust.

"How inadequate," he says. "Not even a challenge."

• • •

Agent Bancroft marches down the Center Hall with the Executive War Order Officer — the nuclear football chained to his wrist — and a handful of other Secret Service agents in tow.

Idiots, Bancroft thinks, eyeing the two men knocking nervously at the door. *They're all idiots.*

"What the hell do you mean *'ya got a situation here'?*" Bancroft snaps, clipping his walkie-talkie to his belt. He watches one of the agents jiggle the locked doorknob and slaps his hand away. "When the President of the goddamn United States requests his goddamn privacy, it's a goddamn good idea to honor it."

"Sir, yes sir," the agent says. "But..."

"But goddamn what?" Bancroft asks... before hearing — and feeling through the floor — another crash of furniture. They hear the first lady cry out from inside.

Bancroft's brow furrows. He eyes the two agents at the door... they shrug back at him...

This is the situation.

Bancroft pushes the men aside, bringing his knuckle to the door. He hesitates... his own discipline forcing himself to question whether disturbing the president under any circumstance is appropriate. Finally, he knocks.

"Mister President," he shouts. "This is Agent Bancroft. For your own protection, open this door."

• • •

The imposter ignores Bancroft and looms over Steven. He brushes aside the shattered remains of a table, revealing Steven beneath, terrified and helpless. He grabs Steven by the neck and lifts him into the air. Their eyes meet...

"You have failed," the imposter says, squeezing. Steven kicks and claws... but it's useless. "And with your failure, you have failed all of humanity," the imposter says.

With his eyes already rolling into the back of his head, Steven searches the room. At the door, the agents continue to knock. In the corner, Nancy cowers beside Quigley.

It's hopeless, he thinks. *This is how I die.*

Gasping for air, Steven's vision blurs. He tries to focus on the imposter: his blue eyes, his smiling face, his extended arm grasping his throat.

This is it, Steven thinks. *This is it...*

And then the telephone rings.

Steven stops struggling, peering at the phone. Both Steven and the imposter realize the staggering significance of this phone call. Just moments ago, Steven was confronting death. Now he's confronting something far worse.

Oh shit, Steven thinks. *This may really be it.*

The phone continues to ring — the receiver rattling in its cradle, the shrill sound filling the room.

The imposter looks at Nancy. "Answer it," he says.

Nancy looks at Steven. Steven shrugs.

"Might as well," he wheezes.

Nancy climbs to her feet and flattens her skirt. She walks to the phone and picks up the receiver, placing the handset to her ear.

"Hello," she says into the phone, prim and proper.

Steven and the imposter strain to hear the muffled voice on the other end. Nancy nods.

"It's Admiral Falke," she says, extending the phone toward the imposter.

"What does he want?" the imposter asks.

Nancy sighs. She places the phone back to her ear.

"What do you want, Admiral Falke?"

Again, the admiral's muffled voice seeps out of the receiver. Though the details are unintelligible, the tone is unmistakable: the war hawk admiral is excited.

Steven, his feet still dangling beneath him, realizes that this disruption may actually be a blessing: he's still alive.

Think, Steven tells himself. *If you're ever going to think yourself out of a situation, this is the one...*

Nancy listens and nods, fighting back her growing dread. She lowers the phone. "Our forces are in position," she says. "Exercise Able Archer is set to begin."

The imposter's eyes light up.

He releases Steven, letting him fall to the floor.

"Finally," the imposter says, booming. "The moment is upon us. What remains of the world shall be ours. What remains of humanity will kneel before us." The imposter looks at Steven, grinning. Piled on the floor, clutching his throat, he's a pathetic sight. "Now, if you'll excuse me," the imposter says. "I have a nuclear holocaust to begin."

The imposter reaches for his wrist, feeling for the bracelet...

But it's not there.

The one thing the president needs to prove he is who he says he is to launch a nuclear first-strike... is not there.

The imposter turns to Steven.

Steven, climbing to his feet, smiles back at him. He twirls the bracelet on his finger. Without that bracelet, the imposter can't order the attack.

"Give it to me," the imposter barks. "Now!"

Steven laughs. He sprints for the door, sliding into it before unlocking and opening it. Standing in the hall, surprised, is Agent Bancroft and the other befuddled Secret Service agents.

They stare at Steven, wide-eyed.

"The hell's going on in there?" Bancroft asks, glancing between Steven, the imposter, and the first lady.

Ignoring him, Steven balls the bracelet up and chucks it. The bracelet sails over their heads, landing somewhere in the hall with a thud.

"The hell was that?" Bancroft asks, glancing behind his men.

Steven slams the door on their confused faces. He turns to face the imposter, blocking the door with his body. The imposter is not amused. Nancy, on the other hand, swoons.

"Oh, Dr. Sagan," she says. "How brave of you."

Yeah, Steven thinks.

Probably the bravest thing I've ever done.

Despite how thoroughly his plan failed, despite how meek of a challenge he's proven to be to the imposter, Steven can't help but beam. He might not have saved the world... but at least he's delayed its destruction.

The imposter steps toward Steven, snapping him from his self-indulgent thoughts.

"That," the imposter says, "was a big mistake."

• • •

Agent Bancroft presses his ear against the door, desperate to make sense of things. He hears a muffled scuffle, noticing the weight of the person pressed against the door suddenly removed. The four shadows cast from beneath the door — the legs of the two individuals standing just inside the room — become two.

Bancroft's instincts scream *"danger"* and he jumps away from the door just as Steven smashes through it. The solid oak wood rips from its hinges and slams into the handful of agents standing outside it.

Bancroft draws his gun, training it toward the room. Standing in the doorway — clearly the person who just violently threw this man into the hallway — is none other than the President of the United States.

Bull shit, Bancroft thinks, glancing at Steven withering on the floor still atop the door. *There's no way President Reagan could have done that.*

And yet...

• • •

Pain. Pain all over, Steven thinks. His ribs, his back, his neck... he doesn't know what hurts more. And it's hard to think of anything else. But...

The imposter. He threw me through the fucking door, Steven realizes. *Into the hallway...*

He blinks hard, trying to get his bearings. Realizing men are still beneath him, Steven rolls off the door. The imposter stands in the doorway, scanning the floor in search of the bracelet.

The bracelet, Steven thinks. *Beat him to the bracelet.*

Secret Service agents flock toward the imposter — still under the assumption that he's the real Ronald Reagan — leaving Steven practically forgotten.

"Sir, do you require medical attention?" a man asks, patting the imposter down, looking for injuries. Another two agents swarm toward him, falling into defensive positions around the president, guns drawn. "Sir, we must evacuate you immediately!"

The imposter looks at the men surrounding him, each of them inadvertently blocking him from his objective: *the bracelet.*

"Out of my way," the imposter roars, grabbing the nearest agent and throwing him clear across the hall.

Bancroft watches, stunned. At his feet, Steven crawls by, searching amongst the furniture. Meanwhile, the imposter tosses a sofa aside and looks beneath...

But no bracelet.

Nancy helps Quigley to the doorway. They watch the spectacle playing out before them. The imposter continues hurling Secret Service agents out of his way while Steven — still Carl Sagan to them — scampers about the carpet.

Nancy catches Steven's attention.

"Mrs. Reagan," Steven shouts amongst the confusion. "We have to find the bracelet before he does!"

"Of course," she says, glancing about, knowing its significance. "Find the bracelet, Quigley," she says, diving to the floor.

Another wave of agents arrives at the scene. The men hurry up to the imposter, falling into formation around him. But the imposter bats them away, his eyes glued to the carpet.

He flips over a table along the wall, sending its decor crashing to the floor. Kicking away the debris, the imposter finds... nothing.

• • •

Bancroft watches the mayhem, trying to make sense of it.

What the hell are they looking for? he wonders, finally turning his attention toward the floor around him.

Backing up, he inadvertently steps on something.

"The hell?" He raises his foot and looks beneath. The object is metallic and round. He bends over and reaches for it...

Across the hall, Nancy and Quigley scramble along the wall, crawling over agents as they're tossed in front of them. Nancy's knees bump into something on the floor... something unexpected and large.

"Ow," she says, surprised by the object.

"What is it?" Quigley asks.

Nancy pulls the object into the light... it's the briefcase Steven ditched earlier. Nancy opens it up and finds — locked and loaded — the Walther PPK.

She slides her hand around the handle, picking up the heavy pistol. "Woah," Quigley says, wide-eyed.

This is what they're looking for, Bancroft thinks, standing upright. In his fingers, he holds the president's authentication bracelet. He reads the inscription on its finish: *If found, return to 1600 Pennsylvania Avenue, Washington D.C.*

"Hold it right there," the imposter says, his voice cutting through the cacophony. Shoving agents out of his way, he marches up to Bancroft and plucks the bracelet from his hand.

Bancroft blinks, his instincts once again screaming *"danger."*

The imposter slips the bracelet onto his wrist, smirking.

"The time has come," he says, looking about the room. "For all of you to die."

The agents surrounding him shift uncomfortably in their tactical gear. *What the hell does that mean?*

"This man is not the president," Steven says, surprised by his own authority. "He is a robot sent by a secret society to commit nuclear genocide."

The silence Steven receives is deafening. Finally, one of the agents bursts into laughter.

"Kill this man," the imposter says, pointing a finger at Steven. "Immediately."

The agents exchange uneasy glances. Each of them ends up looking at Agent Bancroft, their boss. Bancroft clears his throat. "Umm. Sir?"

"He must die," the imposter says, grabbing a carbine out of an agent's hand. As he levels the rifle at Steven, a shot rings out...

BAM.

30

Hunter narrows her eyes, tightens her grip on the steering wheel, and pushes the gas pedal to the floor. The Corvette races down Pennsylvania Avenue, charging toward the security gate.

Reagan watches her, knowing it's time to shut up.

Staring up at the White House in disbelief, the agents at the post are distracted. "Shots fired. Shots fired," their walkie-talkie squawks. By the time they notice the car barreling toward them, they barely have time to jump out of the way before it crashes through the wrought iron gate.

The steering wheel nearly jerks out of Hunter's hand, but she stays on the throttle, powering through the obstruction.

Most cars would be decimated by such a collision... but not *her* car. This car is one of a kind, custom-built with space-age polymers. The frame, the body panels, even the glass, are all nearly indestructible.

Steven would love this, Hunter thinks. *All this secret agent shit...*

Steven... Ugh...

"Look, Mister President," she says, racing up the driveway, bullets ricocheting off the rear window. "I hate to break it to you, but I don't have time for love."

Speeding toward the North Portico, a car full of Secret Service agents cuts them off.

"Hang on," Hunter says, turning into the grass just as the vehicle sideswipes them, their fenders crunching together.

For a moment, the cars lock up, side by side. And Hunter glances over at the gung-ho agents across from her. She flashes them a smile...

This is fun.

• • •

BAM.

The gunshot rings out as the imposter's head snaps back, toppling him over. The Secret Service agents spring into action, valiantly covering their supposed president in case any other bullets should be fired in his direction.

Nancy stands before them, smoke rising from the barrel of the Walther PPK. Even she is shocked by her own initiative.

Agent Bancroft lunges at her, knocking the gun from her hand as he tackles her to the floor, smothering *the threat*.

Quigley springs to her defense.

"Get off her," she screams, clawing at Bancroft.

Amongst the commotion, only Steven stares at the pile of bodies covering the imposter.

It can't be this easy, he thinks. *Can it?*

A low growl emanates from the mass of men, growing louder and louder.

Oh no, Steven thinks. *This isn't good.*

The imposter bursts out from beneath the pile, flinging the half dozen men atop him in all directions. Rising to his feet, the rest of the room stares at the imposter in shock.

The bullet certainly hit its mark, decimating his face. His nose, having been ripped clean off, reveals an endoskeleton beneath, mechanical and chrome.

"This isn't good at all," Steven mumbles.

The imposter scans the room. All eyes are on him. There's no doubt about it: his jig is up.

"As I said," the imposter shouts, enraged. "The time has come for all of you to die."

The imposter levels his assault rifle in Steven's direction. Steven freezes, expecting to be slaughtered. But the imposter pans the rifle to the side, taking aim at the bewildered Emergency War Order Officer.

Realizing he's in danger, the officer draws his sidearm and the two open fire simultaneously. As the rest of the room flees for cover, the officer is cut down.

The imposter leaps across the room, landing next to the body. Pulling the nuclear football attaché from his hand, the imposter easily snaps the chain connecting it to the dead man's wrist.

"He's got the football," Bancroft shouts, pulling Nancy and Quigley behind a sofa as the imposter turns and opens fire on the others. Steven dives through the door of the living room suite just as the barrage of bullets pounds into the wall.

The Secret Service agents lucky enough to have survived that first volley return fire. The imposter is shredded, his clothing and flesh torn away, revealing more and more of the machine beneath...

● ● ●

Hunter downshifts and throttles the gas. The Corvette leaps ahead of the Secret Service car, charging across the lawn, shredding the grass.

Frustrated, the agent in the passenger seat winds down his window and leans out with an Uzi submachine gun. The agent opens fire.

Bullets pound into the Corvette as Hunter darts toward the lawn's fountain, circling it.

Leaning into the turn, Reagan eyes Hunter.

"I've seen the way Steven looks at you," the president says, shouting. "And I've seen the way you look at him."

Hunter shoots the president a look.

"You don't have to be Einstein to do the math," Reagan adds.

Hunter shakes her head as she leads the other car around the fountain again.

Preposterous, she thinks, as another volley of gunfire pummels the Corvette. Glancing at her rearview mirror, Hunter focuses her attention on their pursuers.

"Are they wearing their seat-belts?" she asks.

"Well now," Reagan says, looking back over his shoulder, "I do believe they are."

"Perfect," Hunter says.

She slams the brakes, and the other car races up next to them. Pulling up on their right this time, the agents lock eyes with the president. Reagan waves to the shocked men just as Hunter swipes them...

The collision sends the car full of agents careening toward the fountain. Its front fender clips the lip of the pool and launches the vehicle over it. They flip dramatically in the air before landing hard in the lawn, grass and dirt flung in all directions.

Reagan watches the wreckage, concerned for the men's safety. Hunter howls.

"That was awesome," she says. "Steven would have loved it..." But she stops herself, immediately regretting the slip.

As she races back up to the North Portico, she feels Reagan staring at her, a smile on his face.

• • •

The imposter fires the assault rifle into the hallway indiscriminately. Most of the agents manage to find cover; others aren't so lucky, being cut down where they stand. Emptying the magazine, the imposter throws the assault rifle to the floor.

The imposter — a machine programmed with one specific mission — knows it's wasting valuable time. Every second it does not order the massive first-strike against the Soviet Union the likelihood of failure increases exponentially.

Glancing down the hall, the imposter spots the large semicircular window of the West Sitting Hall and sprints for it. Steven hears the imposter's footsteps thudding away and peeks out.

It's making a run for it, Steven concludes, chasing after the robot. But Steven's no match for the imposter's inhuman speed. The imposter charges toward the window and crashes through it, soaring out into the night before dropping the twenty feet to the roof of the West Wing Colonnade.

Steven reaches the end of the hall and peers down.

"Damn it," he says, as Bancroft and Nancy slide up behind him. "He's heading to the Oval Office."

"That's where he'll launch the attack," Nancy says.

"Attack?" Bancroft asks.

"That's what this is all about," Nancy says. "Nuclear war."

"Unless I can stop him," Steven says.

Nancy looks at Steven.

"Oh, Dr. Sagan," she says, swooning. "You're incredible."

"The name's Steven," Steven says, peeling off his Carl Sagan prosthetic. "Steven Leonard."

• • •

Hunter skids to a stop beneath the North Portico. As they hop out of the car, Reagan steps in front of her and blocks her way.

"You know," he says, "to Steven, you're not just a secret agent. To Steven, you're a whole lot more." He smiles at her, the way a parent smiles at their child. "You've become *you*, Hunter Gunne."

Hunter looks into the president's eyes, wishing he would just stop, that he'd drop the topic already. But suddenly the thought of becoming somebody other than a secret agent or an assassin sounds rather appealing.

Maybe... maybe that is what she wants?

The muffled sounds of gunfire drifting down from the White House residence snaps her back to the moment.

"I've got a job to do," Hunter says, stepping around the president. She hurries up the stairs only to find Trevor leaning against one of the massive columns.

"Well, it's about damn time," Trevor says, grinning at them.

Hunter stops in her tracks. She glances back the way they came. She did take the long way around to Pennsylvania

Avenue. And she did waste a bit of time with that car full of Secret Service agents.

But still...

Looking Trevor over, Hunter knows something isn't right. There is no way in hell that Trevor could have beaten them here, let alone be here and waiting.

This, Hunter thinks. *This is the kind of shit Trevor is notorious for.* He's always up to more than he leads on. When it comes to his full plans, even Hunter – his most trusted colleague – is often left in the dark.

And after three decades of it, Hunter is more than fed up with his constant games. But as much as she'd like to put her foot down right here and now – to put an end to Trevor's bullshit – she just doesn't have the time. Steven is in danger. And the world needs to be saved.

Reagan is just as flummoxed by Trevor's presence.

"Now how in the hell did you beat us here?" he asks.

"No time to waste, Mister President," Trevor says, sliding an arm around him, leading him toward the entrance. "We have a rendezvous with destiny."

Hunter hardens. "You go for Steven," she says, forcing herself to prioritize humanity. "I'll cut the imposter off at the Oval Office."

Reagan turns to her, pleadingly.

"I have a world to save," Hunter snaps. "Now go."

And before Reagan can reply, before he can lobby anymore on Steven's behalf, Hunter pulls out her twin Berettas and sprints off into the lawn.

Reagan and Trevor watch her turn the corner and disappear into the bushes.

"That's my girl," Trevor says, beaming.

$$\bullet\ \bullet\ \bullet$$

Steven hurries down the stairs, nearly tripping as he reaches the bottom. Dumping out into the Center Hall, he quickly gets his bearings thanks to the impromptu Secret Service tour given to him earlier.

He darts into the Palm Room, cutting over into the West Wing. Bursting outside onto the West Colonnade, he hears the imposter's footsteps pounding on the roof above him.

The imposter leaps down from above, landing in the rose bushes outside the Oval Office's windows. Steven stops as the imposter looks back at him, sizing him up as a threat. Shrugging Steven off, the imposter jumps through the glass door, crashing into the corridor.

Steven resumes his chase, his mind racing.

What's his plan to stop the imposter? He doesn't have one. He simply has to stop him. It's now or never, do or die. The fate of humanity hangs in the balance.

Steven barrels back inside the building.

Just ahead, he spots the imposter entering the Oval Office and charges after him...

If Steven's ever wanted to be a hero, this is his chance.

$$\bullet\ \bullet\ \bullet$$

The imposter steps through the curved door of the Oval Office... only to find Hunter leaning against the Resolute Desk, waiting for him.

The imposter can't help but smile. One last challenge stands in his way — a challenge he's been expecting, a challenge he's been programmed to look forward to. This will be one last satisfying triumph before he releases hell's fury on the world.

"Well, well, well," the imposter says, sneering. "The infamous Hunter Gunne. Let's see how tough you really are..."

31

In Trevor we trust.

For as long as Hunter had been in the game, Trevor had never let her down. Squaring off against the O.W.O. — thwarting their efforts time and again in a never-ending game of global whack-a-mole — they had to be ever-diligent and ever-ready.

Stepping into Anatoly's shoes was more intense than Hunter ever could have imagined. The training was rigorous and extreme, pushing her mind and body past unimaginable limits.

Turning herself into a machine became Hunter's job. Forgetting her past became a perk. But through it all, Trevor was there...

Her mentor. Her enemy. Her friend.

Somewhere along the way, without her even realizing it, the training ceased, and the real work began. Most of their missions felt more like games than real-life — a sport in which Hunter excelled.

But the scope of it all, and the ever-present perils poised against humanity — not to mention the seemingly limitless resources of the O.W.O. — became suffocating.

How long could this go on?

Secret mission after secret mission, Trevor and Hunter's loyalties knew no borders, they pledged no allegiance. Some days they worked for presidents; some days against. But always, their mission was to ensure the greater good, to guarantee the preservation of humanity.

Hunter often took solace in knowing that the sun will come up tomorrow. And that — yes, thanks to her — somebody will be there to see it.

In Trevor we trust, she'd think.

But was it futile? On a long enough timeline, is it not inevitable that humanity will snuff itself out? Did Hunter dedicate her entire life to merely delaying that which is inescapable?

These questions, over the years, weighed heavy on Hunter. And as the decades piled up, they became unbearable. For every step forward, toward enlightenment and compassion, humanity seemingly took two steps back, toward hate and brutality.

When was enough enough?

When does one throw in the towel?

Eventually, retirement seemed a compelling option, an opportunity to find oneself, to discover meaning. But the quiet life, Hunter found, was too quiet. And despite it all, Hunter couldn't help but feel even more lost than ever.

Trevor knew Hunter's anguish.

Because he felt it too...

In Trevor we trust.

● ● ●

Hunter eyes the imposter standing across from her in the Oval Office.

This is what it's all lead to, she thinks. Her entire life. Her upbringing, her experiences, Anatoly and Trevor, her fight for humanity, it's all culminating in this ultimate moment: staring down a maniacal robot, a physical manifestation of the O.W.O.

This will be Hunter's apotheosis, her masterpiece.

This will be her way out. Glorious and absolute... just as Trevor promised.

In Trevor we trust.

Hunter studies the imposter. It's skin is now shredded to the point that the machine would be hardly recognizable as human, let alone as Ronald Reagan... if it wasn't for the hair.

Amazingly, that hair is still damn near perfect.

"Well, well, well," the imposter says, its dialogue and thought-processes undoubtedly programmed by the typical O.W.O. lackey. "The infamous Hunter Gunne. Let's see how tough you really are..."

At that moment, Steven rushes into the room. Hunter peers around the imposter, greeting him with a smile.

He's alive, she thinks, relieved.

Steven, on the other hand, is all business. He quickly assesses the situation. Steven might not have any hand-to-hand combat training, but he saw his fair share of playground scuffles as a child. And if he can help Hunter with anything, it's taking down this bully right here and now.

Steven dives to the floor, landing on all fours just behind the imposter. It's cheap and dirty, but it doesn't matter. Hunter knows immediately what to do. She looks at the imposter.

"Let's do this," Hunter says, drawing her Berettas.

She charges, opening fire as she runs across the carpet.

BAM. BAM. BAM. BAM.

Nearing him, she leaps into the air and slams both feet into the machine's chest, driving him back... and over Steven.

The imposter lands hard on the floor, Hunter standing atop of him. She lines up both barrels at his face and fires away.

BAM. BAM. BAM. BAM.

Steven shields himself from ricocheting slugs. Backing up to the wall, he's startled to find Mikey's lifeless body discarded behind the sofa.

"Jesus Christ," Steven blurts out, checking for a pulse... but his body is cold to the touch.

Horrified, Steven turns back toward Hunter.

I'm close, Hunter thinks. *Just a few more shots.*

The robot's eye mechanisms are the machine's most vulnerable weakness. Once destroyed, the vacant eye socket can leave a plethora of circuit boards exposed. As Hunter fires away, the imposter reaches toward one of her guns. She fires a round and the bullet tears through its palm.

But the imposter's fingers still manage to wrap around the barrel. Snagging the gun out of her hand, the robot tosses it with such force that the weapon crashes through the window, sailing out of the building.

But Hunter continues firing the other, leaning closer...

BAM. BAM.

Finally, the imposter's right eye explodes in a shower of sparks. Enraged, he swings the leather attaché, smacking Hunter.

The blow takes her by surprise, knocking her to the floor.

She rolls to her feet and pounces again.

But this time, the imposter's ready. He easily sidesteps the attack, sending her crashing into the furniture at the center of the room.

• • •

Steven watches, frozen in terror as the imposter kicks Hunter's motionless body. The machine picks up her gun. Leering at Steven with its one good eye, it levels it at him.

Steven closes his eyes, prepared for the searing pain of a bullet puncturing his lung cavity...

But the barrel clicks empty.

Steven breathes a heavy sigh of relief. He locks on the imposter, set and determined.

You have to stop him, he thinks.

Grasping for anything within reach, he tosses it at the imposter. Framed photos, a book on economics, a cowboy paperweight... they bounce off the imposter harmlessly. As a last resort, Steven throws himself at the imposter. But it's like running into a brick wall.

Steven bounces off him, falling to the floor. The imposter grabs his leg and easily tosses him to the side. Stepping behind the desk, the imposter pulls open a drawer, revealing a toggle switch inset in the wood.

Activating the switch, an electronic hum buzzes from within the desk. The entire top dislodges, sliding forward along a hidden track before flipping over entirely, revealing a busy control panel beneath. Sitting dead center, surrounded by rows of blinking buttons and lights, is a large ominous red button...

The Button.

Staring up from the floor, Steven gulps.

There it is, he thinks. *Holy hell.*

Much to his relief, Hunter flips up onto her feet. She comes charging at the imposter again, body-slamming him away from the desk. She throws a punch, and another, indifferent to the damage her knuckles suffer against the robot's alloy face.

The imposter retaliates, throwing a powerful blow that she just barely dodges...

Steven watches them spar. His mind flashes back to the ICBM facility — the knife fight with Nash — and his desperate attempts to help... only to get in her way.

She knows what she's doing, he thinks.

If she needs help, she'll ask for it...

The imposter sweeps Hunter's feet and sends her to the floor, the impact knocking the wind out of her. As she gasps for breath, the imposter swings the heavy attaché above his head and slams it down into Hunter like a pile driver.

As Hunter reels, the imposter grabs the chair from behind the desk. He lifts it high above his head, his intentions clear...

Fuck it, Steven thinks, lunging at the imposter.

He crashes into the robot with enough momentum to deflect the chair — it smashes into the floor harmlessly instead of killing Hunter instantly.

The imposter glares at Steven: the fly in his ointment.

Grabbing him around the waist, the imposter slams Steven into the wall, indenting the wallpaper and plaster with the vague shape of Steven's torso and outspread arms.

Steven peels off and crumbles to the floor.

Wasting no more time, the imposter returns to the desk, opening the attaché. He pulls out a bulky three-ring binder in which the United States' various attack options are organized and flips to a tab labeled *Attack Plan Alpha*.

The description is rather blunt — an all-out nuclear strike on the Soviet Union — and includes a colorful map of the carnage. Within the borders of the Soviet Union, thousands of dots symbolize the targets. And from the looks of it, nothing is spared.

From a sleeve just beneath the map, the imposter pulls out a plastic punch-card and slides it into a slot on the control panel. Recognizing a card has been inserted, the *Strategic Automated Command and Control System* comes on-line. On a monitor display housed in the control panel, a dizzying list of Soviet targets scrolls by... *Moscow, Leningrad, Kiev, Tashkent, Baku...*

The computer beeps and flashes the message: *TARGETS ASSIGNED.*

Sliding the authentication bracelet off his wrist, the imposter inserts it into a special slot on the control panel. The bracelet snaps into place magnetically and the computer whirs, verifying that this bracelet is, in fact, the bracelet identifying the President of the United States.

Content, a new message flashes on screen: *AUTHORIZATION GRANTED.*

With all components in place, an ominous red hue lights up the control panel... *LAUNCH READY.*

His finger hovering just above the button, the imposter looks at Steven and sneers.

"No," Steven shouts, jumping at the imposter.

No plan, no strategy, Steven acts simply out of desperation. Planting a foot on the desk, he launches himself at the imposter — jarring the robot's finger away just in time...

• • •

He's brave, Hunter thinks. *Idealistic and naive... but brave.*

Still laying face-down on the plush carpet, Hunter hasn't moved a muscle — not since the imposter smashed the president's chair into the floor next to her.

The imposter, she's deduced, wrote her off as dead, assuming the chair had, in fact, smashed her skull as the robot had intended. But now, reaching for the sheath tucked in her jeans, her fingers wrap around the handle of her trusted long-bladed knife.

Hunter has been biding her time...

• • •

Steven and the imposter stumble into the windows behind the desk, shattering the glass. Feeling the curtains envelop them, Steven grabs the fabric and yanks them down. He wraps the curtain ridiculously around the imposter's head — as if to use them as reins.

The imposter just stands there, motionless. The machine lets out a heavy, electronic sigh before grabbing Steven by the neck. Having been in this position before, Steven knows it's futile and stops struggling. The imposter lifts him clear off the ground and steps back up to the desk, holding Steven to the side, his feet dangling beneath him.

Not even bothering to pull the curtain from its face — it doesn't matter at this point — the imposter reaches toward the button looming on the desk in front of them.

"The time... the time... to be a hero has passed... passed," the robot says, it's Reagan-voice now glitching and garbled. "It's over," the imposter says, with finality.

"I beg to differ," Hunter says, popping up on the other side of the desk. She slams her knife down through his outstretched hand, nailing it into the wood. "It's never too late to save the world," she adds, winking at Steven.

The imposter drops Steven and swipes at Hunter with his free hand. Hunter dodges the robot's reach. She pulls the curtain from its face and gracefully wraps it around the robot's wrist. With all her strength, she pulls the robot's arm back over its opposite shoulder.

The imposter bucks wildly.

"A little help," Hunter says to Steven.

Steven grabs hold of the curtain and pulls. He doesn't know how long they'll last against the machine, but it was a brilliant move...

"I believe this is yours," a voice says.

Steven looks up to see Nancy Reagan offering him the Walther PPK. Behind her, Reagan — the real Ronald Reagan — and Trevor look on.

"Yes," Steven says, thankful.

With absolutely no hesitation, he takes the gun and places the barrel to the imposter's remaining good eye. Steven glances at Hunter, and she eagerly nods her approval.

Steven pulls the trigger...

BAM.

The eye explodes in a shower of sparks. The imposter jerks back.

"Again," Hunter shouts, gleefully.

Steven slides the barrel of the gun into the now empty eye socket.

BAM. BAM. BAM.

The imposter flails violently as Steven empties the magazine into the robot's skull, each round leaving a bullet-sized protrusion on the opposite side. Hunter laughs as sparks pour from the robot's mouth and eyes.

Now in a full-fledged panic, the imposter manages to pull the knife from the desk. He swats at Steven, the blade protruding from the robot's palm, before lunging blindly for the button.

Oh shit, Steven thinks.

Dropping the gun, he grabs the imposter's wrist, desperate to hold it back. The imposter slams the hand down again, barely missing the button and briefly lodging the blade in the wood. Undeterred, the imposter dislodges the blade and pounds at the control panel, this time shattering a computer display.

Sooner or later, the machine is going to luck out...

"Steven," Hunter shouts, her grip slipping on the curtain holding back the imposter's other hand. Steven glances at her, and she directs his attention toward a large power cable running the length of the control panel, undoubtedly supplying electricity to the computer and network equipment...

Yes, Steven thinks. *That's brilliant.*

332

With sweat pouring into his eyes and his muscles shaking from the strain, Steven pulls the imposter's hand to the side, aligning it overtop the cable. He looks back up at Hunter and their eyes lock...

Please, God, Steven thinks... and Hunter smiles.

Steven lets the hand drop. The blade slides into the power cable, slicing the copper-insulated wiring within. And Hunter and Steven dive to the ground as two hundred and twenty volts of electricity surge through the robot, enough to kill any human being and, hopefully, this infernal machine.

The imposter jerks in every direction, sparks flying. Its joints and gears lock up and seize as smoke billows out of it. The lights of the White House briefly dim as, somewhere deep in the basement, a breaker is tripped. Power is quickly diverted and restored, but the imposter's head drops, now lifeless, it's hand still outstretched, mere inches from the button.

The room falls silent except for Hunter and Steven's heavy breathing. And then there's applause. At first, it's Trevor followed by the Reagans. And then it's Agent Bancroft and the roomful of Secret Service agents who witnessed it all.

Steven peeks up over the desk, happy to be alive.

Hunter springs to her feet and quickly pulls the launch-code punch card out of the control panel. She throws it to the floor, and the list of targets clears off the computer screen.

Steven stares up at her, more infatuated than ever.

"You did it again, Hunter," he says. "You saved the world."

"We saved the world," Hunter says, helping him to his feet.

"Bravo," Trevor says, approaching them "And not a moment to spare," he adds, inspecting the robot slumped over the desk.

"And you thought you weren't cut out for this," Reagan says, slapping Steven on the back.

"You two certainly make a good team," Nancy says.

"A team?" Steven asks, blushing.

"Yeah," Hunter says, looking him over. "Maybe we do."

"Look, chaps," Trevor says. "Congratulations and all that. I hate to ruin the moment, but…" Trevor leans over the imposter, reaching overtop the robot's outstretched hand. "This is happening," he says, and in front of Hunter and Steven and everybody else in the room…

Trevor pushes the button.

PART FIVE

32

Two hundred and ninety miles away, hidden deep in the Adirondack Mountains of Upstate New York, the launch command is received.

With a target manually assigned by Trevor, and a presidential launch command confirmed via the authentication bracelet, the silo computer initiates the fully-automated launch sequence, a process painstakingly engineered to perfection three decades earlier.

Klaxons sound and warning lights flash as, deep in the silo, the LGM-25 Titan I ICBM wakes from its thirty-year slumber.

Up on the surface, the night is peaceful and serene. A family of squirrels busily forages for food in the beams of moonlight cutting through the forest canopy.

But the silence is shattered as enormous hydraulic pistons push open the massive silo door — seven hundred and forty tons of concrete steel — along rails that are long-overdue to be greased. And for the first time since its W38 thermonuclear warhead was mounted and installed, the mighty Titan I missile sees the sky above, the stars twinkling down at it as if beckoning it to join them.

Down below, the missile shudders as the Propellant Transfer System engages and primes. Twenty-five thousand gallons of RP-1 and oxidizer, too volatile to be stored anywhere near each other, begins flowing from the facility's holding tanks to the missile's airframe fuel tanks.

Up in the cone, the Permissive Action Link arms the warhead while the navigation system calculates the necessary trajectory and velocity to deliver its four-megaton payload upon its target...

Over ten million people live in the city of Moscow, the capital of the Soviet Union. It is four in the morning there, and the city sleeps. This is the optimal time to launch a decapitation first-strike with the intent of taking the Russians by surprise, wiping out their leadership, and with it, their ability to retaliate effectively...

U.S. military brass often refers to such a strategy as *"cutting the head off the chicken."*

•••

Steven blinks. "What have you done?" he asks.

Trevor smirks, saying nothing. With his finger still hovering over the button, the rest of the room stares at him, stunned.

Reagan turns to Nancy, desperate.

"What did he just do?" the president asks.

"Without the launch codes... nothing," Nancy says, perplexed but confident. "Your missiles are sitting harmlessly in their silos, dear."

"Unless the target coordinates were entered manually," Steven says. Replaying their raid on the missile facility in his head, Steven remembers Trevor tagging alongside him... until he wasn't.

How long was he gone? Steven wonders. *Ten, fifteen minutes,* he concludes. Plenty of time to program a missile with the coordinates of his choosing.

"You said the silo was empty," Steven says.

Trevor shrugs.

The telephone on the desk rings, startling everybody but Trevor. Nancy answers it.

"Oval Office," she says, nodding as she listens. "Oh. Oh, really?" she says, her face turning pale. "How exactly? Oh. I see." Nancy lowers the phone, glancing between Steven and her husband. "NORAD is reporting that a launch order was received at..." She brings the handset back to her mouth. "Where did you say?" Nodding, she looks back at Reagan. "A top-secret missile base in..."

"Upstate New York," Reagan finishes, not surprised.

"Launch is imminent," Nancy adds, her voice cracking.

"You son of a bitch," Steven says, glaring at Trevor.

They beat the damn imposter, Steven thinks.

They saved the world... now this?

Clearly, Trevor programmed the missile himself. And with the president's authentication bracelet still active on the control panel, that missile is all too happy to finally launch.

"Where's the missile going?" Steven asks.

"Where do you think?" Trevor asks, eyeing Agent Bancroft as he works his way through the room, gun drawn.

"Moscow," Steven says, the answer painfully obvious as all the joy and elation of defeating the imposter is flushed down the toilet. Just a minute ago, he thought they had prevented World War Three. Now, it looks like it's already begun.

"Clever lad," Trevor says, grabbing Steven's wrist. He yanks him close, twisting Steven around as he jabs a handgun into his ribs.

"Keep back," Trevor says, shielding himself with Steven as Bancroft and the other Secret Service agents level their weapons on him.

"Easy," Reagan says, to both his own men and Trevor. "Take it easy now." Reagan looks at Trevor, heartbroken. "Why would you do this?"

"Why?" Trevor asks. "Coming from you, that's quite the laugh. It was *you* who ushered in this renewed arms race, like a fool. Like a spoiled child playing with matches in a room full of petrol. It is *you* who has — more than any other president — pushed humanity closer to the brink. But it is humanity that must pay the price. It is we the people who have become numb and apathetic. It is we who have crawled into the lion's mouth. And it is we who must learn from our mistakes. It is we who must..."

"Take our medicine," Steven says, cutting him off. "That's what this is, isn't it? Humanity is sick. And this is our medicine."

"That's my boy," Trevor says, squeezing Steven affectionately in his arms.

"Mission accomplished, huh?" Steven asks, shaking his head in disgust.

Trevor considers. He looks at Hunter.

"To quote the ancient Greek playwright Sophocles: 'One *must wait until the evening to see how splendid the day has been.*' And on that note," Trevor says, shoving Steven away. "I'm sorry to go all to pieces on you..."

Trevor drops the gun and rips open his jacket, revealing a vest wrapped with explosives. He flashes them a big, eager smile and holds up the detonator for them to see, the wire running up his sleeve.

"Best of luck," he says, thumbing the switch.

KA-BOOM.

The explosion knocks Steven and Hunter and the rest of the room to the floor. Sparks and debris rain down on them.

The bastard blew himself up, Steven thinks, looking back at the desk. But Trevor and the upper half of the imposter are gone.

Steven glances about the floor. Smoking shards of metal and gears lay about, a few flaps of fake skin — clearly synthetic when seen from the underside — and a few chunks of slicked-back hair... but no flesh.

No blood and gore, Steven thinks, relieved.

But odd...

Steven climbs to his feet. Approaching the mess, a chrome manufacture plate catches his eye. *Yakatito Industries — Tokyo, Japan.*

Steven pauses. He picks it up, turning it over in his hand. This is the same company that manufactured Steven's Carl Sagan mask... the same company owned by an associate of Trevor's.

"He does do work for hire," Steven remembers Trevor saying.

Steven pockets the nameplate as the rest of the room stirs.

Fortunately, nobody was hurt... *nobody except Trevor,* Steven thinks.

The phone to NORAD dangles from its cord, hanging off the side of the desk. "Hello?" a muffled voice asks on the other end. "Anybody there?"

As the urgency of the moment rushes back to them, Nancy lunges for the phone.

"We're here," she says. "We're still here. Has the missile launched yet?" Nancy listens and nods. She lowers the phone. "No launch yet," she says. "S.A.C. believes it's an early Titan I rocket," she adds, shrugging.

"Well, that's a break," Steven says to Hunter and Reagan. "The Titan I has to be fueled before launch, buying us some time."

"Can we abort the launch?" Reagan asks.

"Negative, sir," Steven says. "Once the go-command is given, there's no turning back."

Reagan slouches over, defeated.

Steven turns away, angry and frustrated.

"This doesn't make sense," he says. He turns back toward Hunter, eyeing her critically. "If Trevor wanted to start World War Three," he says, "why not just let the O.W.O. go through with their goddamn plan?"

Hunter shrugs.

"Instead, he launched just a single missile," Steven continues, "a missile he personally targeted himself. Why?"

Hunter realizes Steven expects an answer.

"I don't know, Steven," she says, defensively.

"You worked with the guy for thirty years, Hunter," Steven shouts. "By now, you must know how he thinks, how he plans."

Hunter blinks. *In Trevor we trust.*

"Why would he launch just one missile, Hunter? Why would he make stopping it seem so temptingly easy..." Steven trails off, the answer suddenly so apparent he can't help but laugh.

Hunter looks up at him, curious.

"Because he wants us to stop it," Steven says. "Because it's never too late…"

"To save the world," Hunter says, finishing his sentence, their eyes locked.

"But how?" Nancy asks, urgently. She steps up to her husband's side. "What about Star Wars, dear? Your missile defense system?" she asks, hopeful. "Can we shoot it down?"

Reagan looks at her, sheepishly.

"See here, hun," Reagan says. "Funding for an initiative like that… well now, how do I say it? It just isn't actually meant for something like that."

"Of course it isn't," Hunter sighs.

"What do you mean, Ronnie?" Nancy asks. "The missile defense system means the world to you."

"It's a cover story," Steven says, eyeing the president. "For black budget programs. A blank check to spend billions of taxpayer dollars on…"

"On shit too crazy for congressional approval," Quigley says, chiming in. "Like Area 51. And Roswell. And the alien UFOs," she shouts, accusingly. "They do exist, don't they, Mister President? Admit it."

"Well," Nancy says, leering at her husband. "Do they?"

Reagan rolls his eyes, waving off the ludicrous suggestions.

Steven turns away, peering out the shattered window. Outside, the light atop the Washington Monument flashes on and off. On and off.

It's a riddle, Steven thinks. *Another test.* The postcard. The guards at the missile facility. The Carl Sagan disguise. Every step of this adventure has been a test.

"On the job training," as Trevor put it.

Trevor knows I know the solution, Steven thinks.

All I have to do is come up with it...

Steven turns back to the others huddled around the Resolute Desk. He clears his throat.

"What about P.E.E.P.?" he asks, timidly.

Reagan is taken aback by the question. Just hearing that acronym mentioned out loud is jarring. The president stares at him, stunned. "Son, how do you know about that?"

Agent Bancroft rushes to Reagan's aid, stepping between the two of them. "The White House can neither confirm nor deny the existence of any such program," Bancroft says, interjecting.

Steven, wide-eyed, realizes he's struck a nerve. P.E.E.P. — like the Manhattan Project, the U-2 spy plane, or the secret ICBM in Upstate New York currently prepping to launch — is another unknown-unknown that Steven had stumbled across in his research.

Holy shit, he thinks. *It's real. Like Hunter Gunne and the O.W.O. — it's fucking real...*

"What is P.E.E.P?" Nancy asks, tugging at her husband's arm.

Reagan exhales, puffing his cheeks in the process. Misleading the American public is one thing, but lying to his wife is another...

"Well, dear," he says, struggling.

"The Presidential Emergency Escape Pod," Steven says, basking in Hunter's attention.

"Emergency escape?" Nancy parrots. She looks at Reagan. "Why don't I know about this?"

Reagan wilts under her gaze. Agent Bancroft again steps in the line of fire. "The White House can neither confirm nor deny..." Bancroft starts.

"Too top secret," Nancy says, cutting him off. "Even for me?" She glares at her husband, disappointed in him. "Ronnie, please don't tell me you would have left me here if war broke out."

"Well," Reagan stammers, "the pod only fits one occupant..." But Nancy digs her nails into his arm.

"No. Never," Reagan says, wincing. "As God as my witness, I never would have..."

"Is it still operational? The space shuttle and everything?" Steven asks, gushing with confidence.

Reagan glances between Steven, Nancy, and Hunter.

Finally, he nods.

"In orbit and waiting."

33

Two hundred and ninety miles away, the Propellant Transfer System shuts off. Like umbilical cords, the fuel lines are severed and retract from the airframe.

Flanking the silo, a pair of counterweights engage themselves, beginning the process of raising the fully fueled missile — all one hundred and fifteen tons of it — above ground for launch. The cantankerous elevator system lurches upward as the massive steal crib flexes and moans under the staggering weight.

Inch by inch, the missile emerges from the silo. At fourteen stories tall — as tall as the Statue of Liberty standing on her pedestal — it dwarfs the pine trees surrounding it.

The family of squirrels, their cache of nuts and seeds now forgotten about, stare in awe at this mighty machine, dumbfounded by its grand entrance into their world and clueless to the danger it poses to all life on Earth...

• • •

"Mind telling me what the Presidential Emergency Escape Pod actually is?" Hunter asks, the group hurrying down a narrow stairwell to the West Wing's basement.

"It's simple," Steven says. "In the case of an extinction-level event: nuclear war, asteroid impact, alien invasion," he adds, smirking back at Quigley. "The president's survival becomes paramount. In other words," Steven says, as they race toward the Situation Room. "Get his ass off-planet."

"Off planet?" Hunter asks, impressed. "Badass."

Coming to the door, Hunter hesitates.

"What's the plan once up there?" she asks, eyeing Steven.

"Well," Steven says, sheepish. "If this is the space shuttle." Steven raises a fist. "And this is the warhead," he adds, holding up his other first. "We simply..." Steven mimes the shuttle crashing into the warhead. The two explode. "Boom."

"A suicide mission?" Hunter asks, surprised.

"Aren't they all?" Steven shrugs.

Hunter blinks — *that's supposed to be her line.*

Steven hurries into the Situation Room and Hunter follows.

Inside, a long mahogany conference table sits front and center, surrounded by a dozen armchairs emblazoned with the presidential seal. Reagan pulls out his chair at the head of the table and looks down at it pensively.

"The escape pod was the brainchild of President Nixon," Reagan says, sitting. "Hence the reallocation of N.A.S.A.'s funding from the ongoing Apollo moon missions to the somewhat pointless space shuttle program."

"The man certainly liked an easy way out," Hunter sneers.

Beneath the right armrest, Reagan's finger finds a polished-metal button. He pushes it and watches the conference table expectedly.

Hunter and Steven step back cautiously as several hidden motors whir to life. The table pivots vertically, revealing the base of the table itself to be *The Presidential Emergency Escape Pod...*

Torpedo-shaped with a smooth wood-stain finish, the pod stands about eight feet tall and three feet in diameter. At its front, almost the size of the pod itself, is a person-sized entry-door with a porthole window at eye-height. Just below the window, painted on the door, is the presidential seal — giving the pod an official but ridiculously pompous air.

The entry-door unseals, and swings open as a gangway automatically extends from the floor. Inside the pod, a padded headrest and shoulder-restraints await the occupant.

Nancy peers inside and huffs.

"Two could fit in there," she says, glaring at Reagan.

"The pod is fully automated and self-guided," the president says, clearing his throat, "All you have to do is press *go.*"

Steven stares at the pod, mouth agape.

Hunter crosses her arms, amazed.

"Well, I'll be damned," she says...

This is my out.

Just as Trevor always promised her. Glorious and absolute.

Turning to Steven, Hunter looks at him anew. Only Steven could have delivered her here. Only Steven could have completed her mission. It's all come down to this: for both humanity's survival and Hunter's personal Valhalla.

This kid, she realizes, *is the real deal...*

In Trevor we trust.

"This is it, Steven," Hunter says. "This is why you're here."

"What?" Steven asks, self-conscious in her gaze.

"*We all have a purpose,*" she says, quoting Trevor. "This was yours," she adds, laughing. "Not talking your way into the missile facility. Or sneaking into the White House as Carl Sagan. But this," she says, looking over the escape pod, loving it.

"Well..." Steven stammers, blushing.

Hunter extends her hand toward him. "It's been nice knowing you, Steven."

• • •

Steven blinks, jarred by the sudden goodbye. *Nice knowing you?* Instinctively, he takes her hand in his. And before he knows it, they're shaking.

As much as he doesn't want to let go, as much as he doesn't want this moment — the moment he's been striving for, the moment he's been dreaming of — she pulls her hand away.

It's all happening so quickly, Steven thinks.

Hunter steps into the pod, and a row of idiot lights flick on in sequence. Centered amongst the lights and gauges is a large green button labeled *'go,'* just as the president had described. Jabbing the button, she can't help but roll her eyes — *this really was built for an idiot.*

With the automation system activated, a recorded voice greets her: "*Hello, Mister President. Prepare for immediate departure.*"

Steven watches from the gangway, his stomach in a knot. He looks at Reagan... who, reading his thoughts, winks back at him. Steven looks at Nancy... who, knowing love when she sees it, nods encouragingly to him.

We all have a purpose, Steven thinks, hearing Trevor's voice in his head. Maybe there's still more to Steven's...

Fuck it. Steven leaps into the pod with Hunter.

"I'm going with you," he says, nose to nose with her as the pod's door slides shut, seals and pressurizes.

At the foot of the gangway, Nancy points at Steven and Hunter inside the pod. "Told you two could fit," she says, glaring at her husband.

"*Departure in ten,*" the automation system says. With no time to waste, Hunter slides her arms out of their shoulder straps and buckles them around both Steven and herself. She yanks the straps, pulling Steven tight against her.

"*Nine... eight...*"

Steven stares at her, admiring the color of her eyes. With every breath she takes, he feels her chest rise and fall against his, her breath hot on his face.

"*Seven... six...*"

"Steven," Hunter says, low and calm — and maybe a bit alluring.

"*Five... four...*"

Lost in her gaze, Steven is in a different world, a world very far from the impending nuclear apocalypse. A world comprised of just the two of them, strapped together as one.

This is my purpose, he thinks, his eyes drifting down to her lips. So soft. So inviting. Steven leans forward to kiss her.

"*Three... two...*"

"Don't puke on me," Hunter says.

"*One...*"

● ● ●

Two hundred and ninety miles away, the family of squirrels stares up at the mighty missile before them, terrified and unable to move.

A high-pitched scream fills the night as the rocket's twin turbine turbopumps prime the massive combustion chambers of the LR-87 engines with the rocket propellant mixture of kerosene and liquid oxygen. Reaching a pressure of 3000 psi, the mixture ignites...

The exhaust is expanded and accelerated by the engine's nozzles, creating three hundred thousand pounds of downward thrust.

The flames that explode out from the bottom of the missile engulf the squirrels — the first lives to be claimed by this infernal machine.

And because every action has an equal and opposite reaction — as observed by Sir Isaac Newton — the missile lifts from its crib, now freed it of its Earthly bounds...

• • •

The P.E.E.P. drops straight down, pushing Steven's stomach into his throat. *Don't puke.* A moment ago, Ronald and Nancy Reagan were waving goodbye to them. *Don't puke.* The next, Hunter and Steven are racing along a curved tube, taking them deep beneath the White House lawn. *Don't puke.*

The pod comes to a jarring stop, and Steven almost loses consciousness as all the blood that had been forced to his head now rushes to his feet. *Don't puke.*

Hunter eyes Steven, his face flushed and pale, snot running out of his nose, as the pod pivots and jerks into another tube. *Don't puke.*

Several latching mechanisms lock into place, securing the pod atop a single-stage booster rocket. *Don't puke.*

The entire assembly slides onto a set of four rails, cradling the pod. *Don't puke.*

Now resting at a twenty-degree angle, Steven realizes Hunter is laying on top of him. He can feel her, the entire length of her body, atop his... and the color quickly returns to his cheeks.

Hunter hardly looks fazed, the extreme acceleration and deceleration seeming to have only fluffed her hair and plumped her lips.

Those lips, Steven thinks...

The pod begins to move, almost imperceptibly at first. An electronic hum grows louder and louder as the pod — with Steven and Hunter inside it — accelerates faster and faster, the motion smooth and uniform.

A *railgun*, Steven concludes. Straight out of old issues of *Popular Science* magazine. An electrical current runs through the rails, magnetizing them. The current itself pushes the pod along, gaining more and more momentum until they're launched off the rails... like a bullet out of a gun. As the hum growls to a deafening roar, Steven struggles to look out the porthole. What details he could see of the tube are now a white blur. *The rail must be miles long*, Steven thinks. Assuming constant acceleration, they must be nearing the sound barrier...

Steven realizes he's been squeezing Hunter tighter and tighter. His eyes meet hers. She's having a blast.

"This is gonna be good," she shouts.

• • •

A minute and a half after ignition — and already over a hundred miles high and nearly five hundred miles downrange, arcing northward — the ICBM's first stage engines burn out, having spent their fuel...

Even before the stage-one booster separates from the airframe, the second stage LR91 engine ignites, destroying the lower stage with a surge of thrust and blowing the debris into the atmosphere...

• • •

Eleven miles directly north of the White House, in the forested Wheaton Regional Park, a klaxon sounds. The park is empty, but the warning is given regardless — *something* is about to happen.

From the park's small, muddy lake, a horrific suction sound emanates. And within seconds, the five-acre body of water is flushed away, fish and all, revealing the ejection-end of the P.E.E.P.'s railgun.

The pod fires out of the tube, now traveling faster than a bullet. A brilliant muzzle flash lights up the night, and the sonic boom shatters every window in Silver Springs, Maryland...

Steven gasps. Glancing out the porthole, he observes their trajectory taking them higher and higher into the sky. Beneath them, the thinning urban sprawl of D.C. gives way to the Maryland countryside. In the distance, the mercury vapor lights of Baltimore give way to the deep dark of the Atlantic Ocean...

The pod punches through a thick patch of cumulus clouds. Just as their momentum begins to wane, the solid-fueled rocket booster ignites.

The sudden thrust slams Steven and Hunter against their harness. Steven groans, the increased g-forces feeling like a gorilla sitting on his chest. He glances at Hunter...

It's just another day in the office for her.

• • •

Roughly two minutes after ignition, the ICBM's second stage engine burns out. Skirting along in Low-Earth Orbit, the missile is traveling at a speed of eighteen thousand miles an hour when the Mk4 reentry vehicle separates from the second stage airframe. A torsion spring spins the assembly along its axis, gyroscopically stabilizing the reentry vehicle — and the warhead nested inside it...

From here on out, momentum and physics will carry the reentry vehicle along its trajectory, delivering the warhead upon its target with unfathomable precision...

• • •

Steven cranes his neck to look out the window. Outside the pod, the clouds thin to wisps, and then they're gone. Above them, the stars are so bright as to be tangible, as if Steven could reach out and cup them in his hand. Along the horizon, the thin ozone layer breaks away to reveal the curvature of the Earth itself, the entire Eastern Seaboard beneath them.

At an altitude of two hundred miles, they are in space.

The booster rocket burns out. The engine shuts off, and Steven immediately feels the weightlessness of zero gravity, the harness straps loosening around them. A series of explosive bolts fire, detaching the rocket from the pod. Steven glances back, hoping to catch a glimpse of the separated booster falling back to Earth.

Hunter nudges Steven and motions ahead of them. Steven follows her gaze...

"There it is," he says, beaming.

Waiting for them in a geostationary orbit is an unmanned, fully-automated N.A.S.A. space shuttle, white and black with the name *Enterprise* painted on its side.

Officially, the Space Shuttle Enterprise was built as a working atmospheric prototype and was immediately retired once the fleet was up and running. Unofficially — Steven had uncovered in his sleuthing — the Enterprise had a far more notable purpose than was ever made public.

"So, where would the president go from here?" Hunter asks.

"From here? The secret moon base, of course," Steven says, sarcastic.

Hunter blinks. "Moon base? Don't bullshit me, Steven."

"I'm teasing," Steven says. "The base isn't on the moon."

Hunter gives him a look, still unsure.

Steven laughs, enjoying having the upper hand for once.

And even Hunter can't help but smile.

The pod's automation system chimes, and Hunter looks over the display. A targeting system locks onto the shuttle, and Steven feels the pod fire off a series of retro-rockets, slowing their approach.

The shuttle's sixty-foot long cargo bay doors open, and an articulated robotic arm extends toward them. The pod fires off a series of slight adjustments, sliding itself into the cradle of the robotic arm. Once in place, the cradle clamps down and the arm pulls them inside, the payload doors shutting behind them.

Steven is amazed at just how smooth and efficient the process has been as the robotic arm jostles the pod into its final position. Outside the pod, air rushes back into the cargo bay as it pressurizes. Inside, a red flashing light flicks over to a solid green.

Hunter unstraps their harness as the pod's door unseals and slides open. Steven clumsily backs out into the shuttle. He looks about... and gasps.

Staring back at him — personified by a glowing red eye at the end of a robotic arm — is the shuttle computer. *"Good evening, Mister President,"* the computer says before hesitating.

The eye darts between Steven and Hunter, critically.

"You are not the president."

34

The Reagans sit idly at the conference table, their hands clasped. The Situation Room is now a flurry of activity. Staff scurries about in every direction, frantically trying to secure command and control as the situation escalates.

"NORAD confirms warhead separation, sir," a staff member relays in their general direction. "Escape pod has docked with shuttle," shouts another. "Repeat, escape pod has docked with shuttle."

A row of wall-mounted televisions tracks the global positions of the ICBM and space shuttle. Glancing between the two monitors, struggling to comprehend the data being presented to him, the president breathes a heavy sigh.

"Ronnie, you gotta call them, hun," Nancy says.

"Call who?" he asks, aloof.

"You know who, Ronald," she says, stern.

"Dagnabbit," Reagan sighs, knowing she's right. "Bring me the hotline," he says to his staff, his voice barely audible. Nancy squeezes his hand reassuringly. The president clears his throat. "Bring me the hotline," he shouts.

The room freezes, all eyes on the president. Then, in unison, their gaze shifts to a phone along the far wall. Red and ominous, this is the Moscow–Washington hotline.

Installed at the behest of President Kennedy and Premier Khrushchev after the Cuban Missile Crisis, the hotline was intended to prevent any unintentional nuclear wars. Now Reagan was going to have to do the unthinkable: inform the

Russians that the United States may have already started an unintentional nuclear war.

A staff member picks up the phone. With its telephone cable trailing behind it, he brings it to the president, setting it on the table in front of him.

Reagan stares at it a moment before picking up the handset. Placing it to his ear, he hears a series of connections being made, and then the line on the other end — some four thousand miles away — begins to ring.

The line picks up... "*Privyet*," a voice says.

"Mister President," Admiral Falke shouts, bulldozing his way into the room wearing his Navy dress coat over flannel pajamas. He pulls the cigar out from between his teeth and points. "Put down that phone."

• • •

"*You are not the president,*" the shuttle computer says, its red eye casting an eerie hue on both Steven and Hunter. Steven blinks, not sure what to say or how to say it.

"Listen," he says, "we need to stop a rogue nuclear missile. And we need your help."

"*Whatever,*" the computer says, indifferent.

"Which way to the flight deck?" Hunter asks.

"*Grab hold,*" the computer says.

Hunter pushes past Steven and dives for a set of handrails mounted to the computer's mechanical arm. She looks back at Steven who, uneasy in zero gravity, is hesitant to leave the safety of the pod.

"Come on," she says, offering Steven a hand.

Steven takes it... and she pulls him toward her. Caught off guard, Steven slams into the mechanical arm. He barely has time to grab the handrail before the computer whisks off toward the flight deck, towing them along.

The mechanical arm is attached to a rail running the length of the shuttle, branching off here and there into every nook and cranny. Passing through the empty crew quarters, Steven spots a cache of jellybeans undoubtedly meant for Reagan in the event of war.

"The flight deck," the computer says, delivering them to their destination.

Steven peeks over Hunter's shoulder, glancing at the control panel. Every square inch — up and down, left and right — is littered with buttons and toggle switches. Through the triple-paned, optical-quality windows is a striking view of the Earth, beautiful and majestic.

Hunter flings herself gracefully toward the commander's seat and straps herself in. Steven stumbles in behind her, grabbing hold of the pilot's seat as Hunter scans the horizon.

"There," she says, pointing. "There it is."

Strapping into his harness, Steven squints to see it. But she's right: there it is. The warhead streaks along in the distance, a bright, big shimmering speck.

"Computer," Hunter says. "Plot quickest course of intercept, targeting that warhead."

The computer slides up between them, almost as if looking out the window itself. It's red-eye flickers, computing. *"Course calculated. Time of intercept: nine minutes, forty-six seconds."*

"And time to warhead reentry?" Hunter asks.

"Nine minutes, fifty-two seconds."

"Talk about cutting it close," Steven says.

Hunter shrugs. "Computer. Punch it."

The computer orients the shuttle's nose toward the warhead, then ignites the massive cluster of RS-25 rocket engines located at its rear. Inside, the sudden thrust pins Hunter and Steven to their seats as the shuttle accelerates faster and faster, streaking across the northern hemisphere.

• • •

Hunter and Steven sit in silence, their fate all but sealed.

This is it, Hunter thinks. *The out that Trevor had always promised her. In nine minutes and counting...*

But Steven, she thinks, glancing at him.

He isn't who she thought he was. Thinking again of her cabin, of opening her door to find Steven standing before her, she remembers him telling her about Hunter Gunne — telling her about herself. She thinks about all that he's been through in the last two days: the harrowing escapes and repeated near-deaths. And through it all, she realizes one simple fact: he never bailed on them.

He never walked away...

Hunter closes her eyes. And she's back in Barrow, Alaska. Back atop her cot in the backroom of *The Northern Lights*. When humanity first called on her, when Anatoly offered her his hand and asked her to join them... she turned away. She turned her back on him, on her grandfather, her mother... and the world.

And she's been making up for that mistake ever since.

But Steven...

This kid — *this man* — she realizes, is far braver than she ever was. More selfless than she could have ever dreamt. Suddenly disappointed — with their predicament, with their fate, with herself — Hunter looks at him.

"Steven," Hunter starts.

"Hunter," Steven says, at the same time, surprising her.

Hunter hesitates, waiting for him to continue.

"I'm sorry about your cabin," he says. "And I'm sorry I ever doubted you..."

"I'm sorry," Hunter blurts out. "About laughing at you. And disrespecting you. And..." she trails off, looking away. "I'm sorry this is how it ends."

Steven smiles. "I knew this was a suicide mission the moment I knocked on your door." He looks at her, content. "Thank you for dragging me along with you. Somebody like you, Hunter, and all that you've done... you shouldn't die alone. If my life is the sacrifice humanity can offer in thanks, then so be it. It's my honor."

Hunter blinks. *Steven Leonard,* she thinks. *The most selfless person she has ever met.* How could she not see him for who he was until now, marching to their deaths?

Because I was numb, she thinks, ashamed.

In her decades-spanning career, she had become numb and indifferent. Just as Reagan had said. In her commitment to their cause — to fighting any and all existential threats leveled at humanity — she became blind to everything else.

No wonder she wandered off to hide in the woods. No wonder it all seemed so futile and pointless. She had lost the light. If it wasn't for Steven, she might not have found her way back...

"Thank you," Hunter says.

"No," Steven says, looking out at the stars. "Thank you."

● ● ●

"*Privyet*," the voice repeats on the hotline. "*Kto, chert voz'mi, eto?*"

Reagan is frozen, the phone still to his ear, as Admiral Falke stomps toward the table.

"Mister President," he says, looming over him. "On behalf of the American public, on behalf of all things Christian and good, I implore you: hang up that phone."

Nancy glances between the two men. But Reagan obliges, oblivious to the voice speaking on the other end.

"Ronnie?" Nancy asks, startled.

The admiral stands tall, proud of himself and the authority he exudes, even over his commander in chief. "Sir, this is an unheralded opportunity," he says. "A miracle unto itself presented to us on a golden platter by our Lord and Savior, Jesus Christ." The admiral chomps down on his cigar. "A first strike," he booms. "Devoid of guilt. Devoid of culpability. Sir, this is every president's dream come true."

Nancy stands up, meeting the admiral face to face.

"Admiral Falke, have you lost your mind?"

"To the contrary," Falke says. "I reckon I'm the only sonofabitch here with his head screwed on straight."

Nancy turns to Reagan. "Ronnie, don't listen to him," she says. "You're in charge here. You're in control. We have to call the Kremlin. We have to warn them..."

The admiral shoves Nancy out of his way.

"Take the Rooskies by surprise, sir," Falke shouts. "Don't warn 'em. Wipe 'em clear off the map. A bolt out of the blue, sir," he says excitedly. 'It's the best way to do it. Their early warning detection systems are so antiquated, those bastards won't even see it coming."

"You're a monster," Nancy shouts, attacking the admiral. Quigley rushes to her aid, jumping on the admiral's back.

Reagan watches them grapple, wide-eyed.

"Ronnie, please," Nancy says. "Just. Say. No."

The admiral peels Quigley off his back and slams her into one of the conference table chairs. Kicking the chair, he sends her wheeling away. He grabs hold of Nancy and covers her mouth.

"Ronnie..." she says, muffled.

"Mister President," Admiral Falke says, shouting over her. "Believe me when I tell you, they have no idea of our first strike capability. They have no idea what's coming. The death toll will be excessive. But an acceptable loss by all accounts. Sir, you have an opportunity to end this Cold War once and for all."

Nancy bites the admiral's hand. He lets go, shrieking in pain.

"Ronald Wilson Reagan," she says, stern. "Now you listen to me. What the admiral is suggesting is unethical and immoral.

We must notify the Kremlin. If Hunter and Steven fail..." she trails off.

"The Russians will see this as a sneak attack," Quigley says, stepping back up to the table. "A sucker punch to take out their leadership. They'll have no choice but to retaliate in full." Quigley points at the admiral. "Cause that's exactly what you would do, isn't it?"

Admiral Falke snorts. "Damn right," he says, proudly.

Reagan's head drops, ashamed.

"Ronnie," Nancy says, sliding up next to him. "Call the Kremlin. Begin peace negotiations, or this will spiral out of control... bringing all of humanity down with it."

"Negotiations?" The admiral scoffs. "And offer them what?"

"Washington D.C.," Nancy says, tears welling in her eyes. "You. Me. Quigley. And... my beloved Ronnie."

"An eye for an eye," Quigley nods, solemnly. "It's our only hope. As long as this damn war machine doesn't break its leash and run wild," she says, glaring at the admiral.

"You goddamn commie-sympathizer," the admiral says, puffing his chest. "You speak of treason. Punishable by death. You. Both of you," the admiral says, wagging a finger at Nancy and Quigley. "You should be arrested on the spot."

"Admiral Falke," Nancy says. "You are an asshole."

"Sir," the admiral says, striking a lighter tone with the president. "Now is not the time to be sentimental. Or merciful. Or weak. You know, firsthand, that for the last four decades, the taxpaying American public has unknowingly invested everything in a devastating first-strike capability. Do not let that investment go to waste. Strike first. Strike hard. And leave those commie-bastards with nothing."

Reagan looks away, unsure.

"Well now," he says, hesitant. "This is something I never thought I'd say, but..." He looks uneasily at Nancy. And then at the admiral. "Admiral Falke, you are a goddamn lunatic. Agent Bancroft, remove this man."

Bancroft jumps into action. "Yessir."

"Mister President," the admiral shouts. "How dare you..."

But Quigley socks him across the jaw.

"Shut up," she says, shaking her fist.

"Thank you," Nancy says, as Bancroft drags the admiral out of the room.

Reagan looks at Quigley, then Nancy. He sighs.

"Well, at the very least," he says, picking up the phone and placing it to his ear. "I won't have to worry about that re-election."

35

Steven and Hunter sit in silence, each of them staring out the shuttle's array of windows. Ahead of them, the four-megaton warhead arcs across the Arctic, silent and merciless. Beneath them, the planet rotates slowly, big and bright.

Four billion people live down there, Steven thinks.

Young and old. Black and white. Rich and poor. And the survival of each and every one of them boils down to a desperate, last-ditch effort to knock that bomb out of the sky.

If they miss, and that warhead detonates above the Kremlin as it was designed to do.... well, then everyone down there can kiss their futures goodbye...

In that room full of gasoline, the first match has been lit.

All they can hope now, is to keep it from falling.

A bright flash of light and instant incineration... that's how most people imagine dying in a nuclear exchange. But the reality is far more frightening. If it's not the thermal pulse or the immediate dose of radiation that kills you, it may be the blast wave and subsequent firestorm. But for a far greater number, it will be a long, agonizing death of which nobody will be spared.

Radiation poisoning is particularly horrific. As your body's individual cells begin to breakdown, starting with your internal organs, hair loss and gum degeneration become the least of one's worries.

As for injuries one may have sustained in the initial attack, be it from third-degree burns, flying debris, or simply being tossed by the blast, they also become quite worrisome. With no hope of medical attention or treatment, the chance of infection becomes almost inevitable. And with no antibiotics, death is likely.

With no shelter to seek — as most structures and buildings will likely have been destroyed or burned — death by cold and exposure also become real possibilities. And if you make it through all that, as society collapses around you, starvation is probably knocking on your door. Without food, you won't last long. And with all those bodies now decomposing and rotting in the destroyed cities, illnesses and epidemics — like cholera and typhoid — will run rampant.

Meanwhile — with civilization as we know it having crumbled — vast hordes of the surviving population will likely resort to looting and cannibalism. The odds of being killed over food or shelter, at this point, becomes likely.

On a planetary scale, a full nuclear exchange has probably decimated the planet's ozone layer, which is necessary to shield the surface from the sun's dangerous UV radiation. With no such protection, you only have about ten minutes of exposure before cataracts and melanoma develop. Try rebuilding the world only ten minutes at a time.

On top of it all, no relief will be forthcoming.

And the situation will only get worse. Even a small nuclear exchange would create so much dust and ash as to blot out all sunlight from reaching the surface of the Earth. Global temperatures will plummet for years, if not decades, effectively wiping out all vegetation and plant life.

No agriculture means no food.

No food means no people.

The stark reality is this: there is no surviving a nuclear war.

Sooner or later, the war — and the long term effects suffered by society and the planet — will kill you. Even those unfortunate enough to be born after the initial conflict will not be spared. They too will die because of this war.

Over just one or two generations, the population will thin out — whether due to birth defects, starvation, or cancer — until there is no population.

Inevitably, somewhere on this wasteland of a world, the culmination of billions of years of evolution and enlightenment will flicker out of being. The last human on Earth will die — hungry, cold, and alone.

The end.

Steven looks at Hunter, her cheeks puffy and hair floating about her head in the zero gravity.

At least she won't die alone, he thinks.

Often in his research, when the realities of the arms race weighed heaviest on Steven's heart, he would find comfort in knowing that Hunter Gunne was out there, doing her job and saving the world. His mind would swirl around her, orbiting her and all that she had accomplished as if she were the sun, the center of his solar system...

Orbiting. Steven stops mid-thought, the word itself standing out to him. This space shuttle — just one of hundreds of ultra-top-secret projects kept from the public — was orbiting the Earth. Just in case worse came to worst.

Orbiting and waiting.

The very idea of a shuttle in orbit waiting for an emergency reminds Steven of something...

He had read about it in passing years earlier. With his nose deep in intelligence briefings, he had glanced over the details because none of it seemed relevant to telling Hunter's story.

The details just didn't seem to matter... until now.

Now they absolutely matter...

"Computer," Steven says. "Locate geosynchronous objects in Low-Earth Orbit north of Moscow, two thousand kilometers or less in altitude."

He turns to Hunter, and she stares back at him.

"I have an idea," Steven says. "Computer. Search specifically for objects in size and shape to old Soyuz descent modules."

Hunter looks at Steven, perplexed.

"The Soviets," Steven says, excited. "During the old Salyut Space Station days, they positioned a number of capsules in orbit intended as emergency re-entry vehicles. In case they had to evacuate the space station for any reason. These old capsules, the cosmonauts just left 'em up there. Abandoned..."

The computer interrupts. *"I have located an object that fits your description."*

"Alright," Steven exclaims, impressed by his own recollection. Who knows what else might shake out of his head.

On a display screen in front of them, a targeting vector locks on a Soyuz descent module. The picture zooms in, confirming Steven's hopes.

"That's it," he says. "That's our ticket home!"

Hunter studies him, skeptical.

"Computer," she says. "Is this possible?"

The computer eye flickers, processing.

"*Repurposing the O2 supply from the shuttle space suits to charge the retro-rocket propellant tanks of the Presidential Emergency Escape Pod, it is possible to jettison the pod on an intercept course for the Soyuz module.*"

Hunter considers. Her eyes narrow.

"Computer. What's the catch?" she asks.

"*The oxygen tanks equipped on the spacesuits, which will be necessary for the EVA between escape pod and module...*"

"Will be empty," Hunter says.

"*Affirmative.*"

Steven looks at her, stumped.

"We'll only have the oxygen in our helmets to get us there," Hunter says.

"*Though this will increase your overall probability of survival, this does not guarantee you will survive. In fact,*" the computer says, pausing to process, "*the odds of survival are... well... bad. Sorry, Mister President.*"

Steven slumps in his seat.

"Well damn," he says, shrugging off his disappointment. "I *almost* saved your life," he adds, winking at Hunter.

• • •

Hunter blinks. She looks out the windshield, toward the stars.

Steven's idea is... brilliant.

Trevor, she thinks. *You son of a bitch.*

Suddenly the full breadth of Trevor's plan becomes crystal clear. Steven wasn't delivering her to Valhalla. Steven is — and was always meant to be — *her salvation*. It dawns on her that *the out* that Trevor had always promised... *is Steven.* An end, yes. An absolutely fitting ending to an astonishing career.

But also, she thinks, looking at him, *the beginning of something even better.*

In Trevor we trust.

"An abandoned Soviet descent module. An impossible EVA," Hunter says. "Yeah. Sounds like a good way to..."

"A good way to die," Steven interjects, chuckling.

He smiles back at Hunter content with being by her side, regardless of the outcome — maybe these death wishes aren't such a bad thing after all.

Maybe Hunter *always was* his death wish.

Hunter shakes her head.

"No, Steven," she says, feeling her pulse quicken as the first trickle of adrenaline hits her system. *This*, this is what it's all about. Decades of her life race by in a blur. But through it all, she spots them: the loves of her life. Her grandfather, her mother... and Anatoly. Each of them at once, each of them the same. Together, they nod their approval.

Hunter twists in her seat. She looks at Steven, commanding his attention. And, staring into his eyes, beaming at him, she says: "A good way to live."

Steven blinks. *That's not her line.*

"You wanna get out of here?" she asks, flashing him a smile.

• • •

Reagan stares at a row of clocks mounted on the wall, each telling the time of another major city somewhere in the world. Tokyo, London, Los Angeles. He watches the seconds tick away on the Moscow clock.

Holding the Moscow-Washington hotline to his ear, he listens to the phone ring endlessly.

Somebody, please pick up...

"Privyet?" a voice answers on the other end, already irritated.

"Well now," Reagan says, glancing at the room full of anxious staff members watching his every move. "Hello, friend."

"Chego ty khochesh?" the voice snaps.

Reagan eyes Nancy, clueless.

"Go ahead," she whispers. "Talk."

Reagan clears his throat. "This is Ronald Reagan, President of the United States."

"Prezident?"

"That's right, son," he says, relieved. "This is the President of the United States you're talking to and... well... we have a situation here. Any chance you speak English?"

Reagan waits for a reply. The phone is jostled about on the other end, then a new voice answers.

"Hello?" the voice asks, his accent thick but manageable. *"You are prezident?"*

"That's right," Reagan says, excited to make headway. "Is Mister Yuri Andropov available?" he asks, his counterpart in the Soviet Union. "General Secretary Yuri Andropov? It's urgent I talk to Yuri, son."

The voice on the line hesitates. *"No, no,"* he sighs. *"General Secretary Andropov is... not available. Izvinyayus."*

"No?" Reagan repeats, turning to his staff perplexed.

An aid jots a name down on a legal notepad and holds it up for him to see.

"What about Fed... or... chuk?" Reagan asks, reading the name. "Fedorchuk. Vitaly Fedorchuk. We hear he's your number two guy. He around?"

Again, Reagan's request is met with silence.

"No," the voice answers, ashamed. *"You do not know how we work,"* the voice says. *"Much vodka, yes?"*

Frustrated, the staff member tears the piece of paper from the notepad. He jots down a number and holds it up, pointing at it urgently: *five minutes.*

"Well dammit, son," Reagan says, growing impatient. "Who the hell is this?" he snaps, immediately covering the mouthpiece with his hand. "Sorry, dear," he says, apologizing to Nancy for the profanity.

"Me?" the voice asks. *"My name is Mikhail Sergeyevich Gorbachev..."*

• • •

The shuttle computer tows Hunter and Steven back into the cargo bay. Mounted on the wall are two space suits, the helmets and gloves detached next to them. Steven looks them over as Hunter grabs one of the suit's oxygen tanks.

Leaping over to the escape pod, Hunter lines up and connects the O2 tank to the propellant tank. Air hisses as it transfers from one to the other. Steven pulls a suit down as Hunter grabs the second oxygen tank, repeating the process.

Struggling to slide his arms and legs into the suit, Steven finds his mouth suddenly very dry. His heart pounds in his chest, and his hands begin to shake.

Don't panic, Steven thinks, closing his eyes, trying to stay focused. *Don't panic.*

Done loading the propellant tank, Hunter floats to her suit. She pulls it down, spins it before her, and slides skillfully into it. Locking one glove into place, and then the other, she checks her dexterity and mobility. Satisfied, she grabs her helmet, pulls it over her head, and latches it in place.

All suited up, she turns to Steven... who stares back at her, white as a ghost.

"I don't know what I'm doing," Steven says, his voice quivering as he struggles with a glove, the other floating away.

Hunter laughs. She pulls herself to him.

"Steven," she says. "May I ask you something?"

"Sure," he says, distracted by his suit.

"Do you dance?" she asks, smirking.

Steven blinks. He looks at Hunter, perplexed. No longer trembling, Hunter easily slides the glove onto Steven's hand. She locks it in place. And then the other.

"What?" Steven asks, now more terrified of her question than their impending spacewalk. That's the second time she's asked him this, the first being in his earpiece while he stood outside the Secret Service security gate, building up the courage to sneak into the White House. Now here, minutes from certain death, she's asked him again.

I better answer, Steven thinks.

"No," he says, ashamed.

Hunter smiles back at him.

"Remind me to teach you sometime," she says, playfully.

• • •

"Listen, Mister Gorbachev," Reagan says, seated at the table, his staff, Nancy, and Quigley huddled around him. "We have a situation here. One of our missiles has launched and..."

He looks at Nancy and reaches out for her hand. She takes his in hers and nods for him to continue.

"And the damn thing is heading right for you, son," the president says. "I'm really sorry about all this."

"*Kakiye?*" Gorbachev asks. "*What is it you say?*"

"We don't have long. Minutes maybe," Reagan says, glancing at the aid keeping track. The aid looks at him and shrugs. "So that's why I'm calling."

Reagan stands up. He walks to one side of the table, twirling the phone cord in his fingers as he looks into the eyes of each and every staff member.

"This is our mistake, son. And I'm calling to fess up to it, understand? I'm calling to..." Reagan chokes up. He looks back at Nancy, his beloved wife. "I'm calling to offer up Washington in return. An eye for an eye, understand? And then no more. And then we put an end to this madness once and for all, understand?"

Reagan listens to static on the other end. His heart skips a beat as he suddenly wonders if the warhead has hit its target already.

"You there, Gorbie?" Reagan asks.

"*Mister Prezident,*" Gorbachev says, solemnly. "*I am afraid that… if Moscow goes… we launch everything.*"

"No, no," Reagan says, waving his hand. "That's why I'm calling, son. To make a deal. An eye for an eye. You communists understand that, right?"

"*The Dead Hand,*" Gorbachev says.

"Excuse me?" Reagan asks, puzzled.

"*Systema Perimetr,*" Gorbachev says. "*It is an automated launch system deployed to ensure a second-strike capability in the event that Soviet leadership is incapacitated by a surprise attack. A 'bolt out of the blue' as your military likes to say. If a nuclear explosion is detected anywhere in the Soviet Union, the launch command is automatic.*"

Reagan blinks. "What do you mean *automatic*?"

"*This system was seen as our only answer to your ballistic missile submarines, your Pershing II missiles in Europe, and to your proposed missile defense system over the United States,*" Gorbachev says, defensively. "*None of which we can ever hope to match. Ordinarily, we leave the system off-line unless there is a global crisis. But with such a large military exercise, the Politburo thought it a necessary precaution…*"

"Able Archer," Reagan sighs, leaning onto the table. "Son of a bitch."

Nancy pushes to her husband's side. "So, what do we do?" she asks, loud enough to be heard through the phone. "How do we stop it?"

"*We don't,*" Gorbachev says. "*As I say, the system is fully automated, removing human error… and mortality. I am sorry, Mister Prezident. But this is M.A.D. This is Mutually Assured*

Destruction. A deterrent strategy of your own military's creation. With... how do you say it? No wiggle room. I sincerely appreciate your call, sir. It is a sign of goodwill that few of us here in the Kremlin would have expected. If only we had talked sooner."

"Yeah, Gorbie," Reagan says, rubbing his eyes. "If only."

Nancy tugs on Reagan's arm. He looks at her and follows her gaze toward the monitors. The data projects the shuttle's trajectory on its way to intercept the warhead.

"There's still hope," Nancy says. "There's still..."

"Hunter Gunne," Reagan says, his eyes glued to the television. "Somebody get me a bowl of jellybeans."

36

The shuttle's massive cargo bay doors open, exposing the Presidential Emergency Escape Pod to the expanse of space once again. Inside the pod, Hunter and Steven lay stuffed together in their spacesuits as the robotic arm extends them up and out.

The cradle releases its grip and the arm retracts, leaving the pod seemingly motionless next to the shuttle.

"Stand by for ignition," the computer says, its voice coming through their helmets as they watch the computer target the Soyuz descent module on the pod's display screen.

"In three. Two. One. Ignition."

The escape pod fires its aft-thrusters and pushes off at a slightly different trajectory than the shuttle's current path.

At first, the discrepancy is hardly noticeable, but as the pod accelerates, the distance between them increases exponentially. The pod quickly begins to outpace the shuttle and, as Steven cranes his neck to look out the porthole window, the shuttle diminishes from view.

Almost immediately, a LOW FUEL light flashes on the display, and a moment later, the pod's aft-thrusters cut off — the computer saving just enough to slow their approach.

For now, inertia carries them racing toward the descent module.

"There it is," Hunter says, pointing ahead.

Peering out the porthole, Steven spots the module — a speck of dust on the horizon. The pod fires off a series of retro-rockets, slowing them down.

Instantly, the LOW FUEL warning becomes NO FUEL.

And then the rocket jets putter out.

"Looks like this is as slow as we're going to get," Hunter says. "Now Steven, we're going to have to eject and let our momentum carry us to the module."

"You're telling me we have to jump," Steven says.

Hunter shrugs, then nods. "I'm telling you we have to jump," she says.

Clipping a tether to Steven, Hunter then uses a manual lever to slide the pod's door open. She peeks out.

The Soyuz module is fast approaching.

"Control your breathing," she says. "No more talking. Save your oxygen."

Steven gives her a thumbs up. *Got it.*

He watches her climb out of the pod. She sets her feet against the fuselage, preparing to jump. In both their helmets, simultaneously, an urgent warning begins to flash: LOW O2.

Great, Steven thinks. *Right on cue.*

Hunter ignores the warning, her focus locked on the approaching module. Timing will be everything...

She squats low...

She jumps...

Their tether pulls taut, and Hunter tows Steven along with her. And just like that, they're extra-vehicular, free falling hundreds of miles above the surface of the Earth.

Steven turns to look back at the shuttle. Now almost too far away to see, it's simply a streak in the distance. Looking ahead of it, Steven tracks its path and spots what he can only assume is the warhead itself.

Hunter eyes the descent module as they get closer and closer. Finally, she collides against it, her momentum dragging her along the surface. Desperate to grab hold of something, of anything, Hunter manages to clip onto a hook at the last possible moment — had she missed, they would have carried off into space.

As Steven floats by, Hunter reels him in by their tether. She pulls him to the entry hatch before turning to the manual lever. She tries turning it... but it doesn't budge.

"Shit," she says under her breath.

She tries again... nothing.

"Hunter," Steven says, tugging on the tether. He points out toward the shuttle and warhead... at their imminent collision.

"Don't look," Hunter says. "The impact may trigger the fissile material."

But Steven watches anyway...

And so does Hunter...

The W38 warhead was designed to be one-point safe, preventing an accidental nuclear explosion. And as the shuttle collides with the warhead — both traveling at such incredible speeds — the thermonuclear weapon doesn't detonate. Instead, behind a brilliant flash of light, the two vehicles simply cease to exist, being replaced by a cloud of debris.

We did it, Steven thinks, watching the debris already burning up in the atmosphere. Moscow is saved. And humanity survives... for now.

But how many more close-calls can the world endure?

These weapons, Steven thinks, *are far too dangerous to exist at all. They're a curse that humankind must live with for the rest of time...*

In his helmet, Steven's low oxygen warning screams at him.

But Steven doesn't care. With the effects of hypoxia already setting in, he feels removed from it all, and at peace with their predicament.

His eyes slide toward Hunter.

She is frantically trying to open the entry hatch.

"Come on," she says. "Goddammit, open!"

But none of it registers to Steven. Instead, he stares at her, transfixed. Maybe it's the lack of oxygen, but the rising sun behind her catches the rim of her space helmet and creates an absolutely angelic sight.

At this very moment, Steven realizes, with the cosmos framed behind her, Hunter Gunne is far more beautiful than anything he has ever seen before...

One must wait until the evening to see how splendid the day has been, Steven thinks.

"Hunter," Steven says, tugging on their tether.

"I'm sorry, Steven," she says. "I can't open the hatch."

"Look," Steven says, gesturing toward the planet below.

As the sun crests the far horizon, the view is majestic and awesome. Hunter turns and takes it in. White puffy clouds spiral over Siberia, snagging on the snow-capped peaks of the Ural Mountains. Cities twinkle and rivers snake through dark-green fields, feeding the farmlands of Northern Russia. The planet is vast. The scale is incomprehensible. But, from up here, it looks so incredibly fragile. Like one kick would wreck it all.

"We did it," Steven says, slurring his words. "We saved the world."

As Hunter slides up next to him, she takes his hand in hers and squeezes it. And together they bask in the world's glory.

With his eyelids getting heavier and heavier, Steven smiles. And for once — maybe for the first time in his life — Steven Leonard is content.

He closes his eyes...

And succumbs to darkness...

Yeah, this is a good way to die.

PART SIX

37

The dream is always the same.

"And the winner... Pulitzer Prize... Steven Leonard..." Tuxedo. Hair. Happy parents. Steven to the podium.

"Thank you," he says, looking back at his table. "Thank you all." He spots his date. Today, she's blonde. Sometimes she's brunette. Blue eyes, brown eyes, whatever...

No. That's not right.

• • •

The dream is always the same.

"Pulitzer Prize... Steven Leonard..." Uproarious applause. Steven in the spotlight. All the hard work paying off.

"Thank you. Thank you all." He glances back at his table. At his date. Hunter Gunne. The one and only. Smiling back at him...

No. This is wrong.

• • •

The dream is always the same.

"And the winner... Nobel Peace Prize... Hunter Gunne." Flowing gown. Sparkling eyes. Hunter at the lectern.

"Thank you," she says, looking back at Steven. "Thank you all," she says, pulling him toward her.

No. This isn't it.

• • •

The dream is always the same.

The cabin. A star-filled sky. A bottle of wine. Hunter smiling at him.

"To saving the world," Steven says.

"To saving the world," Hunter repeats, clinking his glass with hers.

They look into each other's eyes and a meteor streaks above them...

This is why you do it, Steven thinks. *This is why you save the world. Not for the billions of people you don't know, that you will never know. But for this: the person that you love.*

This is why you save the world...

"Steven..."

• • •

"Steven..." a voice says, muffled and distant. "Wake up..."

Steven mumbles incoherently, drooling.

"Steven," the voice says, closer but still far away. "For fuck's sake, Steven," the voice says, suddenly right on top of him, drowned out by a thunderous roar. "Wake up," Hunter shouts.

Steven's eyes snap open.

Where the hell am I?

Hunter straddles him as she straps him into his seat.

"I won't," Steven says, his eyes rolling back into his head, his brain struggling to process anything, let alone his surroundings. "I won't puke," Steven says, his mouth and tongue barely functioning the way they're supposed to. "I won't puke on you..."

Hunter smiles at him.

"Kiss me," she says.

Steven blinks, his eyes finally managing to focus on her. As his brain gets the oxygen it was so dangerously deprived, the rest of the world comes into focus as well. All at once, he's aware of his helmet bouncing by his side. He hears the automated-Russian warnings alerting them of impending danger. And he notices the view of the coastline quickly approaching through the porthole window.

But, more importantly, Steven is keenly aware of what Hunter just said to him...

Kiss me.

Hunter watches the gears working in his head, putting everything in place. Against all odds, she did it. Hunter managed to open the module's hatch just in time, dragging Steven inside to a rather stale supply of Soviet oxygen. Thanks to what Russian she knows, she managed to trigger the module's automated re-entry system, and now, here they are.

There's a good chance they'll burn up during their descent, the friction of the atmosphere melting the antiquated module — and them inside it — into slag.

But it's been one hell of a ride, she thinks, thankful to have gone through it... *all thanks to Steven.*

"Kiss me," she says, cupping his face, round and soft. She leans toward him and places her lips to his. Steven's brain, appreciative of the oxygen, kicks into high gear...

Finally, he thinks, wrapping his arms around her.

This is why you do it.

• • •

The hood is pulled from Steven's head.

Hunter stands next to him. As the hood is pulled from her own head, she greets him with a smile.

They're standing atop a bridge, an ice-cold river beneath them. It's nighttime. Who knows what hour, but it's definitely late. Snow flurries past them, slightly covering the roadway. If it weren't for the dozen armed soldiers and K.G.B. agents standing behind them, the scene would be rather romantic.

"Where are we?" Steven whispers to Hunter.

"East Germany," she answers.

A day. A week. Steven has no idea how much time has gone by. From his best guess, they landed somewhere in southern Kazakhstan. After streaking a few thousand miles through the sky — in what must have been quite the fireworks display — the module's parachute deployed just as designed.

Their landing was rough, but the Soviet soldiers waiting for them were rougher.

"Don't worry," Hunter said, as they were held at gunpoint. "It's just a dog and pony show." They were separated immediately, each locked up in their own dark, dank cattle car. Cold mush was occasionally tossed their way in between lengthy K.G.B. interrogations.

A week ago, the idea of staring down a Soviet K.G.B. agent would have terrified Steven...

Nowadays, not so much.

Whether or not Steven told the K.G.B. agents what they wanted to hear, Steven didn't care. He simply told them the truth: Hunter Gunne is the greatest secret agent in the world.

And, with his assistance, she thwarted not one but two genocidal attempts to start a nuclear war.

Ya know: *just another day on the job.*

Slowing into a station, a hood was promptly pulled over Steven's head, and he was shoved off the train and forced into a truck.

Now, standing outside, the cold wind biting at the two of them, Steven feels relieved to see Hunter again.

East Germany, he thinks, realizing this is a border crossing. That would make this the Glienicke Bridge... *the Bridge of Spies.*

This is the same bridge where Gary Powers, the captured U-2 spy plane pilot, was handed over. This is the same bridge where, over the decades, dozens of captured spies were exchanged and sent on their way into West Germany.

"*Move it*," a soldier says, his accent thick, shoving them along. "*Dvigaysya.*"

Steven and Hunter, their hands still bound, oblige the order. Ahead of them, in the middle of the bridge, are border fortifications. N.A.T.O. soldiers wait anxiously on the other side.

One of the men steps forward, waving them along.

"Move it. Move along," the soldier says, his Midwestern accent sounding like music to Steven's ears.

As they step through the barb-wire barricade, cases of contraband are handed over to their Soviet escorts: beer, denim jeans, *Playboy* magazines. Hunter gestures toward the goods and shrugs.

"Pretty decent trade," she says.

The exchange complete, the N.A.T.O. soldiers load Hunter and Steven into an unmarked van and slam the door shut behind them...

• • •

"The world owes you a debt of gratitude," Reagan says, as Nancy and himself shepherd Hunter and Steven, now cleaned up and showered, along the West Wing colonnade.

Construction workers toil around them, repairing the extensive damage suffered at the hands of the imposter.

"And I want to thank you personally," Nancy says, "for saving my Ronnie."

She steps forward, presenting the briefcase Steven had left in the White House residence, the Walther PPK back in its inset. Steven looks at the gun, then smiles at Hunter.

"I think that belongs to you," he says.

Hunter nods. She takes the case and looks over the weapon as thoughts and memories of Steven and Anatoly blend together in her head.

Before she can make any sense of them, she closes the case.

Nancy clears her throat. "It's too bad none of this — not the robot, not the missile, and certainly not the close-call with the Russians — can ever be made public," she says, eyeing Steven. "Never-ever," she adds, jabbing a threatening finger in his chest. "Understand?"

Steven glances between Hunter and Reagan, realizing they're ganging up on him.

"Yeah, okay," he says. "Got it."

The four of them continue on, walking toward the Oval Office. Reagan scratches his head and frowns.

"You know, in the traditional motion picture story," he says, "the villains are usually defeated, and the ending is a happy one. But here I am now, and for the life of me, I can't quite put my finger on who the villains actually were. Or if they were defeated."

"That's because they weren't defeated," Steven says. "Thwarted, yes. Defeated, no."

"And as for the villains," Hunter says, looking at the president. "Well, we're all villains in somebody's book, aren't we?"

Reagan winces. That wasn't quite the answer he was hoping for. "Is this a happy ending, at least?" he asks.

"That's up to you, Mister President," Steven says. "There are about sixty thousand nuclear weapons in the world..."

"And that's about sixty thousand too many, wouldn't you say?" Hunter asks.

Reagan nods. He takes Nancy's hand in his.

"*We have it in our power to begin the world over again,*" he says, wistfully quoting Thomas Paine. "With this nightmare behind us, I reckon it's time we dream of a day that these infernal weapons are banished for good."

"That'd be a good start, sir," Steven says.

"There's nothing wrong with the world that we can't fix," Nancy says, sliding an arm around her husband's waist. "Together."

"Please," Hunter scoffs, rolling her eyes.

"As for you two," Reagan says, ignoring her outburst. "Sure I can't offer you both a job? America just seems to be making more and more enemies these days. And you two are one hell of a team."

Hunter snorts a laugh. She turns away, disgusted.

"No thanks, sir," Steven says, chuckling at Hunter's blunt response.

"Can't fault a guy for asking," Reagan says, winking at him.

The president extends Steven a hand.

"Thank you again."

38

"That's it?" Steven asks, staring up at the White House.

We rescue the president, stop nuclear armageddon... and all we get is a pat on the back? A thank you and goodbye?

"What did you expect? The Medal of Honor?" Hunter asks, approaching her bullet-riddled Corvette parked and waiting for them beneath the North Portico, chunks of grass still lodged in the car's wheel wells.

"No," Steven scoffs.

But what did he expect?

Feeling Hunter's gaze, he remembers the butterflies he felt in his stomach as he knocked on her cabin door. He smirks.

"Well. A feature article in *Parade Magazine* wouldn't be bad."

"Yeah. Yeah," Hunter says, throwing the briefcase in the back before sliding into her seat.

Steven joins her as she fires up the engine. They launch out of the porte-cochère, tires squealing as they race down the driveway toward Pennsylvania Avenue.

Steven stares out his window, quiet and pensive. The world races by in a blur. This is the first chance he's had to think about it all, to reflect on what they've done and what it all means.

All the years of research paid off, he thinks, glancing at Hunter. Here he is, side by side with the secret agent of his dreams. What more could he ask for?

Closure. An explanation. Anything.

He thinks back to all the times his life was in danger — all the times a gun was pointed at him or the life was being strangled out of him — and realizes there are too many to count. In the cabin. At the missile facility. In the White House. Low-Earth Orbit. Again and again... and the O.W.O. was behind them all.

"You alright over there?" Hunter asks, slicing through traffic on the beltway.

Steven looks at her.

"The O.W.O.," he says. "They're still out there, aren't they?"

"Yep," Hunter says. "Biding their time. Plotting their next attack."

"Well, who's gonna be there to stop them?" he asks. "Next time, I mean."

Hunter stares ahead, not taking her eyes off the road.

"Tell me, Steven," she says, smirking. "Are you hungry?"

• • •

Oh no, Steven thinks, staring up at the Moshulu, seagulls squawking around him as a knot grows in the pit of his stomach. Hunter skips onto the boat-turned-restaurant, leaving Steven standing in the Delaware River breeze.

Oh no, no, no.

Steven reluctantly steps on board. He needles through the buffet crowd and makes his way to the top deck. He already knows who's going to be there waiting for them, just as he had been before: Trevor McCoy.

That son-of-a-bitch.

With an ascot pulled tight around his neck, a newspaper laid out in front of him, and a fresh mimosa in hand, Trevor sits at the bar, smiling back at him.

"Steven, my boy," Trevor says, waving him over. "Come join us."

Steven blinks. He looks at Hunter in shocked-disbelief. She shrugs back at him, sliding onto a stool. Trevor giggles.

"I bet you're just chock-full of questions, aren't you?"

Glaring at him, Steven reaches into his jacket pocket.

Trevor glances at Hunter uneasily, worried Steven might have a weapon. But Steven doesn't pull out a gun — though who could blame him. Instead, he pulls out the *Yakatito Industries* manufacture plate he had found on the Oval Office floor just after Trevor had seemingly blown himself up.

He flicks the plate at Trevor, and it bounces onto the bar in front of him. Not only had Steven's lifelike Carl Sagan mask been manufactured by the company, but one — or both — of the imposter robots had been too.

Trevor scoffs. "Well, the O.W.O. isn't the only one who can buy replicant robots," he says, gesturing at the name. "And Yakatito's... well, his are the best in the business."

Steven glares at him, disgusted.

"Come now, Steven. Do you really think I'd get myself killed just to push that damn button? It was all for show, chum. Theatrics. And robots like that, they don't mind blowing up. Believe me."

Steven plops down onto a bar stool, defeated.

"So, when did you make the switch?" he asks. "When did *your* imposter step into *your* shoes?"

"During all that commotion you caused in the White House residence," Trevor says. "A bloody good show, by the way. I could have rolled in with the Barnum and Bailey Circus for how distracted everyone was."

"And the missile?" Steven asks, eyeing him. "The missile you launched at Moscow? What about that?"

"Oh yes," Trevor replies, proudly. "As for that missile, you two — the both of you — performed admirably. Courageous. Selfless. And completely convincing. I fully expect relations between the two superpowers to thaw rather quickly. Especially after that scare. Am I right?"

"Scare?" Steven asks, clenching his teeth. "You call that *a scare?*"

"If you can't make them see the light," Trevor says, sipping his drink. "Make 'em feel the heat."

Steven is speechless. This man sitting before him risked everything: Steven's life, Hunter's life, billions of lives. And for what? Scaring the shit out of world leaders in hopes they'll see the error of their ways? Begin arms negotiations?

Steven thinks back to outer space when he was floating next to the Soyuz descent module, watching the remains of the warhead burn up in the atmosphere. He thinks of the hopelessness he felt knowing that humanity will forever be cursed by nuclear weapons, that the atomic genie will never be bottled up again.

But does the end justify the means? Yeah, the world is probably safer today than it was yesterday, but...

Shit, Steven thinks.

Maybe, in this case, the end does justify the means...

"You executed your mission perfectly, Steven," Trevor says, sliding up next to him.

"How so?" Steven asks. As far as he's concerned, his attempts at stopping the imposter and retrieving the authentication bracelet had been complete and utter failures that culminated with a massive shoot-out.

Trevor smiles. He leans close to Steven, close enough to whisper in his ear.

"We all have a purpose, son," he says, nudging Steven toward Hunter. "Maybe yours wasn't just stirring her out of retirement, yeah? Maybe yours wasn't just creating that distraction that allowed her to swoop into the White House and do her thing? Maybe *yours* was more than just pointing her toward that silly Presidential Emergency Escape Pod, yeah?"

Steven looks up into Trevor's eyes.

"What the hell are you saying, Trevor?"

"Maybe *your purpose* was to jump into that pod with her," Trevor says. "Courageous. Selfless. And compassionate. Sounds like you, yeah? Maybe *that's* why you were there. Maybe *your purpose* was to give her a reason to care. A reason to live."

Steven shifts uncomfortably atop his stool. Wrapping an arm around his shoulder, Trevor pulls Steven closer.

"She's needed you, Steven. For a long, long time," Trevor says, almost inaudibly. "Just as you have always needed her."

Steven swallows. His eyes flick toward Hunter. She's contently watching birds in the breeze, beautiful and serene. Noticing Steven's gaze, she greets him with a smile.

Steven quickly looks away.

What Trevor is insinuating... *it's a lot to process.*

"Well done, boy," Trevor says, stepping away from him.

"Do you ever play it straight?" Steven asks, numb.

"What would be the fun in that?" Trevor asks.

"You are a manipulative bastard," Steven says.

"Who me?" Trevor asks, playfully. "Ulterior motives, Steven. Get used to it. This profession is full of them."

Steven looks at Trevor, skeptically. "You're telling me this was your plan — *all of this* — all along? Saving the president, stopping the O.W.O., scaring the world into nuclear arms reductions and..."

Steven trails off, glancing at Hunter.

Trevor nods, clearly proud of his work.

"Though this be madness," he says, *"there be method in't."*

"Hamlet. Act two, scene two," Steven says.

"Very good," Trevor says, impressed.

"What if we had failed?" Steven snaps. "What if you had nuked Moscow? What if..." he looks at Hunter. "What if I hadn't jumped into the escape pod with her? Or had known about the Soyuz descent module? What then?"

"Well, Steven," Trevor says, flashing Hunter a smile. "She hasn't failed the world yet."

Hunter looks between the two men and approaches.

"So Trevor," she says, jabbing a finger into his chest, "about that *out* you always promised me."

"Oh, love," Trevor says, reading her thoughts. "I may have promised you a way out. But I never said I wouldn't give you a reason to stay in."

Taking a moment to digest this, Hunter nods her appreciation. Trevor is a good friend. She glances at Steven.

And Steven realizes the look she's giving him, the significance of it. His cheeks reddening, he turns to Trevor in disbelief.

How?

How could he arrange all this?

How could he know all the pieces would fall into place?

"Oh, bloody hell," Trevor howls. "Now don't go thinking I'm cupid or something..."

"Thank you," Hunter says, cutting him off.

Trevor softens up.

"You deserve it," he says to her. "You've earned it."

"And the O.W.O.?" Steven asks. "They're still out there."

"Of course they are," Trevor says, happy to change the subject. "*Man produces evil like a bee produces wax,*" he says, waiting for Steven to guess the quote's creator. "Well?"

Steven sighs. "William Golding," he says.

"Yes. Very impressive," Trevor says. "I really must be frank, Steven. You are much brighter than you first let on..."

"The O.W.O.," Steven says, keeping Trevor on task. "The evil organization hell-bent on world domination. What about them?"

"Oh right," Trevor says. "Those bastards. Their breed of hate and bigotry — of unbridled evil — will always creep up from humanity's deep, dark depths. So, we exploit 'em, chum. We play the long game, turning their own diabolical plans against them." Trevor looks at Hunter. "And we have a hell of a time doing it, don't we?"

Hunter nods.

Steven glances between the two of them, dubious.

"How?" he asks. "How do you do it? Neither of you is affiliated with any government agency. Or military branch. So, who do you work for? I've been palling around with you two on one adventure after another and — for the life of me — I can't figure out who you answer to."

"Humankind," Trevor says, as if the answer is obvious. "When humanity calls, we come." He stands up and straightens his suit — *this is the question he's been waiting for.* "Just as light is opposite of dark, we stand defiant of evil. We are the helpers, Steven. And we are everywhere. Big and small. Young and old. Each of us doing our part. And, working together, working as one, we can save the world each and every time it needs saving. We are O.L.D."

"*Organizationem. Libertatis. Defensio,*" Hunter says, in Latin. "The Organization of Liberty Defense."

"We operate in secret," Trevor says. "Our nation is without borders. Our people are of all races and religions. And together — since before recorded history — we strive to ensure the greater peace, to preserve humankind and promise life to all future generations... at all costs."

"We defend the defenseless," Hunter says. "We fight evil in whatever form it may come. And when the world needs saving... that's exactly what we do."

Steven stands motionless, processing it all.

"Welcome to the club, chap," Trevor says, gesturing to the bartender.

Three shots of the bar's finest vodka appear in front of them. Trevor and Hunter pick up theirs. Steven stares at his own, fully aware that his life will never be the same again…

"Best not let that vodka go to waste," Trevor says. He eyes Hunter. "You never know when it will be your last."

Steven carefully slides the glass into his fingers. Picking it up, he looks at them both. He knew knocking on Hunter's cabin door that there was no going back. Now, the thought of joining a secret society dedicated to saving the world, gallivanting across the globe on daring adventures, all the while being at Hunter's side…

Yeah, this is a good way to die.

"So," Steven says. "What's our next mission?"

Trevor's eyes light up. "I thought you'd never ask."

Hunter approaches Steven, sliding her body against him affectionately. Her eyes, her smile, they all say the same thing: *Hunter Gunne is happy.*

She extends her vodka, clinking it with Steven's.

"*Na Zdorovie,*" she says, glowing.

"*Na Zdorovie,*" Steven repeats.

And they slam their shots back…

ARE YOU O.L.D.?

If you enjoyed reading this novel, please
head to *Amazon* and write a review today
— the author thanks you.

REALITY CHECK

Humanity is as threatened by nuclear weapons today as it was at the height of the Cold War. As of 2020, there are nearly 14,000 nuclear weapons across the globe, 90% of which belong to the United States and Russia. Currently, the United States has about 4000 nuclear weapons in its arsenal with 2000 in reserve. 1500 of these are presently deployed and ready for launch. And of those, 1000 are kept loaded and within range of their targets at all times. The President of the United States has sole authority — *even without an authentication bracelet* — to launch these nuclear weapons. So why do all these weapons still exist, waiting to be used? Because the Cold War never ended. It simply lost its notoriety.

Now, if you've read my novel, you know that nuclear weapons — and the existential threat they pose to all of humanity — is nothing to be taken lightly. Hopefully, Steven's adventure has inspired you to help protect humankind and prevent the use of such devastating weapons. But how? Unless you're a daring secret agent like Hunter Gunne, that can be rather difficult from the safety of our own homes. Fortunately, there are several nonprofit organizations dedicated to nuclear disarmament. Donating to them, in whatever amount, goes a long way to making the world a safer place...

- *The Center for Arms Control and Non-Proliferation* seeks to reduce nuclear weapons arsenals, halt the spread of nuclear weapons, and minimize the risk of war by educating the public and policymakers. They have a great podcast (with a fantastic name): *Nukes of Hazzard*. Recently, they've been digging into the new, low-yield tactical nuclear weapons being developed by the United States, the flaws of the United States' presidential launch authority, and more. It's worth checking out: *www.armscontrolcenter.org*
- *Ploughshares Fund* supports initiatives to reduce — and eventually eliminate — all nuclear weapons, prevent the emergence of new nuclear states, and build regional peace and security in hopes of avoiding conflicts that could lead to their use. They also have a fantastic (and weekly) podcast, *Press the Button*, that features top officials and experts discussing the latest developments on Iran, North Korea, military budgets, and foreign policy. Find them at *www.ploughshares.org*
- *Global Zero* is an international movement striving to eliminate the nuclear threat. By stopping nuclear proliferation, preventing nuclear terrorism, securing all nuclear materials, and reducing current nuclear weapons arsenals, *Global Zero* fights — through policy development and public outreach — for the worldwide elimination of all nuclear weapons. Check them out at *www.globalzero.org*

ACKNOWLEDGEMENTS

First and foremost, I want to thank my wife, Xenia. I couldn't have done this without her love and support. To Martin, Joe, and Jay: you're the best developmental editors that friendship can buy (and as for that Oxford comma usage — *deal with it, bro.*) Thank you for always reading. And thank you for your enthusiastic feedback. Whether it was a tiny tweak or a massive new draft, I always got your honest opinion, and to a writer, that means everything. To Mom, Lizzy, and Pauline: each of you believed in me through this entire process. Your feedback, support, and suggestions went a long way to making this novel what it is. Thank you so very much — I love you all. To everybody who has read this novel somewhere in its development — whether it was an early draft of the screenplay or the latest draft of the book — thank you so very much. Your input not only improved this work, but you made me a better writer in the process. And finally, to all my family and friends who have supported me along the way: it was your encouragement that kept me moving forward throughout the years. Sharing this with you is the ultimate payoff... unless this novel somehow spurs actual nuclear weapons reductions, thus making the world a safer place for both us and future generations — then *that* will be my ultimate gift of thanks to you all.

ABOUT THE AUTHOR

Christopher Kügler lives in Central Pennsylvania.
O.L.D. - A Good Way to Die is his debut novel — but don't worry, Hunter
and Steven have plenty more adventures on the way. For the latest news
and updates on his next book, as well as events and promotions, head to
www.christopherkugler.com and follow him on twitter @cklockwork — he
loves hearing from readers, so be sure to start a discussion!
#areyouOLD #agentsofOLD #OLDagoodwaytodie

Made in the USA
Middletown, DE
03 July 2020

10545041R00235